REVENGE AT LAST

They returned to the little room in the back of the shop and Tuff sat Rabinowitz in the chair once again. The blond man removed a cell phone from his jacket pocket and punched a button.

"Yeah?" came the voice that Tuff knew so well.

"Aaron, it's me."

"I know. I have Caller ID."

"You're not going to believe what I'm about to tell you."

"You're pregnant."

"No, it's better than that. I found her."

There was silence at the other end. "Her? *The* her?"

"Uh huh. She's alive and living in…" he hesitated to scan the newspaper story again. "Lincoln Grove, Illinois. Outside Chicago."

Tuff imagined Valentine doing his little dance of happiness that he did when he got exceptionally good news. "That's wonderful, Emo," his boss said. "Listen. Don't hurt her. I want to speak to her *in person*. You know what I mean?"

SWEETIE'S DIAMONDS

RAYMOND BENSON

LEISURE BOOKS NEW YORK CITY

A LEISURE BOOK®

June 2007

Dorchester Publishing Co., Inc.
200 Madison Avenue
New York, NY 10016

ISBN-10: 0-8439-5859-6
ISBN-13: 978-0-8439-5859-1

The name "Leisure Books" and the stylized "L" with design are
trademarks of Dorchester Publishing Co., Inc.

Printed in the United States of America.

Visit us on the web at www.dorchesterpub.com.

SWEETIE'S DIAMONDS

DAVID'S JOURNAL

Hi.

Mom gave me this journal for my thirteenth birthday so I guess I'll finally write in it. I've had it for seven months but haven't touched it. I'm going to be fourteen next fall, so if I haven't written in it by then and Mom finds out, she might be disappointed. I don't want to disappoint her. So I'm going to write in it and reveal all of my secret thoughts and desires. I'm not really sure why people write private stuff in diaries because the point of a journal is that no one else reads it but them, right? And don't they already know all that secret stuff that they're writing down? Mom says it's "good therapy" to write down our private thoughts. I don't know if she keeps a journal, though. I wish she did.

My name is David Boston and I'm in the Eighth grade. I should really be in the Seventh grade but they moved me up a year when I was younger. I guess they thought I was smarter than the other kids in my first grade class. I stayed in first grade for half the year and then moved up. They said I was a good reader and that I write exceptionally well. I'm good in math, too. I guess I make up for my health problems with a mind for school. The other kids think I'm weird because I take an active interest in schoolwork and would rather tackle a challenging math quiz than tackle another kid on the football field. Besides, my doctor says I can't play football anyway. I can't play any sports. I've been excused from Gym since I started school.

I have what they call Marfan syndrome. I don't totally understand it, but it's "hereditary." I learned how to spell that word when I was six years old. It means you get it from a relative. My Mom says that her father had Marfan syndrome and he died from it. I was born with it. It's a condition where I don't have a certain protein and this causes my body to grow geeky and it gives me bad eyesight. The worst part is I was born with a weak heart. The doctor calls it "aortic regurgitation." I used to have a lot of chest pains when I was smaller, especially when I ran or exerted myself. I still have them if I'm not careful. The doctor says I can get an operation to fix it when I'm older, after my heart stops growing. For now I just have to watch what kind of physical activity I do and I take a pill called Tenormin once a day. It would be really embarrassing to have a heart attack at thirteen years old! Anyway, I'm real tall and skinny for my age—I'm a lot taller than any of the other kids in school and they like to call me "String Bean"—and I wear thick glasses for near-sightedness which really make me look like a nerd. So, you add up all those things—thick glasses, tall and skinny, smart in school, and a wimp at athletics—and you have yourself a founding member of the Nerds of America Club.

You might think I wouldn't have any friends, but I do. Billy Davis is my best friend and he's in three of my classes at school. In fact, he's probably my only friend. He's kind of a nerd, too, I guess. He makes okay grades but he's not too good at Gym. At least he gets to go to Gym.

I can't think of any other guys that are friends. I sure have a lot of enemies, though. Especially that jerk Matt Shamrock. What an asshole. He doesn't deserve to be mentioned in this journal.

My Mom and I live in Lincoln Grove, Illinois, which is a town in the northwest suburbs of Chicago. Mom says it's a "safe place to raise kids." I guess it is. Nothing really happens around here. My school doesn't have metal detectors and things like that. I heard that they have them in Chicago public schools. The kids in my school come from good middle-class families, I guess. And some upper-class ones, too. We're at the lower end of the middle-class group.

Mom and Dad got a divorce a year ago. I was real upset about it at first but I've gotten used to it, I guess. (I guess I say, "I guess" a lot.) It still makes me sad sometimes. The divorce, I mean. I still see my Dad, but not very often. He owns a big car dealership in town and he's one of the Village Trustees. I'm not sure what that means and I don't think I ever will. He goes to these monthly meetings at the Village Town Hall but I have no idea what he does there. He sells a lot of cars though. There's even a radio ad about Boston Ford that people hear all the time. It's on a lot of stations. Dad comes from a long line of Bostons. My Dad's grandfather founded Boston Ford back in the 1940s. Dad's name is Greg Boston. I think he's forty-six or forty-seven years old. I never can remember.

My Mom's name is Diane Boston. She's forty-something years old. She teaches history and social studies at the high school where I'll be going someday—Lincoln High. In fact, she's the head of the Social Studies Department. But her main claim to fame at Lincoln High is with girls' self-defense classes. She does that as an extra-curricular activity. She teaches judo and karate to girls. My Mom has a black belt in that stuff, so unlike me, she's very athletic. Billy thinks she's pretty, too, but I can't say that about my own Mom. He calls her a "MILF"—a "Mom I'd Like to F—." (I figure I can say the F word but I better not write it. Don't ask me why.) Billy says even his Dad thinks my Mom is "hot." Billy's Dad also teaches at Lincoln High, and he's divorced, too. My Mom and Billy's Dad went on a date once but I don't think it went too well.

Mom's really great. She's fun to be around and she's pretty smart, too. I love my Dad, but he can be a jerk sometimes. He doesn't have an open mind. Mom is very liberal and seems to understand everything about people. All the kids at her school really like her. She was voted "Favorite Teacher" two years ago. I feel sorry for her sometimes because of the divorce. Dad moved out of the house and we stayed in it for about a year, but now we have to move to a smaller place. We're going to move this weekend to an apartment because Mom can't afford to keep such a big house for just the two of us. Dad has to pay her some kind of support but it's not enough. I don't really want to move, but I guess we have to.

Mom's usually pretty upbeat about everything, whether it's my medical condition, or her divorce, or problems at school, or whatever. Sometimes, though, she gets real quiet and kind of distant. I guess you could say she gets depressed. She drinks wine a lot at night and sometimes I think she drinks too much. I wish I knew if she had a journal. I'd really like to peek in it and see what kinds of things she would write. I think Mom has some secrets that she hasn't shared with anyone. I can't explain it—it's just something I feel is true. Something happened to my Mom long ago and it makes her a little funny sometimes. I don't mean she's crazy or anything, but she will sometimes sit and stare at the wall for a long time, like she's in a trance. She'll snap out of it eventually. She also doesn't reveal very much about her life before meeting my Dad. That's one reason why Dad left her. He accused her of "not opening up to him" and stuff. If you ask me, I don't think he had very good reasons for leaving, but what do I know? I don't really understand it.

Whatever happened to Mom in the past, I know it bugs her a lot. It's a big deep dark secret and I don't think she'll ever tell anyone what it is.

But I'm going to find out.

CHAPTER ONE

Moses Rabinowitz sighed heavily as soon as the customer left the shop. He had not made a single sale all day and it was nearing closing time. As he had already sent home the help, there was nothing else to do but begin to shut down the store. Being Friday, and Shabbat, it was the one day that A-1 Fine Jewelry closed early. Of course, they were closed all day Saturday and Sunday so the five days a week that they *were* open were precious.

Moses knew better than to complain, though. The store wasn't hurting. He was well aware that he and his brother Hiram did quite well, thank you very much. Hiram ran the home store in New York City, deep in the heart of the diamond district. Moses came west to open the Chicago shop thirty years ago and it proved to be a profitable enterprise.

He had made a lot of important business contacts in Chicago, some of whom were not entirely on the up-and-up. Sure, they did legitimate business with honest customers, but most of the Rabinowitz success came from trade that he wouldn't talk about in front of a policeman. So who was he to question what others did for their livings? As long as they didn't interfere with him, Moses did business with everyone—religious Jews, non-religious Jews, Christians, Muslims, blacks, whites, *gangsters*—he didn't care. As long as the money was good and the transactions were discreet.

The shop was located outside the Loop at a prime location on Lincoln Avenue. The area attracted a lot of pedestrian traffic, so the store did a brisk business with walk-ins. From the street A-1 Fine Jewelry appeared to be a modest long-time neighborhood business—nothing fancy or snooty. Moses liked it that way. It kept the IRS off his back.

Rabinowitz walked to the display windows at the front of the shop and opened them from the back. The routine was to empty them every night. The store had been robbed only once and it was a lesson he never forgot. Some junkie had smashed the windows and taken everything in sight. At his ripe old age of sixty-nine, Moses knew that his health couldn't deal with violent types, the police, or lawyers. Which was ironic, seeing that one of the best-kept secrets in Chicago was that Moses Rabinowitz was a highly respected fence.

He removed one velvet-lined tray of earrings from the window and walked it over to the counter by the cash register. Moses wouldn't open the safe until all four windows were empty and the merchandise was ready to be moved quickly from the counter into the vault. He walked back to the windows and reached for another tray.

That's when he saw her coming. The blonde.

He didn't know her name. He didn't know where she lived. He knew only that she came to him once a month and sold him some incredible merchandise.

Moses quickly ran through the figures in his head to determine if he had enough cash on hand that day. He thought that he just might.

The door opened and the little bell mounted above it jingled.

"Hello, my dear," he said cheerfully.

"Hello, Mister Rabinowitz," she said. She removed

sunglasses to reveal those magnificent cat like green eyes. He was never very good at guessing the ages of women, but he figured her to be in her late thirties or early forties. She was tall and slender, had a healthy figure, and was certainly intelligent enough to know the ins and outs of fencing.

He didn't think she was Jewish, but that didn't matter.

"I didn't expect you until next week," he said, closing the backs of the windows.

"I know, but I wasn't sure if I would be able to visit you next week," she replied. She moved into the store and peered into one of the glass cases. "Ooh, that's nice," she said, pointing to a rose-shaped diamond broach.

"Yes, that's a new piece. We just got that a couple of weeks ago. Beautiful craftsmanship."

She moved down the counter and nodded appreciatively at other items. A necklace caught her fancy and she smiled. "Oh, I like that."

"Would you like to try it on?"

She looked at him and smiled. "Not today. I'm in a bit of a hurry. Maybe next time. I really should treat myself to a piece or two someday, shouldn't I?"

"You most certainly should!" Rabinowitz moved to the front door, flipped the hanging sign so that the "Closed" side faced the outside, and then locked the door. He walked past her and went around the counter.

"Now then," he said. "What have we today?"

The woman opened her handbag and removed a white silk handkerchief. Always the same, he thought. If he were a betting man, he would say that she had two of them wrapped in the hanky.

The woman carefully unfolded the handkerchief on top of the counter. Sure enough, the hanky contained two very large exquisite diamonds.

Even though he had done business with the woman on numerous occasions, the fine quality and sheer splendor of the jewels always amazed Moses Rabinowitz.

"*Oy*," he muttered. It was all he could say.

She laughed. "They're just like the others, Mister Rabinowitz. Not a carat less."

"I don't doubt you, Miss . . . er . . ."

She held up a finger. "Nuh-uh-uh . . . you know the rules. No names. Cash only."

He nodded sheepishly and turned red. "I know, I know. You don't have to worry."

She turned away to admire more necklaces in another case as he went through the ritual of taking a jeweler's glass out of a drawer and examining the stones. He muttered affirmatively as he studied the two gems, verifying that they were genuine and worth three times as much as he was about to offer her for them.

"I can give you five thousand dollars apiece."

The woman turned to him and cocked her head. "Mister Rabinowitz! You know you can sell them for three times that much!"

He gave his trademarked embarrassed laugh and nodded.

"Honestly, Mister Rabinowitz, we go through this every time I come in here!" she said, not without a little flirtation in her voice.

"I know, I know. It's fun to haggle with you," he shrugged and laughed. "Let's see, what was it I gave you for them last month?" He scratched his head as if he were trying to remember.

"Eight thousand each?" she reminded him.

"Oh, yes, uhm, eight thousand."

"Unless of course you want to give me more."

"I'm sorry, but I just can't. Eight thousand is all I can offer you for them."

She stopped smiling and looked at him hard. For a brief moment, Moses Rabinowitz felt as if he were staring into the eyes of a madwoman. He thought he could see something there that could truly hurt him if he weren't careful.

Eventually she broke the spell and smiled again. "Very well," she said.

Moses breathed, nodded, and gestured to the back of the store. "The money's in the safe. I'll be right back."

"Don't be too long," she said. "I might rob you."

He laughed nervously and walked into the back office. He wasn't usually uneasy in dealing with what were obviously stolen goods. After all, they *were* stolen goods, weren't they? Why would this pretty woman come into the shop and sell the same type of diamonds, over and over, for more than twenty years? He had seen this woman grow from being a young girl into this spectacularly confident, mature lady. Who did she work for? Where did she get these diamonds? What was her story?

But one of his jobs as a fence was to not ask questions.

Moses quickly worked the combination and opened the safe. Removing the $16,000 nearly cleaned him out. He had to hope that Hiram could sell the diamonds quickly.

He went back into the shop and found her bending over another case, admiring the wedding rings.

"Thinking of getting married?" he asked.

"Oh, no," she said, turning to him. "Been there, done that." She walked to the counter as he counted the hundred dollar bills. When he was done, she picked up the stack and placed it inside a white envelope that just fit in her handbag.

Moses quickly placed the two diamonds in a velvet-lined box and the woman retrieved her handkerchief.

"Might I interest you in some bracelets? We got some nice items yesterday," he said.

"No, thank you," she said, her eyes twinkling. "But I'll see you soon."

With that, she turned and walked to the front of the shop. Moses followed her, unlocked the door, and held it open for her.

"Good-bye," she said.

"Shabbat shalom," he said, and she was gone.

Moses Rabinowitz looked at the clock on the wall and saw that it was now closing time. He shrugged, locked the door, and finished emptying the front window displays. When he was done, he would make a phone call to his brother in New York and catch him before he went home for Shabbat.

They had new ice to sell.

The nun at Saint Mary's Convalescent Home looked up from her computer and noticed the attractive blonde standing before her.

"Oh, I'm sorry, I didn't hear you come in," she said. "How are you today?"

"I'm fine, thank you," the blond woman replied. "I want to make a payment so I need to see your billing person."

"You can pay me if you'd like."

"No, I want to do this in person. It's a cash transaction. My name is Diane Boston."

"Just a moment." The receptionist picked up the phone and punched an extension. "Julie? I have a Diane Boston at the front desk who wants to make a payment to you personally. Yes. That's right. Okay."

She hung up and said, "Sister Fletcher will see you. Do you know where her office is?"

"Yes, I've done this before," Diane said. "You're new here?"

"Uh huh, I started two weeks ago," the receptionist said.

"Can you tell me if Sister Jarrett is in?"

"I believe she is."

"Do you think I might have five minutes with her?"

"I can find out for you. Why don't you go on in to see Sister Fletcher and I'll let you know."

"Thank you." Diane moved past the reception desk and went through the double doors leading to the rest of the facility.

Saint Mary's was not a hospital. It was a two-story private nursing home for a small number of seriously handicapped and invalid patients. It also served as a rehabilitation clinic for patients that had suffered spinal cord injuries, burn trauma, and other severe problems. There were no doctors on staff but physicians from surrounding areas volunteered their time at the facility. Patient care was performed entirely by the nuns.

Although Diane was not a Catholic, there was something soothing and serene about the way the nuns ran the place. She felt guilty that she didn't get down to central Illinois as often as she should, but at least when she did come to visit it was a pleasant experience. Unlike what it might have been at a hospital.

She walked into Sister Fletcher's office—the one with the door marked "Billing"—and said hello.

"Good afternoon, Mrs. Boston," Sister Fletcher said. "Nice to see you again." She was a nun in her fifties, already developing skin spots on her hands.

Diane sat in front of the desk and said, "I need to make a payment. It's for the next four months."

"I see," Sister Fletcher said. "Let me just pull the file. I take it that you're paying in cash again?"

"Yes."

Sister Fletcher shook her head slightly. She didn't approve of having so much cash lying around. It meant that she would have to run by the bank before it closed and deposit the money.

Diane removed the envelope from her handbag and slid it across the desk.

Sister Fletcher picked it up, opened it, and pulled out the thick stack of hundred dollar bills. She shook her head again and began to count. Diane sat quietly, staring at her lap.

"Sixteen thousand," Sister Fletcher announced. "Just sign here and I'll give you a receipt." She handed over a ledger and the blond woman signed it with a flourish.

The phone buzzed. Sister Fletcher picked it up. "Yes? Oh. All right, I'll tell her." She hung up and said, "Sister Jarrett is waiting for you in her office."

"Thank you. Is that all?"

"That will do it."

Diane stood and walked out of the office. Sister Fletcher shook her head once more and considered that the lady was one of the more mysterious people she had ever dealt with.

Sister Jarrett, the administrator of the home, welcomed the blonde woman warmly. "How are you doing today, Mrs. Boston?"

"I'm fine," she answered. "And you?"

"Very well, thank you. Come in and sit down."

She entered the small space and sat. The nun closed the door and went behind her desk. "What can I do for you?"

"How is she doing?" Diane asked.

Sister Jarrett shrugged. "The same. No change whatsoever. Doctor Patterson was here yesterday to have a look at her."

Diane hadn't expected otherwise yet she sighed with disappointment just the same.

"Have you thought more about what we discussed last time?" the nun asked her.

"Yes, I've thought about it a lot."

"And?"

"I don't know what to do," she said. "I just . . . I just can't pull the plug on my own sister."

"I understand. But let me ask you this. How long has she been here?"

"Twenty-four years."

"That's right. *Twenty-four years.* That's a long time to be in a state of permanent unconsciousness. There have been extremely few cases in which patients recover from a coma of that duration."

"But it's happened."

"Rarely. One in a million."

"Then there's a chance."

The nun leaned back in her chair. "Yes, of course. Prayer and faith go a long way. We will care for her as long as you tell us to do so. Mind you, it is not the Church's policy to condone euthanasia. But this is a special case and the Lord makes exceptions for easing interminable torment. As I explained to you when you first brought your sister in here, we at Saint Mary's like to think of ourselves as progressive. That's why we're privately funded and that's why we're located here in the middle of nowhere."

Even though Diane smiled at the nun's attempt at humor, she knew that Sister Jarrett was also speaking the truth. Saint Mary's was located off the beaten path, in a remote site nearly three hours away from Chicago. The woman had chosen the facility because these particular nuns were liberal-minded, and most importantly, discreet.

Sister Jarrett looked at her papers. "I see that you did enact the Health Surrogate Act three years ago."

"Yes. Just to give me the right to make the legal decisions regarding her care."

"Since that act was passed in Illinois, it's made the process so much easier." The nun looked at Diane and said, "You know, you could make the decision to terminate life support and end this ordeal for you—and her. It *is* an ordeal, isn't it? Our Savior suffered enough for us. There is no reason for you to go on suffering."

"She's my sister. And I'm not suffering."

"Very well. I'm only saying that it's an option. We will gladly care for your sister as long as her body is alive if that is your wish. I'm sure that Christ admires your strength. There are not many people who would have held on to hope for so long."

Diane nodded but then turned away so that the nun would not see the tears well up in her eyes. "Can I see her?" she asked.

The nun answered, "Of course."

Diane allowed Sister Jarrett to escort her out of the office and down the hall to the room where the patient lay.

Sister Jarrett stopped at the door and said, "I'll let you visit with her alone."

"Thank you," Diane said.

The patient was another woman the same age as Diane. She appeared to be asleep, but dozens of wires and tubes were hooked up to her body. A heart monitor by the bed beeped rhythmically. The patient breathed slowly and deeply. Her blond hair had grown out over the side of her skull where they had operated long ago.

Diane stepped to the bed and put her hand on the patient's arm. She squeezed it and said, "I promised I wouldn't let you die, Sweetie, isn't that right?"

The patient gave no sign that she had heard.

Diane stood by the bed for several more minutes and then, without saying another word, turned around and left the building.

CHAPTER TWO

The final bell rang and the students bolted from their desks.

"Don't forget to read chapter seventeen and be ready for a quiz!" Diane shouted above the chaos.

The eleventh graders hustled out of the room and were gone within seconds. One student remained and Diane knew what to expect from him. Carl Dunaway was a timid but good-looking kid whose crush on his teacher was terribly apparent. Diane had noticed him looking at her longingly in class and once found her name scribbled on his notes.

"Yes, Carl?"

"Uhm, I just wanted to ask you about making up my grade on that last quiz?" he asked, swallowing hard.

"You know the policy, Carl. What are you willing to do to raise your grade?"

"Well, I'll be happy to come over and mow your lawn, or help you clean out your garage, or something. You got any weeds to pull?"

Diane almost laughed. "Carl, I appreciate the offer, but that's not what I meant. Students are supposed to do some kind of extra work related to *American History*—an essay on something we've discussed, a book report on one of our topics—that sort of thing."

"Yeah, I know. I just thought I'd offer."

"Well, you think about it and let me know on Monday. Okay?"

"Okay." He smiled broadly and headed for the door. His mission was accomplished. He had spoken one-on-one with the love of his life. Diane didn't want to think about what he would do at home with his private fantasy.

She gathered her things and prepared to leave. It had been a long week and she was glad it was Friday. However, she was not looking forward to the task at hand for the weekend.

Diane glanced at the inter-office phone in her room and saw that the message light was blinking. She picked up the receiver, punched in her code, and listened.

"Mom, it's me," said her son David. "Dad wants to know if I can go see the Cubs with him on Sunday. Let me know as soon as you can. Bye."

She frowned and hung up. Damn Greg, she thought. He knew they had to move out of the house this weekend. What did he expect her to do, haul everything herself?

She lifted the receiver again and dialed the home where she and her son would no longer be living after the weekend.

"Hello?"

"David? I got your message."

"Hi Mom. What about it? Can I go?"

"Listen, David, we have a lot to do this weekend. You *know* we're moving to the apartment tomorrow. We might still have some things left to move on Sunday. I need your help. I can't do it all alone."

"Aw, please? I'll work extra hard tomorrow and we'll get it all done."

"Well, you tell your father that you can go but only on the condition that we get everything finished. That means you have to really help me tomorrow, and no goofing off."

"Sure, Mom. Thanks."

Diane hung up the phone and then dialed the number she knew by heart.

"Greg Boston's office." It was Tina, Greg's secretary. Diane suspected Greg of having had an affair with her but couldn't prove it.

"Is Greg there?" she asked.

"Oh, hi Mrs. Boston," Tina said, much too mellifluously. "Just a sec . . ."

Diane growled to herself as the call was transferred.

"This is Boston."

"Greg, why did you ask David to a ball game on Sunday? You know we're moving out of the house this weekend."

"Oh, hi Diane. Well, I got this extra ticket and he's been at me to take him to see the Cubs. Come on, can't you get everything done before Sunday?"

"Are you going to come over and help us?"

"I can't. I gotta be here tomorrow. It's a big sale on pickups and—"

"I don't care what's on sale, Greg. Look, I told him he could go but only if we get everything done tomorrow."

"Why don't you get some of your students to help you? I'll bet there are dozens of adolescent boys who would love to see you in shorts."

"Very funny." Very true, too, she thought.

"I'm sure you two can do it. There isn't a lot of stuff that the movers aren't moving."

"How the hell would you know? You've been out of the house for over a year. You have no idea how much stuff we have to get rid of and how much we can keep. That apartment is less than half the size of the house, Greg. You know, Scotty was willing to ask the judge for an increase in your support payments so we could keep the house. I told him not to bother."

"Diane . . ."

"And David can't do a lot of work, you know that."

"Diane, I think you protect him too much."

"Yeah? Well, *your* father didn't die from a heart attack at the age of thirty-one!"

"Christ, Diane, there you go again. Will you just take it *easy*?"

She caught herself and shut her mouth. Every now and then she had a temper that sprung from nowhere. It was one of the reasons Greg had left her.

"Look, I'm sorry," she said. "I gotta go. I'll have David call you on Sunday morning to let you know for sure if he can go."

"All right. Good luck with the move."

"Thanks."

Diane hung up and muttered, "Bastard." After fourteen years of marriage, he was the one who had to walk out, claiming that he needed a "new lease on life." She figured that he had been having an affair with his secretary at the car dealership he owned. Typical mid-life crisis bullshit. He had also accused her of "keeping secrets" and "not being totally honest with him." "Distant in bed" was another one. More bullshit.

She picked up her handbag, left the classroom, and walked down the hallway that was bustling with teenagers. Lincoln High School had a student population of nearly 4,200, making it so huge that it needed its own zip code. Sometimes she felt that she was in the middle of a major university campus rather than a suburban high school. Nevertheless, it was a prestigious place to work. Being head of the Social Studies Department had its advantages. She had one less class than the other social studies teachers so that she could attend to administrative duties, of which there were practically none. This usually amounted to an extra free period a day. Diane also felt privileged in that she was generally well liked by the students. She was proud of the Favorite Teacher award that she had received. She was surprised, though, at the jealousy this manifested among her colleagues. People could be so superficial, she thought. It wasn't as if the award meant that she was to be given a raise in salary or anything. It was just a nice thing to hear from the students. She didn't let it go to her head.

One of the school cheerleaders, Nancy Hawkins, approached her. "Mrs. Boston?"

"Hi Nancy."

"Are you going to be teaching the self-defense class for girls again next fall?"

"I sure will. You coming back?"

"You bet. I can throw Brian over my shoulder, you know. That keeps him in line."

"Geez, Nancy, Brian weighs what, two hundred and thirty pounds?"

"Well, he *is* a first string tackle." They both laughed.

"Just be careful."

"Thanks, Mrs. B!" The energetic girl turned and ran off to join her friends.

Diane felt good about the self-defense class. In many ways, it was more fulfilling for her to teach girls to defend themselves than it was to teach social studies. Anyone could teach social studies. It took a black belt to teach a girl how to survive against an attacker. College campuses were the most common places for women to be sexually assaulted. Diane armed her girls with the right amount of knowledge and physical prowess to do a little damage to a bad guy and get away with their lives.

She reached the front office and checked her faculty mailbox. Nothing there. She didn't stop to chitchat with other teachers but instead headed toward the front of the building and the parking lot. Unfortunately, she saw Peter Davis standing at the doors with Heather Cook, one of the more popular seniors. The way he was leaning over her didn't particularly evoke the traditional teacher-student relationship.

Davis looked up and saw her. "Well, there's Mrs.

Boston, the most dangerous teacher alive," he said. Heather giggled.

"Mister Davis. Heather." Diane barely paused as she made straight past them.

"What's the hurry? Got a hot date tonight?" he asked.

Diane quietly shuddered. Peter Davis had been one of those jealous colleagues when she had received the Favorite Teacher award. He had been vying for the position of head of the department for some time as well. When she got the job, his displeasure was not a pretty sight. On top of that, when the word got out that Diane was separated from her husband, he had had the audacity to ask her out on a date. It had not gone well. She had felt obligated to go because Peter Davis was the father of her son's best friend, Billy. The man was slightly younger than she, single, and not bad looking, so she gave it a shot. The guy was more of a jerk off campus than he was on.

Mustering up as much friendliness as she could, Diane answered, "David and I are moving out of the house this weekend. Got a lot to do, boys and girls."

"Oh? Where are you moving to?" Davis asked.

She didn't want him to know, although her address would be readily available in the teachers' directory soon enough. "Just a measly apartment near Town Center."

"You don't say? Those new places that went up over the winter?"

"That's them."

"They're pretty nice. You'll probably like it there."

"They're nice but we're used to a lot more space." She quickly changed the subject. "How are you doing, Heather?"

"Fine."

Heather was one of those gorgeous sexpots that had probably done more than her fair share of experimentation before her time. Her family was rich and she was a spoiled brat. The guys swarmed around her like dogs and she encouraged them. The way Peter Davis was eyeing her indicated that men of all ages were not immune to her charms.

"Where are you going to college in the fall?" Diane asked.

"Northwestern," she said, haughtily.

Of course. One of the more expensive schools in the state.

"Good for you. Well, I must run. Stay out of trouble." She looked at Davis. "Both of you."

As she went out the door, Davis called to her. "You really should get out more, Diane. If you don't, you'll lose your girlish good looks!"

Diane wanted to give him the finger but didn't.

CHAPTER THREE

When they had finished with the pizza that was delivered, Diane and David washed up and began to tackle the unpacking of more boxes. They had spent the day driving back and forth from the house to the new apartment, transporting small items and clothing to save money. The movers were moving only the large pieces of furniture that Diane was keeping—their beds, dressers, the television, and the like. The pepperoni pizza had reinvigorated them, but Diane was feeling the exhaustion. Because David was unable to lift all but the lightest boxes, Diane had ended up doing most of the hard work.

"Why don't we just open the kitchen stuff and call it a night?" she suggested, eyeing the chaos the move-in had created.

"Sounds fine to me," David said. "But can we hook up the TV?"

"I think the movers did it already. Turn it on and see."

David stepped over several boxes and found the remote. He switched it on and sure enough, the TV shot on.

"We don't have MTV," he said, scanning the available channels.

"That's 'cause we don't have cable yet. I'll get it hooked up this week, I promise."

David flicked off the set. "So do I get to go to the game tomorrow?"

Diane sighed. "Oh, David, let's see where we're at in the morning. What time would you have to leave?"

"It's an afternoon game, so I guess by lunchtime."

"Well, let's do a little bit tonight and get up early and unpack some more. If we've made a good dent in it by ten o'clock, I'll let you go."

"Sweet!"

David grabbed a box and ripped the packing tape off, revealing sets of dishes.

"Be careful with those," Diane said. She got up, went into the kitchen, opened a cabinet, and made sure the shelf was clean. "Put them in here, all right?"

As he carried a stack into the kitchen, Diane surveyed the place and had to admit that it was a lovely two-bedroom apartment. The complex was brand new and smelled like it. It was nice to move into a sparkling clean home, even though it was drastically smaller than their house. Besides the two bedrooms, there were two bathrooms, a living room with a fireplace, an eat-in kitchen, and a one-car garage. There was a deck in the back with a barbecue grill, and a nice expanse of yard that they shared with other tenants. Diane figured she would save close to a thousand dollars a month in mortgage payments. She had gotten a very good price.

David carried the dishes from the box to the kitchen and asked, "Mom, what were my grandparents like?"

Diane sat on the floor to open another box. "David, I've told you all about them. What do you want to know?"

"I don't know," he said. "I just wish I had known them. Grandpa and Grandma Boston are okay, but I just wonder what Grandpa and Grandma Wilson were like.

Wilson. The name sounded so foreign to Diane. She hadn't used it in such a long time.

"Well, you know your grandfather died young. I was just a baby, so to tell you the truth, I didn't know him either. He was thirty-one."

"He had Marfan syndrome, too?"

"That's what we think. He had a bad heart. He was tall and skinny like you, and he had thick glasses. Back then they didn't really understand the, uhm, condition like they do today. I imagine he probably exerted himself too much one day and just dropped dead."

David finished with the dishes. "Which box should I do now, Mom?"

She looked around and pointed to the one that contained glasses. "Do that one. The glasses go in the cabinet next to the dishes."

As he started to work, he asked, "What about Grandma Wilson?"

"Well, she was very strict. I guess she had a hard time after my father died. She passed away when I was five. It wasn't much of a family, David."

"What did you do when she died? Where did you go?"

"I lived with an uncle and aunt in Texas until I . . . went to college."

David noticed that his mother had become distracted again. She tended to do that whenever she talked about the past. It was almost as if she couldn't remember certain details.

"Now where was I?" she asked herself, looking at two open boxes.

"I think you were working on the linens," David answered.

"Right." She continued to unload towels and walk them into the hallway where the linen closet was located.

"I thought you went to Harper College before you married Dad," David said.

"I did," Diane replied. "That was later. I went back and got an education degree and my teacher's certificate. The first time I went to college was as a history major."

"Where did you go?"

"What's with all these questions, David? I'd rather not talk about all this."

"Sorry."

They worked in silence a while longer until David sat on the sofa, spent.

"Had enough?" Diane asked.

"I think so," he said. "I might take a shower."

"Sounds like a good idea," Diane said. "We can do the rest tomorrow morning, I think."

After a pause, he asked, "You think you and Dad will ever get back together?"

Diane sat next to him and put her arm around him. "I don't know, honey. I really don't think so."

David nodded resignedly and slipped out from under her arm. He went to another pile of boxes and asked, "Is my PS2 in one of these?"

"Hmmm, maybe."

He picked up a box and tore off the tape, revealing a collection of old, faded newspaper clippings. The one on top was the *Los Angeles Times* and the headline blared, "GANGLAND MURDERS AT PORNO WARE-HOUSE." He lifted the top clipping and saw another headline, "MISSING ADULT FILM ACTRESSES BE-LIEVED DEAD."

"Hey, what are these?" David asked.

Diane wrinkled her brow and stood. She stepped over to him, looked in the box, and gasped. Reacting suddenly, she pulled the box away and closed the flaps.

"That's nothing," she said.

"What do you mean?" David was no fool. He could see that his mother had recoiled in horror at his discovery. "What are they?"

"Just some newspapers I forgot I even had. They're personal. In fact I probably should have gotten rid of them a long time ago. Forget about them, I'm throwing them away. They're garbage."

David looked at her curiously.

"Really," she said, unconvincingly.

He finally shrugged and said, "I'm going to take that shower." He walked out of the room and headed toward his bedroom.

Diane looked at her hand and saw that she was shaking. She really had forgotten that she was in possession of the clippings. They must have been in the crawl space of the house and had been picked up with some of the other boxes down there.

She went straight to the kitchen and found one of the three bottles of wine she had brought from the old house. She then rummaged through one of the boxes marked "Kitchen" and eventually found the corkscrew. After opening the bottle, an inexpensive cabernet, she took one of the wineglasses that David had put away, rinsed it out, and poured a nightcap.

The wine tasted good and would go a long way toward easing her anxiety. She felt her heart pumping hard and fast, so she moved to the sofa and sat. She closed her eyes and tried to will away the unpleasant memories that were evoked when David had unearthed the newspapers.

"Sweetie? What's wrong? You sound—"

"Please . . ."

"Where are you?"

". . . Warehouse . . ."

"My God, what's happened? Sweetie?"

Diane jumped when the phone rang. She picked up the receiver and answered. "Hello?"

"I see your new number works." It was Greg.

"Hi."

"How'd it go today?"

"All right. We still have a lot to do."

"Is David there?"

"He's taking a shower and then he's going to bed. We're both exhausted."

"I can imagine."

"Look, if you're calling about the game, I guess he can go. But really, Greg, you should have known better than to arrange this on a weekend when we're moving."

"I know, I'm sorry, it just came up. I had no control over it."

"Well just keep it in mind for future reference."

"Fine. I was *calling* to see how you were doing, not to get a lecture."

"I'm really tired, Greg, and I have a headache. I don't feel much like nursing your ego."

"Well, fuck you, too, Diane."

"Hey!"

"No, *hey*, to you," he said. She could now hear the alcohol in his voice. She eyed the wineglass in her hand and figured, *it takes one to know one.*

He tried again. "Look, I called to see if your number worked and to see how it went. Why do you have to be such a bitch?"

"I'm not, Greg. If you had paid a little more attention to David's and my needs, we'd all still be living in the same house."

"Are we getting into that again, Diane? Come on, it's been over a year. Can't we be friends now?"

"Why should we?"

"Well, we have a *son* together, for one thing."

"I know, and I promise I can be civil when you're around us. I don't bad-mouth you to him. You're still his father and I respect that."

"You sure don't sound like it."

"Greg, you *left* us! You had your fucking mid-life crisis and walked out of the house. You started screwing your secretary and then—"

"I did *not* screw my secretary!"

"Well, whoever it was, I know it was *someone* at Boston Ford!"

He was quiet for a moment. This confirmed her suspicion.

"You know, Diane," he finally said. "You're a real piece of work."

"What's that supposed to mean?"

"You never gave one-hundred percent to me."

"Sure I did."

"No. You didn't. You held back. I was talking to Steve the other day. You know he and Ann are getting a divorce?"

"I heard that. I'm sorry." He was referring to a couple that they used to hang around with. Since the divorce, Diane hadn't seen either of them. Greg had remained friends with Steve.

"Anyway, Steve agrees with me. He always felt that you were kind of distant and guarded."

"I don't give a damn what Steve thinks. He doesn't know me."

"That's precisely the point, Diane! He *didn't* know you, and yet he *knew* you for six years! The same is true for me, Diane. I don't think I ever knew you."

"I'm hanging up now, Greg. I'm really tired."

Greg paused for a second and then replied, "Fine. I'll pick David up around noon."

"See you then."

"Get some rest. Good night."

"Bye."

She hung up and finished the glass of wine. It was doing the trick, but the phone call had unnerved her some more.

Diane glanced at the box of clippings on the floor. It was too late to do anything with them now. She told herself that she would destroy them the next day while David was at the ball game.

DAVID'S JOURNAL

Tonight is the first night in our new apartment. It's pretty weird being here. I grew up in the old house. I'll miss it. My room here isn't complete yet. I still have to put away all my stuff and put my posters on the walls. It won't feel like home until I do. I guess this is normal when someone moves to a new place.

I've been reading The Catcher in the Rye *and I identify with the main character. I don't think I'm as angry as he is, but I think he's lonely and I am too a lot of the time. My English teacher thought the book might be too adult for me but I told her it wasn't. I've read lots of books that are "adult." I don't see what the big deal is.*

Sometimes I feel very alone. I have no brothers or sisters (which might be a good thing!) but I have no cousins to speak of either. I have cousins, but they're a lot older than I am. My aunt and uncle (my Dad's older sister) had two kids but they're in college. I never see them. I think I wrote before that my best friend is Billy Davis. There's no one else, really. I'm too much of a geek to have many friends. Mom says that will pass as I get older. If I live long enough.

It's weird to think that my grandfather had Marfan syndrome and that he died from it. Things are different today, though. My doctor is confident that I won't die as long as I take it easy until I can have that heart operation. He figures by the time I'm out of high school I'll be able to have it.

Mom seems pretty distracted lately. Tonight I was asking her about her life before she got married to Dad, like I sometimes do, and she went all zombie-like again on me. I mean she sort of stares ahead with this blank look. I think memories are painful to her and she doesn't like to think about them. I wonder what it was that happened to her. Maybe someday she'll tell me.

I found a box full of newspaper clippings tonight when we were unpacking. I'd never seen them before. Mom acted real strange when I found them. She looked like she was afraid of them or something. She says she's going to throw them away. I sure would like to find out what's on them before she does.

Tomorrow I'm going to see the Cubs with my Dad. That'll be fun.

Time for bed.

CHAPTER FOUR

The judge had told the jurors they were to remain sequestered throughout the weekend and then asked if they thought a verdict might be reached if they continued deliberations through Saturday. The jurors unanimously voted to keep working with the hope that they could go home before midnight and still have half the weekend to be with their families. It had been a long trial and they had been deliberating for three full days.

When the news got out at nine o'clock that the jury had reached a verdict, nearly all of the major television and newspaper journalists in Los Angeles swarmed the courthouse. The case had been well publicized, even though the man accused of the numerous crimes had hardly been a household name before the trial. Now the name of Aaron Valentine had joined the ranks of L.A.'s notorious and infamous.

Darren Marshall paid for a cup of coffee and ran out of the Starbucks to join the throng of other reporters filing up the steps and into the building. He had gone through the metal detectors many times over the past few weeks and now knew the security guards by name.

"Howzit goin', Sam?" he asked the sergeant in charge of the detail.

Sam grunted and wiped the sweat off his thick, black brow. "I'm hopin' this is it, Mister Marshall. Maybe we can all go home in an hour."

"Yeah, go home is right. Then I'll have to stay up all night writing my story."

"You best hurry. The courtroom's almost full."

"Thanks, Sam."

Clear of security, Marshall walked briskly down the hall and decided to forego the elevator and take the stairs. The courtroom was not a standing-room-only venue. If you were late, you were late. Tough luck. Marshall reflected that his boss at the *Weekly* would not take too kindly to that. If it were up to Brandon Mertz, City News Editor, then yellow journalists like Darren Marshall would *sleep* outside the courtroom in order to get a seat.

The ironic thing about it was that Marshall knew he probably *would* sleep outside the courtroom if he had to. His colleagues described him as overly ambitious and something of an asshole. That he would do anything to get ahead. At twenty-eight years old, Darren Marshall was already the *Weekly*'s star reporter, but he wanted more. He figured that if he conquered the *Weekly*, then he could move to the *Times* with ease. Unfortunately, the *Times* didn't publish the types of stories Marshall was best at writing. He went for the scandals, the sleaze, the controversial, and the weird. He hadn't cut his teeth at the *National Enquirer* for nothing. Tabloid journalism was ingrained in him and he couldn't help it. Besides, it was *fun*. Writing about addicted celebrities or mass murderers sure beat the hell out of writing about stocks and bonds or the latest traffic snarl.

For years Marshall thought he wanted to be a psychiatrist. The human mind fascinated him and he loved reading about the cases of Freud and other pioneers in the field. He especially enjoyed studying criminal psychology and learning everything he could about what made psychopaths tick. He liked to annoy his friends, and sometimes girlfriends, by performing amateur psychoanalysis on them. He had actually gone to college to study the field but dropped out after two years, mainly because he was too lazy to go the distance. He ended up relegating the practice to a harmless hobby. Falling into tabloid journalism seemed to Marshall to be the next logical step and he loved it.

The only rotten thing about being a journalist was the hours that he had to keep. This was a constant bone of contention between him and Ellie, his girlfriend of three months. She worked as a waitress at Mel's Diner on Sunset, so she had predictable hours. Ellie often complained that Marshall was always out chasing a story. She figured that at the rate their relationship was going she might as well become a nun.

Marshall laughed to himself at the thought of that image. Ellie had pink hair, several tattoos, and a pierced nose. She'd look *wonderful* in a habit.

He made it to the courtroom just in time and was able to claim a seat in the back. Valentine and his lawyer were already seated, as were the DA and his various assistants. Within minutes, the doors were closed and two court officers stood guard.

A large reporter whom Marshall recognized as being from one of the L.A. tabloids was sitting next to him. "I can't understand why Valentine attracted this much attention," he said to Marshall. "It's not a sensational case."

"We made it sensational," Marshall whispered. "Tell the public that something is sensational, and it's sensational. Besides, he's one of those rich pornographers."

"I guess."

The bailiff called the court to order and told those present to rise. Judge Goodner walked in and took his place on the bench. He acknowledged that everyone was present and then asked the bailiff to bring in the jury.

The twelve men and women filed in and took their places. Marshall always tried to read the expressions on their faces and guess what the verdict was going to be. He was never right. This time, though, he figured that Valentine would get off. The prosecution had a weak case and Valentine had mob connections. He *was* the mob, as far as Marshall was concerned.

Aaron Valentine sat calmly and eyed the jurors. He didn't appear nervous at all. In fact, at one point he leaned over to his lawyer, whispered something, and snickered. At sixty-three, Valentine cut a large and imposing figure. His white, bushy moptop made him look as if he were the world's oldest Beatles fan and he continually dressed in out-of-fashion seventies gear. The gold chains and silk shirts the man wore were blatantly kitsch symbols of sexual power. The man had money, he had a lucrative but controversial business, he threw extravagant Hollywood parties, and he had charisma. Those things went a long way, even in the American justice system.

"Has the jury reached a verdict?" the judge asked.

"We have, your honor."

The sacred piece of paper was passed to the judge, who glanced at it without expression, and handed it over. The bailiff took it and read the charges and looked to the foreman for the corresponding verdicts. Marshall scribbled them quickly into his notebook as they were called out.

On the charge of racketeering . . . not guilty.

Pandering . . . not guilty.

Drug trafficking . . . not guilty.

Contributing to the delinquency of a minor (which really meant "employing underage girls in pornographic films") . . . not guilty.

Distributing obscene materials . . . not guilty.

When the last one was called out, Valentine raised both fists in victory. His lawyer audibly expressed his joy, while the folks at the other table sighed and glared at the defendant.

"I'd like to poll the jury, your honor," the DA said.

Standard operating procedure. Marshall listened as each juror repeated the verdicts for the benefit of the prosecution. There was no indication that Valentine's organization had tampered with the jury, although Marshall would have bet on it. The prosecution's case was not the best, but someone like Valentine would have made sure he wouldn't be spending the remaining years of his life in prison. He had an empire to run.

"Too bad they couldn't charge him with the murder rap," said the large man sitting next to Marshall.

"There was no evidence," Marshall replied. "Just conjecture."

"You think he did it?"

"I think he *ordered* it. A guy like Aaron Valentine doesn't get his own hands dirty. He thinks he's above it all. The way his mind works, he believes he's innocent because he doesn't actually do the deeds."

"What are you, his shrink?" the large man asked.

Marshall chuckled. There he was, psychoanalyzing again. The large man said good-bye and got up. Marshall stood and watched Valentine light a big cigar. One of the bailiffs told him he couldn't smoke in the courtroom, so Valentine stubbed it out on the mahogany table surface. He walked out with his lawyer, laughing. Another large and scary-looking man with shoulder-length blond hair and a black eye patch joined them. Marshall knew who he was. The guy's name was Emo Tuff, Valentine's right hand man. It was rumored that Emo Tuff was the muscle behind Valentine's organization and wasn't afraid of doing the dirty work. Marshall had heard that Tuff could crush a skull with the thumb and third finger of one hand.

Marshall squeezed through the crowd and chased them to the elevator.

"Mister Valentine! Mister Valentine!" he shouted over the cries of other reporters. His voice must have carried because Valentine turned and looked at him.

"How does it feel to be cleared of these charges?" Marshall asked, breathlessly.

"These charges were ridiculous," Valentine said in the soft, yet menacing voice that the world had come to know in the last few weeks. "Thank God for the American justice system. I knew a jury of my peers wouldn't convict me. My business provides a service to the public. Some people may not agree with everything I do, but you can't argue with its popularity. My business sold four point three billion dollars worth of merchandise last year. That means that most of the American public likes what I do for a living."

"By that, sir, you mean you sold four point three billion dollars worth of pornography?" Marshall asked.

"Call it what you like, young man," Valentine replied. "This is a free country, and tonight's verdict proves it."

"What do you plan to do now?" Marshall asked as the elevator doors opened. "And can I get an interview for the *Weekly*?"

"I'm going home, where I'll open a nice bottle of champagne and share it with my girlfriends. As for the interview, call my office. Good night." With that, he and his entourage stepped into the elevator. Emo Tuff kept the reporters out of the car and the doors closed.

Marshall was satisfied. He got a scoop. Now he had to get home, write the story, and have it on the editor's desk before dawn.

Then maybe Ellie would have breakfast with him.

As the limo pulled into the gates of Paradise, Aaron Valentine felt a rare surge of emotion. It had been too long since he had been to his beloved estate in Woodland Hills. The exterior lights illuminated the three-story Tudor mansion with the gold and white color scheme, signifying an important event. Valentine had wanted the lighting on the property to reflect his moods. Some nights the house was blue and peaceful. Other nights it was red and passionate. The gold and white scheme was reserved for special nights like this one—Valentine was coming home after seven months in prison. And it felt good. Very good.

"I still don't understand why your lawyer couldn't get you bail," Emo Tuff said. He sat across from Valentine, facing the back of the limo.

"Baxter didn't do shit for me," Valentine said. "First thing tomorrow morning, I'm going to fire him."

"You *did* get off," Tuff reminded him.

"No thanks to Baxter."

Tuff laughed.

"So which juror did you get to?" Valentine asked.

"Make that plural, boss," Tuff answered. "There were three. We picked the ones we thought would have the most influence on the rest of the jury. Hell, we were just hoping for a mistrial, but you got away with the jackpot."

"I wasn't worried," Valentine said. He looked out the window and smiled. "Ahh, Paradise. Long time no see."

The car pulled up to the front of the mansion and stopped. A security guard and Charlie, the black man-servant who had worked for Valentine since 1967, opened the door for him.

"Welcome back, boss," Charlie said.

Valentine got out and smelled the air. "Lavender is the most wonderful scent in the world," he said, referring to his favorite flower that grew in abundance on the property. "Thank you, Charlie. It's good to be back."

He went inside the house, where the staff stood waiting for him. As soon as he was through the door, they all applauded. Everyone was there—the cook, the maids, the groundskeepers, the security guards, his assistants, and his girlfriends.

Valentine bowed dramatically and laughed boisterously. "Hello friends!" he shouted. "Charlie, break out the finest champagne. I believe it's time to celebrate."

The three women—a blonde, a brunette, and a redhead—snaked over to him and draped themselves around his massive girth. He kissed each one deeply, fondling their behinds as he did so.

Emo Tuff stood in the doorway and smiled.

The boss was home.

Valentine stepped into his office but the redhead stuck her head through the open door behind him.

"Aaron! What are you doing?" she asked.

"I'll be out in a minute, baby," he said. He kissed her on the forehead and gently shoved her out. "I have to talk to Emo for a minute. Go dance with the other girls, will ya?"

He shut the door and locked it. Tuff was at Valentine's large desk, eyeing the computer monitor.

"Enjoying yourself, boss?" Tuff asked.

"Emo, before I go upstairs and get the living daylights fucked out of me, tell me something good," Valentine said.

Tuff rolled back in the chair and put his hands behind his head. "The company's doing fine, boss. ESF made a shitload of money this quarter. Forty-six million."

Valentine's eyes moved to the framed poster on the wall behind the desk. It had been Erotica Selecta Films' first feature, back in 1975. *Hot Fruit*, starring Jack Devlin and Terri Tremble.

"That's better than last quarter," he said.

"You're telling me. Suzy Slick is turning out to be a major star. We've got her headlining seven titles this month. Nancy Melons is still selling. Dirk Everwood is at the top of the gay list. We're doing okay."

"How about Sheila?" Valentine asked. He sat on the sofa, beneath the expansive Jackson Pollock that adorned the wall.

"Sheila Rivers is getting old," Tuff said.

"She's thirty-two."

"You know what I mean. She looks fifteen years older. I think the junk has made a mess of her."

Valentine shook his head. "That happens to some of them, doesn't it."

"She nearly screwed up production of one of our gang bang titles. She flipped out on the set and was impossible to handle."

"Guess it's time she retires."

"Yeah. At least her old titles still sell."

The two men sat in silence for a moment. Finally Valentine said, "So, I guess you handled things pretty well while I was gone."

Tuff shrugged. "I did my best. Rudy did his part at the office." Rudy Alfredo, although he was vice president of Erotica Selecta, was basically a figurehead.

"Well, I guess I'll get back to my girls." Valentine started to rise but Tuff held up a hand.

"Wait a sec. I got a surprise for you, boss."

Valentine relaxed back into the sofa. "Yeah?"

Tuff took a small jewelry box out of a desk drawer, stood, and walked to the sofa. He held the box out to Valentine.

"What, are you asking me to marry you?" Valentine asked.

"Open it, boss."

Valentine took the box and flipped the lid. The brilliance of the gem nearly made him choke.

"Is this what I think it is?" he asked in a whisper.

Tuff nodded.

Valentine picked up the diamond and held it to the light. "It is, isn't it! Where the hell did you get it?"

"It surfaced in New York, boss. We think there are more where this came from. There's a dealer there, some Jewish guy who owns a shop in the diamond district. He's getting them from somewhere."

Valentine looked at Tuff. "That means the bitch is alive."

Tuff nodded.

"Find her." Valentine replaced the diamond and shut the box. "Find her and bring her to me."

CHAPTER FIVE

Greg Boston made it a point never to miss the golf course on Sundays. He usually played at the Ivanhoe Country Club, where he, like his father before him, was a member. Being one of the most successful automobile dealers in the county, Greg was treated like royalty. Sam, the golf pro, normally attempted to put together a foursome that included Greg's lawyer, Mark Spencer, but some days it didn't work out. In those cases, Greg usually played alone with Spencer. This Sunday was one of those days.

Spencer drove his ball down the fairway of the seventh hole and looked back at Greg. "What's eating you?"

Greg waved him away. "Aw, nothing. Just the usual stuff."

"Diane?"

"Yeah."

"What's up?"

Greg put his ball on the tee. He didn't speak as he prepared to knock it farther and straighter than Spencer's. He drew his favorite driver from the bag, assumed the stance, and concentrated. He lifted the club back and swung.

The ball shot awkwardly into the trees on the left.

"Well, shit," he muttered.

"Seriously, what's up?" Spencer asked again.

"Nothing really. She and David moved out of the house yesterday. They're in an apartment now."

"You knew that was going to happen."

"I know, but it's depressing. That was a nice house."

The two men began to walk down the fairway carrying their clubs.

"You didn't expect to move back in, did you?" Spencer asked.

"No."

"So what's the problem?"

"It's just . . . oh, never mind."

They walked a good hundred yards before Greg said, "Mine's over *there*." He pointed to the left and veered away from Spencer. He looked at his watch and saw that he had a couple of hours left before he had to pick up David for the ball game. He and Spencer had agreed to play only nine holes that morning.

The divorce still irked him. It had been his idea, it was true, but he never would have done it if Diane had been more forthcoming. After living alone again for a few months, Greg began to realize things that he hadn't fully comprehended when he and Diane were courting and eventually became man and wife.

Diane was one mysterious woman. He never knew any of her family members, and the story was that they were all dead. He wasn't totally sure where she was from. She said she was born and raised in Illinois, but she had some relatives at one time in Texas, too. Diane said she had lived with an aunt and uncle down there after her mother died.

There were gaps in her history that he didn't understand. There was a period in the late seventies and early eighties that he couldn't account for. She didn't go to college until the mid-eighties, after she was in her thirties.

What did she do before then? Where was she during her twenties?

Once Greg had attempted to draw her out but she was evasive and quick to change the subject. Eventually he let it go and tried to enjoy the marriage as it was. But other things gnawed at him.

He noticed that she disappeared after school every now and then. She would be gone for several hours and return to Lincoln Grove in the evening. When he asked where she had been, Diane would reply that she had gone shopping. But she never bought anything.

Greg followed her one afternoon, a couple of years before the divorce. She drove to Chicago and got off the expressway before reaching the Loop. The traffic was heavier there and he lost her, so he never did find out where she went. That evening, he asked about her day and she never mentioned driving downtown. It was as if she were keeping something from him. A few days later he asked her directly about where she had gone and admitted that he followed her. She jumped all over him for doing so.

"I'm entitled to my privacy," she said.

Greg finally decided that she was *too* private. The final straw was her lack of enthusiasm for sex. He filed for divorce.

He and Spencer met up at the hole. Spencer was shooting for par and smoothly knocked his ball into the cup. Greg lined up his putter, took aim, and tapped the ball. It swerved around the hole and came to rest three inches away.

"Shit," he muttered again.

"This isn't your day," Spencer said.

"Tell me about it."

"It's really bugging you, isn't it?"

"What?"

"Diane. The house."

"Yeah. Mostly I want to get David away from her. She's bad for him."

"How so?"

"She's not a very loving person."

This time he knocked it into the cup. The men retrieved their balls and walked toward the next tee.

"Maybe not to you, she wasn't," Spencer said. "From what I can see, she's just fine with David."

"Geez, whose side are you on?"

"Come on, Greg. She's a good mother and she has a respectable job and she's well-liked at school."

"I want custody of David."

Spencer shook his head. "You'll never win. We've been through this before. Courts always favor the mother in custody cases. There's nothing that would suggest Diane's an unfit mother, which is something we'd have to prove. You can't win a custody battle, Greg."

"She's so closed up," Greg said. "She has secrets and I get the feeling that they're not pretty."

"It's not a crime to have secrets."

"What if the secrets *were* crimes?"

Spencer looked sideways at Greg. "Come on. Diane?"

"I don't know," Greg said. "It's something that she doesn't talk about. It must be bad."

"Maybe it's just painful for her. Maybe it has something to do with an old lover or a family member or something. Who knows? Greg, it doesn't matter. Forget it."

"It does matter. I want David, and I'll think of something. Promise me that if I find out anything useful, we'll file for custody."

"It's your wallet, Greg," Spencer said as they reached the tee. "But I reserve the right to refuse the case if I think it's a no-winner."

"Fine."

"You go ahead," Spencer said, indicating the tee.

Greg placed the ball and repeated the ritual of choosing a club, getting comfortable in front of the ball, and concentrating.

This time the ball went straight down the fairway a good three hundred yards.

CHAPTER SIX

A shiver ran up David's spine when the school bell rang at 2:45. It was time to face what some idiot had coined "the music."

David glanced across the room at his friend Billy as he gathered his books and stuffed them inside his backpack. Billy gave him a look that indicated, "I'm glad I'm not in your shoes."

The teacher, Mrs. Brownlove, shouted above the clamor, "Don't forget to do the study questions at the end of chapter seventeen!"

The students poured out of the room, but David remained in his seat. Billy made his way for the door and asked, "You coming?"

David sighed. It was no use trying to hide. "I guess." He got up and joined his friend.

"Have a good day, boys," Mrs. Brownlove said, oblivious to the drama that was unfolding before her.

"Bye," the boys replied in unison.

Billy peeked into the hallway and looked both directions. "All clear so far," he said. David followed him out and went down the hall, straight to his locker.

They heard Matt's voice before he had turned the corner.

"It's clobberin' time!"

"Oh, great," David mumbled. He shut his locker and walked in the opposite direction from where the voice had come.

"If we hurry maybe we can make it out the side door before he catches up to us," Billy suggested.

"Hey, Boston!"

It was too late but they kept walking anyway.

"Hey, Boston, I'm talking to you!"

David winced and stopped. He turned around to face his number one enemy.

Matt Shamrock was the school's biggest and meanest bully. For some reason, he had it in for David Boston since the beginning of the school year. Matt apparently didn't like the fact that David made good grades and it really irked him that David didn't have to take Gym. On the second day of school, Matt had asked him, "Hey, pussy, why aren't you in Gym?"

David had replied, "Doctor's excuse."

"What's the matter, afraid you'll get hurt?"

"No, it's a heart thing."

"A heart thing? What's that supposed to mean?"

David had tried to walk away but Matt kept at it. "Hey, I'm talking to you. Don't walk away from me." He whirled David around to face him. "What's the matter with your heart?"

"I have a congenital disease," David replied.

"You have a genital disease? Hey, everyone, this kid's got VD!" Matt shouted to the others.

"Congenital," David said. "It means I was born with it, you idiot."

Matt's goofy grin disappeared. "What did you say?"

"Never mind. I gotta go."

"Fuck you, you ain't going anywhere."

Luckily for David, the vice-principal came around the corner at that moment and Matt Shamrock changed his tune.

"Hey, we'll see you in Gym, buddy," Matt said, slapping David on the back with slightly too much force.

Ever since that fateful encounter, Matt Shamrock had looked for every opportunity to make David's life at school a miserable hell. The bully especially liked to cross paths with David on the way out of the building at the end of the day. Now that David had moved to the new apartment, David lived close enough to walk back and forth, which he was happy to do. As long as he didn't run and exert himself too much, the walking was good for him. Matt Shamrock hadn't learned David's route yet but it was only a matter of time before he would appear to taunt him.

Earlier, at lunch, David and Billy had been in line to buy a dessert. Matt Shamrock and his goon squad cut in front of them. David spoke up.

"You're not supposed to cut in line, Shamrock," he said.

Matt turned and looked at David as if the tall, skinny boy were some kind of bug. In actuality, David was taller than Shamrock, but the bully was beefier and certainly stronger.

"Why don't you shut the fuck up?" he said.

"You're a real asshole, Shamrock," David said quietly.

Matt's eyes grew big and his three pals gasped.

"You gonna let him get away with that, Shamrock?" the one named Carl asked.

"What did you say, butt face?" Matt asked.

"Look, just buy your dessert and leave us alone," David said.

Matt inched closer to David, fists clenched, but before he could do anything he saw Mrs. Tuttenberg, the teacher assigned to patrol lunch period for the day. She was a few feet away, giving a kid hell for throwing a napkin at his neighbor.

"You're lucky, shithead," Matt said. "If Mrs. Tutti Frutti wasn't right over there, you'd be on the floor."

"Oh well," David said, standing up to his tormentor. "I guess that's too bad."

"But after school, my friend," Matt said, "after school on your way home, it'll be clobberin' time." For some reason, Matt always quoted the Thing from the *Fantastic Four* comic books. David doubted that the bully had read anything in his life, even a comic.

Now the witching hour had come. David faced the enemy but he had one advantage—they were still inside the school.

"Why don't you leave him alone?" Billy ventured. It was the first time Billy had ever stood up for his friend.

Matt Shamrock ignored Billy. "So, Boston, you about to walk home? Shall I carry your books for you? You don't mind a little company, do you?"

David shrugged. "Sure. Come on. When we get to my house we can play something on my PS2, if you can handle the controls." He turned and started walking.

Matt Shamrock creased his brow. This wasn't the reaction he had expected. "I can beat the shit out of you, Boston, anytime, anywhere," he shouted.

"Mister Shamrock?" The voice of Vice-Principal McDonald boomed from down the hall. "Watch your language, young man!"

David and Billy continued to move to the exit. They pushed open the door and went outside just as the most-feared adult at school pulled Matt Shamrock's right earlobe. David and Billy heard the word "detention" mentioned before they were out of earshot.

"I guess you'll make it home in one piece after all," Billy said.

"Yeah. Thanks for sticking up for me."

"No problem. I don't think it did any good, though."

As they walked across the school parking lot toward the sidewalk, David felt his heart pounding. He often got palpitations if something caused his adrenaline to pump. Sometimes it happened if he was excited, nervous, or anticipating something such as a doctor's visit, a test at school, or a conversation with one of the pretty girls. He had to be careful, his doctor had told him. Whenever he had palpitations, David was to stop what he was doing and breathe deeply. He was to relax and mentally push the anxiety away. Sometimes he could do it pretty well. Other times it was more difficult, depending on the situation.

David stopped walking and sat on the curb.

"You all right?" Billy asked.

"Yeah, I just gotta sit a minute," he said. He closed his eyes and breathed.

"You sure?"

"Shhhh."

"I can go get someone if you want."

"Quiet, Billy! I'm trying to meditate. It's okay, really."

"Sorry."

"You go on. Come over to the apartment later. I gave you the address."

"I'll stay if you want."

"No, really. Go on. I think I want to be alone," David said.

"Well, all right. I'll be over in an hour."

"Okay."

Billy walked on. David figured that one advantage to living in the new apartment was that he was closer to Billy's house. They had planned to walk to and from school together, at least until they got into high school.

David continued his breathing exercises and eventually calmed down. The scary thumping in his chest eased up and finally he was able to stand and continue the trek home.

He hoped this wouldn't become a daily occurrence.

CHAPTER SEVEN

David opened the door and found Billy standing on stone stoop where Diane had placed the "Welcome" mat. The apartment was on the ground floor of the complex and in many ways was more like a duplex than an apartment. Each dwelling had its own separate façade that indicated the apartments were individual homes—they were just connected to each other in one large building.

"What's up?" Billy asked.

"Nothing. Come in."

Billy walked inside and David shut the door. "You feeling better?"

"Yeah."

Billy nodded his head in artificial appreciation as he dropped his backpack on the floor and moved through the main room. The apartment was still full of boxes and other signs of a recent move. "So this is the new place," he said. "Nice."

"It's all right. We sure don't have a lot of room."

"What did you do with all the stuff that wouldn't fit?"

"I guess Mom sold it. Remember we had that aquarium?"

"Yeah."

"She got rid of that."

Billy went to the glass door that faced the backyard. "Big yard," he said.

"It's not all ours," David explained. "It belongs to everybody. We have that little deck and the grill, but that's about it."

"Where's your room?"

"Back this way." David led his friend into the hallway and into the first bedroom on the right. His room was almost half as big as his bedroom in the old house and David was having a hard time finding a place for all his things.

Billy looked at the mess and nodded some more. "Nice."

"Not really," David said. "But maybe after we get some shelves on the walls and I get this junk off the floor, it might be."

It was obvious that they really didn't have room to play in there. They moved back into the living room but bypassed the television and went straight to the kitchen. David opened the fridge and asked, "You want anything to drink?"

"What do you have?"

"Orange juice, some sodas, some beer . . ."

"I'll have a beer."

"Yeah, me too." David tossed a Pepsi to Billy and took one for himself.

"So what do you want to do?" Billy asked.

"I don't know. We could go outside, I guess. Or watch TV. But we don't have cable yet."

"Is your DVD player hooked up?"

"I think so. The VCR too."

Billy grinned mischievously. "Great. You won't believe what I've got."

"What?"

"You'll see."

Billy grabbed his backpack and unzipped it. He removed a videocassette housed in a plain, white box.

"What's that?" David asked.

"I found a box of porno movies in our crawl space the other day," Billy said. "They belong to my dad. I watched one of them at home when he wasn't there. Pretty incredible stuff!"

"You're shitting me."

"No, really! They're pretty old. You can tell 'cause the quality isn't very good."

"Is that one of them?"

Billy wiggled his eyebrows. "Uh huh. I haven't seen this one yet. I just grabbed one out of the box and thought we'd watch it together."

"Far out!" His friend's enthusiasm was infectious. David quickly forgot the warnings going off in his head and turned on the television. He slipped the cassette into the VCR and the two boys sat on the couch to watch.

After the initial leader passed, a company logo appeared—Erotica Selecta Films.

"This one's by a different company," Billy observed. "The one I watched before was from some Swedish studio."

David didn't say a word. His eyes were glued to the screen as the main titles came on. The name of the feature was *Blondes Have a Helluva Lot More Fun*. The stars were Lucy Luv, Angel Babe, Karen Klinger, Pete Rod, Jerry Zork, and Paul Stud. The boys laughed when they read the names.

The movie was shot on film and was obviously a low-budget production. Although it was in color, the picture was grainy and had a home-movie quality to it. Still, it was clear enough.

The story opened on a housewife who says good-bye to her husband as he goes off to work. She is blond, of course, and is wearing a dirty old bathrobe. David felt as if the actress was familiar to him, but he couldn't place how. Nevertheless he responded to something about her, for his heart began to beat faster.

The woman sat at the kitchen table and began to look through a fashion magazine. As her blue eyes lingered over the ads of women wearing lingerie, she slowly loosened the front of the robe and reached inside. She began to caress and squeeze her breasts.

"Holy shit!" Billy editorialized.

It didn't take long for the actress to open the robe completely, revealing a completely naked body. She closed her eyes and began to touch herself between her legs, fantasizing about something that only she knew.

"Whoa . . ." Billy murmured.

Before the woman got very far in her self-pleasure, her doorbell rang. She looked up, surprised, and quickly closed the robe. She got up and the camera followed her to the front door. She looked through the peephole and saw the mailman holding a package.

"Yes?" she asked.

"Package, ma'am," he called through the door.

She opened it and saw that he was an attractive young man, well built and tall.

The camera came in for a close-up as she grinned wickedly and invited the mailman inside. The actor playing the mailman adequately conveyed surprise and naiveté as he brought the package inside. The woman closed the door behind her and locked it. She told him to put the package on the table in the entry hall, then led the boy to the sofa in her living room. Before he could protest, she slipped off the robe and stood before him in all her glory.

"I think I'm gonna be a mailman when I grow up," Billy joked. David laughed.

The woman knelt before the mailman and undid his pants. She released him and got to work without another word.

"Look how big that guy is!" Billy exclaimed.

"I don't believe it," David said.

"He's fucking *huge!*"

"Yeah . . ."

But David wasn't getting any pleasure out of watching. Something was definitely wrong and he couldn't quite put his finger on it. He thought that maybe he was feeling guilty for watching a porno tape and that he might get in a lot of trouble if his mom found out. That was probably it.

"I think I better turn it off," David said.

"No! Let's keep watching!"

"My mom will be home soon."

"Come on! Look, she's gonna fuck him now!"

Sure enough, the woman straddled the man's waist and the boys could see exactly how it was done. The camera came in uncomfortably close. The woman's moans and the man's grunts filled the room. The actors began a vigorous rocking that left nothing to the imagination. Then the camera came in for another close-up on the woman.

"Shit, David," Billy said.

"What."

"Do you recognize her?"

"Who?"

"That lady! In the movie!"

"No, why should I?"

"David! Look close!"

"What the hell are you talking about?"

"That's your mom!"

David felt his heart skip a beat. A sudden sick sensation in his stomach nearly overwhelmed him.

"No it's not," he said, weakly.

"Yes it is. Look!"

"It's not her. Don't be stupid."

"David. She's a lot younger but that's definitely her. Don't you recognize her voice? *Look at her!*"

David couldn't help but look and in the process realized what had been bothering him. It must have hit him subconsciously as soon as they had begun the tape but it hadn't registered. Now it was completely clear. As much as he wanted to disbelieve it, as much as he wanted to scream and deny the whole thing, what Billy said was true.

The woman performing sex on the tape was indeed his mother.

Both boys heard the faint slam of a car door. It came from the apartment's one-car garage, adjacent to the kitchen.

"My mom's home!" David cried. He jumped up, stopped the VCR, and ejected the tape. He fumbled with it, trying to get it inside the blank box but couldn't seem to make it fit.

"Here!" Billy said as he grabbed it from his friend. Billy got the cassette inside the case just as the kitchen door opened and Diane Boston walked in. Billy held the tape behind his back.

"Hello boys," Diane said. "What's going on?"

"Oh, uh, we were just watching TV," David said.

She looked and saw that the screen was dark. "What's on?"

David turned and noticed the television. "Nothing," he said. "We really need to get that cable!"

"They're coming next week," Diane said. She put her things on the kitchen counter. "How are you, Billy?"

"Fine."

"How's school?"

"Okay."

She grinned and shook her head. Billy was a boy of few words. "Oh, I left something in the car. Be right back." Diane went out through the kitchen door to the garage. David followed her and watched his mother retrieve some poster board from the trunk.

"You need help?" David called.

"No, thank you, David. I have to prepare some visuals for my sociology class," she said.

Billy used this opportunity to quickly stuff the video-tape into his backpack and zip it up.

When he and his mother were back inside, David turned off the TV and suggested to Billy, "Let's go in my room."

"Okay."

The boys disappeared, leaving Diane to stand and survey the boxes in the living room. "David!" she called. "I'm going to need your help in unpacking some of this stuff!"

"Okay, Mom!" he shouted back.

Diane figured that if they could clear away everything from the living room, they might feel more at home. There was still a lot of work to do.

Billy and David reemerged. "I'm finished with this," Billy said, indicating his Pepsi can.

"Oh, the recycling is in that paper bag in the kitchen," Diane said. She began to pull books out of one of the boxes.

Billy went into the kitchen, dropped his can into the bag, and headed straight for the front door.

"See you tomorrow, David," he said.

"Bye, Billy," Diane said.

"Yeah, see ya," David echoed. He didn't look at his friend. Instead, his eyes were on his mother, who was now kneeling on the floor in front of the box of books. She was in the same position as she had been in the video.

The sick feeling in David's stomach returned full force.

She looked up at him. "What's wrong?"

"Huh?"

"You look funny."

"I do?" He shook his head and said, "Here, let me help."

He bent over a box and ripped it open as a million thoughts cluttered his confused mind.

CHAPTER EIGHT

David twisted the spaghetti with his fork and watched it gather sauce. He sat with his head in one hand, his elbow on the table.

"Anything wrong, honey?" Diane asked.

The fork continued to slowly twirl the pasta.

"David?"

He looked up. "Hmm?"

"Anything wrong? You're playing with your dinner."

"Oh. I'm just not very hungry, Mom." He took his elbow off the table and sat up straight. "Sorry."

"Spaghetti is your favorite. I've never seen you not eat it, even when you had the flu!"

"I guess I just don't have much of an appetite tonight."

Diane looked at him sideways. "Is that bully still bothering you at school?"

He shook his head. "No. Well, yeah, he is, but that's not it."

"Then what is it?"

"Nothing. Really. Don't worry about it." He took a sip of orange juice and looked at his mother, who had resumed eating.

Was this really his mom? he wondered. Could she have

done what he had seen on the videotape? Was it possible? Maybe he and Billy had been wrong. Perhaps it really wasn't her. It was just someone who looked like her.

"What is it?" Diane asked. David realized that she had caught him staring at her. "Do I have something on my face?"

"No. Sorry."

"You were looking at me as if I were an alien."

"Aren't you?" David asked.

She wrinkled her brow. "Huh?"

David snickered and then she smiled. "Oh, you teaser," she said. "Come on, try to eat some more."

"I'm really not hungry, Mom." He pushed the plate forward and sat back in the chair. "I've got a little homework to do."

"David."

"What."

Diane thought about her words before she said them. "I know this is difficult for you. It's difficult for me, too."

"What is?"

"Moving. The new apartment. The divorce."

"Oh. That. Yeah, I guess."

"Your father and I couldn't stay together, David. We were unhappy. Neither of us believed that we should remain unhappy just for the sake of keeping up appearances. You understand that, don't you?"

"We've been through this before, Mom."

"I know, but you seem very down lately. Especially tonight."

"Maybe it's just the move. I'll get used to it."

She nodded and picked up her glass of wine. More and more she had found solace in wine after the sun had set. It eased the anxiety and numbed the pain better than anything else she had tried. Diane had tried antidepressants a while back, when she and Greg had first begun having problems, but she didn't like the side effects. She completely stopped going to the psychiatrist.

Besides, there was nothing wrong with her mind, she told herself. It was a chemical imbalance. That was it.

David got up from the table and left the room without saying another word. Diane was concerned about him. Perhaps the failure of the marriage had done more damage to him than she and Greg had anticipated. Another possibility was that Greg was feeding David's mind with more negativity, which he had been prone to do in the past.

Diane stood and went to the phone by the sofa. She dialed the number she knew by heart and waited until he answered.

"Hello?"

"Greg?"

"Oh, hi Diane."

"What are you doing?"

"Just finishing dinner. You?"

"Us too."

"How's the new place? Settled yet?"

"Not really. But it'll be all right. Once we get used to the lack of space." She hadn't intended for sarcasm to creep into her voice, but it had.

She heard him sigh. "Diane, did you call just to lay a guilt trip on me?"

"No. Have you been saying anything to David? I mean, about the divorce, or anything?"

"I don't know what you mean."

"Well, he's acting pretty strangely. He didn't eat his spaghetti tonight and you know how much he likes spaghetti."

"Jesus, Diane, maybe he's just not hungry."

"That's what he said. But he *always* eats his spaghetti."

"Well, did you ask him about it?"

"Yes. He said he wasn't hungry."

"Well, there you have it. He wasn't hungry."

"I think he's depressed about the move. And about the divorce."

"Well, that makes two of us," Greg said. "Or does that make three of us?"

"Hey, it wasn't my idea," she said.

"I'm hanging up, Diane."

"Wait. I didn't mean to start a fight."

"It seems like that's the only thing that happens when we talk. *You* called *me*, remember?"

She shook her head in frustration. It was impossible to talk to the man.

"Look, I just wanted to know if you had been saying anything negative to him. You have in the past, you know."

Greg cursed under his breath. "Diane, you're too much. I'll talk to you later. Tell David hello for me. Good night."

"Yeah, okay, run away."

"You know it's not like that. I didn't pick up the phone to have a fight."

"Fine. Good-bye."

"Good-bye."

She waited for him to hang up first. When he did, she slammed down the phone.

"Bastard," she muttered.

She reached for her wine and sipped it, sitting and staring at the blank television. She lost herself in the dark screen, unaware that David was peeking around the corner of the hallway and watching her.

DAVID'S JOURNAL

Mom did her spacing out trick again tonight. She had another fight with Dad on the phone and now she's sitting with her wine and staring at the TV. It isn't on.

I think I understand now what her big dark secret is.

Today Billy and I watched one of his dad's porno tapes that he found in his crawl space. I couldn't believe it. I've seen porno before, but this one shocked me more than what I've seen in the past. You know why? I swear the girl in the movie was my Mom.

I can't believe it and I don't want to believe it. But if it's true, then I guess that's it. That's the big secret. My Mom was a porno star. I wonder which one she was? I saw the names in the credits but I didn't know which one was my Mom. This requires some more research.

I wonder if Dad knew about this. Probably not. Unless that's why they got divorced. But probably not. I'll bet I'm the first one who's discovered the big secret.

There are also these strange newspaper clippings that she has in a box we found when we were moving. The box is still in the kitchen. There's another box on top so I bet she just forgot about them. She said she was going to get rid of them but she hasn't yet. Sometimes she gets that way. Sometimes Mom forgets to do something, like she's absent-minded or something. Sometimes I don't know how she teaches the classes she does at school, because at home she can be pretty flaky.

What would my friends do if they all find out my Mom was once a porn star? I sure hope Billy doesn't say anything. I'll have to tell him tomorrow at school to keep quiet about it. It might hurt her job at school.

Actually, I hate to say this, but it's kind of cool, in a way. "My Mom, the Porn Star." How many other kids can say that? How many other kids can look at their Moms and say, "Hey, I've seen her doing the nasty on film."

Probably not many.

CHAPTER NINE

It was past Billy Davis' bedtime. Nevertheless, he was anxious to watch another videotape from his father's stash. Earlier he had replaced the one he had watched with David and taken a different cassette from the box in the crawl space. Even though he was not yet a teenager, his body had begun to respond to erotic stimuli and this made the anticipation even more compelling. He understood, in theory, what was happening to him, and he enjoyed testing the boundaries of his newly discovered adolescence.

He waited in his room until he thought his father had gone to bed. The television in his dad's bedroom was broadcasting the ten o'clock news. It was a nightly ritual for his dad to watch the news until ten thirty and then turn off the light. As a teacher at the high school, his dad had to be out of the house before Billy.

Billy figured it was safe. Surely his dad wouldn't hear the TV in the living room if the volume was low. Billy got out of bed and carefully opened his bedroom door. The hallway was dark. He peeked out and saw the sliver of light underneath the closed door of his father's bedroom. Billy silently stepped into the hall and moved quickly around the corner. Once he was in the living room, he stopped and listened. The illuminated clock on the mantle read "10:30" but he could still faintly hear his father's television. He held his breath and waited until finally he heard the sound of a toilet flushing and then the news snapped off.

Billy crept to the television and turned it on with the remote. He rammed his thumb down on the volume control so that the sound wouldn't blare out when the picture appeared. When it did, the room was bathed in a silver flicker that cast Billy's shadow over the walls and ceiling behind him.

He turned on the VCR and pushed the cassette into the slot. A few seconds later, the television picture changed to the tape's leader. Billy inched up the volume so that he could hear just a little of the soundtrack.

The main credits began. This one was called *Babysitter Brothel* and had virtually the same cast as the other one. Billy watched with anticipation as the credits ended and the movie began. The story opened on a large country mansion where a rich couple was preparing to go out for the evening. The man wonders where the babysitter is. The wife replies that she is on the way.

The bell rings and the man opens the door to reveal the same actress that Billy and David saw in the first film—David's mother. This time she is dressed in a schoolgirl's uniform—plaid skirt, knee socks, white blouse, and her hair is done in pigtails. The man's expression indicates that he is extremely pleased with the babysitter's appearance.

The couple introduces the babysitter to their child, a young boy, and then goes out. The man, however, rubs his hand on the babysitter's bottom before leaving. Instead of being offended, the babysitter winks at him and registers that his advances are welcome.

The scene shifts in time. The babysitter has put the child to bed and is now alone in the huge living room, in front of a fireplace. Once again, she starts the action by focusing on giving herself pleasure.

"What the hell are you doing?"

Billy jumped and almost screamed. He quickly punched the remote and turned off the tape. The picture on the television switched to *The Tonight Show*.

Billy stammered, "Uh, I couldn't, uhm, sleep, so I thought I'd watch television."

"What the hell were you watching?" his father asked. He stood in the archway between the living room and the hallway, dressed in boxer shorts and an undershirt.

"Nothing. Some movie on cable."

"The hell it was. Give me the remote."

Billy was busted. There was no way out of it. He meekly handed the remote to his father. Peter Davis aimed it at the television and pressed "play."

Babysitter Brothel reappeared on the screen. Davis watched for a few seconds, taking in exactly what it was his son had been watching. Then he switched it off.

"Where did you get this?"

Billy stared at the floor, ashamed and humiliated.

"Answer me!"

"David found it," Billy lied.

"David? David Boston?"

Billy nodded.

"Where did he find it?"

"I don't know. It's his mother's."

Peter Davis blinked. "His mother's?"

Billy nodded again. He prayed that his father wouldn't recognize it as being one of his.

Peter almost laughed but didn't. "What makes you think it's his mother's?"

Billy shrugged. "David said he found a box of tapes when they were moving to their new apartment."

His father moved to the VCR and ejected the cassette. He examined it and then took a look at the box it came in. Billy closed his eyes and waited for the yelling, or perhaps the blows that would come.

Peter wasn't sure what he should do with this information. The tape looked like one from his old collection. He hadn't watched them in years.

"Well I guess I'm going to have to talk to David's mother about this," he said. "You know you're not supposed to be looking at this stuff."

"I know."

"We'll talk about it tomorrow. Now you better get to bed. You've got school in the morning."

Billy didn't move.

"Go on," his father prompted.

"Dad?"

"What."

"I don't think it would be a good idea to bring it up with David's mom."

"Why not?"

Billy hesitated and then came out with it. "Well, she's in it."

"What do you mean?"

"She's *in* it. The tape. She's an actress in it."

Peter looked at his son in disbelief. "I don't think so, Billy."

"She is. I think she made a bunch of those movies when she was younger."

Peter examined the box and cassette again, turning it over as if he were hoping that some kind of identifying information would magically appear on it.

Finally, he just said, "Get to bed. Now."

Billy ran past him, down the hall, and into his room.

Peter held the tape in his hand. What did he have here? Diane Boston? In a porno movie? What kind of a hand grenade was he holding?

This warranted closer inspection.

Peter shut off the television and carried the tape back to

his bedroom, where he had his own set, VCR, and DVD player. He shut the door, turned on the TV, and inserted the cassette. The movie resumed where it had left off.

The "babysitter," about to reach her moment of ecstasy, is interrupted when the child's parents arrive back home. The woman instructs the man to pay the babysitter and take her home. The man is all too happy to do so.

After a moment, Peter indeed recognized the video as one he had watched a few times during his bachelor days. His son had lied to him. Billy had been snooping around in the crawl space.

The movie continued. The man escorts the babysitter outside, gives her some money, and then slips her a hundred-dollar bill. He asks her if she'd like to earn a "little extra." The babysitter bats her eyes and tells him that she'd love to. They drive a ways and turn down a deserted road. The man parks the car and then . . . they go to it.

Peter had looked at his fair share of pornography in his time. When he was in college in the seventies, he had made it something of a hobby. He gave it up when he got married but unfortunately his taste for younger women and desire for sex on the side railroaded that venture. After the divorce he had continued to look at and watch porn when he could get away with it, although he hadn't dug out his old collection in years. In many ways, Peter considered himself something of a connoisseur when it came to the pornography industry. He knew who the performers were and he followed the various genres. He could name the classic films and the stars.

And he recognized the actress playing the babysitter as Lucy Luv.

He remembered that Lucy Luv appeared on the porno scene in the late seventies and was around for two or three years and then disappeared. All of her films had been transferred to videotape later in the eighties, once the video boom hit big. He wasn't very familiar with her "work" but he had seen her before and was aware that she had been a promising newcomer, a star of a handful of films, and then she quit the business. If he recalled correctly, there had even been a rumor that she had died.

Peter smiled. Now he understood why he found Diane Boston so attractive. He saw something in her that no one else did. Ever since he had met her, Peter had a sense of *déjà vu* when he was around her. The one time they went on a date he had asked her if they had met before they began working together at the high school. Diane had smirked and said, "Not likely." He had never been able to shake the feeling that she looked familiar.

Now he knew why.

Sure, Diane Boston looked a lot different now. She was older, she wore her hair differently, and she wore contacts to change the color of her eyes.

Nevertheless, it was her. Diane Boston was Lucy Luv.

CHAPTER TEN

Darren Marshall slammed his fist on the desk and screamed at the monitor.

"You piece of shit!"

He looked at his watch and winced. 8:35. He had better get to the office or Mertz would have his hide.

"What's wrong, honey?" Ellie called from the bedroom.

"The damn Internet is clogged up," he yelled back. "Go back to sleep." He closed Explorer and tried opening it again. The blank screen remained frozen, not completely loading his home page.

Wasn't cable Internet supposed to be a lot faster than dial-up? he asked himself. His experience was that this was true only ninety-six percent of the time. There seemed to be periods during the day when everyone and his dog were using the Internet and it slowed to a crawl.

To hell with it, he thought. He closed the window, shut down the machine, and turned off the monitor.

"I'm leaving, Ellie," he called. He grabbed his Starbucks Coffee thermos, picked up his briefcase, and ran to the door. The sun was already warming things up in southern California and he was thankful that every day was Casual Day at the *Weekly*. He could go in wearing a

T-shirt and shorts if he wanted. That would probably have to change if he ever made it to the *Times*.

He got inside his red Saturn, turned on the ignition, and backed out of the drive. He and Ellie lived in a fifty-five-year-old bungalow not far from Echo Park. It was a comfortable two-bedroom abode that he had bought inexpensively because the previous owners had raised cats. The smell of urine could never be eliminated, no matter what kinds of cleaning solutions were tried. This didn't bother Ellie because she was a cat person anyway. She had two of them. Darren was wary at first, but after living in the house for a week he didn't notice the smell. Ellie's cats more than made up for the phantom odors of long-gone felines. The only problem was what to do when they had guests, which thankfully wasn't very often. Ellie usually cooked something with a ton of garlic in it so that he wouldn't have to explain why the house stank.

As he got on the crowded 101, Darren once again considered the project he had decided to undertake. Ever since Aaron Valentine's trial had ended, Darren had become obsessed with the man. He had spent time at the library digging up past news articles on Valentine and utilized his home computer to surf the Internet in search of any dirt he could find about the porn king. It was a terrific idea. An exposé on Aaron Valentine could elevate his status at the *Weekly* and perhaps even lead to a book deal. *The King of Porn*—great title. He had broached the subject with Mertz, who shrugged and said, "It might work. But research it on your own time until you have something concrete to pitch."

Darren wondered if he could really score an interview with Valentine. It was worth a try. Darren had heard, however, that Valentine was not an easy man to see. The man didn't like journalists unless he was in control of what was being said. If Valentine knew that Darren wanted to write an exposé about him, and psychoanalyze him in the process, he probably wouldn't be very happy about it.

Still, Darren was fascinated by what he had learned so far about Aaron Valentine. The man had served a short stint in prison during the sixties for pandering and peddling drugs. He got into the pornography business in the early seventies and apparently found his niche. By the end of that decade he had established himself as one of the kings of the trade. Unlike his competitors, who were based mostly in the San Francisco area, Valentine risked arrest by making his films in southern California. A few of his productions had been busted but many slipped by with the help of the West Coast branches of a couple of Italian families with law enforcement personnel in their pockets. Darren had come across a few articles dated from 1978 inferring that mafia activity in the Los Angeles area was experiencing a renaissance due to the rise in pornography and drug use. Darren was positive that Valentine was mob-connected.

Some of the more intriguing news items Darren had found centered on the mysterious disappearances of a few porn stars who had worked for Valentine's company, Erotica Selecta Films. The first went by the name of Julie Titman. Her body was found in Death Valley months after her disappearance. One older actress, Brenda De Blaze, whose real name was Karen Andrews, had disappeared in the spring of 1979. This would have gone unnoticed if her father hadn't made a big deal out of it and appeared on local television in a plea for help. Valentine's organization claimed that the actress had simply left town. This conflicted with the father's testimony that his daughter had told him she was trying to quit the business but Valentine wouldn't let her. Seven months later, Karen Andrews's body was also found in the desert. She had been shot in the head. The perpetrator was never caught.

Two more starlets who went by the names of Angel

Babe and Lucy Luv went missing at the same time in early 1980. Their real names were Angela Gilliam and Dana Barnett, relative newcomers to the business who roomed together in Santa Monica. Darren got the impression that they were lovers, or at least bisexual. Angela was a pretty young blonde who made less than five feature films before disappearing. Dana, also blond, was more of a star, having been working in the biz since 1977. No one knew what happened to the girls, as their apartment was left with their things still in it. Bodies were never found, if indeed they were deceased. Darren was interested in this case because Angela's brother Eric was also in the porn business, acting under the name of Pete Rod. Eric Gilliam had given a statement to the police implying that his sister wouldn't just leave town without telling him. He suspected foul play and went so far as to insinuate Valentine's involvement. Eric Gilliam left Erotica Selecta Films three years later and began to work for other production companies. Today he was one of the leaders in the business, having produced and directed a line of videos featuring amateurs.

Traffic on the 101 stalled and Darren was forced to use his cell phone to call the office.

"You need to start leaving your house earlier," Mertz told him. It was the sixth or seventh time Darren had called in late in less than a month.

"You won't care when I tell you what I've dug up on Valentine," Darren said. "I think the guy is involved with the mafia and is possibly a murderer."

"So tell me something we don't know," his editor said. "Just be careful you're not setting us up for libel. And get your butt in here."

Darren hung up and the traffic started moving again. What an asshole, he thought.

He figured that a juicy story was just waiting to be uncovered. Missing porn stars? *Dead porn stars?* Mafia connections? Pornography and drugs? It certainly had all the right elements for a bestseller and possibly even a movie deal.

Now if he could just make it happen without incurring the wrath of Aaron Valentine and wind up getting his throat cut, Darren Marshall foresaw nothing but blue skies ahead.

CHAPTER ELEVEN

To Diane, the next few days passed so slowly that she thought time had been altered. School took up most of her activities, of course, and she found that she was too exhausted in the evenings to do much about the unpacking and arranging of the apartment. She was lucky if she got one box emptied and off the floor. Sometimes she would search for a particular box containing something she needed and in the process often picked up one carton and placed it on top of another. This was how the box of newspaper clippings became buried and forgotten. Much later, when Diane eventually found the carton of clippings, she attributed her forgetfulness to her own subconscious denying that they even existed. This was most likely the truth.

David got his room put together much faster and was able to use it as a retreat after school. He spent the time doing homework or listening to music. Billy came over one afternoon and they were able to use the Playstation 2 that had finally been set up in the living room. Billy had not mentioned the video they had seen and David was relieved about that. He hoped that Billy would forget all about it, although he knew this was unlikely.

Diane's schoolwork was therapeutic for her in many ways. When she was in the classroom and faced a group of students, Diane felt empowered and confident. Teaching was something she did well and enjoyed. The days were long and the pay was not compensatory, but other rewards were beneficial to her psyche and self-image. She missed her girls' self-defense class and wished that she could conduct it more often than just during the fall semester. Unfortunately there were so many extracurricular activities available to the students at the high school that space was a problem. She should be happy she got to teach it at all.

When the bell to her last class rang, Diane sat at her desk without getting up. She immediately turned off her energetic teaching mode and slumped. She realized that she had a headache and spent a minute massaging her temples.

Why was she so tired these days? she wondered. She could speculate that it was the stress of moving but she also knew that she was depressed. Diane had been aware of her condition for years but didn't put much stock in the fashionable treatments offered by psychiatrists. She had always been one to believe that matters of the mind could be dealt with by the mind itself. Concentration on work and family made a big difference in how she felt and she wished that more people in this day and age could do that.

Diane finally sighed, stood to gather her things, and noticed that the message indicator light on her phone was blinking. She picked up the receiver and punched in her code to listen.

It was a woman's voice. "Hello, Ms. Boston? This is Trish Hunter with the *Chicago Sun-Times*. I was wondering if you wouldn't mind calling me. I'm doing a story on suburban single moms who are also school teachers." The woman gave out her phone number and hung up. Diane thought she sounded very young.

Diane figured that she didn't have anything to lose, so she dialed the reporter.

"Trish Hunter," the woman answered.

"Oh, hi, this is Diane Boston returning your call."

"Ms. Boston! I'm so glad you called. Hold on just a sec . . ." The woman clicked off for a moment. Diane hated to be put on hold for any reason but the reporter came back within five seconds.

"Sorry about that, I had to get rid of someone," she said. "Now then, can you talk a few minutes?"

"I guess so, if it doesn't take very long. I just finished my classes for the day and I want to get home."

"I can understand that. First of all, how long have you lived in Lincoln Grove?"

"Quite a while," Diane answered. "Let's see . . ." She did the math in her head and replied, "Over twenty years."

"And where were you before that?"

Diane hesitated. Where was this leading? "Excuse me, what's this story about? And how did you learn about me?"

"Ms. Boston, weren't you in southern California in the late seventies?" the woman asked, ignoring Diane's questions.

"What?"

"Southern California. Isn't it true that you came to Illinois from California?" The woman's voice had become more intense the way lawyers on television get when they're cross-examining a witness.

"Listen, Miss, uhm . . ."

"Hunter."

"I'll be happy to answer some questions but I don't want a biography published in the newspaper."

"Is that because you used to star in pornographic movies, Ms. Boston?"

Diane's heart skipped a beat. She suddenly felt a tightening in her stomach that immediately brought on a wave of nausea.

"What did you say?" she asked after what seemed like an hour. The words came out as a whisper.

"Pornographic movies, Ms. Boston. Did you ever star in any?"

"Of course not," Diane said. "I'm hanging up."

".Wait, Ms. Boston, I just—"

But Diane slammed the phone down before the reporter could ask her anything else.

What the hell . . . ? she thought. *How did . . . ?*

She felt herself shaking. All the blood sugar in her body seemed to dissipate and she couldn't stand any longer. Diane fell back into her chair and stared ahead, a million thoughts racing through her head. The nausea increased and she could have sworn that the room had tilted. It was like one of those bad television science fiction programs in which the protagonist has been drugged. All she could see was a blurry classroom that seemed to be twisting in two directions at once.

My God . . . my God . . . what was happening?

She attempted to breathe deeply, the technique she had used many times to combat anxiety and paranoia. It seemed to work but only after she had sat at the desk for several minutes. When she finally felt closer to her normal self, Diane looked at the phone and considered calling the woman back. She would tell her to go to hell and that she was barking up the wrong tree.

Whoever she was, this Miss Hunter-Doo-Dah, she was dead wrong. She didn't have the facts. She didn't know the truth.

Isn't that right, Sweetie?

What should she do? Diane wondered. Should she call the reporter back and explain that she was never a porn star? She had promised to never reveal the actress' true identity. Was the secret she had kept for over twenty years finally going to come out?

Diane brushed away the bombardment of doubt and stood once more. She picked up what she needed to take home with her and headed for the door. Once she got halfway down the hall, the nausea returned with a vengeance.

She made a beeline to the girls' bathroom, ran into a stall, knelt, and vomited.

CHAPTER TWELVE

Diane parked her '97 Honda Civic in the one-car garage, opened the door, and jumped out of the vehicle. Breathless, she unlocked the door to the kitchen and burst inside, slamming the door behind her.

"David?" she called. "Are you home?"

There was no answer but she noticed a note on the kitchen counter. It told her that her son was at Billy's house and that he'd be back before dinnertime.

That was a relief. She could do her business without having to answer questions. Diane eyed the remaining boxes piled in the kitchen. The top one was a box of books. She shoved it off the pile and the carton landed on its side, tipping over. As the top flaps had been opened previously, the books came tumbling onto the floor. Diane ignored them and continued down the totem pole of boxes until she found what she was looking for.

The carton of newspaper clippings was second from the bottom. Why hadn't she destroyed them the other night when she had said she would? How could she have forgotten? It was unthinkable. She attributed it to simply being over-exhausted and stressed out. She refused to imagine that something in her subconscious kept her from throwing away the clippings. She didn't want them. To her they didn't exist. Why she still had them she would never know. She should have burned them years ago. Why hadn't she?

Never mind. Get rid of them now, she commanded herself.

When David walked into the apartment, he found his mother stoking a fire in the fireplace. This was very strange, he thought, since it was a beautiful spring day outside. The dregs of Chicago winter had faded away a month earlier.

"Hi Mom," he said.

"Hi," she said. Her eyes were intent on the fire as she stirred a mass of burning debris with the iron poker.

"What are you doing?"

"I lit the fireplace," she said blankly.

"I see that. How come?"

"I wanted to make sure it worked. We're going to need it next winter, you know." It was a gas fireplace installed with fake logs. One didn't need kindling to light it.

"Oh," David said, unconvinced. He looked closer at the ashes and asked, "What are you burning?"

His mother answered, "Just some junk. How was school?"

"Fine." David knew what it was. He could see the remains of paper—*news*paper. She had burned the clippings from that box he had found.

The room was very warm. David noticed that his mother's forehead was damp with sweat. "How long are you going to do that?" he asked.

Diane inexplicably came out of her trance as if she had been awakened by an alarm clock. "Oh. I suppose I'm done. The fireplace works fine, doesn't it?"

"Looks to me like it does."

She reached for the metal key on the left side of the fireplace and turned it, shutting off the gas. The flames diminished and fluttered out, leaving piles of white ashes over the fake logs.

"I'm going to my room now," he said.

"Okay. I'll open up a couple of TV dinners for supper."

David turned and went to his room, leaving her to clean up.

Dinner was another awkward affair. This time Diane was the one who was quiet. She played with her food and seemed distracted. David figured that if she had burned those clippings, then she knew exactly what she had destroyed. He was mature enough to appreciate that the clippings represented a part of her life that was perhaps painful.

They had to be related to the porno movie he had seen with Billy.

"You okay, Mom?" David asked after chewing a piece of rubbery fried shrimp from the microwaved frozen dinner. They often lived off of TV dinners and take-out during the school week.

She looked up and smiled. "Hmm? Sure. Why do you ask?"

"You're miles away."

She nodded. "I suppose I am. I'm sorry. I have a lot on my mind. School and stuff."

"What stuff?"

"Oh, just finances and things. Never mind. Nothing for you to worry about."

David tilted his head slightly and squinted at her sideways, the way she sometimes eyed him when she didn't believe something he had said.

Diane laughed. "No, really. I was just in my own little world. Tell me about your day."

They spent the rest of the dinner talking as if nothing were the matter.

But David knew better.

DAVID'S JOURNAL

Tonight while Mom was doing something else, I got on our computer to see if I could find out anything about what she used to do. The computer is in the living room so both of us can use it. We finally got cable today so both the TV and the computer are hooked up.

I'm not supposed to look at porn sites but we don't have any kind of parental control on the computer. As long as Mom doesn't see, I guess I'm okay. Anyway, I used Yahoo to search for "porn stars" and "pornstars" and came up with about a zillion websites. I didn't know where to start. I started clicking through the search results until I came across one that appeared to be something more than just pictures. The site was called "Porn Star Legends" and it had a big database full of porn stars' biographies since the 1970s. The problem was that I wasn't sure what name my Mom went under. I couldn't remember all the names of the ladies who were in the video that Billy and I saw, but I remembered a couple. One was Karen Klinger and the other was Lucy Luv. I looked up Karen Klinger first. There was a picture of her face and some bio information and I could see immediately that it wasn't my Mom. There were other pictures of Karen, too, if you know what I mean!

Then I looked up Lucy Luv and I hit the jackpot. There she was. My Mom, in all her GLORY. It sure is weird for me, her SON, to be looking at this stuff. I mean, I can sort of pretend that the lady on the website isn't my Mom because she doesn't really look like her now. She was so young then. It's like she's a different person, but I know it's her.

While I was looking at the site I heard Mom coming down the hall. I quickly clicked the mouse to close the window. The site disappeared and left a website about video games in its place. I had set that up first so that it'd be on the screen underneath what I was really looking at.

Mom asked me what I was doing and I told her I was looking for game hints. She went on about her business and I brought the porn site back up.

It said that Lucy Luv's real name was Dana Barnett. But that's not my Mom's name. My Mom's name is Diane and her maiden name was Wilson. Did she use a different "real" name as well as her "porn star" name? I don't know much about these things but it seems weird.

The website listed several movies she was in, produced by some company called Erotica Selecta Films. I recognized Blondes Have a Helluva Lot More Fun on the list of about eight titles.

Lucy Luv arrived on the porn scene in Los Angeles in 1977, made a few movies, and then disappeared in 1980. It said that there was talk in the industry that she had been murdered at the same time as another porn star named Angel Babe. No one knows what happened to them. There was very little investigation done because the police didn't care about porn stars and no family members came forward to make waves. Lucy Luv and Angel Babe made a few films together and were apparently girlfriends.

Oh. My. God. I don't know WHAT to think about that. My Mom was a LESBIAN? Could that be possible?

You know, maybe I've got it all wrong and this porn star is

just someone who happens to look like my Mom. Maybe Billy and I are wrong about the whole thing.

Of course, I'd like to believe that but something in my gut tells me that it's all true.

Yuck.

CHAPTER THIRTEEN

Hiram Rabinowitz sighed heavily as soon as the customer left the shop. He had made only two sales and it was nearing closing time. As he had already sent home the help, there was nothing else to do but begin shutting down the store. Being Friday, and Shabbat, it was the one day that A-1 Fine Jewelry closed early.

Summer had come early to New York. It was blazing hot outside and Rabinowitz didn't look forward to walking to the subway. It was worse underground, waiting in the crowded station on the platform was more like standing in a sauna. Hopefully he would get a train that was air-conditioned. Most of them were, but every now and then you got an old one and the A/C was faulty. That was murder, especially when the train was packed like sardines. Rabinowitz didn't like crowded trains. It reminded him of that terrible day a week after he had turned six years old. He and his family were herded out of their Berlin home by the Nazis and forced to stand in a smelly, crowded train. The ride to the death camp had been long and torturous. Rabinowitz and his brother Moses miraculously survived the ordeal because they were strong, healthy boys who could work, but their parents were not so fortunate.

Hiram Rabinowitz surely hated crowded trains but it was the only way to get home to Queens.

At four o'clock he finished unloading the display windows and securely locked the merchandise away in the safe. He stepped out the front door, locked it behind him, and then pulled down the flexible metal security wall. It was painful to bend over and lock the padlock. It wasn't much fun being seventy-two years old and still having to work. Sometimes he envied his brother for moving west to Chicago for a change of pace, but the winters there were deadly. Winters in New York were bad enough.

The sun was still shining brightly and he would make it home in plenty of time before dusk. He ceased being religious years ago but there were certain traditions that were difficult to get out of his blood. One of those was observing Shabbat by closing early and having a nice dinner at home with candles, challah bread, and prayers. It reminded him of happier times when his late wife and his three children, now grown, were still around.

The jewelry store was located in a prime location and had been since he and his brother started the business in the fifties. Forty-seventh Street was known as "Diamond Row" and it was lined with nothing but jewelry shops and diamond brokers. Most of them were Jewish, not that it mattered, but Rabinowitz felt at home on the street and that was important. His routine after closing was to walk east to Fifth Avenue and then downtown to Forty-second Street so that he could catch the number seven train. By doing so, he avoided changing trains to get home. It was a bit more walking but anything was better than standing body-to-body with some stranger in a moving subway car.

As expected, the station underground was blisteringly hot and Rabinowitz was sweating before he had completed descending the stairs. Luckily, the train was pulling into the station just as he swiped his Metro card and went through the turnstile. He stepped through the open doors and squeezed in, careful not to look anyone in the eye or improperly rub against a woman.

The ride took about fifteen minutes and thankfully there were no delays. He got off at the Sixty-first Street and Woodside stop, ascended the stairs, and was happy to be in the open air again. Oddly, it felt cooler outside of Manhattan. He walked north, crossed Broadway, and within minutes was standing outside his apartment building.

He didn't notice the stranger lurking a few feet away.

Rabinowitz opened the outer door and entered the lobby. He used a key to open his mailbox and found nothing but bills. He then used a different key to unlock the security door and as he did so, the stranger stepped inside the building and held the door open.

"Here you are, sir," the man said.

"Thank you," Rabinowitz said as he turned to see who the gentleman was. The sight of the tall man with shoulder-length blond hair and an eye patch startled him so badly that he gasped.

"Take it easy, Mister Rabinowitz," the man whispered. "I have a knife. Don't say a word, just take me up to your apartment like we're old friends."

Rabinowitz felt his heart flutter. "I . . . I don't have any money with me . . ." he stammered.

"Shhh," the man with the eye patch said. "We'll talk about that upstairs."

The two men walked through the empty lobby to the elevator. The man with the blond hair put his arm around Rabinowitz as if the old man were his grandfather. When the elevator door opened, an elderly couple stepped out and recognized Rabinowitz.

"Hello Hiram," the man said. "How are you?" They looked at the intimidating figure with his arm around their friend.

"Hello Abe," Rabinowitz managed to say. "Ida." He could see that they were expecting him to introduce them to the younger man. "Uh, this is . . . uh . . ."

The man with the eye patch held out his hand and said, "John Hancock. I'm Mister Rabinowitz's nephew."

The couple cheerfully went "Oh!" and the man called Abe shook his hand. "Are you here visiting?" the woman named Ida asked.

"Yes. I'm here from Cincinnati. Great city, New York," the blond man answered.

"Well, enjoy yourself. *Shabbat shalom*, Hiram," Abe said as the couple nodded at them and walked on.

Smiling, the blond man put his arm back around his "uncle" and led him into the elevator. "Nice work, Mister Rabinowitz. You handled that real good."

The elevator stopped at the third floor and the two men walked out. Rabinowitz was shaking so badly that he could barely stand. The man with the eye patch had to help him.

"You can make it," the blond man said. "Just a little farther." When they were in front of apartment 3G, he commanded, "There. Now, the keys."

Rabinowitz struggled with the key ring and couldn't manage to insert the appropriate one into the lock. The man with the eye patch took the keys and did it himself. The door opened and the blond man shoved Rabinowitz inside. The old man fell to the floor as the door slammed shut.

"Who . . . who are you?" Rabinowitz whispered.

"Call me Emo."

"What do you want?"

"Information. About some diamonds you've been selling. Do you recognize this?" Emo Tuff reached into his pocket and stooped by the old man. Tuff brought out a small, black velvet bag and opened it. Inside was a large, sparkling diamond.

Rabinowitz saw the gem and winced.

"Well?" Emo Tuff asked. "You sold one like this recently, correct?"

The old man nodded.

"How many like this have you sold?"

Rabinowitz whispered something.

"I can't hear you. Speak louder."

"I don't remember," the old man coughed. "Ten . . . twelve . . ."

"Oh, really?" Emo Tuff grabbed the man by his jacket, pulled him off the floor, and slung him into an easy chair. "Here, get comfortable."

The old man began to whimper.

"Now then." Emo Tuff stood over him. "How long has this been going on? The diamonds. Selling these stones. How long?"

Rabinowitz shook his head.

"Listen, old man, I'll circumcise you a second time if you don't talk." As he spoke, Tuff slipped on a pair of Sap gloves—black leather gloves that were lined with metal. A blow by a man wearing Sap gloves was tantamount to receiving a punch with brass knuckles.

"Please . . . I don't . . . know . . ." Rabinowitz said.

The first blow broke the old man's jaw and sent his glasses flying across the room. Rabinowitz cried out in pain.

"That's just to show you I mean business," Emo Tuff said. "Now, how long have you been selling these diamonds?" Tuff allowed Rabinowitz a few minutes to regain his composure. He handed the old man several tissues from a box on the coffee table so that his victim could sop up the blood.

"Ten years, I think," Rabinowitz finally struggled to say, as his mouth was swollen and his jaw had ceased to work. "I really . . . don't remember. It might be twelve years. Not more than fifteen."

"So that means you've sold a lot more than ten or twelve, doesn't it?"

The old man nodded.

"What was it?" Tuff asked. "One a month. More?"

Rabinowitz nodded again. "On the average. One a month."

"That's a lot of fucking diamonds. All right, next question. And this is the real important one, so you better do real good on this one. Where do you get them?"

Rabinowitz desperately wanted to keep his brother out of this. Whoever this maniac was, Rabinowitz knew then and there that the monster would never let him live. It was best to stay silent. If he were going to die anyway, then why should he expose Moses?

"They come from an unknown source," Rabinowitz said after coughing more blood out of his mouth. He spoke slowly and deliberately. "There's a black man who comes in to the shop. He sells them to me. I don't know who he is or where he lives. I swear."

Tuff considered this and said, "I'm not sure I believe that, Mister Rabinowitz. You say a *black man* comes into your shop and sells you these diamonds? And you do business with him but you don't know his *name?*"

Rabinowitz nodded. "It's the truth. I swear it!"

The knife appeared in Tuff's hand the same way a wand might materialize in a stage magician's palm. It was actually a seven-inch stiletto that he must have had sheathed under a trouser leg. Rabinowitz had no idea where it had come from.

Tuff grabbed the old man's right wrist and held it down firmly on the arm of the chair. "Think again, Mister Rabinowitz. Where do you get them?" Tuff asked calmly.

"I told you!" the old man whimpered. "I swear, a black man—"

The stiletto sliced through Hiram Rabinowitz's little finger, cutting it off at the second joint. The old man screamed bloody murder.

Tuff left the man in the chair and went into the kitchen. He found a cloth that was used to dry dishes and then walked back into the living room. Rabinowitz was on the floor, crawling toward the door and leaving a trail of blood on the carpet. Tuff stepped over the man, wrapped the towel around his victim's head, covering the mouth, and tugged it tightly.

"You're not going anywhere, my friend," Tuff said. He kneed the man in the back and forced him down. "It's no use protecting whoever it is. I'll get it out of you eventually. You may as well save yourself a lot of grief."

The towel muffled Rabinowitz's cries.

Tuff placed the stiletto over the fourth finger of the old man's right hand. "You have anything to say before I relieve you of another finger?"

Rabinowitz nodded his head furiously. Tuff pulled down the towel just enough for the old man to speak.

Rabinowitz told him everything. His brother Moses in Chicago got them from someone and sent them on to him. Since he had the better black market connections, they brought in a better profit out of New York. Moses supplied them from the Chicago store and they were sold out of the New York store. Where Moses got the diamonds he didn't know and didn't care to know.

Emo Tuff believed the story. He got up, went back into the kitchen, and rummaged around until he found a bottle of kosher red wine and a glass.

"Hiram, where do you keep your corkscrew?" he called. There was no answer. "Never mind, I'll find it." He opened drawers until he found the silverware. The corkscrew was there.

Tuff opened the bottle of wine and poured some into the glass. He returned to the living room and found Rabinowitz sobbing in his blood.

"Here's to you, Mister Rabinowitz," Tuff said. He drank a little and spit it out. "Peeewww! What the hell is this shit? It's way too sweet. Don't you have any *real* wine?" He took another sip and rolled it around in his mouth. He swallowed it and said, "I guess it's not so bad.

I'll drink it." He downed the glass and put it on the coffee table.

"Well, Mister Rabinowitz," Tuff said. "You've been very helpful. I thank you for your hospitality. It's been a pleasure meeting you." He got the stiletto ready and squatted beside Rabinowitz's face. "Now it's time to say good-bye."

CHAPTER FOURTEEN

The first period bell rang as Diane rushed into the class-room. The students were being rowdy and most of them were not in their seats.

I don't want to deal with this today, she thought.

"Sit down and shut up!"

As their teacher had never used that sort of language or tone of voice before, the teens looked up in surprise and froze. After a moment they slowly moved to their seats and settled down.

Diane moved into the room and shook her head. "Sorry. Forgive me, I didn't mean to shout. I have a lot on my mind this morning."

"It's okay, Miz Boston," said Jeffrey, one of the African-American students whom she thought was one of her brighter pupils.

"Thanks, Jeffrey. Okay, class, let's forget it and get started with your oral reports. We have a lot to get through today." She gathered some materials from her desk and moved to the rear of the room. She was thankful that all she had to do that period was listen. As each student went to the front of the class, however, Diane found that her mind wandered. She just couldn't concentrate on the reports no matter how hard she tried. Halfway through the period she realized that she hadn't written a single note on two of the students' presentations.

What had they spoken about? Diane sighed to herself and decided to give them A's. The two pupils were smart but timid boys who might be called bookworms. They probably *did* make A's but their presentation skills were sorely lacking.

Miraculously, she made it through the first hour. At the beginning of the ten-minute break she ran to the office to check her mailbox. She subscribed to the *Chicago Sun-Times* but the office staff didn't get around to stuffing mailboxes until sometime during first period. As expected, the paper was there along with other assorted flyers and school announcements.

She stood and flipped through the newspaper but found nothing that might remotely pertain to her. She wasn't sure why she thought there might be. That reporter's phone call the other day had unnerved her.

I'm becoming paranoid, she thought. But there was no reason to be, was there? It was all a big mistake. Had to be.

Second period was more of a challenge since it was Sociology and she actually had to get up in front of the class and lecture. As she spoke, Diane could see that she wasn't reaching the students. They were completely zoned out. She knew she was normally an engaging speaker and could hold the attentions of a classroom full of antsy teenagers. Today, though, she choked—big time—and had to do her best to cover for it.

During the lunch period she chose to remain in her room. It had been a hellish morning and she finally had a few moments in which to relax. Diane sat at her desk, checked the phone for messages, and opened the brown bag she had brought from home. As she bit into the tuna fish sandwich, she listened to an automated message from the principal's secretary regarding a meeting later in the week. When it was done, she erased the message and put down the receiver. Since it was usually off during classes, she clicked on the ringer and then continued to eat.

The phone rang ten seconds later.

"Diane Boston," she answered, her mouth full of food.

"Diane Boston?"

"Yes?"

"My name is Gordon Walton and I'm a reporter with the *National Enquirer*." It was a young male. Diane thought it might be one of her students, playing a prank.

"I beg your pardon?" she asked sarcastically.

"This is the *National Enquirer*. I'm doing some fact checking on a story that we're running in this week's paper."

The guy was for real. Diane felt her pulse quicken as her stomach lurched. She put down the half-eaten sandwich and tried to talk but found that her throat had tightened.

"Mrs. Boston? I'm sorry, I didn't catch that," the man said.

She cleared her throat and tried again. "What's this about?"

"It's about you, Mrs. Boston. We're running a story about you in the *National Enquirer*. That you're a suburban mother and high school teacher who is really the former porn star known as Lucy Luv and whose real name is Dana Barnett."

The room suddenly darkened. All Diane could hear was the pounding of her heart. The dreaded anxiety flooded her chest and she could feel bile rising in her throat.

"I need to do some fact checking," Gordon Walton said. "May I ask you a few questions?"

"No, you may not," Diane managed to answer. "I don't know what you're talking about."

"Ma'am, if you refuse to answer any questions, the

story will run anyway. I'll just have to say that you were unavailable for comment."

"Where the hell did you get this story?" she demanded.

"I'm sorry, we can't reveal our sources."

"It's not true, you know. You may be looking at a libel lawsuit," she said, her voice wavering. She knew that it wasn't a very convincing threat.

"So you have no comment?" he asked again.

"That's right," she answered weakly. "No comment."

"Fine. Thank you for your time."

After he had hung up, Diane sat there with the receiver to her ear, completely stunned.

Peter Davis appeared to be waiting for her when she came out of the faculty ladies' room but it was obvious that he attempted to feign reading his mail as he leaned against the wall. Diane knew better.

"Oh, hi Diane," he said, smiling.

Since she had just thrown up, Diane didn't feel up to the usual sparring. "Hey Peter," she mumbled and started to walk back toward her room.

"Whoa, Diane, wait. Are you all right?"

She stopped and looked at him but she didn't answer.

"You, uhm, look a little pale," he said.

"I don't feel well," she said and started to walk on.

"That's too bad," he said to her back. "People in the news have to put on a good impression."

Diane stiffened.

What did he know? What did he mean?

She whirled around to confront him. "What did you say?"

He shuffled his feet and laughed. "Hey, I'm sorry. I just meant, you know, you're a celebrity here. Teacher of the Year and all. You should always be happy."

Diane wasn't sure if he was on the level. "That's what you meant?"

"Well, yeah."

"Sorry to disappoint you, but Teachers of the Year can have bad days too." She started to walk away once more.

"You're full of surprises, Diane," he said, lowering his voice a little. This time she could swear that he was insinuating something. "And the whole world's going to find out about them someday, huh?" he continued.

She halted and turned back to him.

He moved to within a foot from her and he wasn't smiling. "You know, Diane, I like a woman who gives good head. You sure you don't want to reconsider going out with me?"

Diane was too shocked to react. After he walked away she realized she should have slapped him but there were students in the hall. As the man disappeared into the teachers' lounge, Diane had to steady herself against the wall.

My God, what is going on? What is happening?

She didn't know the answer but at least she had a good idea who might be behind it all.

CHAPTER FIFTEEN

*She was in the warehouse . . . dead bodies everywhere . . .
Sweetie with blood in her hair . . .*

*No, it wasn't the warehouse, it was the barn at the ranch . . .
They were up in the hayloft . . .*

*Sweetie wanted her necklace . . . "It's mine, you can't have
it!"*

*Oh my God, Sweetie, there's blood in your hair! There's a
bullet in your head and THERE'S BLOOD IN YOUR HAIR!*

Diane almost screamed but her body jerked, waking her
from the nightmare. After a few seconds of disorienta-
tion, she sighed with relief and sank back into the bed.

The bad dreams had begun again. She thought she
had gotten past that stage of her life but ever since the
phone call from the reporter at the *Sun-Times,* she hadn't
had a decent night's sleep.

She lay in her bed for a few minutes, slowly shaking
away the remnants of the nightmare. Her stress had not
lessened in the past two days. It was as if she were waiting for a heavy ball to drop—some new revelation that
would destroy her peaceful existence.

Before she could will herself to get out of bed, the

phone on the night table rang. It startled her, causing adrenaline to burst through her body. She reached over and picked up the receiver.

"Hello?"

"Mrs. Boston?" A woman. She sounded familiar.

"Yes?"

"This is Trish Hunter with the *Chicago Sun-Times* again. How are you this morning?"

Diane suddenly grew livid. "Why are you calling me this early? What do you want? I don't want to talk to you."

"I'm sorry to call at this hour but I wanted to get your opinion on the story about you in the *National Enquirer*."

Once again Diane felt the dreaded surge of anxiety flow through her chest cavity. It was a sensation quite like being unable to breathe.

"What story?" Diane asked, although she knew what the answer would be.

"The story claims that you're really a former porn star known as Lucy Luv. Is that true?"

Diane shut her eyes. "Don't you people have anything better to do than snoop into people's private lives? No comment." She slammed down the receiver and jumped out of bed.

Quickly, she pulled on blue jeans and a T-shirt, put shoes over her bare feet, grabbed her purse and car keys, and ran out of the bedroom. David's door was still closed. She didn't have to get him up for another half-hour.

Diane went through the kitchen and into the garage. She punched the button for the automatic garage door and moved around to the driver's side of her Honda. By the time the garage door was up she had settled into the car and started the ignition. She looked through the rear windshield and noticed a white van in the driveway. There were two men and a woman standing beside it, apparently removing equipment from the side door.

Diane stopped the car and got out.

"What are you doing in my driveway? I need to back out," she called.

The woman looked up and said, "Look, there she is! Is the camera ready?" The woman carried a microphone with a television *Channel 7* logo attached to it. She was young and attractive, probably someone that Diane had seen before on the local news.

No, not this!

Diane yelled, "Get the hell out of here!"

The woman approached the open garage with microphone in hand, followed by a man holding a large camera.

"Mrs. Boston, could we please have a word with you?" the woman asked.

Diane didn't answer. She got back in the car, put it into reverse, and backed out, barely missing the reporter and her cameraman.

"Is it true that you used to work in porn films?" the woman called.

The van was a good ten feet back from the garage opening. Diane jerked the wheel to the right so that the Honda's rear angled toward the front lawn. She continued in reverse at a particularly unsafe speed. The car's front wheels screeched on the driveway and then the Honda plunged onto the lawn, missing the van.

"Mrs. Boston!" the woman pleaded. "Please wait!"

Diane put the car into drive and stepped on the gas. The Honda kicked up grass and dirt as Diane turned the wheel away from the complex. The car flew off the property, over the sidewalk, and into the street. It then sped away, leaving behind the bewildered camera crew.

David saw the entire thing from his bedroom window.

Diane pulled into the little strip mall that was less than a mile from the new apartment. The White Hen Pantry convenience store would surely carry copies of the *National Enquirer*.

She got out of the car and went inside. The cheery middle-aged woman behind the counter greeted her but Diane went straight to the magazines and newspapers that were on display and quickly found the *Enquirer*.

At least she wasn't on the cover. It was a picture of Michael Jackson doing something strange again along with other blurbs announcing that various celebrities were having affairs or entering rehab clinics.

Diane turned the pages one by one, quickly scanning the stories and pictures for anything that looked familiar. She found it on page fourteen. It was a quarter-page story and there was a picture of Lucy Luv from the late seventies. The headline read "CHICAGO SUBURB MOM AND TEACHER WAS PORN STAR."

Her heart pounded as she read through the story. She was identified as Diane Boston of Lincoln Grove, Illinois. She was a teacher at Lincoln High and the story even included the bit that she was Teacher of the Year. The facts were correct regarding her divorce from Greg Boston and that she was the mother of a thirteen-year-old boy.

Thank God they didn't print his name, she thought.

The story went on to speculate how her name was really "Dana Barnett," and that she had used the screen name of "Lucy Luv" when she had made porn films for the Erotica Selecta company in the late 1970s. Lucy Luv had disappeared in 1980 and many people in the industry suspected that she had been murdered. The mob had been heavily involved in the pornography industry at that time, and still was, but there was much more criminal activity associated with it then.

The story ended on a somewhat positive note that "wished Mrs. Boston the best" and that the *Enquirer* was "pleased to learn that Lucy Luv was indeed alive and well."

Damn, damn, damn.

She took the paper to the counter and paid for it, then went outside to look at it again.

They've got it all wrong. How was she going to correct this horrible mistake? How were they going to react at school? Could she lose her job? What should she DO?

One thing was certain—she was no longer safe. Diane knew that *they* would come after her as soon as the word got out that "Dana Barnett" was still alive.

CHAPTER SIXTEEN

David watched from his bedroom window as the TV van pulled out of the driveway and parked on the street in front of the apartment buildings. The crew didn't go away, though. The female reporter and her cameraman gathered materials for a second assault on the house and after a few minutes they went to the front door to ring the bell. David was too terrified to answer it. Instead, he got dressed and went into the kitchen. Attempting to go through the motions of a normal day, he got out the Rice Krispies and fixed himself a bowl of cereal with milk. He sat down to eat at the counter but wasn't very hungry.

A few minutes later he heard the garage door open and the Honda drive inside. After the car door slammed, he heard his mother scream, "I told you to get out of here! I'm calling the police!"

The key turned in the lock and David's mother came in carrying the *Enquirer*. He could see that she had been crying, for her eyes were red and her cheeks were flush with anger.

She saw him at the table and stopped, struggling to tell him something. He decided to prompt her.

"What's going on, Mom?"

"Oh, David," she said. She came closer and put a hand on his head. He allowed her to hold him to her stomach for a moment, and then she released him and sat down in the other chair.

"I guess I have something to tell you," she said.

"I think I know what it is," David admitted.

She looked at him curiously. "You do?"

He nodded and looked at the floor. He didn't want to get Billy in trouble so he skirted around the whole truth. "When you were gone one day, I, uhm, was looking at some porn sites on the computer. I found this one site that had your picture on it. It said you were in some movies."

Diane sat back in the chair. "I see."

"I'm sorry, Mom."

"I know, honey. Listen, I want you to know something. That's not me in whatever you saw."

"It's not?"

"No. I know it . . . it looks like me," she said. David eyed her closely but she wouldn't meet his eyes. "It's someone else. I've been protecting her for over twenty years. I always hoped that I'd never have to reveal this terrible secret. It's been a heavy burden for a long time."

"Who . . . who is she?" David asked.

"Honey, there are some things in your mother's past that have come back to haunt me. I'd like to keep all of it secret but it doesn't look like I'll be able to. But I'm going to try until I'm absolutely forced into revealing everything. I have to ask you to trust me and believe me. It's not me."

David didn't know what to think. He didn't want to say that he doubted what she was saying.

"Okay." He shrugged. It was all he could come up with.

"David, did you tell anyone else about this?" she asked.

David looked at the floor, not knowing what to say. Should he tell her about Billy? If he did so then it would come out that he had seen one of the movies and that Billy had provided it.

"No," he lied, and he immediately felt a sickening flush flow from his chest into his face.

"You promise?"

David wasn't sure what to do. If his mother could lie, why couldn't he? She was obviously lying about the porno stuff. It *was* his mother in the tape he had seen.

He nodded. "I promise," he said.

His mother frowned and said, "Well, someone else found out about it. I have a feeling it might be Billy's father but I can't prove it."

David was alarmed. "Mister Davis?"

"Maybe. I don't know. This could be a very serious situation. I have to think about what to do."

The two of them sat silently for a good three minutes until Diane broke the stillness. "Well. Come on, we both have to get to school. Are you going to finish your cereal?"

"I'm not hungry."

She sighed. "I don't blame you. Come on, let's get ready to go. I'll take you."

David stood as she took his bowl to the sink. He felt as if he could cry. He had never lied like that to her before.

Diane washed out the bowl and put it in the dishwasher. She turned and saw him standing there. "You all right, honey?" she asked.

He went to her and threw his arms around her waist. "I love you, Mom," he said.

She embraced him in return. "I love you too, honey. Don't worry. We'll get through this."

When she got to Lincoln High, there was a message in her mailbox to see Principal Morgan. Diane looked up at the clock on the office wall and saw that she still had twelve minutes before her first class.

The butterflies returned to her stomach and the constriction in her throat was worse than ever. Nevertheless, she held her head high and moved toward Jim Morgan's office. She reminded herself that he was a good guy. He was a little older than she was and he seemed to like her. Morgan had told her on several occasions how good it was that the students responded so well to her. Surely he would support her through this.

"So what's next, Diane? Jerry Springer?"

Peter Davis. He was behind her, collecting his own mail. She decided to play dumb.

"What are you talking about, Peter?"

"You mean you don't know?"

"Know what?"

"There's a very interesting article about you in the *National Enquirer*," he said as if it were some kind of holy revelation.

"Is that so? Oh, that's right, I forgot that rag *is* the most appropriate material for your reading level, Peter. I wouldn't want you to attempt anything more challenging."

He glared at her but she walked on. Before she rounded the corner to the administrative offices, she saw Davis leave the office and join the senior, Heather, in the hallway.

Why was he always hanging around that girl? Diane wondered. She watched them through the glass wall for a moment. Davis obviously told her what had just occurred and Heather laughed. Heather placed her hand on the older man's arm in an affectionate manner—but Davis was quick to subtly remove it.

Jerk, Diane thought as she moved on.

Sylvia, the principal's secretary, appeared nervous when she saw Diane. "Oh, Mrs. Boston. I'll tell Jim you're here." She picked up the phone, punched a button, and spoke softly into the receiver. When she hung up, Sylvia said, "You can go on in, Mrs. Boston."

"Thanks, Sylvia."

Diane knocked on the door and heard Principal Morgan call for her to enter. She did so and found him at his desk, looking at a copy of the new *National Enquirer.*

"Close the door, Mrs. Boston," he said.

She shut the door behind her and said, "My, news travels fast."

He gestured for her to sit down. "I'll stand," she said. "I have to get to first period and it's over in J hall. Uhm, you wanted to see me?"

"Diane, I don't normally read this rag but it was brought to my attention this morning. What's the meaning of this story?"

"It's not true," she said.

"It's not?"

"No."

"Then why are they reporting it?"

"Sir, that's the *National Enquirer.* That should be enough to raise your eyebrows."

He looked at her for a long time and then said, "Fine. We'll discuss it later. You need to get to class. There is an emergency school district board meeting after classes tomorrow in the teachers' lounge conference room. Your attendance is mandatory."

"I take it that the agenda concerns me?" she asked.

"That's right. You can do your explaining then. That's all, Diane. Thanks for coming in."

"Thank you, Mister Morgan."

She turned, left the room, and strode into the hallway, avoiding the stares of the staff and other teachers who were gathering their mail.

CHAPTER SEVENTEEN

"If your warranty has expired, then there's not a whole lot I can do about it," Greg Boston said into the phone. "I'm sorry, Mrs. Zakowski, but that's the cost to replace the battery. I guarantee you that it's a competitive price and you probably won't find a better deal in the Lincoln Grove area. I'll be happy to send one of my men to your house to change out the battery and get your car started, but I can't do it for free."

Some people, he thought. Why did they think that just because they purchased the car from his dealership then they were entitled to free service for the rest of their lives? Mrs. Zakowski's Ford Tempo was ten years old. There was no way he was going to give her a free battery.

After listening to her bitch and moan for another minute, Boston said, "All right, Mrs. Zakowski, I'll knock off twenty percent from the labor charge. That's the best I can do."

Suddenly, that seemed to satisfy her. *Sheesh*, he thought. All it took was to give *just* an inch.

After hanging up he went back to last month's sales figures that had been placed on his desk that morning. They weren't bad but they weren't great. Damn economy, he mulled. No one was buying these days. At least no one who wanted to spend a lot of money.

The phone rang and he hesitated before answering it. *Why do I think this is bad news?* he mused.

He picked up the receiver and said, "This is Boston, how can I help you?"

"Greg, it's Mark."

Mark Spencer, lawyer extraordinaire and golf partner.

"Hi Mark. What's up?" Boston answered.

"Have you *heard the news?*" his lawyer asked. He sounded very excited.

"What news?"

"You're never going to believe what's in the *National Enquirer* this morning."

Boston winced. "Are you shitting me, Mark? Who reads that crap?"

"Well, my wife does, for one. She has a subscription."

"I see."

"Listen, you're not going to believe this."

"I don't believe most things in the *National Enquirer.*"

"There's a story about your ex-wife."

That got Greg Boston's attention. "What did you say?"

"Your ex-wife is in the *National Enquirer,*" Spencer said. "My wife pointed out the story to me this morning. Un-fucking-believable!"

Boston sat forward in his chair. "What's it say?"

Spencer read the story to him. Boston listened to it without making a sound and when his lawyer was finished he still had nothing to say.

"Greg? You there?"

"Yeah, I'm here. I don't believe it."

"It's bizarre, ain't it? Where did they get this if it's not true?" Spencer asked. "I mean, think about it. No one knows who Diane Boston is except the people in Lincoln Grove, Illinois. She's a hotshot schoolteacher and all that but why should a national rag like the *Enquirer* give a shit about her? Maybe it's because it's a story that grabs a reader's imagination. *And* maybe because it's a story that must be true. Think about it, Greg. They usually write about crazy celebrities. They can write just about anything about those people and get away with it. The celebrities either don't care or they end up suing them. So why would they pick on a suburban woman that no one outside of her community knows? *Because it's a true story.*"

Boston was struck dumb. It was so utterly *out there* that it couldn't be true. And yet . . . it would explain a lot. He always suspected that Diane had a big fat dark secret and that she was afraid of opening up to him. Could this be it? Was this the reason why he could never get to know the *real* Diane Wilson? Could this be why their marriage eventually broke up?

"You know, Mark," he finally said, "there's something about this that does ring true."

"I thought you'd see it that way," his lawyer said.

"This is . . . this is really weird." It didn't take a lot to shake up Greg Boston, but this time he knew he wouldn't get much work done that day. He rubbed his hand through his hair and asked, "Sheesh, what do I do about this?"

"Not much you can do, buddy," Spencer said. "But I tell you one thing though."

"What?"

"This could put a whole new light on the custody case."

Boston leaned forward. "Yeah?"

"You bet. This could be just what we need to show that Diane is an unfit mother. All we have to do is get hold of some of her movies and show them to a judge and you just might get custody of David."

Boston drummed his fingers on the desktop and considered the ramifications. It would be an embarrassing court procedure for all parties concerned. And he hated to drag David through it all. Speaking of David, did he know? He was bound to, sooner or later. The school would know, everyone would know. The best strategy for Greg Boston would be to play the outraged father and ex-husband. Shock and awe. Humiliation and pain. It could work.

"All right, Mark," he said. "Go for it."

Darren Marshall slipped out of bed quietly so that he wouldn't disturb Ellie. She was snoring softly, something he figured might have a bit to do with her pierced nose but he wasn't too sure. At any rate, it didn't bother him because he thought it was cute. He probably snored a hell of a lot louder.

Marshall slipped on his house robe and tread softly out of the bedroom. He went into the kitchen to turn on the Mr. Coffee and then went outside to collect the newspapers. He subscribed to three different L.A. papers even though he barely had time to get through one of them. It was important for him to keep up with what everyone else was doing, though. Marshall felt that he had to be familiar with the different styles of writing in the various papers.

Today was a bonus because the *National Enquirer* had been delivered. Marshall still had a soft spot in his heart for the tabloid. He had cut his teeth writing scandalous tomes of libel for the paper and he continued to enjoy reading it. Since he had worked for the publication, he knew that most of the stories weren't true. The editors gambled that the celebrities involved wouldn't bother pressing charges—most of them ignored the paper as harmless junk. The few who did take issue with what the *Enquirer* reported went through a lengthy and expensive process to sue and in the end they rarely found the experience worth the trouble. As for the small percentage of plaintiffs that did succeed in collecting a sizable payoff, the *Enquirer*'s phenomenally high circulation more than made up for what the publication had to pay in damages.

Marshall made his coffee and glanced at the clock. He could take his time that morning. He had no deadlines and Mertz was away. Marshall could afford to come in late. No one would notice.

He sat at the dining table with the papers and coffee and started on the *Enquirer* first. Ellie's two cats appeared from nowhere and meowed for their breakfast.

"Get the fuck outta here," he told them. They seemed to understand and ran into the bedroom, most likely to wake up Ellie.

Marshall turned the pages of the rag slowly, scanning the articles and noting that there was really nothing new. Same old celebrities, same old trash. Then the name "Lucy Luv" jumped out at him from a headline and he took notice. Since he had been researching the life of Aaron Valentine, Marshall had become something of an authority on the history of the pornography industry. He had compiled a database of porn stars who had been affiliated with Valentine and was intrigued by the number who had gone missing or were found deceased. There seemed to be a whole lot of them who had died of "drug overdoses," or of "suicide." Only two were flat out ruled homicides but nothing had ever been pinned on the porn tycoon. The case of Lucy Luv had particularly sparked Marshall's interest.

He read the article twice and scratched the stubble on his chin.

So Lucy Luv was alive. . . . He wondered if he could find her and talk to her. What kinds of stories would she have to tell? Why did she leave the business? Why did she disappear in such a mysterious fashion? Did she know anything that could link Valentine to the other disappearances or the murders? Could she provide him with facts that could help him prove that Valentine was linked to the West Coast mob?

Marshall once again saw visions of the Pulitzer Prize.

He got up and went to the kitchen phone. He dialed Directory Assistance and held the *Enquirer* in front of him. When the operator answered, he said, "Yes, in Lincoln Grove, Illinois, please, do you have a number for a Diane Boston?"

The operator told him to hold a moment, and then, "Nothing for a Diane Boston."

"How about Dana Barnett."

"Nothing for a Dana Barnett."

Marshall shrugged and thought he'd try it. "How about Lucy Luv? Spelled L-U-V."

"Nothing for a Lucy Luv, sir."

"Okay, thanks." He hung up the phone and went back to the table.

Ellie wandered in, rubbing the sleepies from her eyes. She was dressed in a tattered long T-shirt that came down to the middle of her thighs. She yawned and asked if there was any coffee.

"I just made some," Marshall said. "Hey, look at this, honey. That porn star Lucy Luv is alive. She's some schoolteacher in Illinois. Isn't it weird?"

"Who's Lucy Luv?" Ellie asked as she shuffled to the Mr. Coffee.

"You remember, we were talking about her the other night. One of those porn stars that disappeared. She used to work for Aaron Valentine."

Ellie could care less. "Oh yeah."

"I need to talk to her. I wonder if she has any dirt on Valentine. This could be what I need to get the scoop."

"I'm happy for you," Ellie said with absolutely no enthusiasm. She poured her coffee and sat at the table across from him.

Marshall noted who was responsible for the story and said, "Gordon Walton. I don't know him. Must have started working there after I left. Hey, I better get dressed and go to the office. I want to call this guy and find out where he got the story."

"I thought you didn't have to work this morning."

"This isn't work," he said, gathering the papers. "This is *fun!*"

CHAPTER EIGHTEEN

The following day all the major Chicago newspapers reported what had been in the *National Enquirer*. Diane simply put on a good face, got David ready for school, and went to Lincoln High prepared to face whatever degradation might be thrown her way. So caught up in her own torment that she didn't consider what could happen to her son.

David had spent the first day after the *Enquirer* news broke anxious and distracted. He wanted to confront Billy about the videotape but ultimately decided to wait. However, on the second day, he knew he couldn't delay any longer. His mother was in trouble and was visibly upset. He still didn't know whether or not to believe her story that the accusations were false but what mattered was to get to the bottom of how it all got out.

"Billy," he said as the two boys sat down for lunch in the school cafeteria. No one else had joined the table yet so David felt as comfortable as he could possibly be before bringing up the subject. "Did you tell your dad about my mom in that videotape?"

Billy looked at him with wide, defensive eyes. "No, man," he answered. "Of course not!"

"Are you sure?"

"Yeah, I'm sure. What do you mean? I told you I wouldn't tell anyone."

"It's just that someone found out about it and my mom thinks your dad may have had something to do with it."

"My *dad?* He doesn't even *like* your mom!"

"Exactly my point," David said.

"I can't believe you'd say that, David," his friend said, frowning. He looked away and concentrated on his lunch. David could usually read Billy pretty well and he could see that something wasn't right.

"Look, I just want to find out what happened, that's all," David said. "My mom is in a lot of trouble. She could lose her job."

Billy looked up and spat, "So you're blaming *me?* Typical, Boston. Your best friend. Your *only* friend, from what I can see."

"Billy—"

"I'll see you later." Billy got up with the remains of his lunch and left the cafeteria. David didn't bother going after him. Instead he finished his own meal as other kids reluctantly took seats at his table. Sitting with the freaky tall, skinny boy with thick glasses was a last resort when no other chairs were empty.

After school David avoided Billy and started the walk home without him. The rest of the day had been a blur because he was so upset. In retrospect, David suspected that Billy had lied to him. He knew his friend well enough to figure it out. At the time David wanted to believe him and was thus blinded by his loyalty. Looking back at the incident, David could see that Billy had shown all the telltale signs of deceit.

David got just beyond the school parking lot and thought he was clear of running into anyone he knew. Fortunately, no one had said anything about his mother.

Perhaps they didn't read the newspaper. People would know soon enough, though.

He kicked a long forgotten empty soda can ahead of him and planned to make a game out of it for at least another block when he heard the dreaded voice.

"Hey, Porno Boy! You! I'm talking to you, Boston!"

David crumpled inwardly but kept walking as if he hadn't heard.

"Hey! What's the matter, you deaf?" Matt Shamrock's lumbering presence approached David from behind. The bully's massive hand grabbed David's backpack and held on.

"Let go, Shamrock," David said. "I have to get home."

"What for, so you can watch your mom suck some dicks?"

David whirled around and barked, "Shut up!" Then he saw that Shamrock had brought along two of his henchmen.

"Whoa, big tough Porno Boy! You going to make me? Or are you going to get your porno star mom to lick me? Get it? *Lick* me?" He laughed at his sick joke and stood his ground. David was certainly taller than the lummox but he knew he was no match for the boy's strength.

That didn't stop David from taking a swing at the creep. His fist landed hard on Matt Shamrock's chin, taking him by surprise. The bully jerked back, blinked several times, and rubbed his jaw. David had actually hurt him! If he had been a more experienced boxer David would have known to take advantage of his opponent's confusion and gone on the offensive with more punches. Unfortunately, David, being the timid and insecure boy that he was, stopped right there and wanted no more to do with the fight. The sudden rush of adrenaline had also set his heart pounding. It was the uncomfortable sensation of tachycardia his doctors had warned him about. He needed to sit down and catch his breath.

Matt Shamrock didn't share David's sentiment for

pacification and came at David with everything he had. A punch to the stomach and a blow to the face sent David tumbling to the sidewalk. He fell on top of his backpack, cushioning the descent somewhat, but the straps painfully jerked his shoulder joints.

David saw stars. His heart raced and the wind was knocked out of him. He gasped for breath and at the same time fought to regain control of his heart rate. Matt Shamrock stood over him, beckoning him to get up but the image was blurry. David's hand involuntarily went up to his face and he realized that his glasses had been dislodged.

"Come on, you freak. Let's finish this!" the bully yelled. "It's clobberin' time!"

David wheezed loudly, attempting to draw in air as the light around him dimmed. The figure above him tilted and the sky beyond him rotated in the opposite direction. He thought he heard voices shouting around him but they soon faded into oblivion along with his consciousness.

David became fully cognizant in the nurse's station inside the school. He vaguely remembered regaining his senses on the sidewalk and was aware that a group of kids had gathered around the scuffle. Then Coach Driggers appeared and broke up the mob. David heard the coach order Matt Shamrock to report to the office immediately and then the man's voice was closer.

"David? Are you all right?"

David didn't remember what was said but the coach helped him stand and together they went back to the school. Along the way David heard some of the kids' comments.

"Wow, Matt Shamrock knocked out David Boston!"

"Did you see Shamrock knock the crap out of Boston?"

"Shamrock KO'd David Boston!"

David wanted to protest. Matt Shamrock didn't knock

him out. He had fainted. His heart rate had increased to the danger level and his condition of aortic regurgitation reduced the flow of oxygen to his brain. He had passed out, which was the body's way of protecting itself from overexertion.

As the school nurse, Miss Hatchins, examined him, he overheard the coach and the principal talking a few feet away.

"Should he go to the hospital?"

"What do you think, Miss Hatchins?"

David did *not* want to go to the hospital under any circumstances. If his doctor had known that he had fainted from overexertion, he'd be in serious trouble. The last time this happened they admitted him to run some "tests" and he ended up staying in the hospital for two horrible nights. His mother would be worried sick and he would have to eat that crappy food. No way. Better to throw the blame elsewhere.

"I don't need to go to the hospital," David said. "Shamrock got in a lucky punch, that's all. I guess he knocked me out for a second."

"What were you two fighting about, David?" the principal asked.

"He said something about my mother," David replied.

The coach tapped the principal on the shoulder and pulled him to the corner of the room. David heard the coach murmuring but the word "newspaper" was the only thing that was discernible. The principal looked at David grimly and then came back to him.

"All right, David, we'll deal with Mister Shamrock. In the meantime I think we should get you a ride home. Shall we call your mother?"

"That's okay, I can walk home."

The nurse spoke up. "I don't want you walking home. You had a nasty blow. You need to rest a while. Maybe even stay home from school tomorrow."

"That's not necessary," David said. He really was feeling much better. The spot on his cheek where Shamrock hit him barely stung. He was certain that the punch he had given his nemesis hurt far worse.

"We'll call your mom anyway," the principal said.

"She won't be there," David remembered. "She has a meeting at the high school this afternoon." His mother had warned him that she'd be home a little later than usual.

"What about your father?" the nurse asked.

"He's probably at work."

"We'll give him a call."

It was 4:30 by the time Greg Boston arrived at the middle school to pick up his son. He was not in a good mood. David carried his backpack and threw it into the back of his father's Jaguar and got in the passenger seat.

"Why the hell did you get into a fight?" was the first thing his father asked.

"I'm fine, Dad. Don't worry about it," David replied.

Greg realized he had come on too strong and backed up. "I'm sorry, son. Are you okay?"

"Yeah."

His father pulled away from the school and headed toward his dealership. "It figures they couldn't reach your mother. We have to go back to the shop, son. I was in the middle of something. I'll get a message to your mother to come pick you up there. Is that all right?"

"You can't drop me off at home? It's not that far."

"No, there isn't time. Besides, I want to talk to you."

David didn't understand why they couldn't talk and also go to the apartment but he didn't question his father's reasoning. He waited a few moments before his dad said anything.

"How would you like to come live with me?" his dad asked.

David almost did a double take. "What?"

"You know. Come live in a nice big place with me instead of that dinky little apartment with your mother."

"I don't know, Dad. I like living with Mom all right."

"You don't think she's too protective, do you?"

David didn't like where this conversation was headed. "No. Come on, dad. I don't want to talk about this."

"Listen, son, I think you should come live with me."

"I don't want to, Dad. I mean, I love you and all that, but I think that would kill Mom."

His father sucked in his lips as if he were thinking of the right way to say what was next. "Well, she just might have to learn to deal with it anyway."

"Why?"

"I've filed for custody. You know what that means?"

David was alarmed. "Yes."

"I think we have a good case. Do you know why?" Greg Boston looked at his son, probing the boy's face for a sign that he knew what was going on.

"Because of what was in the newspaper?" David offered.

His father turned back to the road. "Yeah. I can't believe that, son. Can you believe your mother did that? It's just incredible. I can't tell you how much that hurts me."

"Dad, it was a long time ago. And I don't know if it's even true. She says it isn't."

"She would say that."

"Well, save your money. I don't want to move in with you," David said.

"Son, sometimes things are not up to you. I'm your father and I have your best interests on the table here."

"You just want to punish Mom," David said softly.

"What?"

"Nothing. I don't want to discuss this."

"Fine, but I'm just giving you a heads up. Your mom is going to find out today that I've filed. So let's put a good face on it, all right?"

David was appalled. Was this man beside him really his father? How could he be so vindictive? What was the matter with him?

"You know, David," his father continued, "your mother shelters you way too much. She keeps you from having fun. You should be out more at your age. Playing sports, getting interested in girls, doing more things outdoors . . ."

"I can't do that, Dad, you know that. My condition—"

"Condition conshmition," Greg Boston said. "It's all a lot of bunk. Your mom just made up that stuff about your condition so she could keep you at home. I don't want to see you be a mama's boy anymore."

"What do you mean she made it up?" David asked.

"Your so-called heart condition. I never believed it. She made it all up."

"But the doctor said—"

"That's her doctor and he'd do anything to keep the insurance payments coming in. I'm telling you son, you're as normal as the next fellow. You just need to exercise more and build up your strength. When I get you out of her home and into mine, we're going to fix you right up."

David didn't know what to think. His father's words terrified him. As the Jaguar pulled into the Boston Ford lot, David realized that he was gripping the seat as tightly as he could and that his heartbeat had increased once again.

CHAPTER NINETEEN

At the same time that David was defending himself against Matt Shamrock, Diane Boston was preparing to face a sea of unfriendly faces at the school district board meeting. All day long she had considered her options on what she should tell them. How much of the truth should she relay? How dangerous could it possibly be after all this time? Was she being overly paranoid?

Near the end of the last period she came to the conclusion that it was indeed still unsafe. She knew those people in Los Angeles. She was well aware that they were ruthless and vindictive. They also had long memories.

To be prudent, Diane made a call to Scotty Lewis, the lawyer who had represented her so splendidly in the divorce. He was also a dear friend, one who chose to remain on her side when she and her husband split up. He advised her to go to the board meeting and listen to what they had to say. She was to answer their questions as truthfully as she could and then call him back later.

At precisely 4:00 Diane stepped into the faculty conference room located off of the teachers' lounge. The board had already assembled—the four officers and seven members. Principal Morgan was present but only as an observer since he wasn't a board member. Diane nodded to everyone and then sat at the table next to Morgan. A few of them said, "Good afternoon Mrs. Boston."

A few seconds later Peter Davis came into the room. Diane was surprised to see him and was bewildered as to why he would have any business being there.

"Sorry if I'm late," he said, taking a seat across the table from Morgan and Diane. He wouldn't look her in the eye.

Board president Judy Wilcox was a tough-minded conservative Republican in her fifties. Her late husband had been a state representative until his untimely heart attack four years earlier. Judy Wilcox was well connected in the district and was also on the Lincoln Grove Village board of trustees along with Diane's ex, Greg. Diane wasn't sure if Mrs. Wilcox's association with Greg would be in her favor or not. Most likely the latter.

Mrs. Wilcox didn't stand, opting to address those present from her seat. "Meeting is called to order. We're here to discuss what we have learned about Mrs. Boston and give her a chance to explain herself. After that we will deliberate and vote on appropriate action, if any. Are there any questions before we begin?"

Diane spoke up. "Is this a trial of some kind?"

Mrs. Wilcox answered, "Of course not, Mrs. Boston. It's just that we're faced with a . . . well, a *delicate* situation that might cause some unwanted negative publicity for Lincoln High School. We want to discuss what we should do about it. Call it a hearing if you must. That's all."

"Is my job in danger?" Diane asked.

Mrs. Wilcox frowned. "Why don't we move along and get to the heart of the matter. I believe that question can wait until we're finished today. All right?"

Diane nodded. She wished that Scotty were with her for support but hopefully she wouldn't need him in the long run. Perhaps everything would turn out all right.

Mrs. Wilcox addressed Peter Davis. "Mr. Davis, why

don't you begin since you were so adamant that we meet today to discuss this."

Davis inadvertently met Diane's eyes at that point and he blushed. Now she knew. He *was* behind it all. The bastard wanted her job. The prick was still sore that she wouldn't date him and now he was having his revenge. Whatever the motive, she hated the man more than she could fathom.

"Thank you, Mrs. Wilcox," Davis began. "As you all know, there were disturbing articles in the newspapers today involving Mrs. Boston. The original story was reported by, I believe, the *National Enquirer*. The local papers picked up the story from that. Now I don't know about you all, but I'm terribly distressed by this revelation that Mrs. Boston used to work in the, uhm, pornography industry. She is a role model for the students here at Lincoln High and I believe that this seriously undermines her position. Frankly, now she's become a joke. You should hear what the students are saying in the hallways and classrooms. She's become a laughingstock. What kind of message does this send to the kids? We can't have a scandal like this infecting our school and community."

"And what is it that you propose, Mr. Davis?" Mrs. Wilcox asked.

"I'm afraid I have no choice but to recommend suspension," he said. He continued to avoid looking at her but Diane stared straight at him. If her eyes had been equipped with laser beams he would certainly be made of ash by now.

"Thank you for your comments," Mrs. Wilcox said. "That will be all."

Davis looked around the room. That was it? He didn't get to stay?

"Thank you, Mr. Davis," she said again.

He got the message and stood. "Thank you." He

glanced at Diane and said quietly, "I'm sorry, Diane." Then he left the room. Diane would have liked to tell him to fuck himself but she remained quiet.

"Principal Morgan?" Mrs. Wilcox spoke. "Do you have anything to say?"

"Not at this time, Judy," Morgan said. "I think we all need to hear from Mrs. Boston on the matter before anything drastic is done. Don't you agree?"

"Of course. But I understand you've received some phone calls?"

Morgan squirmed in his seat. "Yes. The office received eight calls yesterday after the story appeared in the *National Enquirer*."

"And what was the nature of these calls?" the president asked.

"That Mrs. Boston be fired immediately."

"I see. And did you receive any phone calls today after the story appeared in the daily newspapers?"

"Yes."

"How many?"

"Last count was one hundred and fifty-six."

"All for the termination of Mrs. Boston?"

"All but six. Those callers expressed admiration for Mrs. Boston."

There was a marked silence for a few moments and then Mrs. Wilcox looked at Diane. "Mrs. Boston?"

"Yes?"

"Suppose you tell us what all this is about."

Diane took a breath and began. "The stories being printed about me are false. It's true that there was an actress in those adult movies that looks like me, or rather, how I looked over twenty years ago. But it's not me."

"Is this one of these movies?" Mrs. Wilcox held up a videocassette in a plain white box. "I'm told that the actress in it is you."

Diane was startled. "Where did you get that?"

"An interested party turned it over to us," the president said. "I understand there were a few of these movies back in the seventies."

Davis, she thought. It had to have been him.

"Mrs. Boston, I'll repeat the question. Are you or are you not the actress in the movie?"

Best to get it out in the open. There was no turning back now.

"What I'm about to say can't leave this room," Diane said.

Mrs. Wilcox paused and said, "I can't guarantee that. You're a high school teacher at a public school. This business is already in the news, Mrs. Boston. I think you had better tell us the truth."

"The actress in the movie was my twin sister, Dana," Diane replied.

The reaction in the room was palpable. Already the other board members were shuffling their feet and looking embarrassed as if they really did have egg on their faces. One man murmured, "Oh my God," while another said, "Ooops."

Mrs. Wilcox looked at Diane and indicated for her to continue.

"My sister Dana had gone to Hollywood in the late seventies to try to be an actress. Needless to say she got involved with the wrong crowd and started making those movies. When I found out, I was mortified and I tried to get her out of it. But the West Coast mafia ran the entire operation. They had her hooked on drugs and it wasn't a pretty picture. When she finally tried to leave the business she just disappeared. I believe she was murdered."

Diane calmly looked down at her hands on the table. The room was beyond silent. She had completely shocked them with this bombshell.

It seemed that several minutes went by before Mrs. Wilcox spoke again. "Mrs. Boston, I'm very sorry to hear this. I assume that you plan to hold a press conference to clear your name?"

"No."

The board president was clearly taken aback. "Why not?"

"Because I've protected my sister's name all these years. I shall continue to do so."

"But if she's dead and your name is being smeared . . . wouldn't you want to correct that wrong?"

"Frankly, I don't care," Diane said. She couldn't help angrily speaking her mind. "I'm appalled that I was dragged in here to bring up these painful memories. If you ask me it's Peter Davis who should be in here facing suspension."

Mrs. Wilcox asked, "Mrs. Boston, is there anything else you would like to tell us? I'm afraid I don't find it satisfactory that you're unwilling to clear your name. It just doesn't make sense."

"A lot of things in life don't make sense," Diane answered. "It didn't make sense that my sister was murdered, but she was. Am I free to go?"

Mrs. Wilcox looked around the room and got a few indications of uncomfortable acquiescence.

"Yes, you are. Could you just wait outside for a few minutes?"

"Certainly." Diane stood and left the room. In the teachers' lounge she got herself a cup of coffee, sat on a couch, and waited an interminable seven minutes before Principal Morgan emerged from the conference room.

He came over to her and said, "Diane, the board has agreed to look into this matter further over the coming week. There will be another meeting here at this same time a week from today. That's when they'll let you know what action they'll be taking. I suppose what you do in the meantime will influence their decision."

"I see," she said. He looked sheepish so she added, "There's something else, isn't there."

He nodded. "You're suspended with pay until next week's meeting."

She looked away and fought back the tears welling in her eyes.

"I'm sorry," he said. "It wasn't my idea."

"Thank you, Jim," Diane replied. She stood and moved toward the door. "I'm just going to my classroom to get some things, okay?"

"Sure."

Devastated, Diane left the lounge and walked quickly through the labyrinthine halls back to her room.

DAVID'S JOURNAL

I'm sitting in one of the offices at Dad's workplace, Boston Ford. I'm in Happy Jules' office because he's out sick today. I don't know why they call him Happy Jules. His name really is Jules but I don't know where they get the "Happy" part from. He's always in a bad mood every time I've seen him. Maybe it's a joke that the other salesmen play on him.

My Mom is still at school and I have to stay here until Dad can get word to her to come pick me up. Apparently he's too busy to take me home. I don't know why. It looks to me like he's just in his office on the phone and stuff. It would take ten minutes to drive me home and ten minutes to drive back. He could have dropped me off after he picked me up from school but he didn't want to. I have a feeling he brought me here just so Mom would have to go out of her way to pick me up. That would give him an excuse to start a fight with her or something. He seems pretty sore at her for the porn movie stuff. I guess I don't blame him. If I found out my wife used to be in porn movies and I didn't know it before I married her, I'd be upset, too. But she keeps saying it's not true. Isn't there a thing in this country that everybody is innocent until proven guilty? Even though I saw the tape with my own eyes and it sure looked like my Mom when she was young, I suppose I will wait to pass judgement until all the facts are in.

Gosh, I guess I sound like a lawyer or something.

I sure feel stupid about the fight I had with Matt Shamrock. What a jerk. He's a real asshole. He has shit for brains and he's got his head up his butt. At least I punched him a good one. I really hurt him, I could tell. He didn't hurt me much. I don't even feel it anymore, but I do have a red spot on my cheek. My stomach kinda hurts where he hit me there. I hated having to say he knocked me out. He really didn't. It was my goddamn heart that did it. I KNOW there's something wrong with it, I don't care what my Dad says. Dad told me today that I didn't have a heart condition and that Mom made it all up to protect me. Protect me from what? I don't get it. Why would he say that? He knows I have a heart condition. He was there when the doctor told us all about it. I was really little but I remember being in the hospital. I was three years old and I remember it. It was awful. I was in the hospital again when I was seven. That was even worse because they did all kinds of weird tests on me. I got poked by needles a hundred times. I never want to go back to the hospital. It smelled bad. It smelled like DEATH.

I wonder what I should do about Billy. I think he lied to me about the videotape. But what the hell, I lied to my own Mom about it. I guess it's human nature to lie. Probably the best thing to do would be for me to go up to him tomorrow and tell him that it's okay and for him not to worry about it. Maybe then he'll tell me the truth. THEN I can be mad at him. LOL!

I sure hope Mom is okay. I could tell this morning that she was nervous about going to school. There were probably lots of jokes going around in the halls. I heard them in MY school. I can just imagine what it was like at hers. It's really stupid that people have to act that way about something that happened twenty or thirty years ago to someone. If it really did happen.

Maybe I should tell Mom the truth about Billy and the videotape. I'll have to think about it.

CHAPTER TWENTY

Moses Rabinowitz was amazed by what he saw in the *Sun-Times*.

There she was in black-and-white, the mysterious blond woman who had been selling him the diamonds all these years. The photo was not too good and it was very old but it was definitely the same woman. She looked about twenty in the photo and was just as good-looking then as she was now. Diane Boston was her name. A schoolteacher in the suburbs. Very interesting.

And she was some kind of porn star back then. Very interesting indeed.

Rabinowitz wondered if there was a connection between that porno business and the diamonds. She had always been careful to conceal her true identity and she had made him swear to keep their transactions a secret. The paper intimated that organized crime on the West Coast controlled the porno industry back then and that she had gone missing. What if those gangsters were looking for her? It would explain a lot of things.

What it didn't explain was why his brother was murdered.

Rabinowitz had returned to Chicago the previous day

after attending Hiram's funeral in New York. He was still in shock from what had happened. When Hiram hadn't answered his home phone over the weekend, Moses wasn't too worried. But on Monday Hiram hadn't picked up the phone at the shop either. Moses called Hiram's son Julius, a banker who lived in Manhattan, and asked him to find out where the young man's father was. Julius called back a few hours later with the bad news.

The New York police were baffled by the crime. They questioned Moses at length about the business. Of particular interest to them was whether or not they had any enemies. Could they have made a bad business deal? Was someone out for revenge? There weren't too many other possible motives that could fit the savage stabbing of an old Jewish jeweler who kept to himself and was no trouble to anyone. It couldn't have been a robbery gone badly because Moses attested to the fact that Hiram never kept jewelry at his apartment. Given the brutal aspects of the slaying, the police didn't believe it was a robbery anyway. They called it a "personal" killing—that there was evidence of torture involved. In other words, the murderer had wanted to know something from his victim and by killing the poor man the killer was sending a message. The police wanted to know to whom the message was directed.

After talking to the police Moses Rabinowitz had spent a sleepless night at his nephew's home on the Upper East Side. He worried that perhaps some of the black market dealings he and his brother made over the years *had* come back to haunt them. The problem was that there were so many! Could it have been this diamond business?

Rabinowitz knew the police would never solve the crime. He had to bring in some outside help. The only thing he could do was to call in a favor. Rabinowitz had hoped that he would never have to do so but if ever there were a situation that called for drastic action, this was it.

Before leaving New York, Rabinowitz made the phone call and spent an hour with the only man he could trust with the Rabinowitz secrets.

Now that he was back in Chicago, Rabinowitz felt nervous and afraid. What if Hiram's killer came to Illinois? Surely Hiram would not have talked about their business. He was a tough old boy and had survived a lot over the years. But could he have withstood the torture inflicted upon him? Moses didn't know. He wasn't sure if _he_ could.

The old jeweler looked up at the clock and realized that the afternoon had passed quickly. It was closing time and he wanted to get home before the Wrigley Field traffic got too bad. The Cubs were playing that evening and the streets near the store were always a mess.

He went around the counter and began the routine of emptying the display windows. The street outside was noisy and crowded. Rush hour was in full swing, pedestrians dashed back and forth in front of the shop, and traffic was already jammed. Rabinowitz appreciated the fact that he didn't have far to go to his little brownstone near Addison. He didn't have to use any expressways and he could get through the traffic by using side streets. He could be home in fifteen minutes.

The tinkling of the bell above the front door made Rabinowitz jump. He hadn't noticed that someone had approached the shop. The open door revealed a tall man with shoulder-length blond hair. He had on a black eye patch and wore matching black leather clothes. The guy looked scary as hell.

"Good afternoon," Rabinowitz said. "M-m-may I help you?"

The blond man closed the door and said, "Maybe you can, my friend. Are you the only one here?"

Rabinowitz hesitated. "My assistant just went out for something. He'll be right back."

The man with the eye patch smiled. "And you're lying,

my friend. You work alone." He flipped the sign so that the "Closed" side faced the street. He then turned the dead bolt on the door. Turning back to Rabinowitz, he said, "You resemble your brother, Mister Rabinowitz."

Rabinowitz felt a tremor of panic. The angel of death had arrived.

"What do you want?" he whispered.

Emo Tuff put his arm around the old man and walked him toward the back room. "Let's go somewhere nice and quiet, shall we? We don't want nosy people looking in the windows and seeing us conduct business, now do we?"

Rabinowitz walked with the man but he was so frightened that he may as well have been a puppet. When they were in the office, Tuff pushed Rabinowitz into the chair and then reached into his jacket pocket. He pulled out the black leather pouch and removed one of the diamonds.

Rabinowitz's heart sank. Hadn't he been pondering a possible connection between the porn star schoolteacher, her diamonds, and Hiram's murder? Was this the coincidence to end all coincidences?

"You recognize this?" Tuff asked.

Rabinowitz nodded.

"I need to know where it came from. And the others like it."

"Did you . . . ? My brother . . . ?"

"I'm asking the questions, my friend," Tuff replied. "But since it might help to refresh your memory, yes, I was the last person to see your brother alive. I sliced his throat open after cutting off a few other parts of his body. You don't want that to happen to you, too, do you?"

Rabinowitz shook his head.

"So why don't you tell me about these diamonds."

Rabinowitz nodded. "It's a woman. She's in her forties. Blond. Very attractive. She lives in the suburbs somewhere. She's a schoolteacher and I think she's got a family. About fifteen years ago she came in here and showed me two of those diamonds and asked if I could fence them. I don't know how she got my name but my brother and I, well, we've been doing that kind of work on the side for a long time. I gave her a fair price for the diamonds and she's been coming back ever since. Maybe once a month."

Tuff was pleased. "Very good, old man. That wasn't difficult, was it? Now comes the important part. Who is she? What's her *name?*"

Rabinowitz shook his head. "I don't know. She always kept her identity a secret. We had . . . an understanding."

Tuff frowned. "Tch, tch, tch . . . that's not a good answer. I need to know her name." The stiletto appeared in the man's right hand. Where it had come from Rabinowitz couldn't say.

"Wait!" he cried. "The paper! Today's paper. It's on the counter inside the shop. Her picture is in it. She's some kind of porn star or something. She's in the news!"

Tuff's one eye flared brightly. "Did you say . . . porn star?"

"Yes. Go look, I'll show you the page. It identifies her!"

"All right. Let's see." Tuff gestured for the old man to get up. Rabinowitz walked quickly into the shop, grabbed the *Sun-Times*, and opened it to the page with the story. Tuff picked it up and stared at the photo. He read through the text and smiled.

"Well, well, well. So she's alive and living in suburbia. Un-fucking-believable." Tuff dropped the newspaper on the counter, put both hands on Rabinowitz's head and pulled it forward so that he could kiss the old man's forehead. "This is great news, Mister Rabinowitz," he said. "Thank you."

Rabinowitz smiled. He almost laughed. Was the killer going to spare him? Had he done the right thing?

Tuff took the paper and said, "Let's go back in your office. I need to make a phone call." They returned to the little room in the back of the shop and Tuff sat Rabinowitz in the chair once again. The blond man removed a cell phone from his jacket pocket and punched a button.

"Yeah?" came the voice that Tuff knew so well.

"Aaron, it's me."

"I know. I have Caller ID."

"You're not going to believe what I'm about to tell you."

"You're pregnant."

"No, it's better than that. I found her."

There was silence at the other end. "Her? *The* her?"

"Uh huh. She's alive and living in . . ." he hesitated to scan the newspaper story again. "Lincoln Grove, Illinois. Outside Chicago."

Tuff imagined Valentine doing his little dance of happiness that he did when he got exceptionally good news. "That's fucking wonderful, Emo," his boss said. "Listen. Don't hurt her. I want to speak to her *in person*. You know what I mean?"

"Yeah. I'll get her to California somehow. Talk to you later."

"Right. Good work."

They hung up and Tuff put away his phone. He smiled at Rabinowitz once more. "You did all right, my friend. You made the boss really happy."

"I'm glad," Rabinowitz said. He looked at his watch. "I guess I should finish closing the shop. Got to get home before that Cubs traffic gets too bad."

Tuff chuckled. The stiletto was back in his right hand and he used the point to clean the fingernails of his left. "I don't think so, my friend. Your brother wants to see you."

"M-m-my brother?"

"Yeah." Tuff stood over Rabinowitz. "He misses you."

CHAPTER TWENTY-ONE

Scotty Lewis was expecting her when Diane pulled up in front of his Arlington Heights office. She had been near hysterics on the phone after the school board meeting and he agreed to see her right away.

Scotty first met Diane Wilson at Harper College in Palatine, where she had gone to school in the eighties to get an education degree. They were roughly the same age and had dated a while. For several months Scotty thought it was fairly serious. He was never entirely sure what had happened between them, but Greg Boston entered her life and she gradually changed the relationship from a romance to a friendship. Surprisingly, Scotty had remained close to Diane and became not only her legal advisor but also a sounding board for various personal problems. When she and Greg eventually separated, Scotty came close to regretting that he had married in the interim. However, he convinced himself that his wife was infinitely more stable than Diane was. Scotty always suspected Diane of having a dark past and of not being totally forthcoming about herself—just as her former husband had thought—and Scotty figured that perhaps it was for the best that they hadn't ended up together.

Still, he admired her a lot and would do just about anything for her.

Diane got out of the Honda and waved at him when she saw him watching her through the glass door. He held it open for her and she went straight into his arms.

"Scotty," she said, sounding as if she were on the verge of tears.

"Come inside, Diane," he said. He let her squeeze him as they kissed cheeks, then she moved indoors.

Scotty's office was a one-man show. He had a secretary who had gone home for the day but he did practically everything himself—he even changed the light bulbs and replaced toilet paper in the unisex bathroom. Despite the fact that this made him appear to be a hard luck lawyer, Scotty Lewis was highly respected in the Chicago suburbs. Specializing in family court, Scotty was one of the best divorce lawyers in the area and was rapidly becoming a top-notch custody attorney as well. His fees were unusually modest and he preferred a client base that was strictly lower to middle class and he also did a lot of *pro bono* work. If ever there were an honest lawyer, Scotty Lewis was it.

"Sit down, honey," he said to Diane. "Want something to drink? Soda? Something stronger?"

"Oh, just some seltzer if you have it," she replied. "I'm afraid that if I drink something stronger I won't stop and then I wouldn't be able to drive home." She sat in one of the big comfy chairs in the outer office. There was no need to retire to the inner sanctum.

"It's been a tough couple of days, huh," he said.

"You're telling me."

He got a couple of cold bottles of sparkling water from a little refrigerator behind his secretary's desk and gave her one. "You want a glass?"

"That's all right." She opened it and had a drink.

Scotty sat opposite her on the couch and studied her. "You're looking no worse for wear."

She waved him off. "Stop. I'm a mess. My makeup is all smeared. I feel like shit and probably look it, too."

"No you don't."

She smiled and said, "Thanks." Diane thought he was pretty nice on the eyes as well. A man of Irish descent, Scotty had flaming red hair and freckles and resembled Howdy Doody but was infinitely more handsome and masculine. He had put on some weight in the past few years but was still an attractive man.

"So what's going on, Diane?" he asked.

"Oh, Scotty. Jesus." She shook her head as if the whole thing was merely a nightmare.

She told him about the videotapes starring her twin sister and that someone mysteriously got wind of them. "Maybe it was David or one of his friends," she said. "I just don't know. Peter Davis instigated the school board meeting, I think. You remember me telling you about him?"

"The teacher who hates you but wants to go to bed with you."

"That's the one." She continued to tell him about the meeting and what was finally decided. "And so I'm suspended for a week, and the way things look I'll probably be fired. Parents are phoning the school right and left with complaints."

Scotty rubbed his chin. "Well, Diane, I have one thing I need to ask. Is it true?"

"I'll tell you what I told them. The woman in the tapes was my twin sister, Dana. Except I told them she was dead."

His eyebrows raised. "The Health Surrogate Act you took out three years ago?"

"Yeah."

"I'd almost forgotten about that," he said. "Well, then you have nothing to worry about. All you have to do is provide them with the truth that she exists."

"I can't do that."

"Why not?"

"Because you're the only one I want to know she's alive!"

Scotty wasn't sure what to think. Once again he could see that she was not being totally straightforward. It was as if a wall had suddenly been erected between them. "Well, Diane, I'm sure we can fight this thing. After all, you don't have a black mark against you. This porn stuff was a long time ago, right? You've moved on, you got an education degree, you've made a name for yourself at the school. . . ."

"You don't believe me, do you?"

"I didn't say that."

"Then what do we do?"

"Diane, if we have to sue the school board, then we'll sue the school board. I'm going to have to consult some colleagues about this. It's not really my expertise. The best thing, though, would be for you to come clean and tell everyone the truth. It simply *can't* be that difficult!"

Diane sighed. It was the last thing she wanted to do. Talk about opening a can of worms. . . .

Scotty cleared his throat and shifted his weight. "Diane, there's something else I have to bring up."

"What's that?"

"You're not going to like it."

"Tell me, Scotty."

"I heard from Mark Spencer today."

Greg's lawyer. Diane got one of those sickening jolts in her stomach that indicated imminent bad news.

"Yeah?"

"Greg has filed for custody of David."

"What?" She sat upright. "He can't do that!"

"He can, Diane. He can do whatever he feels like doing. And he's using this porn movie business as leverage."

"I can't believe it!"

"We'll have to develop a strategy, Diane. Whatever we use for the school board we'll have to use with him, too."

Diane stood and paced the room. "He's not taking

David, never, no way. He's out of his mind if he thinks he can do that. That son of a *bitch!*"

"Sit down, Diane. Take it easy. It's going to be a tough fight for him. Even Spencer thinks so. It won't be easy on our part either, but it's not a slam-dunk for them. We'll beat them."

"Jesus, Scotty," she said, taking her seat again. She put her head in her hand and struggled to keep from crying.

After an uncomfortable silence, Scotty asked, "So what about your sister? I don't understand why you can't tell the truth about her. Where is she, anyway?"

"She's hidden. No one but me knows where she is."

"Right. I forgot."

"Look, I got that Health Surrogate Act done to make me the decision-maker for her because she's mentally and physically incapacitated but being kept alive. It basically gives me the right to pull the plug, right?"

"Yes."

"She's been in a coma for over twenty years and I can't decide if I want to do it or not. Basically I'm very pro-life and I keep thinking that someday a miracle will happen."

"You didn't answer my question," he said.

She sighed and said, "The reason I can't let anyone know she's alive is because they'll come and kill her."

"Who?"

"*Them.*"

CHAPTER TWENTY-TWO

"You bastard!" Diane yelled into the phone. "Why are you doing this?"

Greg Boston replied, "Why do you think, Diane? I don't want my son living with you. No respectable father would."

"Oh, give me a break. You don't know the *first thing* about any of that stuff. None of it is true, Greg."

"Well, I hope it isn't. But that's not going to change my mind."

Diane had stormed into the apartment after the meeting with Scotty only to find David not at home. A message on the answering machine, from her ex-husband, indicated that her son was at Boston Ford and she should come and pick him up. Instead, Diane picked up the phone and called her former marital partner.

"You'll never win, Greg," she said. "Scotty and I will fight you on this, make no mistake about it."

This time Greg blew up on the other end of the line. "Then fight me! You're the one who's lied to me all these years, not telling me the truth about yourself. You know what? I think a judge will take my side on this one. I'm an upstanding member of the community, a village trustee, and I go to church. And you? You were once a porno star and you never revealed this to anyone, even the man you married. What else have you done? Were you a drug addict, too?"

"Stop it, Greg, you're being a real asshole! And you had no right picking up David from school and bringing him to the dealership. You were just looking for a confrontation, weren't you?"

"For your information, Diane, he *needed* to be picked up because he got into a fight at school! He was knocked out!"

"What?"

"Yeah! Your son was knocked out. The school tried to call you but you were too busy being raked over the coals by your own school board to pay attention to your son."

"That's not fair, Greg, and you know it! Is David all right?"

"He's fine, no thanks to you."

Diane had to slow down and breathe. Finally she said, "I'm on my way."

She hung up and cursed to herself. She felt like picking up a glass and throwing it across the room but she managed to control her anger. *This is getting out of hand*, she thought. Something had to be done. If it called for legal battles, then so be it. Scotty would need to be paid and she might even need other representation beyond him.

Diane went to her bedroom and pulled out the dresser drawer where she kept the small velvet-lined jewelry bag. She took it out, sat on the bed, and carefully unzipped the bag. There were three diamonds inside.

Damn, she thought. She needed to go to the bank and retrieve more from the safety deposit box.

She replaced the bag, shut the drawer, and left the apartment. It took her fifteen minutes to drive to Boston Ford and that gave her plenty of time to replay the phone conversation in her head. She managed to work herself up again in the car by imagining various scenarios in which she and her ex-husband had it out in court. By the time she arrived she was livid.

Diane stormed into the dealership and didn't bother to say hello to the various salesmen and staff who could see and hear everything in the store. She found David in one of the offices.

"Hi Mom," he said.

She saw the bruise on his face and immediately went to him.

"Honey, are you all right? What happened?" When she put her arms around him, David squirmed away.

"Nothing. I'm okay."

"What happened at school?" she demanded to know.

"Matt Shamrock and I got into a fight. He hit me and I guess I got knocked out for a few seconds. I hit him back good, though."

"Oh, David." She looked up and saw Greg. "*You*, mister, have got a lot of nerve!"

"Keep your voice down, Diane," he said. "Everyone is watching."

"I don't give a damn what they see. They should know what a *prick* you are! You are *never* going to get custody of my son, Greg. *Never*. I'll *kill* you if you go through with this, I swear it! Let's go, David."

David gathered his school things and left with his mother. He and his father exchanged looks and Greg said, "We'll talk soon, son." The rest of the employees stood gawking and David couldn't blame them. He had never seen his mother so angry before.

After the Honda drove away, Greg apologized for his ex-wife's behavior and told his staff to get back to work. He shut himself in his office and tried to finish the work he had to do.

He was the last one out of the dealership at nine thirty, long after the place had closed. Greg knew he wasn't about to get any more done that night so he might as well head home. After locking up, he got into his Jaguar

XK8—one of the perks of owning a Ford dealership—and drove the eight miles to the other side of Lincoln Grove, where he rented a small house. When he moved out of the family home Greg spent a few nights with Tina, his secretary. He had been seeing her before the separation, an on-again, off-again affair that had been going on for three years. Tina's cousin owned the house and he was happy to rent it. He had never been sure if Diane knew about the affair.

Greg pulled into the driveway, got out, and locked the Jaguar. He walked in the moonlight to the front porch, jingling his set of keys. Greg liked the fact that the house had a wooden porch with a railing. There was also a porch swing, an item he thought would be nice to sit on with a new girlfriend. To date that hadn't happened. Tina had never come over since he was in the house and there certainly weren't any new girlfriends.

As he stepped onto the porch, Greg thought he smelled tobacco, the same odor that permeated the area behind the dealership where some of the salesmen had their cigarette breaks.

Odd, he thought. Who could have been smoking on my porch?

He put the key in the door, turned it, and was startled by the flick of a cigarette lighter over by the porch swing. A man was sitting there in the dark.

"Hey!" Greg said. "Who the fuck are you? What are you doing on my porch?"

The man lit his cigarette and shut the lighter. He stood and the swing creaked on its chains.

"Greg Boston?"

Greg attempted to peer through the darkness to see who it was. "Yeah? Who's there?"

Emo Tuff was a good six inches taller than Greg was. When the man moved closer, Greg could make out that this was one scary-looking dude.

"Where's your wife?" the man asked.

"My wife?"

"Diane Boston."

Greg felt a shiver of fear but he managed to speak with bravado. "Get out of here before I call the cops." He continued to unlock and open the front door, which was perhaps the biggest mistake of his life. He stepped inside and said again, "Go on, get out of here."

"Directory assistance said I could find Mrs. Greg Boston here," the man said.

"Well it was wrong. I live alone. We're divorced. Her number isn't listed," Greg said. "Good night."

He started to close the door, but Tuff's boot prevented him from doing so.

"What the—" Greg started to say but the man with the long blond hair shoved the door open and stepped inside.

CHAPTER TWENTY-THREE

Diane spent most of the next day alone with her thoughts while David was at school. He had shown no ill effects from his encounter with Matt Shamrock and appeared to be fine at breakfast. After he had left, Diane didn't really know what to do with herself. She was a creature of habit and routine.

Who was taking over her classes? she wondered. Would her students miss her?

Perhaps it was time to begin thinking about something else to do with her life. She really didn't want to leave Illinois. She couldn't abandon her sister. There was no one else who could take care of her and keep her alive.

That was the other question . . . *should* she keep her sister alive? After all this time her sister had shown no sign of gaining consciousness. Diane couldn't bear the thought of giving an order to kill her but perhaps it was time to do so. She just didn't know. It went against everything she stood for.

By mid afternoon, David had come home and was busy with his homework. Diane decided to take the drive downtown and get rid of the three diamonds she had in her possession. She also needed to ask Mr. Rabinowitz about the possibility of doing business long-distance in case she had to leave the state.

Diane took the Edens Expressway, merged into the Kennedy, and slowly made her way into northwest Chicago. Traffic was always dense, especially as the day approached rush hour. Diane cursed herself for not going sooner—the round trip was going to take longer than she had planned.

After exiting at Diversey, Diane went a few blocks east until she came to Lincoln Avenue. She got lucky and found a metered parking space a block down from A-1 Fine Jewelry. Diane locked the Honda, walked toward the shop, and noticed that a police car was parked in front. When she got closer she saw the yellow tape across the storefront.

Full of apprehension, Diane peered through the display windows to see inside. There were three men—a uniformed policeman, a fellow who appeared to be a plainclothes detective, and another man who looked like a hippie. This third man was very hirsute with long Christ-like hair and a beard. He was dressed in shabby clothing that might have been recently picked up at a flea market. He looked clean, though, so that eliminated the possibility that he was a street person. So far the men hadn't noticed her in the window. Should she knock? What had happened here?

A fourth person came out of the back room and joined the others. He was younger, a man in his twenties. He wore a suit and a *yarmulke*. Possibly a relative?

The young man saw her and said something to the others. The uniformed policeman turned and came outside.

"Can I help you, ma'am?" he asked.

"Is Mister Rabinowitz here?" Diane asked.

"Are you a relative?" the policeman inquired.

"No."

"A friend?"

"Well, sort of. I've known him a long time. I'm a regular customer."

"I see. I'm afraid I have some bad news. Mister Rabinowitz was found dead this morning."

"Oh dear!" Diane suddenly wanted to cry. She really liked the old guy. "What happened?"

"Would you like to talk to his nephew? He just got here from New York."

"Well, sure."

The policeman went back inside and after a moment the young man with the *yarmulke* came out.

"Hello, I'm Julius Rabinowitz."

"Hi." She suddenly realized that she had never given the old man her real name. "I'm Suzie Thomas," she said. It was the first thing that popped into her head.

"Can I help you?"

"The officer just told me about . . . your uncle, was he?"

"Yes." The young man seemed to be in a quiet state of shock but he had his wits about him.

"I guess you could say I'm a long time customer. What happened?"

"My uncle was murdered last night," the young Rabinowitz said.

"Oh my God!" She took a moment to compose herself and asked, "Was it a robbery?"

"No. It doesn't appear so. The killer didn't take a thing. He just slit my uncle's throat and left."

Slit his throat?

"Oh, I'm so sorry," Diane said.

"The killer killed him just like he did my father a few days ago."

"Your father?"

"He ran the jewelry shop in Manhattan," Rabinowitz said.

"Oh, yes. You mean they were both murdered?"

The young man nodded grimly. "By the same person

or persons, so it seems. I can't understand who would do something like this. Two old men who wouldn't hurt a fly. The police think they may have made a bad business deal."

A slit throat? That reminded Diane of something from the past. *It couldn't be him, could it? Had he found her?*

"I'm so sorry to hear this, I really am," she said. "Is there any other family besides you?"

The young man shrugged. "Just me and my sisters. My uncle didn't have children. None of us are in the same trade as my father and uncle. I'm a banker."

"I see," she said. "You poor thing, you must be so distraught."

He seemed relieved to be able to talk about it to someone. "This has been some day. As soon as I get to work this morning there's a call from Chicago. The police say my uncle is dead. I got the next flight out of LaGuardia that I could. I arrived here an hour ago. The ambulance has already taken the body away and now the detective and other policeman are, I don't know, asking questions and things."

"Well I won't take up more of your time. I'm truly very sorry," Diane said.

"Thank you." He turned and went back inside the store.

Diane walked back the way she came. This was all too bizarre, she thought. Both men killed by the same murderer. Why? And the method . . . it struck her as too familiar. She prayed that it wasn't who she thought it might be. If so, then it wouldn't be long before her own door was kicked in.

She had gone fifty feet from the store when she felt her neck tingle. Diane turned around to face the shop again and saw the shabby longhaired man standing outside on the pavement, watching her. Who was he? Surely not a detective. He was staring directly at her as if he were memorizing every feature.

Diane turned back around and kept going toward her car.

Nicholas Belgrad watched the blonde get into her car, which was parked a block away from the jewelry store. He scratched his chin under the beard and went back inside the shop. He didn't say anything about her to Detective Sharp or Officer Logan. This was information he wanted to keep to himself.

"I'm sorry," Sharp said. He was the man wearing plain-clothes, scribbling notes into a small notepad. "Mister Belgrad, tell me again what your relationship with the deceased is?"

Belgrad nodded. "Close family friend. To both Moses and Hiram."

"You and Mister Rabinowitz flew from New York together?"

The young man said, "No. Mister Belgrad and I just met."

Belgrad offered an explanation. "I'm afraid I never had the pleasure to meet Hiram's children. But I've known Moses and Hiram since I was a child. I flew from JFK."

Detective Sharp was confused. "But who contacted you about Mister Rabinowitz's death?" he asked.

"No one. I was coming to see Moses. I didn't know that this had happened."

The detective nodded as he scribbled more notes. "Right, I understand now. May I ask what your business was with Mister Rabinowitz?"

"No business. Just a friendly get-together," Belgrad answered.

The detective mulled that one over and finally said, "To tell you the truth, whoever let you come into the crime scene earlier went against procedure. I'm sorry that you saw your friend's body in that . . . state."

"I am too, but don't knock yourself out. I'm just glad Julius here didn't have to see that," Belgrad said.

"Okay, I have your contact details if I need you. I guess we're done for today. Forensics did a thorough sweep of the place and now we'll just have to wait for the results." The detective then ignored Belgrad and addressed the only blood relative to the deceased. "In the meantime I have to get the file from New York on your father's case. I guess I'll be working with New York to solve these two crimes. From what you've told me it sounds like the same perp."

"I'd say you're right," Belgrad interjected. "Detective Sharp, do you still have the evidence bags or were they sent to the lab?"

"I have a couple of things in the car. Why?"

"The newspaper that Mister Rabinowitz was clutching in his hand. May I see it again?"

The detective frowned. "I don't know, since you're not a relative. . . ." He looked at the younger Rabinowitz, who shrugged. Sharp said, "Come on," and he brought Belgrad outside. He opened the trunk of the police car and removed a plastic bag with a *Sun-Times* inside of it. There was dried blood splattered on the paper.

Belgrad took the bag and examined the newspaper through the clear plastic. It had been opened to a story about a woman living in the suburbs who had been accused of being a porn star. A photo of the woman accompanied the text.

Belgrad's instincts had been right. The woman he had just seen outside the shop and the woman in the story were one and the same.

DAVID'S JOURNAL

I feel shitty.

Today when I got home from school, I found that someone had vandalized the front door of our apartment. Someone had painted "Porn Mom Lives Here" and "Teacher Got an A+ Sucking Cocks" in big red letters. Sheesh. Very depressing. I didn't know what to do about it. Mom wasn't home and I really didn't want her to see it. I let myself into the apartment, went to the kitchen, and got a wet sponge. I tried to erase the paint but it wouldn't come off. It was some kind of enamel or something. I guess Mom would have to see it after all. I went inside and watched TV.

I feel like this is all my fault. If Billy hadn't watched that stupid videotape probably none of this would have happened. I haven't spoken to Billy since our fight in the lunchroom. He avoids me at school. I know his Dad has something against my Mom and he's involved with her school trying to get rid of her. I bet Billy's Dad told him not to talk to me. Great. Now I've lost my only friend.

Mom came home and looked as depressed as I was. She came over to me, turned off the TV, and said, "I'm sorry, David." I told her I was sorry, too. We kinda hugged each other for a minute and then she said she needed to find something to clean off the door.

Then she told me there was a possibility we might have to move. Not to a new place, but to a new town. Maybe even a new state.

I told her I was all for it. I don't want to stay in Lincoln Grove. I don't even want to stay in Illinois. She just nodded and went into the kitchen to look for some turpentine or something.

Mom got the door cleaned before dinnertime and we ordered a pizza. I wasn't able to eat very much of it. Sometimes I wish I had a dog that I could give food scraps to. That would be cool. Maybe if we move somewhere and start over in a bigger place I can ask Mom if I can have a dog.

CHAPTER TWENTY-FOUR

Diane crawled out of bed the morning after her upsetting day in Chicago and found that she had overslept. David had already gone to school. She sighed and was thankful that he was getting old enough to take care of himself. She still worried about his health and how he was going to function in the world with his condition, but at least he had the brains to get past nearly any obstacle.

She went into the bathroom, looked at herself in the mirror, and was horrified. Diane couldn't believe it was her image staring back at her. Bags under her bloodshot eyes, hair unkempt . . . Then she remembered that she had consumed a bottle of wine before going to bed the night before. Coming home to find the graffiti on the front door was enough to drive anyone to drink.

Damn them all, she thought.

Diane put on her bathrobe that was becoming more and more tattered and wandered into the kitchen to put on some coffee. She stood in a daze while the machine did its thing and eventually she took a cup into the living room, turned on the television, and sat on the sofa.

A local morning news show was on and she numbly focused on the screen as the commentators droned about the president, foreign crises, and unrest at home. After a while they switched subjects to local news and Diane saw her photo suddenly appear on the screen. A caption beneath it read, "The Porn Star Mom—Diane Boston."

That woke her up.

"There's a new development in the ongoing story of the so-called Porn Star Mom in the Chicago suburb of Lincoln Grove," the male anchor said. "We've received word that Diane Boston is planning to file suit against the Lincoln Grove School District for unlawful suspension. According to our sources, the school board gave Mrs. Boston a week to clear up the allegations that she appeared in adult films in the late nineteen seventies. When Mrs. Boston refused to do that, she was put on suspension with pay until the board did some further investigation into the matter. Mrs. Boston has denied the allegations but doesn't seem to want to prove that they're false."

The screen changed to video of none other than Peter Davis with a reporter's microphone held to his face. The caption read, "Peter Davis—Teacher at Lincoln High School."

"I work with Mrs. Boston in the Social Studies Department," he said. "Of course we were all very shocked by these allegations. The thing is, if she doesn't have anything to hide, then why doesn't she produce this 'twin sister' that she's claimed to have. It's very peculiar. If you ask me, she's making it up."

"Fuck you," Diane muttered to the television.

The screen switched back to the anchor. "Channel Seven learned about the pending suit a day after Mrs. Boston's former husband, car dealer Greg Boston, filed for custody of their son David. As the story develops, we'll keep you informed."

Diane grabbed the remote and shut off the set.

There was no way she could pick up and leave now. There was all this *legal* crap to deal with. The court battle with Greg was certainly worth staying for but Diane was beginning to wonder if the school board fight had any merit. Sure, it was the principle of the thing but, at this point she didn't *want* her job back. She knew she couldn't go back into those halls and resume her status as a "Favorite Teacher" after everything that had happened. There were probably plenty of students who would support her—and even think she was "cool" for being in adult films—but that's not how she wanted to be thought of.

Damn it, it's not even true!

But there was nothing she could do but sit, drink her coffee, and wallow in the gloom and doom.

David didn't know how he got through classes that day but somehow he had. His mind was not on his schoolwork and his math teacher even called attention to him in class.

"Please stop daydreaming, Mister Boston," he had said. It wasn't too bad of a reproach. Everyone was well aware of what David was going through. Still, it had embarrassed David and made him angry. All the kids in class turned to look at him. Not only was he the Porn Star Mom's son, but he was the kid who got into a fight with Matt Shamrock and was knocked out. His classmates surely had pity on him for the latter situation—no one liked Matt Shamrock except the bully's own little gang of hoodlums. Actually, it wasn't really "pity." It was more like they were thinking, "You poor sucker."

As for his reputation as the Porn Star Mom's son, that was becoming more and more humiliating. He could hear the whispers behind his back and the giggles as he passed through the halls. Once there was a piece of paper stuck on his locker that displayed his new moniker—Porno Boy. Matt Shamrock or one of his flunkies must have coined the epithet. Even though Shamrock had been suspended for the fight, his groupies were still at school. One of them called him that at lunch and an entire table of kids laughed.

It was becoming increasingly demoralizing for David to appear in public.

When the final bell rang he slipped out a side exit and hurried across the parking lot to the street. He wanted to avoid Shamrock's goons in case they were ready to retaliate for their leader being suspended. David got a block from the school without any problems, way ahead of any other kids, and he breathed a sigh of relief. He hoped that every day was not going to be like this one. Something had to give, and soon.

"Hey, Porno Boy!"

The voice came from directly ahead. David had been looking at his feet and not paying attention to what was in front of him. There he was, thirty feet away. The Thing.

"It's clobberin' time again, pal," Matt Shamrock said, walking swiftly toward David. "You got me suspended and you're gonna *get it*."

David was in no mood to repeat what had happened before. His heartbeat was already increasing and he felt lightheaded. He held his hands in front of him and said, "Hey, Matt, come on, give it a—"

But before David could finish his plea for peace, Matt shoved the tall boy hard in the chest. David went down on the pavement, falling once again on his backpack. Matt kicked his prey in the leg.

"Get up, pussy. Or do I have to kick you while you're down?" the bully taunted.

David wasn't about to get up. He closed his eyes and prepared himself for the coming pain. Maybe if he kept his eyes shut then the whole thing would just go away magically, as if he had been dreaming.

"What's going on here?"

It was a masculine voice, one that David didn't recognize. It came from across the street but was loud enough to be heard. He opened his eyes and looked up. Matt Shamrock had turned to face the speaker, who was standing by a white van. The man was quite striking. He was tall, had long blond hair to his shoulders, and everything he wore was black. The most distinguishing feature was that he had on a black eye patch.

The man crossed the street and came over to the two boys. He addressed Shamrock. "You always pick on fellows smaller than you?"

Shamrock snickered. "Smaller than me? Look how tall he is! And who the fuck are you?"

Emo Tuff's hand slapped Shamrock's face so fast that neither boy saw it happen. The sound, though, reverberated in the air around them.

"Oww!" Shamrock said, stepping back.

"Watch your language, kid," Tuff said. "He may be taller than you, but you know damn well that you're tougher than him. He's no match for you. As they say, why don't you pick on someone your own size? Go on. Get out of here."

Shamrock didn't know what to think of the creepy stranger. He backed off a few feet, then turned and ran down the block.

Emo Tuff held out his hand to David. "Can I help you up, son?" he asked in a kindly voice.

David hesitantly gave him his hand and the man helped him up. "Thanks, mister," David said.

"Sure. Glad to be of assistance."

"You don't live around here, do you?" David asked.

"Nope," Tuff said. "I'm just passing through. That kid pick on you a lot?"

"Uh huh. He's a real asshole."

Tuff chuckled. "That he is, son, that he is. Listen, would you like a ride home? My van's right there. You look a little shaken up."

David *did* feel woozy. His heart had gone into overtime for a few minutes and he didn't want to pass out again. The man looked scary but he seemed pretty nice. After all, he broke up the fight.

"I don't know. . . ."

Tuff laughed. "Oh, I see. You're not supposed to accept rides from strangers, is that it?"

"Well, yeah."

Tuff held out his hand. "My name is Emo. What's yours?"

David shook hands and replied, "David."

"Well, David, we're not strangers anymore, are we?"

"I guess not."

"Come on, that punk might be hiding up ahead to finish what he started. Let me give you a ride home. It's not far, is it?"

"No. Just a few blocks down toward the village center. Where the apartments are."

"I think I passed 'em earlier," the man said. "Come on, I'll get you home real quick."

David followed Emo Tuff across the street. The man opened the side of the van, a Chevrolet Astro Cargo RWD, and said, "Hop in, David." He climbed in and sat in the passenger seat. Tuff closed the door and walked around to the other side. He looked up and down the street and saw that other school kids were coming down the road now but they seemed to be paying no attention. David had been at least five minutes ahead of everyone else leaving the school. They hadn't been seen.

Tuff got into the van, closed the door, and pressed a button. There was a click that echoed around the van and David had the uncomfortable supposition that something bad was happening. Had the man just locked all the doors? David then became aware that the van had no windows other than the driver's, passenger's, and front windshield. Solid white paneling covered where there should have been rear and side windows.

"Better buckle up, David," the man said as he started the van. "It's the law, you know."

David did as he was told. "Listen, uh, Emo, I think I can walk. It's okay, you don't have to—"

"Nonsense. It's right up here, isn't it? Just settle back and I'll have you home in a jiffy."

The van pulled out into the street and drove the six blocks to the center of town. David pointed to the apartment building. "That's it, right there. You can pull over here."

But Emo Tuff drove on past.

David spoke louder. "What are you doing? I said that . . ." And then he realized that the driver wasn't paying any attention to him.

As fast as he could, David unbuckled his seat belt and pulled the door lever beside him. Sure enough, it was locked.

"Like I said, David, you'd better buckle up," Emo Tuff said. "It's the law."

CHAPTER TWENTY-FIVE

What was she going to do about finding another fence?

Diane left Scotty Lewis' office after discussing strategy for her upcoming legal battles and was faced with this dilemma. Lewis had secured another attorney from Chicago to help with the school board case, as this was something he wasn't comfortable handling alone. The new lawyer's name was K. R. Harp and a preliminary meeting between the three of them was scheduled for the following day. Harp's fees were frighteningly high and Diane realized that she desperately needed to cash in more diamonds before she could even begin to pay the retainer.

It was late afternoon by the time she got home. Coming into the kitchen through the garage, she called, "David?" When there was no answer she went to his bedroom, expecting it to be closed with music playing inside. The door was open, however, and David was not in the apartment.

She figured he was probably out with Billy Davis and that he'd be back before dinner.

* * *

Darren Marshall put a portable digital tape recorder on the table and asked, "Do you mind if I tape our conversation?"

"Naw, go ahead," his subject said.

Marshall turned it on, stated the date and time, and announced, "I'm sitting in Starbucks with Mister Eric Gilliam and he's agreed to answer a few questions about his days at Erotica Selecta Films." He addressed the man across the table from him. "Say something so I can check the level."

The man replied, "Roses are red, violets are blue, her pussy is sweet, and her tits are new."

Eric Gilliam was fifty-one years old but had a lean, muscular body. He had sandy blond hair, blue eyes, and could pass as a beach bum surfer. He was tan, clean-shaven, and sported several tattoos. Still a handsome man, Gilliam was a major player in the adult film industry and had been involved in it since the seventies. In the business, everyone knew him as "Pete Rod." He began his own line of amateur adult videos in the early nineties and they had made him a rich man.

"Mister Gilliam, tell me how you got into the business and when you first met Dana Barnett," Marshall began.

Gilliam rubbed his chin. "I guess I met Dana in nineteen . . . seventy-seven. I had been working for Valentine for about a year. He started Erotica Selecta, I don't know, nineteen seventy-five?"

"That's right."

"Anyway, I think I started acting in adult films at the end of seventy-five. My so-called Hollywood career just wasn't happening. I had made two lousy teenage beach movies and I didn't have any lines. Someone suggested that I get into figure modeling, you know, for art classes, and I did that. That led to someone asking me to do some photo shoots for a gay magazine. It was pretty good money so I did it, even though I'm not gay. After that, this rep signed me and I started making loops."

"In those days adult movies were shot on film," Marshall stated.

"Right. There were feature films being made by a select group of producers, mostly in San Francisco, but L.A. had its fair share of work available. Other companies made loops—those are short films, ten to twenty minutes, and these were made for adult peep shows and bookshops to run in viewing booths, you know?"

"I know."

"Anyway, I was doing that and made a few loops for Erotica Selecta. Aaron Valentine was getting into feature film production by then and I starred in his first two flicks, *Coed Dormitory* and *Doggy Day Afternoon.* Dana Barnett appeared one afternoon at the studio as my leading lady for my third flick, *Blondes Have a Helluva Lot More Fun.* It also had Karen Klinger and Jerry Zork in it, as well as my sister."

"Angel Babe?"

"Yeah, Angela." Gilliam made a face that indicated he didn't like to talk about his sister. He took a sip of coffee.

"What was Dana like?"

"Smart," Gilliam answered. "Smart and beautiful. Nothing 'dumb blonde' about her. I had the feeling she could do anything she wanted. A lot of actresses who get into the adult business have shit for brains. Dana could have been a lawyer, she was that smart. I have no idea why she wanted to get into porn. I think she was escaping her past, although I don't know what that was. She never talked much about it. Angela told me once that Dana's parents had died when she was young and that she had grown up in Texas. She was raised by an aunt and uncle and I have a feeling her uncle must have abused her. I'm not sure about that, though."

"Do you know where in Texas?"

Gilliam rubbed his chin. "It was a small town. Somewhere in the western part. Let me think on that one."

"Did you have a relationship with Dana outside of business?" Marshall asked.

"We were great friends," Gilliam said. " 'Course you know she was with Angela from the get-go. Those two hit it off so fast that it made your jaw drop. They had a girl-girl scene in *Sgt. Pecker's Lonely Hearts Club Band* and from then on, they were a couple. Angela moved in with Dana and they were roommates until they disappeared three years later."

"Do you think Dana was a lesbian or was she bisexual?"

"I imagine she was bi, but when I knew her she definitely preferred girls. Angela was the only girl she preferred, too. Anyway, the three of us often hung out together. Angela and I were always pretty close so it was natural that we'd all get together. If there was a girl I was seeing, we'd go out as a foursome."

"Do you think the fact that Angel Babe—er, Angela—was blond had anything to do with Dana's attraction to her?" Marshall asked.

"Hell, I don't know," Gilliam answered. "Maybe. They looked alike, you know, and they liked to pretend they were sisters. They were cast as sisters three or four times and that was a major selling point for Erotica Selecta."

Marshall made a couple of notes in a notepad and asked, "When did you begin to think things weren't so rosy at Erotica Selecta? When did all the disappearances and murders start?"

Gilliam frowned and said, "You know, none of that was ever proven. The police got involved and all those cases were eventually dropped. Valentine was brought in for questioning a few times but he was never charged with anything. So what I'm about to say is pure conjecture. You can't quote me as stating facts."

"I understand."

"It was in nineteen seventy-eight, around Thanksgiving, when Julie Titman disappeared. You remember her?"

"Yes."

"Lovely brunette girl. She had the sweetest smile. Anyway, she just didn't show up one day. After a few days someone went around to where she lived and there was no sign of her. All her stuff was still there but the car was gone. She was reported as a missing person."

"And then her body turned up six months later in the desert."

"Right. At least they *thought* it was her. Nothing but bones there and the skull was gone. Some of the clothing that was still on the skeleton was probably Julie's, or so they said. No one was ever charged for the crime."

"What do you think happened?"

"Julie was in a dispute with Aaron over her contract. She wanted more money and was threatening to leave for another studio. I think he threatened her and when she didn't budge, he had her killed."

"Why do you think that?"

"That's the way Aaron Valentine is," Gilliam said. "He's a cold-hearted, mean son-of-a-bitch. He's a sadist. He likes to control people. He had *me* under his thumb for several years and he threatened *me* when I tried to get out of my contract. I stuck with it until it expired and I didn't renew. That was in nineteen eighty-three. I did work for other studios and then in nineteen ninety I started my own line of videos. Valentine didn't like it that I left, but I left fair and square, you know? I stuck it out with him. Even while suspecting him of having my sister killed. I never confronted him about it, though."

"Do you get along with him now?"

"We're cordial on a business basis. He respects what I've done with my career. I'm a star in the industry and he likes to think he discovered me. He invites me to some of his parties. We get along okay."

"What other things led you to suspect Valentine was a murderer?"

"Well, after Julie disappeared, it seemed that more and more of his acting stable went missing, and they were all stars who wanted out or something. Another body was found in the desert in nineteen seventy-nine, remember? They think it was Paul Stud. All they found was a pile of bones but they linked the teeth to Paul Stud's dental records. Brenda De Blaze—her real name was Karen Andrews—she disappeared in seventy-nine and then *her* body was found in Death Valley. That was definitely labeled a homicide but nobody was ever charged. Anyway, it was getting pretty weird around Erotica Selecta. There was a rumor going around that Valentine would have you burned up in an incinerator that he kept at his warehouse if you didn't tow the line. Valentine kept up the gloss, though. By then he had moved into that big mansion of his and started throwing the extravagant parties. He had some hit movies and was making a lot of money."

"He became one of the kings of porn."

"Yeah."

"Do you think the mafia was involved?" Marshall asked.

"Absolutely. There were these greasy Italian guys always hanging around the mansion and sometimes at the studio. They looked like they were right out of *The Godfather* only they wore Las Vegas-style glitzy shit. It was no secret that the West Coast mafia was controlling all the distribution of the films and stuff. They had an interest in the adult bookstores and peep shows and all the sleaze that went with them. No question that it was all organized crime. Not like today. Today it's all legit. My production company is completely clean. I pay my taxes and no one bothers me. A criminal element might still exist in some circles, but not in the mainstream adult business. That was a thing of the past." Gilliam lowered his voice and added, "Although I think Valentine is still in bed with those guys."

"I guess you've seen the reports that Dana Barnett is alive and well and living in Illinois?"

"Yeah, I heard that," Gilliam said, shaking his head.

"What do you think of that?"

"I don't know what to think. All this time I was sure she was dead. She and Angela. They disappeared together. I'd like to ask Dana a few questions, like what the fuck happened to my sister?"

"They're saying that the woman in Illinois claims she's not Dana Barnett. She says that Dana Barnett was her twin sister. Do you believe that?"

"I tell ya," Gilliam said. "Dana never said *anything* about having a twin sister. I don't believe that for a minute. I saw a picture of that woman and I'm convinced it's Dana."

"Thanks, Mister Gilliam." Marshall shut off the tape recorder.

By dinnertime David had not come home and Diane had become concerned. She and her son had an agreement that he was to be home for dinner and if there were a problem he was to call.

She picked up the phone and punched the speed-dial button for Billy Davis' house. Unfortunately his father Peter answered.

"Peter, it's Diane," she said quickly. "Is David there?"

"Well, hello, Diane," Davis said cheerfully. "How's life treating you?"

"Is David there, Peter?" she repeated with a touch of impatience in her voice.

"No, he isn't. Actually Billy doesn't want to see David much anymore, Diane. I can't imagine why."

Cut the sarcasm, you bastard.

"Fine," she said and hung up.

Where could that boy be?

She dialed Boston Ford and spoke to the hated secretary.

"Tina, is Greg there?"

"Oh, hi Mrs. Boston," the girl said, ever so sweetly. "No, he didn't come in today. In fact, he wasn't here yesterday either. We don't know where he is."

"Really? That's odd," Diane said. "He's not at home?"

"He doesn't answer the phone, Mrs. Boston."

"I see. Well, leave a message for him if he calls in. Ask him to call me, it's about David."

"I will," Tina said. There was a playfulness in her voice that Diane didn't like, as if the girl—Diane didn't want to think of her as a woman—was laughing at her at the other end of the line. Everyone else was laughing at her, why not her ex-husband's mistress?

Diane hung up and drummed her fingers on the counter. She went out to the garage through the kitchen, raised the garage door, and got into the Honda. She pulled out of the driveway and spent the next half-hour driving around the neighborhood looking for her son. She circled his school and found no trace of him.

By seven thirty she was really beginning to get worried. Diane drove back to the apartment and he still hadn't shown up. She went inside, picked up the phone, and dialed her ex-husband. His answering machine came on.

"Hi, this is Greg, leave a message," the voice announced.

At the beep she said, "Greg, it's Diane. Listen, it's seven thirty and I don't know where David is. When you get this message please give me a call."

She hung up and wondered what else she could do besides wait in torment. As she considered turning on the TV, the phone rang loudly, startling her.

"Hello?" she answered, picking up the receiver.

"Hello Dana."

It was a male voice. Confident. Sinister.

"You have the wrong number," she said.

She was about to hang up when the caller answered, "Don't hang up, Mrs. *Boston*."

Probably a prank call. "Don't call here again," she said.

"Hang up and you'll never see David again," the man said quickly.

That got her attention. "What did you say?"

"David is safe. You're not to call the police, do you understand?"

Oh my God. They found me. They found US. Oh my God!

"Do you understand, Dana?" the voice asked again.

"This isn't Dana, but yes, I understand," she replied, her voice shaking.

"David won't be harmed if you do what we say."

"May I please speak with him?" she asked.

"That is not possible. He isn't with me. He's with someone else."

"Who is this?"

"You should know. I am to deliver this message and you must heed it if you want to see your son alive again."

"What's that?"

"Aaron Valentine requests the pleasure of your company. At his home. As soon as you can get there. That's all."

The man hung up.

Diane held on to the receiver until the dial tone began to beep, indicating that she must hang up. She dropped the phone in its cradle and began to shake uncontrollably.

"David," she sobbed as tears ran down her cheeks. "David, I'm so sorry . . . David . . ."

CHAPTER TWENTY-SIX

The van crossed the state line into Iowa as the sun was setting. For the last few hours since he had been abducted, David carefully considered his options. Unfortunately there weren't very many. While the van was on the road the man named Emo kept the doors and windows locked, so David couldn't pull a Hollywood stunt and jump out of the van. His only hope was to try and get away when they stopped. Eventually they'd have to stop, wouldn't they? What about bathroom breaks or the need to fill up with gas? Where the hell were they going, anyway?

"Where are we going, anyway?" David asked.

"Hollywood, David," Emo Tuff answered. "Ever been to Hollywood?"

"No."

"The City of Angels, it is. You'll love it."

"How long will it take?"

"Just a couple of days," the man answered. "I don't need much sleep, you know. I can drive straight through. We'll be stopping for food and gas but not much else. Don't you worry, I'll get you there safe and sound."

"I'm not worried," David said. Actually he was very

worried. The medicine he took for Marfan syndrome was at home. He had to be careful and not become too agitated. "Why are we going to Hollywood?"

"There's a man out there who wants to see your mother. He figured this was the only way to get her to come out and see him."

"You're not going to hurt me, are you?" David asked.

Tuff smiled. "Nah, I ain't gonna hurt you, David," he answered. Then he turned and looked at David with absolutely no warmth. "Not unless I have to."

A shiver went down David's spine. Now he was sure this guy was dangerous. He was nice during the trip so far but David could sense that underneath the friendly exterior there resided an evil person. Hell, he *looked* like a pirate. And he had kidnapped David in broad daylight. No, David told himself, this man was not a friend.

"I just thought of something, David," the man said.

"What."

"Do you have a cell phone?"

David wished he did. "No."

Tuff nodded. "That's good."

The van passed an exit warning sign that displayed the icons for food and gas. David figured it was now or never.

"I have to go to the bathroom," he said.

"Already?" Tuff asked. "Can't you wait until we have to fill up?"

"No."

Tuff frowned and moved into the right lane. "Now listen, David. We gotta have some ground rules on these stops. You understand?"

"Yes."

"You can't try to get away from me. I'll just catch you again, I promise you. And if you try anything like that, I can't keep my word that I won't hurt you. It'll make me real mad if you try to contact a cop or someone else. It'll make me real mad if you try to escape. You don't want to know me when I'm mad, you understand?"

"Yes."

"Good."

He took the next exit and the van moved off the highway. An Amoco gas station that was also a convenience store stood at the end of the ramp. Tuff pulled into the driveway and parked on the side of the building. There were no other customers.

"The bathroom's inside. I'm going in with you," Tuff said. "Maybe if you're good I'll buy you a candy bar."

"I'm not supposed to accept candy from strangers," David said. Their eyes met and a smile played on David's lips.

Tuff laughed. "That's good, David! That was funny!" He hit the button that unlocked the van doors. They both got out and went inside the convenience store.

A large African-American man was behind the counter. David thought he might have been asleep before they walked in. The man eyed them but showed no sign that he thought anything was suspicious. Just a father and his son—but that was one weird looking father, though.

"Where's your bathroom?" Tuff asked.

The man gestured behind him. The Men/Women signs were displayed in an alcove near the self-service coffee counter. Tuff pointed the way to David and said, "I'll wait out here."

David went into the Men's and locked the door behind him. It was a one-room affair, just a toilet and a sink. And a window.

He was just tall enough to reach it. It wasn't a large window—it was rectangular in shape and was hinged at the top so it could be opened to ventilate the room. A crank at the bottom apparently opened it. Could he climb up there and get through it?

David looked around and determined the only thing

that might assist him was the trashcan. He grabbed it, turned it upside down, and placed it against the wall underneath the window. He stepped onto the bottom of the can and had a much better angle with which to turn the crank. At first he couldn't budge it—the crank was stuck. He put his full weight into it and hung from the handle, hoping gravity would do the trick. The crank gave a little as David bounced in the air, his feet dangling off the trashcan. Finally, the crank slipped and turned, creaking as it went. David fell to the floor, knocking the can against the wall.

A knock at the door. "David? You all right?"

"Yeah."

"What are you doing?"

"I gotta do number two," he said. "I'll be out in a minute."

"Okay. Hurry up."

David quietly got off the floor and put the trash can back in place. He returned to the top and continued to crank the window until it was open as far as it would go. Now for the hard part.

He grabbed the bottom sill and heaved himself up the wall, trying not to grunt too loudly. The traction of his tennis shoes helped considerably. He got to where his head and shoulders were in the open window and now all he needed to do was worm his way through. The bottom sill was uncomfortable against his chest and stomach as he slid out to his waist but he clenched his teeth and kept going. There was no eloquent way to do it; he couldn't bring his gangly legs through the window with his torso. All he could do was dive out, head first.

David used his hands to cushion the fall and the impact on the pavement stung like hell. He did an awkward body roll and managed to land without hurting himself further. He had done it!

The window emptied out to the back of the store, where the trash dumpster was located along with a single Ford pickup, probably belonging to the cashier on duty. The only thing beyond the property was a wide-open grass field. On the other side of the store was the highway. He certainly couldn't go that way. Where was he going to hide?

The sun had set and the field was partially illuminated by the three-quarter moon. Maybe he could get far enough away and Emo wouldn't be able to find him without more light. Maybe there would be a place to hide in the field. He had to take the chance.

David took off running into the darkness.

Inside the shop, Emo Tuff was becoming impatient. He knocked on the bathroom door again. "David? Come on, we gotta go." When the boy didn't answer after a couple more knocks, Tuff went to the cashier and asked, "Hey, do you have a key to the bathroom? My boy, he's, uh, he's been sick. I'm afraid he might have passed out or something."

The man nodded and handed him the key. Tuff walked back to the alcove and unlocked the door.

"Shit," he said, eyeing the empty room, the overturned trash can, and the open window.

Tuff ran through the store, tossed the key to the cashier, and burst out the door. He bolted around the building and found the spot underneath the window where David would have fallen. He looked around the property and realized the only direction the boy could have gone was out into the field.

"David!" he called.

One advantage to losing an eye was that the remaining one naturally compensated for the lack of 20/20 vision. Emo Tuff's one good eye saw exceptionally well, even in the dark. He scanned the moonlit horizon and detected movement some hundred yards away at an angle of thirty degrees. The kid was running.

Tuff took off after him.

David wanted to call for help but knew that no one

would hear him out there. Besides, he was already out of breath. He couldn't run much more. His heart was pounding and his chest hurt. Nevertheless, he heard Emo call his name—he just couldn't stop now.

Please, please, find a place to hide!

He kept running but his pace slowed. His lungs screamed in agony as he attempted to draw a decent breath of air. It's what happened when his heart had to work overtime. He couldn't get enough oxygen and he passed out.

No! Not that!

An excruciating pain ripped through his chest, causing him to stumble and fall. He hadn't felt anything like it since he was a small child, back when they had first discovered he had a heart problem. He had just done what his doctor had told him not to do—exerted himself beyond his capability. He needed his medicine badly.

David rolled in the grass and lay face up, gasping for air and clutching his ribcage. That's how Emo Tuff found him.

"You little shit, I'm gonna beat you senseless!" the man yelled over him as he squatted by the fallen boy. Tuff pulled David up by the shirt and made a fist, ready to knock the kid's jaw loose. Then he saw that the boy was not well.

"David? What the fuck is wrong?"

David gasped for air, unable to speak. He looked at Emo Tuff with wide eyes, the whites shining in the moonlight. The way the kid was holding his ribcage prompted Tuff to ask, "What's the matter? Is it your heart? Nod your head if it's a yes!"

David nodded.

"Okay, take it easy," Tuff said. "Sit up." He helped the boy into a sitting position. "Calm down. I'm not gonna hurt you, David."

But David lost consciousness and drooped forward into his arms.

"Aw shit," Tuff said. "Don't die on me, you stupid kid." Valentine would have his hide if the boy died en route to California. Tuff looked back toward the gas station and saw no indication that the cashier had followed him outside. Tuff cradled the lanky boy in his arms and picked him up. He carried David across the field and back to the van. After opening the door, he placed David in the back seat and strapped a seat belt around the boy's waist. He shut the door, locked it, and then went to peer through the glass front of the shop to see what the cashier was doing.

The man's eyes were closed and his head was cradled in his arms on the counter.

Tuff went back to the van, got inside, started the ignition, and drove back to the highway.

CHAPTER TWENTY-SEVEN

Diane parked the Honda in the lot next to the bank and got out of the car. Carrying her purse and a few towels in a shopping bag, she went inside the bank lobby and approached the first available teller.

"I'd like to get into my safety deposit box, please," she said quietly.

"Sure," the teller said. "I'll need identification and your bank card, please."

Diane produced the two items from her purse and the teller signaled one of the men who sat at desks on the bank floor. A vice president-type, the young man walked over to Diane and said, "I'll be happy to help you, ma'am. Come this way." He led her through double doors into the surprisingly small room that contained the boxes. With the appropriate authorization given to him by the teller and the correct key, he unlocked the little door, pulled out the box, and handed it to Diane. He then led her through another door into a room furnished with a table and a couple of chairs.

"You can have some privacy in here," he said.

"Thank you," Diane said as she placed the box on the table.

The man gestured to a phone on the table. "Just punch seven if you need any assistance."

He closed the door behind him, leaving her alone with the elongated metal container. Diane carefully opened it and saw that everything was as she had left it—when was it? Three months ago? It was an eternity.

She lifted the heavy black velvet bag and untied the drawstring. She spilled the diamonds onto the table and counted them, guessing as to what she might get for them if she went to a straight jeweler. Actually, she had no idea. She was so used to the black market prices that Moses Rabinowitz offered her that she didn't have a clue what they were worth in a legitimate market. Perhaps in California she could find a fence that would give her something reasonable. If her plans worked out, someone she knew would be able to point her in the right direction.

Diane scooped the diamonds back into the bag and tied the drawstring. Weighing it in her left hand, she reflected on the fateful day that she acquired them and the dreadful phone call that came after midnight. . . .

"Hello?"

". . . Help me . . ."

"Sweetie? What's wrong? You sound—"

"Please . . ."

"Where are you?"

". . . Warehouse . . ."

"My God, what's happened? Sweetie?"

". . . Shot . . ."

"What? I can't hear you! Did you say—?"

Then there was the sound of the receiver dropping. The line went dead.

"Shot"—that was the last word Diane had heard her speak. She had gotten out of bed, dressed quickly, and sped to Valentine's warehouse. The place was well lit but eerily quiet when she arrived. She found a window, near the loading dock where Valentine and his men always entered, and that's where she crawled in. Diane feared that she might find something terrible inside but she never expected to encounter the bloody tableau on display in the creepy old place. Bodies were strewn here and there, full of gunshot wounds. Four black men. Three of Eduardo's thugs and Eduardo himself lay on his back, his chest ripped open by several rounds of ammunition. Diane called out for her sister but didn't see her. Where was she?

Her sister.

Diane. Dana. Sisters.

Who was who? The events of that night were jumbled in her mind. What was memory was not necessarily fact. Or was it? What had happened? Where was her Sweetie? She liked to call her Sweetie. It wasn't her real name but it had stuck. (*When they had been little girls, the twins called each other Sweetie for the fun of it.*)

Her head hurt. She reached up, felt the back of her head, and then examined her hand. There was blood on it. How did she get hurt? She wasn't at the scene of the massacre when it happened, she had been at home in bed.

Or had she?

Look, she thought. There was a trail of blood on the concrete floor. Perhaps she should follow it?

"Sweetie?" she called again as she slowly traced the red-streaked trail into the rows of stacked boxes that filled the building. Diane found her, unconscious, in the small office that was located near the stockpile of videotapes waiting to be distributed around the country. Sweetie had found a phone on a desk there and must have used every bit of strength she had to make the earlier call.

There was a gunshot wound in Sweetie's head. The blond hair was matted with blood.

Diane examined her carefully and saw that she was still breathing.

Got to get help, she thought. Or would they be coming after her? They would come soon, they surely would!

With this kind of carnage at the warehouse, they would want revenge.

Diane carried Sweetie back to the central area of the warehouse, where Eduardo and the black gangsters lay sprawled about like broken dolls. On the table was an open briefcase. Diane stopped to look and gasped. It was full of sparkling gems. Diamonds. (*"Eduardo is making a big haul tonight,"* Sweetie had said.) Even after the shock of seeing her sister with a gunshot wound to the head, the sight of the dazzling baubles made her gasp.

What should she do? Could she risk taking Sweetie to a hospital? Think! Think! How could she turn this situation into an advantage for the two of them?

The incinerator was going full blast. Had they disposed of someone? That was where they did it, Diane knew that. If Valentine wanted to get rid of somebody, Eduardo or one of the other goons would throw the victim into the incinerator. Then there was no trace.

Diane looked at the incinerator and then at her sister. That's when she was suddenly aware of intense pain in the back of her head. Diane touched her hair and felt a wet stickiness.

Why was her head bleeding? For a moment she had to lean against the table to regain her equilibrium. Then she knew what she had to do to complete her mission.

Near Eduardo's right hand was a gun—a Colt .45. Diane picked it up and put it in her purse. She then closed the briefcase with the diamonds inside and took it with her. . . .

That was what had happened, wasn't it? At least that's how Diane remembered it. It was so long ago that the details were all mixed up, just like they were in her dreams. *Best not to dwell on that night,* she thought.

Diane snapped out of it and realized she was in the private bank room, the empty safety deposit box in front of her. She opened the shopping bag, placed the bag of diamonds inside, and wrapped a couple of the towels around it.

Then she reached into the safety deposit box and pulled out the only remaining items—a Colt .45 and a box of ammunition. Diane briefly examined the handgun to check that it wasn't loaded and then put it and the ammunition in the shopping bag. Again, she wrapped them in towels to hide the bag's contents.

Diane closed the bank box and stood, ready to head out of town. There was one more thing she had to do, though.

It was a short drive to Scotty Lewis' office. She went to the door and looked inside. His secretary, Delores, was on the phone but the outer office was otherwise empty. As Diane stepped inside, Delores waved to her and smiled. "Yes, sir, I'll have Mister Lewis call you as soon as he's finished with his meeting," Delores said into the phone. "Uh huh. Bye." She hung up and said, "Hello Mrs. Boston. How are you?"

"Fine, Delores. Is Scotty in there?"

"Yes, but he has a client with him. Did you have an appointment?" Delores wrinkled her brow and looked at her calendar.

"No, he's not expecting me. I just wanted to tell him one quick thing and then I have to leave. Is there any way I can speak to him?" Diane asked.

"Just a second, I'll see." She picked up the phone and pressed an extension. "Scotty? Mrs. Boston is out here and she'd like a quick word with you. No, I don't think so. That's right. Okay, I'll tell her." She hung up and said, "He'll be right out."

Diane didn't sit. She preferred to gaze out the glass window at the street. There wasn't much activity for a weekday morning, but then who was she to judge? She usually spent her days in the classroom.

"Diane?" Scotty had come out of his office.

Diane turned and went to him. "Hi, Scotty, listen I won't take up much of your time. I have to leave town for a few days."

"You do? Why?"

"I can't tell you. Listen, you have my cell phone number, right?"

"Yes, but—"

"Then call me if you need me. Although I may be out of touch at times."

"Diane, what's going on?" Scotty asked. "We have a meeting with Harp on the school board case in three days. Will you be back for that?"

"I doubt it. I'm just going to have to count on you to represent me at that. Tell him I had some unexpected business to attend to. Tell him it was a family crisis."

"Diane, are you all right? Something's wrong, I can tell."

"Leave it, Scotty. I'll be in touch when I can." She turned and made for the door, stopped, and faced him again. "Sorry to do this, Scotty, but it has to be done. Thanks for everything. I promise I'll be in touch as soon as I can."

And she was gone.

She couldn't think of anything else that she might need. She had a packed bag in the trunk, she had some money, and most importantly, she had the diamonds and a weapon. As she drove back to Lincoln Grove from Scotty's office, Diane decided to make one last stop before heading west.

Greg Boston's little house stood quietly on a street full of homes that were built in the fifties. It was a lower middle class neighborhood and she was well aware that Greg hated living there. He could afford a better place but he had gotten a good deal from someone he knew at the dealership. Diane imagined that Greg would move to a nicer house in a more upscale area of town once the dust was settled between them. She was determined, though, that David would not be living with him when Greg did move.

Greg's Jaguar was parked in the drive. Odd, she thought. According to Tina, he wasn't home and hadn't been for a couple of days. Where would he go without his car?

Never mind, she thought. She would just leave him a note to say that she had gone out of town for a few days and had taken David with her. She looked in the glove compartment, grabbed a notepad and pencil, and scribbled the message. Diane got out of the car and went to leave the note on the door. She considered knocking just to see if her ex-husband was home but she didn't really want to see him.

Then she noticed that the door was ajar.

She peered inside. "Greg? Are you home?" No sound. "Greg?" She knocked loudly. "Hello? Anyone there?"

She opened the screen door and gently pushed the front door wider. "Greg?"

When she saw what was lying on the living room floor, Diane stifled a scream. She put her hand to her mouth and gasped, nearly choking herself. The sight was so shocking that she stumbled backward into the door, slamming it shut.

Greg Boston's body, or what was left of it, was spread over the Oriental rug that covered the living room floor. What was irrevocably imprinted on her brain was the sight of blood—lots of it—dried to a dark ruddy color and covering a great deal of the floor space.

In a panic, Diane turned, struggled briefly with the front door, and ran out of the house. She got to her car, started it without thinking, screeched out of the driveway, and sped down the road like a banshee. With her cell phone, she dialed 911 to report what she had seen but hung up before giving out her name.

She didn't realize that old Mrs. O'Donnell, the kind

lady who lived across the street from Greg, was looking out her window when Diane ran out of the house. Mrs. O'Donnell had taken a shine to Greg after he had moved in and occasionally brought him cookies or cakes when she baked them. She felt sorry for the divorced man, especially now that his ex-wife had received such awful publicity in the newspaper.

The old woman recognized the blonde rushing out of Greg Boston's house as the former spouse.

Another person also saw Diane run out of the house and take off in her car. Nick Belgrad sat in a silver Lexus three houses down from Greg's home. He had been following Diane all day—first to the bank, then to her lawyer's office, and now here.

Belgrad started the ignition and pulled out into the street. He wasn't about to lose her, no matter where she was going.

DAVID'S JOURNAL

I can't believe what I just heard on the radio. Even Emo is amazed. I just can't believe Mom would do something like that.

I better back up since I haven't written in my journal for a couple of days.

To make a long story short, I've been kidnapped and I'm being taken to California by a strange guy named Emo Tuff. He has long blond hair and he wears an eye patch. He kinda looks like a pirate. So far he's been pretty nice to me but I can tell that he's probably mean when he wants to be.

I'll bet he's killed people.

We're in a van that has special doors on it that he locks. I couldn't get out if I wanted to. He stops every now and then to let me go to the bathroom and we get food to eat in the van. He hasn't stopped driving and he doesn't get tired.

Last night I tried to escape. Boy, that was a mistake. We were at a gas station in Iowa and I snuck out the bathroom window. I ran into a field but my heart started doing its bad thing again and I fainted. Emo caught me and took me back to the van. I slept the rest of the night. This morning when I woke up I felt awful. I was very weak. I need my medicine but it's at home. I told Emo about my condition and he actually apologized. He said that he'd try and get me what I needed when we get to L.A.

We got McDonald's for breakfast and I felt better. We drove on through the morning and now it's just after lunch. We stopped at a Wendy's and got hamburgers. I feel pretty good now. I think that Emo must have been a little scared when I was sick. He says that he's under orders to deliver me to L.A., so I guess I have to stay alive.

Anyway, I convinced Emo to put on the radio because the drive is so boring. We're in Nebraska and there's nothing to look at but flat fields. The radio is okay. I tried to find a decent station and there was something coming out of Omaha that played some good alternative stuff. After a while the news came on and I was surprised to hear my Mom's name mentioned. Even Emo became alert and turned up the volume.

They said that my father was murdered in his house and that my Mom was seen leaving the scene in a hurry. The police are looking for her and they think she left town and—get this—they think she's taken me with her!

Well, I figure since they got that part wrong, maybe the whole thing is wrong. I can't believe she'd kill Dad. That's just crazy.

They said Dad is dead. Maybe it's not true. I don't want it to be true. I love my Dad. He wasn't a bad guy. I know he and my Mom had their problems but I never had a problem with him. It got a little strange the last time I saw him when he told me that I wasn't really sick and that Mom made it all up. I know now that he was lying. Why would he do that? I guess he just wanted me to live with him and not Mom.

I got out my journal to write this stuff down but now I don't think I can focus my eyes on it. I'm tired and I feel depressed. I'm gonna lie down again in the back seat.

And I don't want Emo to see me cry.

CHAPTER TWENTY-EIGHT

Diane was so tired by the time she reached Des Moines that she had to stop. She pulled in to a Days Inn motel and spent a fitful night in a dank room that was barely worth the forty-two dollars she had paid for it. The alarm she set jolted her awake at six o'clock and she estimated that she'd had about three hours of sleep. It was enough.

The drive was monotonous and she spent most of the time wondering where David was. Was he traveling by car? Did they fly him to L.A.? Wouldn't it be ironic if it turned out they were driving along the same route as she? Maybe she would catch up with them and she'd pass them on the highway. *That would be something*, she thought. She prayed they wouldn't hurt him.

The radio kept her awake. She had forgotten to take some cassette tapes for the journey. Her Honda didn't have a CD player so a lot of her music consisted of tapes from the eighties and nineties. It was difficult to find cassette tapes in the stores now. Everything was CDs. Even though she had a CD player at home, and David did, too, she owned very few compact disks. She never had time to listen to music anyway.

When the news came on, Diane nearly turned the dial to find more music but something made her stop. What was going on in the world? She had been so preoccupied with her own problems that she had no idea if the country was still at war or if some famous celebrity had recently died.

She didn't expect to hear a story about her.

Wanted for murder? How could that be? She didn't kill Greg! What was wrong with those people?

The story suggested that she had been seen "fleeing" from the scene of the crime. Apparently one of Greg's neighbors had seen her run from the house after she had discovered the body. Didn't they figure out that it was *she* who had called 911? Who else could have done it? The police were idiots. They were idiots in L.A. and they were idiots in Illinois.

When she reached Omaha, Diane had to stop to get something to eat and use the bathroom. She got off the Interstate and drove a ways into the city, hoping to find a place where she could chill out and have a quiet meal. In the end she decided not to waste much time, so she picked a Taco Bell. It was situated in the large parking lot of a strip mall full of shops and a grocery store.

On the way inside she noticed several newspaper dispensers—one featured the *Chicago Tribune*. She hesitated a moment and then dropped the coins in the slot. She went inside the restaurant, ordered three hard shell tacos and a Pepsi, and sat down to look through the paper.

Sure enough, buried in the Metro section was a picture of "Lucy Luv" with Diane's name plastered beneath it. The headline read: "Porn Star Mom Wanted for Murder."

Jesus. What was she going to do now?

The story spelled it out. Greg Boston had been found in his home, his throat slashed, and his ex-wife Diane Boston was seen fleeing the scene. A neighbor spotted her and had spoken to the police. Apparently they didn't know who had dialed 911, for a "mystery caller" had phoned the police just minutes before the neighbor did.

The police were looking for her and her thirteen-year-old son, David. Apparently they believed that she took him with her. That wasn't good.

Diane ate her meal way too quickly, giving her heartburn followed by nausea. The anxiety of the last two days exacerbated it and she spent the next ten minutes in the ladies' room throwing up.

After tidying herself and sitting in the restaurant for a few minutes to get a grip, she returned to the car and got out her cell phone. She dialed Scotty Lewis, who had left six messages on her voice mail since she left Illinois.

"Scotty, it's Diane."

"God, Diane. Where are you?" Scotty sounded alarmed.

"Let's see, right now I'm in Omaha, Nebraska."

"What are you *doing*? Diane, do you know what's going on here?"

"Yeah, I just found out. I'm wanted for murder."

"The police are looking for you. You need to get back here right away! Didn't you get my messages?"

Diane took a breath and continued. "Listen, Scotty. I didn't kill Greg. You should know I didn't kill Greg."

"Well . . . well, of course I know that."

"You don't sound convinced."

"Diane, if you say you didn't do it, then I believe you. It's just that this old lady who lives across the street—"

"Scotty, I *found* Greg's body, or what was left of it. I panicked and ran out of the house. I wasn't thinking. I dialed 911 and reported it, but I was on my way out of town, remember? I just kept going. I know, I know, I should have stayed. It would have looked less suspicious."

Scotty sounded flustered. "Christ, Diane. That's the worst thing you could have done. You need to get back here and clear all this up. Otherwise you could be in a lot of trouble. A lot more trouble than *I* can help you with!"

"I know, Scotty, but I can't."

"Is David all right? Everyone is freaking out that you took him with you."

"I didn't take him, Scotty. He's not with me."

"He's not? Where is he?"

Diane knew it was risky telling him. "He . . . ran away. That's why I'm on the road. I'm looking for him."

"Ran away? Why?"

"Oh, you know. Teenagers."

"Do you know where he went?"

"I have a good idea," she answered. "That's where I'm going."

"Where is that?"

"Scotty, I'm counting on you not to tell the police."

"All right."

"California. L.A."

"David went there? Whatever for?"

"After I find him I'll explain everything," she said. "Just tell the police and anyone else who's concerned that David is missing and that's why I left town. Tell them I'm innocent of Greg's murder and that I'll be back to face the music."

"I'll do that, Diane, but I'm not sure how it's going to fly."

"It's going to have to for now. Thanks, Scotty, you're a savior."

"Diane, you *call* me. Let me know what's going on. I can cover for you for just so long. You know they'll be looking for you."

"I understand. Good-bye Scotty. Wish me luck."

She hung up and started the car. Perhaps it was a good thing the police would be made aware that David wasn't with her. They'd start looking for him and take some of the heat off of her. Maybe they would find him before she did.

Diane drove out of the Taco Bell parking area in order to get back on the main road leading to the Interstate. Out of the corner of her eye she saw a sign above a store-front that read "Perlman Fine Jewelry."

She swung the car around and drove past the store. It

appeared to be fairly upscale and there were no customers inside. Better yet, another sign claimed that fine jewelry was "bought and sold." Diane parked the car again, grabbed her purse, and got out of the Honda.

Inside the store a good-looking man in his thirties said, "Hello! I'm Mike Perlman. Can I help you?"

"I'd like to sell some diamonds," Diane said.

Perlman raised his eyebrows. Apparently he wasn't used to strangers walking in off the street with diamonds. "I'd be happy to take a look at them," he said.

"Believe me, you'll like them." She walked over to the counter and with her back to the man she opened her purse and removed four gems from the velvet bag. She placed them on the mat, closed her purse and stepped back so that he could see.

His eyes widened and he blinked three times.

"Those are real?" he asked.

"Listen, Mister Perlman, if you're not experienced with this sort of thing, I'll have to take them elsewhere," she said.

"No, no, I'm very experienced," he said, his voice cracking. He cleared his throat and went around the counter to get his glass. He turned on a lamp and examined each diamond carefully.

"Where did you get these?" Perlman asked after several minutes. It was obvious that he was awed.

"They've been in my family for a hundred years," she replied. "They belonged to my great-grandfather. Now I want to sell them."

He looked at her soberly. "They're not stolen, are they?"

She did her best to look affronted. "I should say not!"

"I beg your pardon. Well, ma'am, I'm not sure I have the kind of money that you would want for these," he said.

"I appreciate your honesty. What *can* you give me for them?"

Perlman removed his glass and scratched his head. "I can give you ten thousand dollars for the four of them."

"Cash?"

He blinked again. "I would have to go to my bank."

"I'm kind of in a hurry."

"It's here in the strip mall. You wouldn't have to wait long."

Diane knew they were worth four times that much but she needed the cash quickly. "All right. Go get the money. You want me to wait here?"

"Uhm, actually . . ."

She put up a hand. "I understand. I'll wait outside. In fact, I'll go to the grocery store and come back in twenty minutes. Will that give you enough time?"

Driving on the main road back to the Interstate, Diane stopped at a Car Max and went inside the dealership. She looked for and found an overweight salesman who just might be charmed by a beautiful blond woman.

"Yes ma'am, can I help you?" he asked, all smiles.

"I want to sell my car and buy a used one," she told him.

"I'm sorry?"

"See that Honda out there? I have my title and everything right here. I want to trade it in and get a new car."

"Why would you want to do that?" the man asked.

Because the police are looking for this one, you idiot. "Because I'm sick of it and I want something new. Is that all right?"

The salesman shrugged. "Well, sure. Let's take a look at it."

She had gotten the idea of trading cars from that Alfred Hitchcock movie, *Psycho.* Janet Leigh was on the run with a lot of stolen money and she became paranoid when a policeman began to tail her. She pulled into a used car joint and created a great deal of suspicion when she tried to trade her car. Unfortunately, her scheme didn't work. The cop who was tailing her saw the entire transaction from across the street.

In Diane's case, however, no policeman was watching. And no one was the wiser when she drove out of Omaha in a used green '97 Chevy Malibu.

CHAPTER TWENTY-NINE

Darren Marshall was ecstatic over the news that Diane Boston was wanted for murder. Even Brandon Mertz was beginning to show some interest in the story. The city editor gave Marshall more leeway for time out of the office. There was still a lot of research to be done and Marshall was busy tracking down everyone who had known Dana Barnett when she was doing adult films. Unfortunately, there weren't a lot of folks left—they had either died, disappeared into obscurity, or didn't want to talk. The latter was the case with Aaron Valentine himself. Marshall had called the offices of Erotica Selecta and requested an interview. When Valentine learned that Marshall wanted to talk about Dana Barnett, Marshall was told to go to hell.

Pete Rod, AKA Eric Gilliam, had provided the best stuff so far. There were enough leads there to keep Marshall busy for a while. Marshall especially wanted to track down Dana Barnett's roots in Texas. Someone had to remember her. It wasn't that long ago.

Marshall got up from his desk at the *Weekly* and stretched. He had been surfing the Net for hours, compiling every bit of fact and fiction that had been written about Erotica Selecta, Aaron Valentine, and Lucy Luv. There was a surprising amount of information, which just proved Marshall's long-time adage that "if it had been conceived and written down, then it was on the Internet somewhere."

The phone rang. He picked it up and said, "Marshall."

"Uh, hi, it's Eric Gilliam."

"Eric, how are you?" Marshall went around the desk and sat.

"Fine. Listen, I got to thinking after our conversation the other day."

"Yeah?"

"And I went and got out some of my sister's stuff from storage. I started to go through it and there may be some shit here you might want to see."

"Really?" Marshall felt as if he had just been given a raise in pay. "What do you have?"

"Well there are some letters and a diary. She writes a lot about Dana in it."

"Fantastic. When can I come by?"

Gilliam replied, "I'm shooting today but you could come by tomorrow after noon. But listen, since you're gonna profit by all this, I'm gonna have to ask you for a piece of the action."

Marshall wasn't sure how to handle that one. "Well, gee, Eric, like I told you, I'm gonna write an article for the *Weekly* and hopefully turn it into a book. I don't get anything for the article except my regular salary. The book is another story but that's way down the line. I have no idea what that's gonna be or if it will even happen."

"Don't bullshit me, Marshall," Gilliam said. "You and I both know that this is a helluva story. The book will be a bestseller and it'll be a major motion picture, too."

Marshall sighed. He had to have Angela Gilliam's things. "All right, what is it you want?"

"I want in on the movie. Associate Producer or something. With a salary. And I'll play myself in the picture. It's my ticket out of the adult business and into mainstream."

"Whoa, Eric, how can I guarantee you something like that? Let's say that this article does become a book. Then let's say that the film rights are sold. Once that happens, I have no control over what Hollywood does with it. It'll be out of my hands. Some producer will hire a scriptwriter and a director and they'll probably change the whole thing and I won't have any say. You know how it works."

"So don't sell the film rights unless you have some creative input in the project. Believe me, I'll bet you can do it. They're gonna want this story and they'll give you what you want."

Gilliam had a point. Marshall imagined his name in lights on a marquee. He just might be able to get away with it.

"All right, Eric, we'll do it this way. We can even put it in writing. We'll have an agreement, but there's gonna have to be a lot of 'ifs.' *If* I get creative input, *if* the thing sells, *if* they'll even take you. *If* that's okay by you, then we have a deal."

"That's a lot of 'ifs.' How about you pay me five thousand dollars flat and I'll turn over all the stuff to you."

"Sold."

Nick Belgrad kept the silver Lexus at least six car lengths behind Diane's new Chevy Malibu. With years of experience tailing people, Belgrad was confident she was unaware she was being followed. He had kept tabs on her since she left Illinois and had witnessed the exchange of cars in Omaha. He, too, was reminded of the Hitchcock movie.

Her trip to the jewelry store was puzzling. What was that all about? And where was the boy? The whole thing was one big mystery, but Belgrad thrived on mysteries.

He made his living solving them. Pieces were slowly falling into place and he was beginning to understand something about the woman he was tailing. Her lawyer had quoted her extensively, saying she was innocent of killing her ex-husband and that she was on the road looking for her runaway son. The chief of police in Lincoln Grove, a man named Grabowski, didn't believe it and he was frothing at the mouth to catch her.

But Belgrad had seen her run from her ex-husband's house. She had appeared frightened and hysterical, and in Belgrad's experience that was not the demeanor of a murderer after committing the crime. In his opinion, she looked like she had just seen something horrible, which is what the lawyer claimed. Belgrad bought it.

What he didn't believe was that she was looking for her runaway son. Belgrad was convinced that something bad had happened to the kid. And Diane Boston knew what that was.

All this was leading Belgrad nearer to closing the gap between this woman and what had happened to the Rabinowitz brothers. That was the main objective. Belgrad had a job to do and he had promised Moses he would do it. When the phone call came after Hiram's funeral in New York, Belgrad felt that he owed it to the Rabinowitz brothers to see it through. Moses' death had been another shock but Belgrad wasn't particularly surprised by it. He had warned Hiram time and time again that they played with fire and were likely to get burned. Even Belgrad's father had reproached the brothers about their shady dealings and the elder Belgrad was their dearest and closest friend.

It all had something to do with Diane Boston and her association with the pornographers in Los Angeles, Belgrad was sure of it.

He had done his homework. Diane was really Dana Barnett, an actress who worked for Erotica Selecta Films in the late seventies as "Lucy Luv." She was most likely involved in a lesbian relationship with another actress, Angel Babe, the sister of a male porn star named Pete Rod. The pair disappeared in 1980 at the same time as a gang shoot-out that took place at Aaron Valentine's warehouse in Van Nuys. According to a police report that Belgrad was able to get hold of through a business contact in California, Valentine had a younger brother named Eduardo. Police believed that Eduardo was the liaison between Valentine and the mob. Eduardo had been arrested once for drug trafficking but got off thanks to his brother's connections. Belgrad figured that Eduardo probably supplied drugs for the porn actors and actresses.

Eduardo Valentine and three other Erotica Selecta employees were found shot to death at the warehouse. Several slain members of a black gang that operated out of Nigeria were also discovered at the scene. The police never could figure out what the gunfight was about but it was highly probable that it had to do with drugs. It made sense. Aaron Valentine had been questioned at length but he convinced the authorities that he knew nothing. What was not reported in the media but was mentioned in the police account was that evidence was retrieved at the scene indicating Lucy Luv may have been present. Police feared that she and her girlfriend Angel had been thrown into the incinerator.

The sun had finally set and Belgrad saw the Malibu pull off the highway. He figured that she was calling it a day and would check into a motel. That meant another night of sleeping in the car, staking her out. He had to be able to hit the road as soon as she did and the only way to do that was to keep an eye on her car.

What fun. Lots of coffee. Maybe a cold sandwich or a pizza. A little shut-eye in the dead of night. An aching back in the morning. Ibuprofen. More coffee.

It was all part of the job.

CHAPTER THIRTY

They made it in good time.

Los Angeles was waking up when the van rolled into town. The trip took two nights and not quite two full days. David was dead tired but Emo Tuff seemed to be as alert as ever. *Was the guy human?* David wondered. The man never once yawned or gave any indication that he needed sleep.

"Welcome to the City of Angels, David," Tuff said. "Too bad we got into town just as rush hour's starting."

"Where exactly are we going?" David asked.

"To Aaron Valentine's house. You know who he is?"

"No."

"He's a millionaire. Movie producer. You'll like him."

The van made its way through the dense traffic onto the Hollywood Freeway and headed west on the Ventura, crossing the 405. Eventually Tuff took the exit to Woodland Hills. He drove through the better part of town and then turned left onto a road that circled up into the hills. David watched with interest as they passed several spectacular homes hidden at the back of private roads or behind security fences.

"Is this Beverly Hills?" he asked.

"Nah, that's farther south. This is Woodland Hills," Tuff said. "But a lot of rich celebrities live up here, too. And a lot of starving artists and just plain folks."

David lost all sense of direction as the van transgressed the winding, narrow road that ascended through a thick forest. Finally Tuff turned into a driveway blocked by an iron gate with a sign above it proclaiming the place as "Paradise." He stopped and lowered his window so that he could punch a code on a keypad. The gate slowly opened.

A paved drive snaked up and around a hill past elegant fountains and statuary. Dense foliage of trees and vines blocked any view beyond the road but David thought he was entering the palace grounds of a Roman emperor. A fully bloomed male peacock crossed the drive at one point and Tuff had to slow down and honk the horn. When they reached the top of the hill the greenery opened up, revealing the three-story Tudor mansion to the right and a vast lawn to the left.

"That's where people park when there's a party," Tuff said, indicating the lawn.

"Wow," David said. For a moment he forgot that he had been kidnapped. It was the most beautiful place he'd ever seen.

The van pulled around a circular courtyard and stopped in front of the mansion. Two bulky men dressed in black and wearing handguns at their waists met them in front of two large double doors. Tuff opened the van and got out.

"Let's go, David," he said.

David nervously stepped out.

"Damn, he's tall, ain't he?" one of the men said.

"You play basketball, kid?" the other asked.

"No," David replied.

"Leave him alone," Tuff said. "Where's the boss?"

"In his study," the first man answered.

"Come on, David," Tuff said, leading the boy through

the double doors and into what David always imagined an English duke's residence might be. Or maybe it was more like a king's country home.

As they walked through the mansion, David saw several servants and more men dressed in black. There were also a few women—gorgeous model types—wearing very little clothing. One of them smiled at him and said hello. David was too flustered to speak.

"Close your mouth, boy," Tuff said. "Your jaw is hanging open."

David snapped out of it and followed Tuff up a flight of circular stone stairs. "Who are those girls?" he asked.

"Actresses."

"Really? Were they in anything I've seen?"

"I doubt it. Not until you're eighteen. Twenty-one in some states."

They walked past a suit of armor on display in a hallway and went through an opening that led to yet another passage. At the end of the corridor was a closed wooden door. Tuff knocked on it. A man's voice within told them to enter.

Aaron Valentine was not what David expected. He didn't know what he had expected, but he didn't think the man would have such a thick head of white hair. The guy was big, like a wrestler, and he wore an abundance of gold chains and jewelry.

"David, this is Mister Valentine," Tuff said.

"Hello, David," Valentine said, offering his hand. David meekly shook it.

"Hi."

"Welcome to Paradise," the man said. "Don't you worry, you're going to be just fine. As soon as your mother gets here, she and I are going to have a little talk. Depending on how that turns out, well, that will decide how soon you'll get to leave. But in the meantime you can have whatever you want. You'll have to stay in one room, I'm afraid, but it's got a television with cable, and

I have a library of DVDs that you can pick from. Oh and there's a Sony Playstation installed there, too, and I've got all the latest games. You like video games, David?"

He shrugged. "I guess."

"Is there anything you need right now? Are you hungry?"

"I need my medicine," David replied.

"He's got a heart condition," Tuff explained.

"Oh? What do you take, David? I'll see that we get it for you."

"It's called Tenormin," David answered.

"Fine. We'll get hold of it right away. What would you like for breakfast?"

"I'm not hungry."

"Suit yourself. Emo will show you how to call someone to bring you food. I'll see you later, okay?"

David nodded but refused to look the man in the eye. It was certainly an adventure being in such a palace, but he didn't like Aaron Valentine. There was something incredibly . . . *smarmy* . . . about him. Emo Tuff was nice, to a point, and David could sense that he was dangerous and was probably the muscle behind whatever dirty work this Valentine character might want. On the other hand, Aaron Valentine exuded an aura that David could only call menace. The man smiled and was gracious but it was all an act. Valentine no more wanted David in his house than he wanted a horsefly.

"Let's go see your room, David," Tuff said.

They went back through the corridor and into the main second floor hallway. They passed a large picture window that faced the back of the mansion, where David could see a tennis court, a swimming pool, and a vast lawn sculpted with hedges and flowerbeds. A couple of girls in bikinis were frolicking in the pool. A huge tent had been erected on a portion of the lawn and there were tables and chairs beneath it. David followed Tuff up another flight of stairs to the third floor, where an abundance of doors lined a long corridor. Displayed prominently along the hallway were a series of colorful erotic paintings culled from various decades throughout history. David gawked at the blatantly sexual ones but others were simply too surreal. Finally, Tuff unlocked a door halfway down the corridor.

It was a spacious bedroom with a four-poster queen-size bed, a large-screen television, a dresser, and a huge window covered by colorful drapes. Tuff pointed out a call bell on a nightstand. "Just push that if you need anything. Someone will come shortly." He pointed to a door on one side of the room. "That's the bathroom. Feel free to run a bath or take a shower, whatever." Tuff opened a clothes cupboard, revealing several shirts and shorts. "I estimated what your sizes were and called ahead. These are some things they bought for you since what you're wearing stinks now. I hope they fit. If not, well, hopefully you won't be here long. Just dump your dirty clothes in the hamper by the door and someone will wash them for you. I'll see you later. I'm going to get some shut-eye!"

Tuff went out and closed the door. David heard it lock.

The first thing he did was look out the window. It appeared to face the side of the house, around the corner from the expansive backyard and swimming pool area. The good news was that he could unlock and open the window if he wanted to. The bad news was that the window was three stories high and there was nothing attached to the side of the building that he could use to climb down.

The excitement of being in "Paradise" quickly faded. He was, without doubt, a prisoner.

CHAPTER THIRTY-ONE

The day after David's first night in Paradise, Diane reached Los Angeles. The first thing she did was look up Pete Rod. She knew that the actor's real name was Eric Gilliam and he had been a close friend of Dana Barnett. The actress known as Angel Babe was Gilliam's sister. Hopefully he would know what she could expect when she went to see Aaron Valentine. Diane felt she needed an ally, someone who could serve as backup. She was determined that Valentine was not going to get away with intimidating her. He probably wanted compensation for the theft of his diamonds. He also most likely wanted to exact some kind of revenge on Dana for taking the gems and disappearing.

It wasn't difficult to track down Gilliam. His production company was listed and was located in Van Nuys, along with many other adult film businesses. She didn't know why the industry gravitated to that particular suburb but it was so.

Pete Rod Productions turned out to be just an office. A woman who looked as if she might play the lead role in a movie called *Biker Chicks From Mars* manned it. She wore black leather and a lot of metal, had a pierced nose, tongue, and eyebrow (and probably other body parts that weren't so visible), and short pink hair. Her name was Louise.

She told Diane that Gilliam rarely showed up at the office. He worked out of his home and shot his videos at various clandestine hotel rooms around the city. Diane paid her fifty dollars for his address, which Louise was more than happy to give out.

Gilliam's residence was certainly not the estate that Aaron Valentine's was but it had a lot of class. It was a large ranch house built in the sixties and elegantly placed in a neighborhood lined with palm trees. A security fence surrounded the property, prompting Diane to press a button on an intercom when she arrived.

"Yeah?" came a voice.

"Is Eric Gilliam at home?" she asked.

"Who wants to know?"

"Diane Boston."

"Who?"

"Dana Barnett's sister."

Silence.

Diane looked up and noticed the security camera pointed at her. She gave a little wave.

"Drive on in," the voice intoned. There was a click and the gate opened. Diane got back in her car, which had been idling in front of the gate, and drove forward. Once she was within the walls, Diane decided that the property was not much different from upper middle-class houses in the Chicago suburbs. She pulled up and parked in the driveway beside a Porsche, got out, and went to the open front door, where Eric Gilliam was standing.

"Hi," she said. "I understand you knew my sister." She offered her hand.

Gilliam stared at her in disbelief. "I'll be goddamned," he said. "You're Dana's sister?"

"Yep."

He shook her hand. "Pardon my astonishment but you look just like her. Well, I mean, you're older of course. I haven't seen Dana in over twenty-five years."

"I know. No one has. She's dead," Diane said.

"I didn't know that Dana had a twin sister," he said. "And I knew her pretty well."

"She kept it quiet, especially in the business she was in. May I come in? I hope I'm not disturbing you?"

"No, no, I'm sorry, come in. I'm kind of in shock." He stepped aside so that she could enter the house.

He led her past a "reception area," where, he said, he interviewed potential actresses for his amateur adult videos. Diane was familiar with what those were. Girls who wanted to break into the adult film industry usually started out in amateur productions, of which there was a proliferation—Gilliam wasn't the only "older" male adult film actor who had begun his own amateur business. It was highly lucrative and it also kept him in the public eye, mainly because it was usually he who had sex on camera with the beginning actresses. If he didn't set up a stationary camera to film himself with the girl, he might employ one other person as a cameraman; otherwise it was strictly a one-man operation.

He took her into a large den where his television, stereo equipment, and a bar were located.

"Sit down somewhere. Something to drink?" he asked.

"Just some ice water if you can manage that," Diane said, sitting on a large, denim-covered comfy chair.

As he fixed her a glass and got himself a beer from a refrigerator, he said, "So I understand you've been in the news lately."

"Does it travel this far?" she asked. "My, my."

"You're in a lot of trouble."

"Yeah, I guess so. None of what you heard is true, you know. I *am* Dana's sister. And I didn't kill my ex-husband."

"Hey, I don't care." He handed her the glass. "What I'd like to know is what happened to *my* sister."

"I don't know," Diane said.

He squinted at her.

"Really," she insisted. "Your sister disappeared with my sister."

"All right, I suppose I'm prepared to believe you. So what brings you to my door?" He sat across from her on a sofa.

"Aaron Valentine," she replied. "He heard about me and he thinks I'm Dana. There was some bad blood between him and my sister and I suppose he wants to kill me."

"So you came to L.A. to let him do it?"

"No. He's kidnapped my son and is using him as bait."

"Your son?"

"He's thirteen. David."

Gilliam whistled. "Geez, why don't you call the police?"

"That's exactly what he told me not to do."

"Right, right. So . . . why did you come to me?"

She sat forward in the chair. "I've come to ask you for help. You know Aaron Valentine. I don't. You know his business, his cohorts, and you know his mansion. I don't want to just walk in there without some kind of plan, some kind of security for myself and for David."

"Why me?"

"Because of Dana, of course. And Angela. Valentine had them killed, you know. Along with several other actors and actresses who didn't want to go along with his business terms."

Gilliam sat silently for a few moments and then asked, "How do you know that?"

"Dana was my sister," Diane replied.

"So how come she never talked about you? How come Angela never mentioned it? You know they were tight, Dana and Angela. Lovers. You knew that?"

"Yes."

"You'd think Dana would mention that she had a twin sister."

"You'd think. She chose not to."

"So what's your story?" he asked. "I want to know everything you know before I say anything about helping you. Aaron Valentine may not be as bad as he was in the seventies and early eighties, but he's still a dangerous guy. He's powerful and he's got powerful friends. He was just acquitted on charges of racketeering, pandering, and using underage actresses. If you ask me, the DA's office had him in the bag."

"What happened?"

"His goons must have got to one or more of the jurors. He walked."

"I'm not surprised."

"So you tell me about you and Dana. I want to know some things before I get involved."

She sighed. "Dana and I lost our parents when we were kids. First my father, when we were three, and then my mother two years after that. We were sent to live with my aunt and uncle, my father's brother, down in Texas. My uncle was not the nicest nor most intelligent of guardians. We split as soon as we got out of high school and headed west. Dana was dead set on becoming an actress. I was into physical education and wanted to work in a gym. Dana tried to get an acting agent but wasn't successful, and before long she started running with the wrong crowd. Drugs and stuff. She moved out and lived with some drug dealer for a while. I think it was through him that she got into porn."

"We call it the *adult film industry*," Gilliam said.

"Whatever. Anyway, she and I, well, we lost touch. I didn't know what she was up to. Then one day she shows up at my apartment and she's been beaten. She had a bloody lip and a black eye. I was appalled. She told me that she was working in the adult film industry and Aaron Valentine sent some guy to beat her up because she wanted more money or something, I can't remember. Maybe she wanted out, I really don't know."

"I remember that!" Gilliam said. "I remember when she had the black eye and busted lip. She couldn't work for three months until her face got back to normal."

"Yeah. Well, I told her to get out of that business and come back to live with me. She wouldn't do it. I found out later that she was hooked on drugs. She was living with your sister by then."

Gilliam nodded. "They were both using heroin and cocaine," he said. "I guess we all were back then. Coke was very big in the late seventies. Dana OD'd one night."

Diane concurred. "That's the next part of the story. One night I got a call from Cedars-Sinai Hospital. My sister was admitted with a drug overdose. I went to see her and she was barely alive. She pulled through, though, and I begged her to get help. I pleaded with her to get out of that business. That's the first and only time I met Angela, by the way. She was there in the hospital room and she looked pretty strung out herself."

Gilliam merely nodded.

"Anyway, after Dana got out of the hospital she went back to her old ways. Then one night I got a call from her and she said that she and Angela were finally going to quit the business and run away. She said that unless they left L.A. then one of Valentine's men would kill them. Do you know who worked for Valentine then that was capable of doing that?"

"Sure," Gilliam said. "He's still around, too. A guy named Emo Tuff. He's Valentine's right hand man, enforcer, and whatever. I wouldn't be surprised if he was the guy who nabbed your kid. Very scary guy. But there are others, too, I suppose. Valentine always had some shady characters around him. Go on."

"Anyway, then she told me about Valentine's brother."

"Eduardo?"

"Yeah, that's him. She said that Eduardo was the one who supplied all the actors and actresses with drugs."

"That's right," Gilliam said. "He was real good at his job. He did a lot of Aaron's scumbag work."

"Apparently Eduardo was closer to the organized crime thing than his brother was."

"You could say that, but Aaron knew all about it. Eduardo always acted on Aaron's orders. Did you know about Eduardo and Angela?"

Diane cocked her head. "What do you mean?"

"They were an item for a while. And she was still living with Dana. Eduardo was fucking her. I imagine it was a sex for drugs thing because from what I could tell, she was devoted to your sister. Dana didn't see it that way. She was pretty upset about it."

"I didn't know that. That explains some things."

"Keep going."

She sighed. "On the phone that night, Dana told me that she and Angela planned to rip off a bunch of diamonds from Valentine. Eduardo had apparently made some kind of drugs for diamonds deal with some gangsters from Africa or someplace."

"The warehouse massacre," Gilliam said. "That was big news."

"Yeah." Diane looked away and had to compose herself. Telling the story had unearthed some dormant emotions. "Sorry."

"That's okay. Angela and Dana were never heard from again after that."

Diane looked back at him. "Dana called me from the warehouse just after the shootings. She had been hit and begged me to come and get her. I found the warehouse and got there before any cops knew what happened. I saw all those men, dead. Dana and Angela weren't there. It looked like—" She hesitated and nearly sobbed. "There was this incinerator in the warehouse."

Gilliam held up a hand. "I know. It looked like both girls had been thrown into it."

She nodded. "But no one knows for sure. I never saw Dana again."

Gilliam crushed his empty beer can in his hand. After a moment of silence he said, "All right. I'll help you."

Diane smiled and exhaled loudly. "Thank you. Maybe we can both get a little payback for our sisters."

"As a matter of fact we have a golden opportunity tonight."

"What's that?"

"Valentine is throwing a big party at his place. I'm invited and I can bring a guest. Wanna go?"

Diane smiled. "You bet your ass."

"There's just one other thing I want to know," he said.

"Yeah?"

"What happened to the diamonds?"

Diane smiled wickedly. "Oh yeah. That was something else I wanted to ask you. Do you know any good fences in this town?"

CHAPTER THIRTY-TWO

"Why the fuck did you have to kill him?" Valentine roared.

Emo Tuff shrugged. "It seemed like the thing to do. You know, he'd seen me."

"Damn it, Emo, it just puts more heat on *her*. The police are looking for her and that makes what we have to do riskier. Wasn't there another way to find out where she was without knocking off her ex-husband?"

"I was trying to expedite things. She wasn't listed and he was. Look, I found her, I got the kid, you should be happy."

Valentine fumed at his desk. If Tuff weren't such a reliable enforcer, Valentine would have him canned. But the guy had been with him since the beginning and taken care of most of the dirty work. He had to keep Emo happy.

"All right, forget it," Valentine said. "When do you think she'll be here?"

"I can't imagine that she'll make as good time as we did. She couldn't have driven straight through without stopping. I wouldn't put her in L.A. until tomorrow at the earliest."

Valentine stood and went to a window that faced the back of the mansion. The staff was busy preparing for the party by decorating the tables beneath the tent and arranging flowerpots around the pool. Men were setting up food and beverage centers at key locations around the property and portable toilets were being erected on one side of the house to accommodate the thousand-plus guests.

"How many are we expecting tonight?" Tuff asked.

"Too many. I've brought in extra security. Talk to Julio, he'll fill you in on everything."

Julio was head of security at Paradise but he reported to Tuff. For all intents and purposes, it was Emo Tuff who really ran the security operations but he usually had to be in a million places at once during a party. Bouncers handled problem guests but Tuff had to step in occasionally. He had received a reputation in the industry as a man no one should mess with at Valentine's parties. Those outside of Erotica Selecta who knew him feared him and the Paradise staff steered clear of him.

"What about the kid?" Tuff asked. "With all these people here tonight—"

"Don't worry about it," Valentine replied. "Keep him locked in his room. We have security guys guarding the stairs on the first floor. Floors two and three are always off limits to party guests, you know that. Check on him a couple of times during the evening but otherwise leave him alone. He doesn't exist."

Tuff considered this. "I'll have a guy posted outside his door, just in case."

"Do what you want. By the way, those jobs you did in New York and Chicago . . . everything taken care of with regard to our privacy?"

Tuff acted offended. "What? You doubt my work? You think I'm gonna slip up after all these years?"

"Take it easy, Emo. It was just a question."

"Aaron, I wore my gloves, I cleaned up afterwards,

and nobody saw me. Those two old men were the only ones who got a look at my face and they sure ain't telling no tales."

"I wonder how many diamonds are left?"

"From what the old man in Chicago told me, it sounded like she didn't sell them too many. Unless she had 'em fenced somewhere else. I can't believe she'd go to the trouble. She probably made enough dough off of one measly diamond to last quite a while. I bet she still has over three-quarters of the entire lot."

"Let's hope so. What she's willing to give back and what she's willing to compensate me for will determine what happens to her and the kid."

"You'd let her go?"

Valentine gave him a hard look. "She won't be leaving California."

"I figured. And the boy?"

"I haven't made up my mind. He's old enough to make trouble if we set him free."

"Yeah, I know."

Valentine rubbed his chin. "I guess we should take care of him, too. I'll leave that to you. Make it quick and painless. But as for *her* . . ."

"I read you loud and clear," Tuff said.

Darren Marshall buckled his seatbelt and took a look at the in-flight magazine that was in the seat pocket in front of him. Thumbing through it, he wondered how writers got articles in it and if the pay was any good. He never read the damn things. Did anyone? Marshall put the magazine back and settled back for the flight to Texas. His flight was direct to El Paso and then he had to change planes and go to Midland-Odessa. Looking at the area on a map, it appeared that there wasn't much to look at in West Texas. The towns were few and far-between. Garden City, his ultimate destination, had no airport and Midland-Odessa was the closest one. He'd have to rent a car and drive what he estimated to be a little less than an hour.

Eric Gilliam's material was not as exciting as he had expected. There were no shocking revelations there except the clue that Dana Barnett had lived in Garden City. Angela had written in her diary that Dana once told her Garden City had the "silliest" name for a town and that in actuality it was the "armpit of Texas." Marshall had to believe this was where Dana's aunt and uncle lived, the ones who raised Dana and her alleged twin sister. Marshall intended to find them, and if they weren't alive, he meant to locate someone who had known them. One way or another, he was going to track down the truth behind the twin sister business.

DAVID'S JOURNAL

I'm stuck in this room on the third floor of Aaron Valentine's mansion in California. It's somewhere in a suburb called Woodland Hills. I'm a prisoner and we're waiting until my Mom shows up. I sure hope she gets here soon. I'm going crazy in here. I wish they'd let me out so I could walk around the place. I'm getting tired of watching TV and playing games.

Last night Emo brought me my medicine, so that's good. They're treating me all right. No one has tried to hurt me. The bed is comfortable and I slept pretty good. The food sure is great. For dinner last night they gave me steak and lobster. I couldn't believe it. I asked for chocolate cream pie for dessert and I got it. I'm beginning to think that if I asked for monkey brains for dinner they'd find a way to give it to me.

But I still want to get out. No one likes being a prisoner even if it's in a palace. Through my window I've seen workers doing stuff outside and it looks like there's going to be a big party tonight. I wish I could see the backyard and swimming pool. I'd be able to signal someone. But there's nothing down below my window but purple flowers. Maybe someone will walk down there and I can drop a message to him.

I tore some pages out of my journal and wrote a bunch of notes. They say, "David Boston is a prisoner upstairs on the *third floor—Help!" Maybe there will be a good breeze tonight and I can scatter them out the window. Somebody is bound to see one.*

I just noticed that one of the lenses on my glasses is scratched. I can still see out of it but there's this weird line across my vision. That's all I need. My eyesight isn't very good to begin with.

It's lunchtime and I'm hungry. I guess I'll punch the call button and ask for a hamburger or something. Maybe a milkshake.

I'll write more later.

CHAPTER THIRTY-THREE

Nick Belgrad lost Diane Boston when the Lexus had a blowout just as he crossed the state line into California. Cursing his bad luck, he wasted precious time changing the flat and then driving the car to a garage to have the tire repaired. She had gained a three-hour lead on him and by then she was in the heart of Los Angeles. Belgrad couldn't remember ever losing a mark and wondered if it was a harbinger of things to come.

Once he was in the city, Belgrad checked into a hotel in Hollywood and took an afternoon nap for a couple of hours. He hadn't slept much on the trip from Chicago so it was just the thing he needed to shake the cobwebs out of his brain. Nevertheless he had a vivid recurring dream that was not particularly pleasant. In it, he was back in Israel, twenty years ago, creeping up the old rickety staircase of a condemned building. General Security Services had identified the three men squatting in an empty room on the top floor as Israeli traitors cooperating with Palestinian terrorists. He had volunteered for the mission to take them out before the police could arrest them. It was thought that the men deserved to be killed rather than go on trial and later be used as another excuse for Palestinians to protest imprisoning more radicals.

The scene was just as he remembered it. Sunlight streamed through slats in the walls and he could hear the traffic on the main highway down below. The snores of the men were audible half a flight below their floor. Apparently the militants felt safer sleeping during the day and doing their notorious work at night.

Belgrad readied the gas-powered Galil ARM assault rifle and prepared to burst through the boarded door. But unlike what had really happened, the men in the dream were ready for him. As soon as he kicked in the door Belgrad was met by a barrage of gunfire from the traitors. The bullets ripped into his body, knocking him back— and awake. His body jerked abruptly, forcing him to sit up. He almost expected to see blood on the front of his shirt but there was nothing. He realized where he was and relaxed.

Belgrad got up, went into the bathroom, and splashed cold water on his face. Normally when the dream occurred—nightmare, really—he felt disoriented and shaky afterwards. This time, though, the adrenaline made him feel surprisingly rested.

By four o'clock he was ready to track down Diane and finish putting the puzzle pieces together. He considered looking up the actor known as Pete Rod, AKA Eric Gilliam, since the guy was Angel Babe's brother. However, he thought that perhaps the best course of action would be to visit the Erotica Selecta administrative offices. Perhaps he could get an audience with Aaron Valentine himself.

The company's office was located in a four-story building on Highland Avenue, between Sunset and Hollywood Boulevards. It was strictly a paperwork facility, as any kind of production activity would be done on the sly at various locations around the city. A young and attractive receptionist that might have been cast as a live-action representation of Betty Boop sat at a circular desk and greeted him when he entered. Belgrad noted that access to the rest of the suite was behind her, through a glass door.

"May I help you?" she asked in a voice that matched her looks. Belgrad was amused.

"Perhaps. Is Mister Valentine in?" He flashed a New York private investigator license at her. He figured she wouldn't know that it was useless in the state of California. For that matter, it was just as unusable in New York since he wasn't really a PI. It was just something he used for intimidation.

"Uhm, I don't think so," she replied, her eyes widening when she saw the ID. To her it was probably the same thing as a police badge. "I'll have to ring his office and see. He rarely comes here, though." She picked up the phone and inquired about the boss' presence. She said, "Uh huh," a few times and hung up.

"No, Mister Valentine isn't in," she said with a pout. Then she brightened and said, "Mister Alfredo is here, would you like to see him?"

"Mister Alfredo?" Belgrad asked.

"Rudy Alfredo. He's the vice president."

Before he could answer, the phone on her desk rang. "Excuse me," she said as she answered it. The girl said a few more "Uh huhs" and then hung up. "I'm sorry, I have to do something that will only take a second. I'll be *right* back." She stood up, revealing an extremely short black skirt, long white legs, and heels. The girl went through the glass door and disappeared, leaving Belgrad standing in front of the desk.

As was his proclivity, he scanned the various items on the desk for anything interesting. A stack of cards caught his eye and he casually picked one up. It was an invitation to a party at Valentine's home in Woodland Hills. That night.

Belgrad pocketed the invitation and waited for the receptionist to return. She reappeared not ten seconds later, carrying a stack of FedEx packages.

"Sorry," she said. "I had to get these ready 'cause the FedEx guy is downstairs."

"Quite all right," Belgrad replied.

"So did you want to see Mister Alfredo?"

"No, that's okay. I'll come back another time. By the way, what's your name?"

"Betty!" she beamed.

Belgrad nodded, smiled, and left the office.

"Have a nice day!" the girl called sweetly.

Darren Marshall drove his rented Mazda 626 into Garden City on Highway 158 and laughed at the sparseness of the town. It appeared to be about a mile long and the highway itself became the main street passing through. The town reminded him of the locale in *The Last Picture Show* only it was smaller. Garden City was built on a flat, rugged plain with very little that could be called a garden. Mesquite grew in abundance and the dust blew between the ramshackle buildings as if it were an old Western ghost town. There was no one in sight.

Marshall pulled into a gas station and stopped. A skinny old man wearing overalls came lumbering out and smiled, revealing an incomplete set of teeth.

"What can I do fer ya, mister?" the man asked.

"This is Garden City?" Marshall asked after he rolled down the window.

"Yes sir, this is Garden City."

"Where is everybody?"

"Whatcha mean?" The man was puzzled by the question.

"There's no one around," Marshall said.

"Sure they are. Everyone's at work. It ain't rush hour yet."

Marshall couldn't imagine what rush hour would be like in a town of this size. "I see," he said. "Listen, is there a place in town to look up public records? A library or something?"

The old man nodded. "Yes sir, the public library is near the high school." He pointed down the road. "Take a left at that intersection there, by the drug store. A few blocks down you'll see the high school on the right. The library is 'cross the street on the left."

"Thanks," Marshall said. He rolled up the window and drove away.

Apparently Garden City also consisted of little patches of civilization that spread out from the main highway, but the town still seemed like Nowheresville to Marshall. He found the library, which was a tiny square building the size of a garage, and parked in one of the two available spaces in front.

The interior was a one-room affair with fewer books than Marshall owned personally. A little old lady who looked as if she might be the gas station attendant's sister was the librarian.

"May I help you?" she asked.

"Uhm, yes, do you have any old phone books for the area?"

The lady nodded and waddled to a file cabinet. She opened a drawer and asked, "How far back you wanna go?"

"Er, the sixties. Maybe the fifties."

She shook her head. "Sorry, the oldest one we have is from nineteen ninety-seven."

Marshall wanted to laugh again. "Really?"

"What is it you might be looking for?" she asked.

"Well, I'm trying to track down a family that was here back then. Does the name Dana Barnett mean anything to you?" he asked.

There was a flicker of recognition in the old gal's eyes. "Was she one of Edna Barnett's nieces?"

Marshall felt a sudden thrill of discovery. "Maybe. Was there more than one?"

"Yep, there were two girls. Twins."

Twins!

"Is anyone from that family still around?" he asked, hoping against hope.

The old lady went, "Tch tch tch, no, not really. Roy Barnett died nearly thirty years ago. Edna, well, she's still alive but I don't think she could help you much. She's in a home on the other side of town. Poor thing has dementia."

"Their names were Roy and Edna Barnett?"

"That's right."

"What do you know about the twins?"

"Nothing, really. I just know there were a couple of girls living with them for a while," she said. "You know, their property is still there and I think Manuel still takes care of it. Edna left the house to him and his family."

"Manuel?"

"Manuel Delgado. He was one of the ranchers. Roy Barnett was a rancher. Raised cattle. The ranch is north of here about seven or eight miles. If Manuel's there he might be able to help you."

Marshall gave her a slight bow. "Thank you, madam, you've been a tremendous help."

This made the lady smile. She, too, was missing several teeth.

CHAPTER THIRTY-FOUR

"You sure no one is going to recognize me?" Diane asked as she pulled down the Porsche's windshield visor so she could look at herself in the vanity mirror. She had applied heavy makeup with an abundance of silver and blue eyeshadow and dark mascara, and she wore a metallic silver wig with bangs that had straight strands reaching just below her jaw line on the sides and back. The wig matched a costume she picked out of Gilliam's closet—he kept a variety of clothes for the fresh actresses that starred in his amateur videos. Diane was dressed in a silver and white bra, panties, garter belt, and stockings combo with a sheer wrap that came down to her knees. At Valentine's parties, the dress code went by the adage that less was more. Most of the women wore lingerie or other revealing ensembles and the men dressed in pajamas, boxers and T-shirts or Hawaiian shirts open to expose their chests.

"You look great, and no, I don't think anyone will recognize you," Gilliam said. He was wearing gym shorts and an open Hawaiian shirt decorated with topless hula dancers.

The party officially began at nine o'clock and they

aimed to arrive at ten. If things went the way Valentine's other parties usually did, the soiree would last until dawn. Gilliam took the Woodland Hills exit off the Ventura freeway and began the trek into the hills. Already there was a line of cars and limousines snaking up the narrow road toward Paradise. It took them longer than Gilliam expected but eventually they were cleared by security at the gate and were ushered toward the great lawn that served as a parking lot.

The place was bustling with hundreds of beautiful people. Apparently everyone who was anyone in the adult film industry was there, as well as quite a few legitimate celebrities from Hollywood. Diane recognized several top-drawer actors and actresses, musicians, and athletes. Most of the guests were young and virile but there was also a contingent of older, established luminaries from days gone by. As expected, the women were dressed in audacious, revealing outfits. The hostesses that walked through the party carrying trays of *hors d'oeuvres* wore nothing but body paint.

A DJ supplied loud dance music that already had an appreciative audience participating on a dance floor underneath a separate tent. The swimming pool was also a popular attraction. Men and women were cavorting in the water and wearing, in most cases, nothing at all.

"Wow," was all that Diane was able to say.

"Amazing, isn't it?" Gilliam responded. "This is nothing. I imagine the size of the crowd will double by midnight."

"I don't think there are this many gorgeous people in the entire state of Illinois," she said.

"So what's our plan?"

"I don't know," she said. "We have to figure out a way to get inside the house."

"That shouldn't be a problem. I know the owner. However, I doubt we'll be able to go past the first floor.

Usually the second and third floors are off limits during parties."

"See if you can use your celebrity status, Eric," she suggested.

"I'll do my best. Come on, let's get a drink."

When Nick Belgrad presented his invitation to the guard at the gate, the man eyed him through the Lexus window.

"What's your name?"

"Nick Belgrad." He figured there was no reason to hide his real identity. No one here would know him.

The guard scanned the list and shook his head. "You're not on here. How do you spell it?"

Belgrad spelled his surname and said, "I might not be on the list. I was a late addition. I just got my invitation today by FedEx."

"Who sent it?"

"Betty at the main office on Highland."

The guard nodded. "Are you with a company or something . . . ?"

Belgrad answered, "I'm an agent. I handle men's magazines."

The guard looked up and saw the long line of cars waiting to get through the gate. "All right, go ahead," he finally said.

Belgrad rejoiced to himself as he drove into the property and was directed toward the lawn to park. He locked the Lexus and strolled toward the crowd around the mansion and realized he was overdressed. He had on khaki slacks, a black short-sleeved turtleneck knit shirt, and a tweed jacket.

Oh well, he thought, he was always a bit off-fashion. He just hoped he wouldn't have to use the Browning 9mm tucked neatly in his left armpit underneath the jacket.

* * *

"Eric! Glad you could make it!"

"How are you, Aaron?" Gilliam said.

Aaron Valentine held court like a mafia don, sitting in a large wicker chair with a tall rounded back. With him were four gorgeous starlets—two stood at his side running their fingers through his white hair and rubbing his neck, while the other couple sat at his feet, their arms draped over his legs. He wore a white Arabic cotton tunic that covered his massive body down to his feet. Gold chains around his neck glistened in the colored lights that were strategically placed beneath the tent. Such was his regal manner that Diane's first instinct was to bow to him.

Valentine didn't stand to shake Gilliam's hand. Instead he eyed Diane and asked, "Who's your lovely friend?"

"This is Carol," he said. It was a name that he and Diane had agreed on.

"Nice to see you with someone closer to your age," Valentine remarked, laughing.

"Now, now, Aaron. Look who's talking!"

Valentine addressed her. "Welcome, my dear. Do you live in Los Angeles?"

"No, San Diego," she replied. "I'm just up for the weekend."

"How do you know Eric?"

Gilliam answered for her. "Would you believe we met at a bar? I was down there doing a shoot and we all ended up at this terrific little place downtown. Carol here was our waitress."

"It's a pleasure to meet you," Diane said. "It's a wonderful party."

"Thank you. Go and enjoy yourselves," Valentine said, waving his hand and dismissing them.

As they walked away, Diane noticed the tall man with long blond hair and an eye patch, dressed in black. He was watching them closely.

"Eric, there's a creepy guy over there looking at us," Diane whispered to her escort.

Gilliam glanced at him and replied, "That's Emo Tuff. He's the guy I told you about. I should probably go say hello but you had best steer clear of him. Why don't you go get something to drink at the bar?"

"All right."

"Get me a vodka with ice."

She nodded and walked away. Gilliam approached Tuff and they shook hands. Diane watched them out of the corner of her eye as she stood in line at the bar. The two men obviously knew each other and conversed like old pals. At one point Tuff gestured toward her and Gilliam looked her way. They spoke some more and Tuff nodded, satisfied with Gilliam's explanation of who his date was.

Diane turned away as the line drew closer to the bar and glanced at the second line running parallel to hers. She blinked twice and immediately faced forward again.

The man with the long hair and beard! From Chicago! The one who had watched her outside of Rabinowitz's jewelry shop! He was standing in the other drinks line but he was staring at her.

My God, who is he? What's he doing here? Had he followed her from Illinois?

She attempted to keep her cool until she got Gilliam's vodka and a glass of wine for herself. She walked quickly back to her date, who was in conversation with a nearly naked brunette.

"Ah, here she is," Gilliam said, taking his drink from Diane. "Carol, this is Tawni Pebbles, one of the biggest adult film stars on the planet." Diane thought it was an apt description, given the size of the woman's breasts. "Tawni, this is my friend Carol."

The actress shook hands with Diane and said, "Pleased to meet you." She immediately turned her attention back to Gilliam. "So when are we going to make that movie together, Eric?"

Gilliam laughed. "Come on, Tawni, you know I'm too old to be in feature films. They'd rather pair you up with one of the new young bucks."

"Honey, we should all look as good as you at your age," Tawni said, batting her eyes. "I think you'd be surprised if you talked to Felix about it."

Gilliam turned to Diane and explained, "Felix is her producer. One of Aaron's rivals." Back to Tawni. "Is he here?"

"Somewhere. I saw him earlier. Well, nice talking to you both. Call Felix, Eric, all right?"

"I'll think about it."

"Bye, have fun!" She slinked away, leaving Gilliam alone with Diane.

"So are you having fun yet?" he asked her.

"Eric, there's this guy over by the bar who's watching us. Look, he's the one in the jacket with long hair and a beard. See him?"

Gilliam looked up surreptitiously and nodded. "Yeah."

"I saw him in Chicago the day before I left town. He was . . . well, it's a long story but I saw him at a jewelry store where I usually sold a diamond or two every now and then. The old man who ran the shop was murdered and this guy was there with the police. Now he's here. What do you think it means?"

"I don't know," Gilliam said. "Is he a cop?"

"He doesn't look like one."

"And the way he's dressed indicates that he's new to these parties. Now that you point him out, he sticks out like a sore thumb."

"You see how he keeps looking at us?"

"Yeah. Well, try to relax and we'll keep an eye on him."

"Shit, he's coming this way!"

Sure enough, Belgrad had decided to throw caution to the wind. He walked over to the couple and addressed them both.

"Don't be alarmed, I'm on your side," he said. He

looked at her and said, "Hello, Diane. I saw you outside of A-1 Jewelry in Chicago. Remember?"

"Who the hell are you?" she asked.

He held out his hand, which they each shook hesitantly. "My name is Nick Belgrad. I'm working for the Rabinowitz family. Well, actually I'm working for Moses and Hiram. The rest of the family doesn't know me."

"But the Rabinowitzes are dead," Diane said.

Belgrad nodded. "Moses called me in New York the day of his brother's funeral. I promised him that I'd solve Hiram's murder. After Moses was killed I was more resolved in fulfilling that obligation."

"Are you some kind of cop?" Gilliam asked.

"Not really," Belgrad replied. "You could say I'm sort of a private investigator, but I'm not a P.I. Call me a mercenary-for-hire. I'm a troubleshooter, a fixer. I do dirty work for people who don't want to mess up their clean hands."

"Pardon me, but you look like a rabbi," Gilliam said.

Belgrad smiled and said, "I'll take that as a compliment. I mostly work for clients in the Jewish community. When I was much younger I worked in Israel for many years as a special operative for Israeli intelligence. Now I mostly work in New York."

"How do you know the Rabinowitzes?" Diane asked.

"Ah, that's a story," Belgrad said. "They knew my father in Berlin, back in the days of the Nazis. They were children together. The two brothers saved my father's life in a concentration camp. They became lifelong friends after that and my father always told me that should one of them ever ask me for a favor, I should perform it with no questions asked. In their later years, my father did a lot of business with the Rabinowitz brothers, mostly selling black market gems in Israel. He died a few years ago."

"I'm sorry," Diane said.

Belgrad shrugged and said, "Thank you. He lived a

full life." He looked around to make sure no one was watching them. "Now that you know who I am, I just want to say I'm here to help you. My main objective is to find Moses' and Hiram's killer and I'm pretty sure it has to do with you, Diane. I've been following your case in Chicago and I believe you didn't kill your ex-husband."

"I didn't."

"I said I believe you. And personally I don't care if you made porno films or not. Now where's your son?"

"I think he's here somewhere," she said. "He was kidnapped. Valentine thinks I'm Dana Barnett and he had David abducted in order to bring me out here. So far no one knows I'm here yet. I'm still trying to figure out what to do. I'd like to find David before I present myself to Valentine."

"Why does he want you here?"

She sighed and looked at Gilliam. He nodded to her and she answered, "I have some diamonds that once belonged to him. The Rabinowitzes fenced them for me."

Belgrad said, "I figured it was something like that. A guy like Valentine probably holds a grudge."

"Speaking of Valentine," Gilliam said, "he's looking at us." The other two casually looked toward Valentine's throne and saw that the big man was eyeing them and speaking to Emo Tuff.

"We better split up," Belgrad said.

"We're going to try and get upstairs in the house," Gilliam said.

"Good. See what you can find out and let's meet back here in an hour." Belgrad shook hands with them, making it appear as if he were one of Gilliam's fans, and then he walked away.

"Come on," Gilliam said to Diane, pulling her toward the house.

Before the party began, Emo Tuff had entered David's room and removed the light bulbs from all of the lamps.

"Sorry, David," he had said. "Can't have you signaling any of the guests from the window. I'll leave you with a candle on the table there and you can still watch TV, but no lights."

Since then they had left him alone. David knew that a guy was stationed outside his door—if he tried to open the window and shout to someone on the ground, he'd be heard. At this point it would have done little good anyway. So far no one had appeared on his side of the mansion. The party activity was directly in back, in front, and on the opposite side of the house where the portable latrines were set up.

Nevertheless, David opened the window and stuck out his arm. There was a weak breeze, but was it sufficient to deliver his messages? It was certainly worth a try.

David gathered the tiny pieces of paper containing his SOS and dropped a few out the window. They scattered in the wind and fluttered away into the darkness like confetti. He waited a little while and dropped some more. Ten minutes later he let loose with the third and final batch.

Diane followed Gilliam into the back parlor of the house where yet another bar had been set up. Most people were outside but there were a few who had chosen to lounge within the walls of the palace. Beyond the parlor was a game room, a large dining room, a screening room, the kitchen, and what was referred to as the Grand Hall. This was the first room guests encountered if they came in through the front door. From there dual circular stone staircases led to the second floor.

The Grand Hall was empty except for two security men standing at the foot of each staircase. Gilliam approached one of them.

"Hi," he said.

"Good evening, sir," the guard said.

"I'd like to show my date Aaron's collection of erotic paintings upstairs. May we go up?"

"Sorry, sir, the second and third floors are off limits during the party."

"Aw, come on, you know me, don't you? I'm Pete Rod. Aaron and I are good friends. I come here a lot."

"Sorry, Mister Rod. I can't let you up unless Mister Valentine accompanies you."

Gilliam shrugged. "Okay." He turned to Diane and said, "Come on, honey, I guess we have to go complain to Aaron." He took her arm and led her out of the Hall.

"What now?" she asked.

"Let me think," Gilliam said. They went back through the house to the parlor, stopped to get two more drinks, and went outside. "Let's circle the house and take a look at the windows. Maybe he's up there and we'll be able to see him."

"Okay," she said. Arm in arm, they strolled past necking couples in the shadows. In other dark corners of the grounds they noticed guests using coke spoons and smoking pot. A tent with flaps covered a space strictly reserved for an orgy, already in progress. When Diane peeked inside, a woman beckoned her to join them.

"No thanks," she said and quickly closed the flap.

The party was obviously becoming more and more decadent. Gilliam said, "By two o'clock it'll be like ancient Rome."

They went to the side of the house where the Port-O-Johns were located and looked up at the house. The windows were dark.

"Let's try the other side," Gilliam suggested.

On the way they passed two girls looking at a tiny piece of paper. "Who the hell is David?" one of them asked.

Diane perked up and said, "Excuse me, can I see that?"

One of them handed the note to Diane and said, "We

found it over there on the ground. There's a whole bunch."

Diane felt her heart rate increase as she recognized her son's printing.

David Boston is a prisoner upstairs on the third floor!—Help!

"Eric," she said breathlessly, "we've *got* to figure out a way to distract those guards and get upstairs!"

CHAPTER THIRTY-FIVE

David had an idea. If he were to get his heart pumping fast but not enough to hurt himself, perhaps he could fake an attack. They'd have to supply him with medical attention. They wouldn't let him die, would they? It wouldn't be a pretty picture for Aaron Valentine if a kid died during one of his parties. Then, as they escorted him out of the room, he'd make a break for it.

It just might work.

He left his position by the window and stood by the bed and nightstand where the call button was located. He figured that if something really did happen to his heart, he'd be right there to punch the button.

David began to run in place, slowly at first, and then he increased the speed until he could feel his heart thumping in his chest.

Diane and Gilliam met Belgrad at their rendezvous and showed him David's message.

"I found one, too," Belgrad said.

"He must have managed to get them out one of the windows," Diane said, "but we couldn't figure out which one. I think it's on the other side of the house. At any rate, we have to get upstairs."

"There are two guys guarding the staircases," Gilliam added.

"Then those two guys need reasons to leave their posts," Belgrad said. "What's inside the house?"

"There's a bar in the parlor leading to the backyard," Diane replied. "Beyond that it looked like, what, Eric, a screening room? Dining room?"

"Yeah, several places where Aaron entertains guests. The kitchen's on the first floor. I don't think there are any bedrooms."

Belgrad stroked his beard. "Are there a lot of guests in the house?"

"No," Gilliam answered. "Not many at all."

"All right, I'll cause a diversion at the bar in the parlor," Belgrad said. "I'll bet those two security men come to see what's going on. That's when you make your move. You'll need to be ready because there won't be a large window of opportunity."

"What are you going to do?" Diane asked.

"I'll make a nuisance of myself and hopefully they'll throw me out. I'll get my car and park it outside the gate. And I'll wait for you. If you don't show up in another hour, I'll leave." He told them the name of his hotel. "I'll go there and wait to hear from you if we don't connect. I'll assume that if I don't hear from you by tomorrow morning that something went wrong. In that case I'll call out the cavalry."

"Sounds like a plan," Gilliam said. He held out his hand for Belgrad to shake.

"Thank you for helping us," Diane said.

"My pleasure. I just want the scumbag who killed the Rabinowitzes."

"If I were to make a wager," Gilliam said, "I'd say it was Emo Tuff, the guy with the eye patch."

"Yeah, I've been checking him out," Belgrad said. "My sources told me that he's someone on the police 'watch' list but so far they've never been able to pin anything on him. He's suspected of everything in the book, including murder."

"I *know* he's a murderer," Gilliam replied. "I can't prove it, but I just know. You know?"

"Yeah. Look, I'm going to go do my thing. Good luck getting upstairs."

"Be careful," Diane said. "Try not to get hurt."

He winked at her. "Don't worry about me." Belgrad walked away and went into the house.

"Come on, we better get in position," Gilliam said. They followed Belgrad into the parlor but kept moving through the house, past the screening and dining rooms, finally stopping to hug the wall just beyond the Grand Hall. A drape had been pulled apart and tied on opposite sides of the archway, allowing them to huddle in the bunch of fabric adjacent to the wall. Gilliam peered through the drape and saw that the two men were still standing firm.

Meanwhile Belgrad approached the bar and asked for a rum and Coke. When the bartender gave it to him Belgrad asked, too loudly, "Why did you do that?"

"Sir?"

"Why did you spit in it?" He purposefully slurred his words and staggered.

"I beg your pardon?" The waiter was puzzled.

"I saw you!" Belgrad yelled. He pointed at the bartender and addressed the other guests in the room. "This bastard spit in my drink before he gave it to me! I saw him do it!"

"Sir, please lower your voice," the bartender said. "I did not spit in your drink."

"The hell you didn't!"

A security man standing outside the parlor came in

and approached Belgrad. "Sir, you're going to have to calm down. I'm sure he didn't spit in your drink. Perhaps you've had a little too much . . . ?"

"Oh shut up!" Belgrad said, belligerently. Then, without warning, he tossed his drink into the security man's face. "I think you've had too much, too!" He laughed obnoxiously as more guests looked into the open door to see what the commotion was. Belgrad set the empty glass down on the bar and waited for the moment he knew was coming—the guard finished wiping his face and lunged at him. Before the man's hands made contact with him, Belgrad let loose with a right hook that sent the guard flying backwards. A couple of women screamed and a man shouted, "Hey!"

Belgrad turned back to the bar and with a sweep of his arm knocked a row of clean empty glasses to the floor, shattering them. "Oops! Somebody made a mess!" he shouted and laughed hysterically. By then the guard had recovered and spoke into his headset. He then got on his feet and threw a bear hug around Belgrad in an attempt to restrain the unruly guest.

Diane and Gilliam watched the two staircase guards react to the call for assistance in the parlor. One of the men said, "I'll go. You better stay here." The guard nearest to them walked toward the archway. Gilliam threw the drapery over their bodies as he went past.

"What now?" Diane mouthed. There was still a man obstructing the passage upstairs.

Belgrad allowed the guard to wrestle with him for a few seconds and then he made his move. He slammed his right elbow into the guard's stomach and then back-kicked the man in the kneecap. The guard yelped in pain and released Belgrad. By then the staircase guard had come into the parlor and rushed at Belgrad. Belgrad bent his body just enough to avoid the man's outstretched arms and at the same time grab hold of the assailant's waist. Using the guard's forward momentum, Belgrad swung the man around and slammed him into the bar. Now guests were running out of the house.

"Why don't you guys crash your own party?" Belgrad slurred.

The noise of the fight could be heard all the way in the Grand Hall. The remaining guard spoke into his headset. "Is everything all right? Do you need me?"

Gilliam looked at Diane and said, "Shh." He left her there and rushed into the Grand Hall. "Hey," he said to the guard. "They need your help in there. Some guy's gone crazy!"

The sole security man followed Gilliam through the archway, leaving the staircases wide open. Diane emerged from behind the drape and quickly ran up to the second floor.

Gilliam entered the parlor and watched in amusement as the three guards attempted to subdue Belgrad but the hairy man was too slippery for them. Still maintaining the fiction that he was drunk, Belgrad managed to slither out of their grasps, deliver a punch, and spin around to break another piece of furniture.

Finally, the first guard said, "Aw, to hell with this." He drew his gun, a Heckler & Koch semiautomatic, and pointed it at Belgrad. "Freeze, asshole. I mean it!"

Belgrad stopped moving and slowly held up his hands. "Gee whiz, fella, there's no reason to get personal," he said.

At that moment, Emo Tuff entered from the backyard, followed by Aaron Valentine. Tuff said, "What the fuck is going on here?"

The first guard kept his gun on Belgrad. "This guy's had too much to drink," he said.

"Frisk him," Tuff ordered.

One of the other guards patted down Belgrad and

found the Browning. "The guy's carrying!" he exclaimed. He held it out to Tuff, who took it and examined it.

"Who are you?" he asked Belgrad.

Belgrad shrugged. "I'm the fiddler on the roof. Don't you recognize me?"

"He's a cop," Valentine said. "Throw him out."

"I'm not a cop," Belgrad said. "But throw me out anyway, it's a lousy party."

The three guards took hold of Belgrad and forced him out of the parlor toward the front of the house. Tuff started to follow but Valentine stopped him.

"He was talking with Eric and that girl earlier. As soon as you get rid of him, find them," Valentine ordered.

Tuff nodded and went after the men. Outside the front door he emptied the Browning of its ammunition, put the bullets in his pocket, and gave the gun to one of the guards.

"Don't give it back to him until he's in his car and out the gate," Tuff said. He turned to Belgrad and warned, "I don't ever want to see you again."

"But can we still be friends?" Belgrad asked sweetly. The guards roughly escorted him to the parking lot.

Upstairs, David had run all he could. He felt dizzy and had to sit on the bed to catch his breath. His heart pounded furiously and he thought he might have overdone it. He didn't want to *really* have a heart attack!

Suddenly the pain ripped through his chest and he gasped for air. It was like the night in the field when he ran away from Emo Tuff. He couldn't breathe. His lungs wouldn't cooperate no matter how hard he tried to inhale. He was unable to take in the amount of oxygen his heart needed to sustain the exertion.

Don't faint! he willed himself. *Take it easy!*

But the shadows crept in from the sides of his vision.

At first he thought he didn't have his glasses on but when he felt his face, they were there.

David knew he should call someone, and quickly. He reached for the call button, but as he did so he slipped off the bed to the floor. As darkness overcame him, David wasn't sure if he had pushed the button or not.

CHAPTER THIRTY-SIX

Diane went down the second floor hallway, listening at doors and softly calling David's name. She found a massive library full of books but devoid of humans, an art gallery that displayed numerous photographs and paintings of nudes and other erotic works, and rooms that served as offices. A corridor hidden behind a curtain led to what Diane presumed to be Valentine's private study and master bedroom but the door was locked. There were two other bedrooms on the floor and both were empty. Satisfied that her son wasn't on this level, she made her way back to the staircase and ascended to the top floor.

As soon as she was on the landing she saw the security guard sitting outside one of the doors in a long hallway. The corridor was lined with several wooden doors, much like a hotel. Guest bedrooms, she thought.

Could that be David's room? The one where the man was posted? It made sense. How could she get him away from there? She moved around a corner so that he wouldn't see her and considered her options. She could approach him and try to talk him out of leaving his position. She could break something on the stairs and perhaps he'd go to investigate but she would still have to get past him on the way down.

To hell with it, she thought. She'd worry about getting out once she had David.

All of a sudden she heard a bell ring, much like a telephone. The guard looked up and turned his head toward the door. He stood, knocked, and called a name.

Did he say "David"? Diane peered around the corner and watched him closely.

The guard took a key out of his pocket, unlocked the door, opened it, and went inside. Diane held her breath. Was this her chance?

The man came running out of the room with a look of panic on his face. He was speaking rapidly into his headset as he made his way for the stairs, but he had left the door open. Diane flattened herself against the wall as he passed her on the landing and descended the stairs, two at a time.

It was now or never. Diane ran down the hall and looked in the room.

"David!" she cried when she saw the unconscious boy lying on the carpet by the bed. She closed the door, knelt beside him, and took his arm. She felt a pulse and muttered, "Thank God." She shook him and gently patted his face. "Wake up, David, it's Mom! David!"

His color was pale but she could see he was breathing, although it was shallow.

"Please, David, wake up!"

She shook him again and the boy seemed to stir. "David? Can you hear me?"

"Mom . . . ?" he whispered. He inhaled deeply and his eyes fluttered.

"Oh, David, thank God!" she cried as she raised his limp torso to her chest and hugged him. Then she remembered they had to get out of there—fast. "David, can you get up? We have to get out of here. Can you do it?"

"Mom?" He was attempting to focus on her. Diane re-

alized that his glasses were on the carpet beside them. She picked them up and gently placed them on his head.

He could see her now. "Mom?"

The wig. She laughed for a second and tore it off. "Sorry, it was a disguise. Yes, it's me!"

"How did you get in here?" His voice was weak and fragile.

"Long story. Listen, David, we *have* to get out. They'll be coming any second. Can you stand up?"

"I'll try." He put a hand on her shoulder to support himself as she helped him up. He leaned against her and took another deep breath.

"Gosh, David, I'd forgotten how tall you are," she said. "What happened, did you have an attack?"

He nodded. "Let's go."

"Are you sure?"

"We have to, don't we?"

She walked him to the door, opened it, and peeked into the hallway. So far, so good. "Hurry," she said.

He was barely able to keep up with her. She held on to his waist and let him lean into her as if they were in a three-legged race. Just as they made it to the landing she heard voices below, and they were growing louder.

"Damn," she muttered. "Quickly, David, this way!" She took him back down the corridor and could now hear the men on the stairs between the second and third floors. She tried the first door on the opposite side of the hall from David's room and was relieved to find it unlocked. Diane pulled her son inside and closed the door just as Emo Tuff, David's guard, and another man stepped onto the landing.

It was another bedroom, probably one used for guests. Apparently someone currently occupied it, for there was an open suitcase on the floor, clothes were thrown about, and the bed was unmade. The inhabitant was thankfully not there—most likely at the party, Diane thought.

She heard the men pass by the door on the way to

David's room. "Sit here," she said to David as she helped him to the bed. "Wait just a second." She then went to the door and quietly opened it a crack.

The men were just going into David's room. Three seconds later she heard shouting and Tuff stormed back into the hallway, followed by the other men.

"He tricked you, you fool!" Tuff said. "Find him. Search every goddamn room! I'm going downstairs to look."

Diane shut the door and went back to David. "Quick, David, let's get under the bed! Hurry!" It was a king so there was plenty of room. Once they were underneath, she reached up and pulled a loose sheet down so that the space between the box springs and the floor was covered. They could hear doors opening and closing up and down the hall as the men searched for the missing boy. Finally, the door to their room opened. Diane held her breath as she heard footsteps enter, circle the room, move to the bathroom, then back and out the door. She waited a few moments and then whispered, "Okay." They slid out from under the bed.

"Are you all right?" she asked.

David nodded.

She went to the door and once more opened it a crack. The men had finished searching the rooms in the hallway and were now heading to other parts of the house. She shut the door and turned back to her son.

"Now we have to find a way to get downstairs without being seen," she said. "Got any ideas?"

David pointed to the window. It was on the opposite side of the house than his had been. "Try that," he said.

Diane went to the window and pulled back the drapes. She could see the Port-O-Johns down below and several people milling about waiting for their turns to use them. She unlatched the window and opened it.

"There's a trellis attached to the wall," she said. It was made of metal and covered with vines. She took hold of the top strip and tried to shake it. It was sturdy and strong. "David, I think we can climb down this thing. Can you do it? Are you strong enough?"

He nodded even though he wasn't sure. He still felt woozy and a little nauseated. The excitement of the escape, though, had activated his adrenaline supply and this was doing him a world of good.

"Then let's do it," she said. "You want to go first?"

"It doesn't matter."

"You go."

He stood by the window and put one leg out and over the sill. He found a foothold on the trellis and then swung his other leg out. The breeze of the night air felt good and it helped to invigorate him even more.

"Can you do it?" Diane asked.

"Yeah. Come on," he answered as he worked his way down the ladder-like structure.

Diane watched him go a ways and then she said, "I'm throwing my heels out, watch your head!" She removed them and tossed them out the window, not caring if she hit anyone other than her son. Then she, too, put a leg over and out the window, and began the descent. It was much easier than she had expected.

"Look up there!" someone shouted.

Great, she thought, they'd been seen. Oh well, it couldn't be helped. She just hoped that none of them were security men.

"Hey lady, you need help?" someone else called out.

No, but it was damn chilly, she realized. After all, she was wearing very little.

By the time David got to the ground a group of men and women were standing and watching the whole thing. When they saw the lanky boy and the older woman in lingerie above him, they put two and two together and got five.

A man patted him on the back and said, "Nice work, kid. I like 'em older, too."

"What's the matter, kid, did her husband interrupt you?" another fellow asked.

A woman said to her date, "You know, that happened to me once. I had to climb out a hotel room and I almost broke my neck!"

Diane got to the ground and hugged David. "We made it, honey!" she cried, and the small crowd applauded.

Now they had to find Eric Gilliam and get off the grounds without being caught.

CHAPTER THIRTY-SEVEN

Eric Gilliam watched the men take Nick Belgrad toward the parking lawn and was confident that his new friend would make it out of the property all right. He went back inside to the Grand Hall to find that the staircases were still unguarded. Was Diane upstairs? Did she make it? Did she find her son?

Gilliam glanced around to see if anyone might notice and then decided to ascend the stairs. He got to the second floor landing when he heard angry voices on the level above his head. As the men descended the stairs, Gilliam recognized one of the voices to be Emo Tuff's. He quickly reversed direction and took the steps two at a time but he was too late.

"You!"

Gilliam froze at the foot of the stairs and looked up. Emo Tuff and another man were above him.

"Hi, Emo, what's going on?" Gilliam attempted to ask, oozing innocence.

"Don't move," Tuff said. He and the other guard hurried to the bottom floor and then, on Tuff's signal, the guard drew his Heckler & Koch and pointed at Gilliam.

"Hey, Emo, what's the idea?" Gilliam asked.

"Raise your arms," Tuff ordered. Gilliam did so and allowed Tuff to frisk him.

"Do you do this to all your guests?"

"Shut up," Tuff said. "Where's the girl you came with?"

"I don't know. I was just looking for her. Maybe she went to the potty."

"She's Dana Barnett, isn't she?"

Gilliam did his best to act put out. "What? Dana Barn—are you mad? Dana's dead and you know it."

"Is she, Mister Gilliam?"

"Look, where's Aaron? I can't believe I'm being treated this way. You *do* know who I am, Emo, or have you lost some of your marbles?"

Emo grinned, turned away from Gilliam, and then swung back with a lightning right hook that sent Gilliam to the floor. At that moment, Aaron Valentine entered from one of the corridors, followed by another security man.

"Did you find the girl and her kid?" he asked, ignoring his guest on the floor.

"Not yet," Tuff said. "But this wise guy is trying to act like a big star and get preferential treatment."

"Go find them," Valentine said. "I'll deal with him." As Tuff left the room, Valentine turned to the other security man, told him to stand in the archway and prevent any guests from entering the Grand Hall. He then turned to Gilliam and said, "Eric, I'm disappointed in you. I thought we were friends. Now I see that you're conspiring with that *woman*."

Gilliam sat up, rubbing his face. "I don't know what the fuck you're talking about, Aaron," he said. "As for your man Emo, I'm speaking to my lawyer in the morning. Jesus, there was no call for an assault."

Valentine told the guard with the gun to call for backup and then addressed Gilliam again. "I'm afraid you won't be speaking to *anyone* in the morning, Eric. You've crossed me and I don't like it."

Gilliam tried to stand but the guard clubbed him hard on the shoulder with the gun butt. The sickening snap of Gilliam's collarbone echoed in the Hall and the actor screamed in pain. He fell to the floor and writhed in agony.

"You fail to see how serious I am about this, Eric," Valentine said.

Gilliam sucked in air and gritted his teeth. After a moment he was able to spit out words in broken sentences. "Who do you think you are, Aaron? . . . The fucking godfather of porn? . . . Have you finally joined up with your mafia family? . . . You can't get away with this!"

Valentine knelt and spoke softly to his victim. "You should know by now that I deal with unpleasant problems by doing something equally unpleasant. Now I regret I must handle you the way I should have handled you those many years ago when you didn't renew your contract with me."

"You going to kill me, Aaron? . . . Is that it? . . . I'm not some obscure, unknown runaway that made a few loops . . . The heat'll come down on you so fast that you won't know where your ass is."

"Oh, don't worry, Eric. We'll make it look like suicide or something. No one will have a reason to suspect me or any of my men."

"Fuck you, Aaron," Gilliam groaned.

"And to think I'm the one who gave you your start in this business," Valentine said. "So ungrateful." Two more security men came in and approached the group. Valentine stood and spoke to them. "Take him to the warehouse and wait for me and Emo." The two new men grabbed Gilliam by the shoulders to pull him up, causing the actor to yelp with distress. His damaged shoulder appeared misshapen.

Once he was on his feet and supported by the two brutes, Gilliam recovered from his pain enough to ask, "Aaron, there's one thing I have to know."

"And what's that, Eric?"

"Did you kill Angela?"

"Angela?"

"*My sister.* Did you have her killed?"

Valentine shook his head. "Of course not. Ask your friend Dana. Angela disappeared when she did." He nodded at the guards and they pulled Gilliam toward the front door.

"You fucking murderer!" Gilliam shouted. "I'll see you in hell, you bastard!"

When they were out the door and the room was silent once again, Valentine wiped his hands on his tunic and sighed. He then turned, went back to his party, and pretended to enjoy himself as if nothing had happened.

CHAPTER THIRTY-EIGHT

Diane and David peered around the house into the backyard. The number of people in attendance had doubled and the party was at peak performance. The music seemed louder, the revelry more intense, and the inhibitions were gone with the wind.

Diane didn't see Gilliam but with that many people to scan he was a needle in a haystack. Perhaps he was inside the house.

"Where do we go, Mom?" David asked.

"I'm looking for someone," she answered, but she knew they couldn't dawdle. They should stick to the plan and just head to the front of the house and try to get out the gate as soon as possible. Gilliam could make it on his own.

"Come on, let's go this way," she said. They turned around, went past the portable latrines and the guests waiting to use them, and walked quickly to the edge of the house. Diane stopped and carefully looked around the corner.

Emo Tuff and two men were standing not ten feet away. One guard was pointing toward the parking lawn and Tuff appeared angry. As she watched, a black limousine drove into the circular drive in front of the house and stopped. She wasn't able to see the front door but she had a full view of the drive. After a moment, Tuff broke away from the two guards and went to the limousine. He opened the back door and looked toward the house.

Diane gasped when she saw the three guards hoisting Gilliam down the walkway and into the limo. He appeared to be badly hurt. She heard him yell in pain when the men shoved him into the car. The three guards got in with him and then Tuff slammed the door shut. The limousine pulled away from the house and drove toward the front gate.

Where were they taking him?

Then Emo Tuff strode in their direction. She heard him call to the two guards he had left standing near the corner, "We're going to circle the grounds, starting with this side."

Damn! They were coming!

"Come on, David," she whispered. She took his hand and they ran along the side of the house toward the backyard once again. They emerged in the midst of the party, just on the edge of the dance floor. Men and women occupied every inch of space, gyrating to the pounding rhythms blasting from gigantic speakers set up near the DJ. Diane looked back and saw Tuff and the two guards come around the side of the house.

His eyes met hers. Tuff said something and pointed to them.

"David!" she urged as she tugged him onto the dance floor. David followed her as she slithered through the dense crowd. At one point a man attempted to engage Diane in a dance but she pushed him away. They eventually got to the other side of the dance floor and broke out of the crowd.

"Can you run, David?" she asked, speaking into his

ear. The music was so loud that he wouldn't have been able to hear her any other way.

He nodded, so she took his hand and they ran toward the big tent. It was the opposite direction from where they needed to go but Diane had no other choice. Two couples carrying plates of food and drinks walked into their path without seeing them and David charged right into them. The people dropped their plates and yelled, "Hey!"

"Sorry!" David called back as he and his mother kept running. They entered the tent where guests were dining at tables. The place was standing room only so they had to decrease speed and carefully navigate a course through people once again. But two guards stood waiting for them on the other side of the tent. Tuff had apparently signaled them through his headset. One of them spoke into his mike and pointed at them. The entire security force was looking for Diane and her son.

"Damn, not that way," she said. She doubled back with David in tow.

"Mom!" He pointed to the front of the tent, where Emo Tuff and his two men had entered. They were trapped.

The buffet was laid out on tables to their right. An unguarded side of the tent was beyond that. Diane pulled David to the ground and they crawled underneath the food tables. Servers on the other side of the buffet looked at them with confusion when the mother and son emerged.

"Excuse us," Diane said breathlessly. Then they took off out of the tent.

Tuff saw what they had done and spoke into his headset. He left, ran around the tent, and held his hand out to one of the armed guards.

"Let me have your gun," he said. The man gave it to him and Tuff pointed it toward the running couple. He fired once, kicking up the grass at their feet.

Female guests in the vicinity screamed. Couples pulled back and cowered, wondering what was going on. Tuff paid no attention to them; instead he chased after Diane and David.

Diane pointed to the smaller tent that had no visible openings in the flaps. She could see that there were people inside because of the silhouettes darting about the sides of the tent, projected by the light inside. She steered David toward it but he stumbled and fell to the ground.

"David!" She stopped to help him up. He was hyperventilating. "Are you all right?"

He nodded but she knew he wasn't. He couldn't take much more running. "Come on, honey, you can do it. We have to get out of here!"

He got to his knees and stood up. His face was full of pain. "Okay," he gasped. She squeezed his hand, pulled him to the tent, and grappled with the sides until she found a flap that opened.

David had never seen an orgy before. The sight of two dozen naked men and women writhing and cavorting on cushions nearly stopped his heart then and there. Diane shuddered in embarrassment and said, "Don't look, David!" He paid no attention; he was wide-eyed as she pulled him along the sides of the tent. The revelers were too busy to notice them.

They exited on the other side of the tent and saw a clear path to the swimming pool. They were now closer to the house and thus nearer to the front.

"Run, David!" she said.

They sprinted across the lawn, dodging guests and a body-painted hostess. Diane was aware that David was wheezing and fighting for air.

We're going to make it, David, just hang on!

He fell again, clutching his torso. Tears ran down his face and she knew that he was in agony. "Come on, sweetheart, just a little farther! You can do it!" she pleaded. Diane looked back and saw Tuff and his goons running toward them.

Diane summoned as much strength as she could and picked up her tall, dangly boy. Holding him in her arms, she moved the twenty yards to the pool where dozens of guests were swimming and lounging. She collapsed at the edge of the pool, releasing David onto an empty lounge chair next to a round patio table with a closed umbrella jutting out of the center. David moaned and gasped for breath as she turned to face their pursuers.

Tuff and the two men were fifteen feet away. He grinned and gestured with a curled index finger for her to come, and then the men walked slowly toward her. Suddenly, a very large guest jumped off the diving board and hit the water, creating an enormous splash that doused everyone on the perimeter of the pool. The torrent hit Diane and David, as well as Tuff and the men. Using the surprise to her advantage, Diane turned to her left and took hold of the umbrella. She lifted it out by the pole and then swung it at the three men with all her might. The umbrella slammed into their sides and knocked them into the pool.

"David! Now!" she cried, pulling him off the lounge chair. He was barely able to move with her as they limped toward the house. Tuff screamed at them from the water as guests looked on, horrified and fascinated by the spectacle.

Diane and David trotted along the side of the house where David's room had been and made it to the front without a problem. The lights were bright on the circular drive as several limos and taxicabs either dropped off guests or picked them up. The mother and son scooted between two limousines and walked quickly up the paved road to the gate.

"We're almost there, David!" Diane panted. Her son was fighting for oxygen, weakly keeping up with her.

The gate was opening to let a white stretch limousine inside. Perfect timing.

Diane grabbed David's hand as they ran out of the property and into the street. A line of cars was backed up on the road, waiting to get inside the gate.

Where was Nick?

Diane looked around frantically. Should they hail a taxi?

"Diane!" The voice came from across and down the road, where it was dark. She could just make out a hand waving from a car window. The headlights flashed twice. She waved in return and the car pulled out of its hiding place. The silver Lexus screeched to a stop beside them.

"Get in," Belgrad said, opening the passenger door. Diane took David, ran around the car, and helped her son get into the back seat. After she got in on the passenger side and shut the door, Belgrad stepped on the gas and they were away.

CHAPTER THIRTY-NINE

The Lexus sped down the hill but Belgrad had a difficult time controlling it. The road was narrow and the line of ascending cars was lengthy. Belgrad couldn't go as fast as he needed to without risking the dissection of another automobile.

"Is there another way down?" Diane asked.

"No," Belgrad replied. "How's David?"

Diane turned to her son in the back seat. "How are you feeling, David?" she asked. The boy was lying down but he was so tall that he had to bend his legs in a fetal position His breathing was shallow and his eyes were closed. Diane reached back and felt his head. His skin was cold and clammy.

"David?"

His eyes fluttered open but they were blank.

"Can you say something, David?" She became frantic, as she had never seen him in this condition, and shook him hard. "David! Please say something!"

David whispered, "Can't . . . breathe . . . good. . . ." The escape from Valentine's party had taken its toll on him.

"Nick, we have to get him to a hospital," she said. "He's got a bad heart."

"I'll do my best," Belgrad said, "but now we've got company."

Diane looked through the rear windshield and saw two bright headlights coming at them. She was unable to see who or how many men were in the car. The pursuing vehicle tailgated them for a while and then slammed into the Lexus' back bumper, jarring David onto the floor. Diane shrieked and fell into the dash.

"Damn it, Diane, put on your seat belt!" Belgrad ordered.

She had to help David back into his seat first. "Can you put your seat belt on, honey?" He struggled weakly with it until she leaned over her seat to buckle it for him.

The Lexus was rammed a second time, knocking Diane backward into the dash again.

"I don't care who I hit, I'm letting loose," Belgrad said as he increased the Lexus' speed. Diane fastened her belt as the silver car stormed around a curve and scraped the side of a stretch limousine. The driver honked at them.

"Sorry, pal," Belgrad said, "I'm afraid I don't have time to stop and give you my insurance details."

Then they heard gunfire and a piece of the back windshield exploded inward.

"Shit!" Diane cried.

"Get down!" Belgrad commanded. "And keep David down!"

Diane crouched in her seat and looked back at her son. He appeared to be unconscious. At least he had the seat belt around his waist. Diane brushed the broken glass off of him and then faced forward.

The Lexus screeched around another curve and finally made it to the foot of the hill. Belgrad opened up, running a red light in order to beat a mass of cross traffic before it got in the way. He looked in the rearview mirror and saw that their pursuers had no choice but to stop. With the aid of the streetlights he could discern that it was a green Mercedes with three men inside.

"That'll put a little distance between us," he said. He sped toward the freeway entrance, zigzagging through traffic until he got to the ramp. Ignoring the metered light, Belgrad shot out onto the 101, heading east.

"Where's the nearest hospital?" Diane asked.

"To tell you the truth, I'm not sure. Do you know?"

"The only one I know is Cedars-Sinai."

"Where is that?"

"Uh, West Hollywood. Near Beverly Hills."

"Can you be more specific?"

"I think it's Beverly Boulevard and . . . damn, I can't remember. San Vicente?"

"Okay."

He shot around a slow-moving truck and veered right onto the Hollywood Freeway toward Universal City. Diane heard a sharp report behind them and saw that the Mercedes was gaining.

"Nick—"

"I see them." He gripped the wheel and inched the speed to ninety-five miles per hour. One of the guards leaned out the Mercedes' passenger window and aimed a handgun. Belgrad saw him and warned Diane to keep down just as a bullet smashed his side mirror, startling them both. "That was way too close," he said and proceeded to cross lanes and weave in and out of traffic.

The Mercedes attempted to mimic the Lexus' maneuvers but the driver couldn't anticipate the lane changes before Belgrad performed them. Belgrad managed to maintain a distance of approximately four car lengths between the two racing vehicles but that wasn't enough for him.

"I have to get off the freeway," he said. "It's the only way to lose these jerks." The Highland Avenue exit was next, so he took it. "This will get us closer to your hospital, at any rate," he observed.

The line of cars on the exit ramp was substantial but that didn't keep Belgrad from driving onto the curb, half-off the road, in order to get in front of the line. Angry drivers honked at him and some cursed from open windows.

"Let's just hope we don't run into a cop," he said as he ran the red light at the intersection. A taxicab nearly collided with the Lexus but Belgrad slammed on the brakes, causing a deafening screech. The car skidded and turned completely around.

"Whoa," Diane said softly. She was clenching the arm rest so tightly that her knuckles were white.

"Everyone okay?" Belgrad asked.

"Yes, just go," Diane said. She looked back at David and saw that he was still unconscious.

The Lexus sped south on Highland, crossing Hollywood Boulevard, and then it reached a red light at Sunset. Belgrad looked into the rearview mirror and couldn't see the Mercedes. He stopped at the intersection.

"You think we lost them?" Diane asked.

"I don't know," he answered. He drummed his fingers on the wheel, waiting for the light to turn green. "Come on . . ." he urged. Then he saw the Mercedes in the mirror, just as the cross-town light turned yellow. He didn't wait for his green.

The Lexus tore out across Sunset, again missing tardy traffic by a hair. Unfortunately, the vehicles on Highland were moving slowly as they approached Santa Monica Boulevard. Belgrad was stuck in the line, with cars in front and back of the Lexus. The only good thing about it was that the Mercedes had the same problem a half-block behind them.

When the light turned green, traffic crawled across Sunset. Belgrad slapped the wheel and barked, "Oh, come *on!*" As soon as he reached the intersection, Belgrad made a sharp right and went west on Santa Monica. It was a wider boulevard but traffic was just as thick. A median separating the two directions of transit made the passage more difficult to navigate.

"This was not a smart move," he said. He looked into the mirror and saw that the Mercedes had followed them. Belgrad reached underneath his jacket and drew his Browning. He handed it to Diane and said, "Here, I reloaded this while I was waiting for you. See if you can knock out one of their tires. Or the driver. Anything."

She held it in her hand and swallowed hard. Diane had considered removing the Colt from her handbag and attempting that very thing. She decided to use the Browning instead.

The window went down and she leaned out. The Mercedes passenger was already balancing himself on the door and aiming straight at them. His gun fired and Diane felt the heat of the bullet whisk by her head, so close that it forced her back inside. She clutched the side of her face in pain.

"Diane?" Belgrad called. "Are you all right?"

She looked at her hand and saw there was no blood. She pulled down the visor and looked in the mirror. She was fine apart from a red streak on her cheek.

"Damn," she said. "I thought he had me. I'm just a little burned."

"Maybe you'd better stay inside the car."

"No, I'm gonna try this." She leaned out the window again, took a bead on the Mercedes, and fired. One of the headlights burst. She fired again and saw a spider-web form on the windshield. The Mercedes swerved momentarily but quickly got back on track. Diane returned to her seat and re-fastened her belt.

"I hit something," she said.

"Good girl," Belgrad said. "I'm getting the hell off this road." At the next intersection he pulled a left turn from the right lane, confusing and annoying all the other drivers. The Lexus was now on Fairfax.

The Mercedes attempted the same daring maneuver but was hit broadside by a Corvette going thirty miles per hour above the speed limit. The Mercedes spun in place and then tottered, two wheels off the ground, threatening to topple onto its side. It didn't, though; the car fell with a thud on all four wheels. The driver's side of the car was smashed in but the vehicle was still operable. It dodged the other traffic and followed the Lexus onto Fairfax.

Belgrad slapped the wheel again and said, "Oh, man, I thought that was it." Determined to end the chase once and for all, he floored the pedal and the Lexus shot forward, practically lifting itself off the road.

"Look, there's Beverly!" Diane pointed.

"I see it." Belgrad turned a sharp right onto Beverly Boulevard with the wounded Mercedes hot on his tail. Diane unbuckled her belt again and leaned out the window, the semiautomatic in hand. Pointing it at the Mercedes, she squeezed the trigger several times, releasing a volley of rounds. Flinching, she was unable to see what damage she caused but the Mercedes swerved sickeningly. Then it ran up onto the sidewalk and crashed into the back of a parked Ford pickup.

"Yes!" she cried and got back in her seat.

"Did you hit the driver?" Belgrad asked.

"I don't know."

He watched in the mirror until he saw the Mercedes back out of its predicament and resume the chase, but it was definitely a dying animal.

"You didn't hit him," Belgrad announced.

"Nick, there's the hospital!" Diane pointed. Sure enough, the massive Cedars-Sinai campus was up ahead on the right, beyond San Vicente, just as Diane had guessed.

"Maybe we can lose those bastards here," Belgrad said as he swung into the emergency room drive. The path curved behind a building, out of the Beverly traffic sightlines. He pulled the Lexus up to the emergency room doors, stopped, held his breath, and watched the drive behind them. The Mercedes failed to appear after a couple of minutes.

"Nick, you did it!" Diane cried. She threw her arms around him and kissed him on the cheek.

Belgrad laughed uncomfortably and then got out of the car. He opened the back door, unfastened David's seat belt, and pulled him out of the car. Carrying the boy in his arms, Belgrad ran inside the hospital with Diane at his side.

Diane sat in the emergency waiting room for nearly two hours before learning anything about David's condition. In the meantime, Belgrad had parked the Lexus in the hospital's garage, made some calls, and returned to find her wringing a magazine as if it were a wet towel.

"I think you killed that poor magazine," Belgrad remarked.

She smiled when she realized she had nearly obliterated it. "I guess I'm pretty anxious." It was worse than that, though. She had gone into her trance-like state while Belgrad was gone and felt as though the stress she was under would surely kill her. Being in the hospital reminded her of the two times long ago when Sweetie was there. First the drug overdose . . . and then later with the gunshot wound in the head . . .

"We're twins, aren't we, Sweetie? You have to pull through!"

Sweetie didn't say anything. Sweetie didn't move.

Diane expected to find blood on her clothes, the way she had that night, but there wasn't any. She was still wearing the gaudy bra/panties/garter belt outfit and was drawing a great number of stares from other hospital visitors.

"Here, I brought you something," Belgrad said, handing her a bag from the hospital gift shop. Inside was a large, white knee-length T-shirt decorated with candy canes. It was meant to be a sleep-shirt.

"Oh, thank you," Diane said. "You'd think I was sitting here naked from the way people are ogling me." She slipped it on and covered herself, feeling immensely less vulnerable.

"Any word?"

"Not yet."

Belgrad looked at his watch but didn't mention how late it was. He could see that Diane was terribly upset and it reminded him of his own personal baggage. Like him, the woman had a past that had exacted a price from her, both spiritually and emotionally. He knew this was so, simply by looking into her eyes. She was damaged and he empathized with the destruction he saw. He had gone through analysis for years and at the very least he understood why the demons of his own history fueled what he did for a living today. He worked on the edge of danger and death because that's what it took to confront the devils and face his fears.

He wondered if Diane understood it, too. His gut feeling told him that she didn't have a clue. It was too bad that he found her damnably attractive. Or was it?

A man wearing a white coat emerged from the swinging doors, looked around, and focused on them. He came over and asked, "Mr. and Mrs. Boston?"

"I'm Mrs. Boston," Diane said.

"I'm Doctor Crane," the man said. He was probably in his late thirties, good-looking, fit. He sat in a chair beside them. "David is fine," he said.

"Oh, thank God," Diane muttered. She put a hand to her mouth and the tears flowed.

The doctor held up his hand and warned, "But he's not out of the woods. To tell the truth he's had a terrible strain on his heart. The aortic regurgitation that he's experienced in the past is much worse. We've got him on oxygen and a sedative, and he's going to need rest. I'd like him to stay in the hospital for at least twenty-four to forty-eight hours so we can observe him. I don't think there're going to be any problems but I want to make sure. Cardiac arrest is a distinct possibility with Marfan syndrome, but I suspect you know that."

She nodded and took a tissue from her purse to wipe her face.

"I understand you're not residents of California?" the doctor asked.

"That's right."

"Then I suggest as soon as you get home that he see his doctor. I think the time has come for him to have that aortic valve repaired. You'll find he'll be able to live a much fuller life once that's done."

"Thank you, Doctor. Can I see him?"

"Sure. Try not to excite him. I've already told him that he'll be here overnight and possibly tomorrow night."

Belgrad said to her, "You go on. I'll wait here." Diane stood and went with the doctor back into the treatment area. David was lying with an IV in his arm and an oxygen mask on his face. His eyes were open and they brightened when he saw her.

"Honey, how do you feel?" she asked, putting a hand on his forehead.

"Okay," he said through the mask.

"You're going to have to stay here a while, is that all right?"

He nodded.

"I'll bet you're exhausted. Get some sleep. I'm probably gonna go to a hotel and I'll be back to see you tomorrow. Okay?"

He nodded again.

"Don't worry about those awful men. They don't know you're here. You'll be safe. And our new friend Nick will be watching out for us."

David nodded once more.

She leaned over to kiss his forehead. "I'm glad you're

okay. We're gonna get through this. And I want to say, well, I want to tell you that I'm sorry this has happened. It should never have involved you."

Tears welled in his eyes.

"And I'm sorry about your father," she continued. "You know it wasn't me that did that, don't you?"

He nodded as a drop rolled down his cheek.

She kissed him again. "I love you. Feel better. I'll see you tomorrow."

Belgrad gave her a comforting hug when she returned to the waiting room. "Thank you," she said. "For everything."

"Do you have a place to stay?" he asked.

She shook her head. "I was staying with Eric. Where do you suppose they took him?"

"I don't know. We really should try to find him."

Diane got an idea. "The warehouse. They probably took him there."

"The one in Santa Monica?"

"Yes. If it's still there."

Belgrad said, "His company's warehouse is still there, all right. I did a lot of checking up on Valentine before I came out here. Let's go take a look."

DAVID'S JOURNAL

I'm in the hospital in Los Angeles. I asked the nurse for a piece of paper to write on because I don't have my journal with me. Mom's got it in Nick's car. He helped us and he seems like a good guy.

I'm really tired and I'm going to sleep in a minute but I wanted to write down some thoughts before I forget them.

Mom came and rescued me from Aaron Valentine's mansion. I got very sick and something bad happened to my heart. I might need an operation soon. Despite all that, this has got to be the most exciting day of my life. Mom was incredible. She was like some kind of superhero. I couldn't believe that she climbed down that thing outside the window at Valentine's house. And then she whacked Emo and those other guys with that umbrella and they fell into the swimming pool. I was really out of it but when we were in the car being chased on the freeway, it was right out of a movie. I remember some of it. I think Mom fired a gun. She's really brave and I'm proud of her.

I don't care if she was a porno actress. She's the best Mom in the world.

CHAPTER FORTY

They stopped by Gilliam's house in Van Nuys just to make sure he hadn't escaped from his captors and gone home. Diane got her hopes up when she saw the Porsche in the driveway beside her Malibu. She let herself in with the key he had given her, but as she feared, found no one at home. How did the car get there? While pondering that puzzle, she took the opportunity to change into blue jeans and a blouse and then rejoined Belgrad in the Lexus.

"I take it he wasn't there?" Belgrad asked as they drove away.

"No. How did his Porsche get here?"

"I imagine they brought it here. If anything happens to Mister Gilliam then they can claim he left the party."

Belgrad pulled into a gas station a few blocks away from Gilliam's house.

"Are we out of gas?" Diane asked.

"No, there's something I need to do," he answered. Belgrad popped the trunk, got out of the Lexus, and took a moment to examine the scrapes and scratches the car had sustained during the chase. He shrugged and then went around to the rear of the vehicle. Diane got out and joined him as he removed a five-gallon plastic container for gasoline. She noticed that there was also a crate of empty Coke bottles and a pile of rags.

"What's all that?"

"For emergencies," he said, winking at her. He swiped his credit card in the gas pump and began to fill the container. Diane, puzzled, picked up one of the empty bottles.

"I don't understand," she said.

"You will later." He topped off the container, sealed it, and placed it back in the trunk. "Ready to go?" he asked.

They got in the car and took off for Santa Monica.

Darren Marshall had to drive the thirty-five miles back to Midland to check into a hotel. Garden City was such a wasteland that there weren't any commercial hotels in sight.

He had spent the rest of the day in Glasscock County attempting to track down Manuel Delgado, the man the librarian had told him about. There was no phone number listed in the tiny Garden City directory, so Marshall obtained a rough sketch of the surrounding areas from the woman and an approximate location of the Barnett ranch. A barbed wire fence lined Highway 33 North and there was supposed to be a break in it "seven or eight miles" from the center of town, where a cattle guard and a dirt road jutted off to the left. Marshall drove ten miles on the highway but never found the turnoff she mentioned. Since the sun had set and visibility was nil, Marshall figured he might have better luck during daylight hours.

He was beginning to wonder if he was on a wild goose chase.

"You think David will be all right?" Diane asked.

"Sure. He's in good hands," Belgrad replied. "Has he ever been in the hospital before?"

"Yeah. He doesn't like it much."

"Who does? But he knows the ropes. He'll be fine."

"I hope so. I'm worried."

They drove into Santa Monica and headed west, closer to the ocean.

"Have you thought about what you're going to do back in Illinois?" he asked after a few minutes of silence.

"What do you mean?"

"Well, I mean eventually you're going to have to go back and face the music. You're wanted for murder, you know."

"Yeah, I know. It's so stupid. You'd think by now they'd have figured out I didn't kill Greg. That's my ex-husband."

"I know. And what about your job at the school?"

She cocked her head and eyed him. "You sure know a lot about me, don't you?"

He shrugged. "It's what I do, Diane. When you became the major link to solving the Rabinowitzes' murders, I did some homework. But there's a lot I *don't* know about you. Like, for instance, this business with a twin sister. No one seems to know for certain whether you had a twin sister. Is it true?"

"Yes, it's true. Her name was Dana."

"And she was the porn star, right?"

"That's right."

"And she's dead."

"As far as I know."

Belgrad stroked his beard as he drove.

"What?" she asked. "You don't believe me?"

"It's not that. I just find it strange that you're unwilling to provide proof of her existence."

"You're beginning to sound like my lawyer."

"Where did you and your sister grow up?" he asked.

Diane crossed her arms and turned away. She stared out the window and sighed.

"I can't ask you that question?" Belgrad inquired.

"I don't want to talk about it," she answered. "It's a painful part of my life."

He merely nodded and continued to drive.

She turned back to him and said, "Look. I just want to finish my business here, get rid of these diamonds for some hard cash, and make sure Aaron Valentine and his organization leave my son and me alone for the rest of our lives. Then I'll go back to Illinois and I'll do what I can to clear things up. One thing at a time. It's all I can handle right now."

"I understand," he said. "I'd like nothing better than to take care of Aaron Valentine and that goon Emo Tuff, too. I doubt seriously that they'll ever be prosecuted for the Rabinowitzes' murders. They've perfected their crimes to a fine art. Look how long they've been going on and those guys have never been convicted of anything. It's a case that calls for unorthodox methods."

"What does that mean?" she asked.

He looked at her. "What do you think it means?"

Diane didn't say anything. They both knew what would happen if they found Gilliam at Valentine's warehouse.

"I have a gun," Diane said.

"I figured you might."

"I want to help you."

"I thought you would."

After navigating the streets toward the beach he pulled the Lexus over and parked in the shadows. He pointed to a building across the street. "There it is," he said.

The memory of the place came back to Diane in a flood of emotion. She felt the familiar anxiety well up within her chest and she suddenly felt nauseated. Images of blood and death flashed before her eyes and she had to take a deep breath to calm herself.

"Are you okay?" Belgrad asked.

"Yeah," she said.

The warehouse was the size of a small airplane hangar and was made of steel and wood. It was set apart from other buildings on the street and looked as if it might be a storage center for construction equipment. A sign in front of the main entrance proclaimed, "A.V. Enterprises." The building was dark except for faint illumination in the rear of the structure, where the loading dock was located.

"See that limo?" Diane asked. She pointed to a black limousine, a portion of which was visible, parked at the back of the warehouse.

"Yeah."

"That's the same car I saw them put Eric in. They're here, Nick."

"You said there were three guys with him?"

"Uh huh."

A pair of headlights appeared in the rearview mirror. "Get down," he said, ducking in his seat. Diane did the same as a white stretch limousine went past them and pulled into the drive behind the warehouse. "Looks like we were just in time." They watched as Aaron Valentine and Emo Tuff got out of the limo. Tuff was still dressed in black, as he had been at the party, but Valentine had changed into street clothes. They casually glanced up and down the street, didn't notice the Lexus in the dark, and then went inside the building.

Belgrad popped the trunk, got out of the car, and quietly closed the door. Diane followed and watched as he took two empty Coke bottles from the trunk and filled them with gasoline. He stuffed rags in the bottle openings and then asked, "You ready?"

"Sure."

"Oh, by the way," he said. "I can find someone who'll pay you good money to take those diamonds off your hands."

"Really?"

"Sure thing. Come on, let's go."

CHAPTER FORTY-ONE

Diane and Belgrad crept along the side of the warehouse until they got to the rear edge of the building. Belgrad peered around the corner and confirmed that the two limousines were the only vehicles present. The loading dock door, a heavy steel shutter that rolled down from the ceiling, was open at the bottom. A man could duck and enter the warehouse through there or use a standard door that was up a small flight of steps.

"I know another way in," Diane said.

"Yeah?"

"It's on the other side of the building. It's how I got in before."

"Show me."

They went around the building, retracing their steps to the front and then moving down the opposite side until they came to a series of windows.

Diane frowned. "There used to be a bunch of boxes and crates here. I climbed up and got in through that window. It goes to a storage room that's closed off from the rest of the place."

"I can give you a boost," Belgrad said. "See if you can get the window open."

She put a foot in his cupped hands and he lifted her as high as he could. Diane pushed on the hinged window, opening it after a few good thrusts.

"Can you climb in?" he whispered.

"I think so. What will you do?"

"I'll find another way in. Wait until I make a move in there, all right?"

"Okay." She put her head in the window and surveyed the place. It was just as she remembered it. The room contained tools and janitorial equipment, as well as a slop sink and cleaning supplies. Diane jumped to the floor, using her self-defense training to land lightly. The place was dim and dusty but enough illumination seeped in from the building's exterior lighting to allow visibility.

Damn! She had forgotten to retrieve the Colt out of her purse. That's just great, she thought. There she had been, boasting to Belgrad how she could hold her own and now she was stuck in the warehouse without a weapon. Alas, there was no turning back now. On with it.

She carefully crept to the door and opened it a crack. The warehouse interior hadn't changed much and seeing it brought back that terrible night with such ferocity that Diane recalled the smell of the incinerator and the sound of her voice echoing through the grand building.

"Sweetie? Are you here?"

The place was filled with Erotica Selecta products—boxes of videos and DVDs, magazines, and adult books. The warehouse served as a shipping center to retail outlets all over the world. The incinerator, located in the wall opposite where Diane was hiding, roared as if it were alive. Its doors were open, revealing flames that shot up from the lower depths of the warehouse, where unwanted material was disposed of. Such as bodies.

The men were gathered thirty feet away, beneath a work light that hung from the ceiling on a single electrical cord.

Two guards held Eric Gilliam up by the arms, his hands tied behind him. Diane could see blood and bruises on Gilliam's face. Emo Tuff and Aaron Valentine stood in front of him. The third guard was standing near the incinerator, holding a milkshake and sucking on the straw.

Tuff wore black gloves that she knew were lined with metal, if she remembered correctly. A blow by a man wearing those gloves was like getting hit with a sledgehammer. *Sweetie had told her about the man with the metal-lined gloves . . . "Watch out for that guy," she had said.*

Valentine stepped closer to Gilliam and addressed him. "Look, Eric, we can make this as unpleasant as possible for you, or we can end it right now. Just tell us where we can find Dana and the boy."

Gilliam mumbled something that Diane couldn't make out but she was certain that it was some kind of insult. Valentine made a face, backhanded Gilliam, and then wiped the blood off his hand onto his victim's shirt. He nodded to his henchman and stepped back as Tuff struck Gilliam's face and stomach with pile-driver punches.

Diane shut her eyes and resisted the urge to cry out and stop them. Was there anything she could do to help her friend?

Tuff stopped the pummeling and then squeezed Gilliam's cheeks, causing the actor to cry out in pain.

"Is your jaw broken, Eric?" Valentine asked. "Becoming hard to talk, isn't it? You better tell me what I want to know. Otherwise in a little while you won't be able to talk at all and then we'll just have to put you in the incinerator. We'll have no further use for you. I'll find the stupid woman eventually, with or without your help. I was just hoping you could save me a little time."

Diane could barely understand what Gilliam said in reply. It sounded as if his mouth was full of cotton. "People saw me . . . at your party . . . if I disappear . . . you'll be a suspect . . ." the poor man said.

"Nonsense," Valentine replied. "You forget what kind of influence I have over my friends. There are plenty of people who will testify that they saw you at my party, drunk and disorderly. They'll say you left of your own volition. Your car is no longer at Paradise. It'll be found parked in front of your house in Van Nuys. I believe it's already there. No, Eric, I'll be able to provide plenty of evidence that after you left my party, you went home. What happened there is anyone's guess. Perhaps you simply left town. No one will find your body. I know we made mistakes in the distant past but I've learned that to properly dispose of someone then we have to obliterate every single piece of tissue associated with it."

As if on cue, the third guard tossed his empty milk-shake cup into the incinerator. The flames brightened as the furnace bellowed with hunger.

"I'm going to tell you something, Eric, and it's the truth," Valentine said. "You think I had something to do with your sister's disappearance, don't you. You think I had her killed. You believe I had Emo here throw her into the incinerator. You believe that, don't you? Answer me!"

Gilliam nodded his head.

"I'll tell you what I think happened to your sister. She and Eduardo weren't getting along. You remember my little brother, Eduardo? He didn't like the fact that Angela lived with Dana Barnett and had a lesbian relationship with her. They often fought about it. This is what I think. The night my brother was shot to death by that Nigerian gang, he brought your sister here to talk some sense into her. Things probably got out of hand and she ended up in . . . well, you know. . . ." He gestured with his head toward the incinerator. "And I believe Dana was here that night as well. She waited until the shooting was over between my men and the Nigerians. When every-one was dead, Dana came out of hiding and stole my di-amonds. And that's why I want to catch her. She ripped me off and tried to get away with it. Maybe she had something to do with Eduardo's death, I don't know. All I know is Dana Barnett was here when my little brother died and I hold her responsible. I could be wrong, but you see, things never went very smoothly when she was around. The girl was schizophrenic. You worked with her. You saw her during the shoots. She was a whacko, wasn't she? Sometimes she was so drugged out she didn't know who she was. Once when she had a starring role, she reported to the set so wasted that she insisted she wasn't Dana Barnett. She claimed that her 'uncle' would kill her if he knew what she was doing.

"You want to know what I think, Eric?" Valentine continued. "I think Dana was jealous of Angela's relationship with Eduardo. I think *she* killed Angela."

"Not true . . ." Gilliam managed to say. He spit blood and tissue onto the concrete floor.

"Are you sure you won't tell me what I want to know?" Valentine asked with menace in his voice. "Last chance."

Gilliam did his best to have the last word. "F—f—f . . . uuu . . . ck y—y—ou. . . ."

Valentine turned to Tuff and held up his hands, as if to say, "I give up." He nodded and then walked toward the administration office so he wouldn't have to watch Tuff and the three guards drag Gilliam toward the incinerator.

CHAPTER FORTY-TWO

After helping Diane climb through the window, Nick Belgrad moved back to the rear of the building, crouched low, and made his way to the loading dock. Positioning himself at eye level with the warehouse floor, he could see through the opening in the door and observe what was going on inside—the men holding Eric Gilliam, Valentine interrogating him, and the killer Emo Tuff beating the victim senseless.

Belgrad waited until all eyes were turned away and then he slipped onto the loading dock platform and darted underneath the partly open door. He moved quickly to the side and squatted behind a stack of cartons. He looked for the storage room where Diane would be but the section was blocked by rows of boxes waiting to be shipped to retailers. Directing his attention back to Gilliam and the men, Belgrad watched and listened as Valentine gave the victim a final chance to talk. Belgrad was well aware that Gilliam couldn't take much more and if there was a time to make a move, it was now.

The men began to drag Gilliam toward the incinerator as Valentine walked away. Belgrad took one of the Molotov cocktails out of his trouser pocket, set the second one on the floor beside him, and removed a cigarette lighter from his jacket. He flicked the lighter and held the flame to the rag in the bottle. Belgrad stood, drew his arm back, and prepared to throw the hand-made firebomb.

But as the men got within five feet of the incinerator, Emo Tuff surprised everyone by turning quickly and flashing a stiletto at Gilliam's throat. The maneuver was so fast that he looked like a painter making three dynamic brush strokes on canvas. The paint, however, became blood as it gushed from Gilliam's neck like water from a spigot.

"Nooooo!"

It was Diane. She had screamed from her hiding place and emerged from behind the boxes. Tuff shouted an order and pointed. The men dropped Gilliam, drew their guns and turned to face the woman.

Belgrad threw the Molotov cocktail so that it burst on the floor between Diane and the men. The gasoline spread over the concrete and created a wall of fire that prevented the gangsters from moving closer to the woman.

"Diane!" Belgrad shouted. "Get out! Go back the way you came!"

Diane looked up and attempted to locate him through the thick smoke that filled the warehouse at an alarming pace. Belgrad waved and shouted again but it was too late—he saw the massive shape of Valentine behind her. The big man grabbed her and put a guard's Heckler & Koch to her head.

The men, aware of Belgrad's presence, directed their guns at him. Belgrad took cover behind the boxes again as bullets zipped past him with deadly precision. He picked up the second Molotov cocktail, ignited the rag, and stepped out on the other side of the boxes. He scanned the right side of the warehouse for Diane and Valentine and spotted them moving back to the storage room.

Belgrad took aim and threw the cocktail so that it

burst on the stacks of boxes directly behind Valentine and Diane. The cartons of videotapes and DVDs exploded into flame, quickly and sufficiently blocking their escape.

He then drew the Browning and dropped to the floor. Peering around the boxes, he saw two of the thugs moving closer. The smoke obviously burned their eyes and hindered visibility. Picking them off was easy. Belgrad squeezed the trigger twice and the two men flew backwards as if an invisible force gave them sucker punches.

Now Belgrad had trouble seeing through the black smoke. The flames were spreading faster than he expected. He estimated that they had no more than a couple of minutes to get out or they would be overcome.

Where were Emo Tuff and the third guard? Belgrad crouched as low as possible but he couldn't see any movement. Fine, he thought. Concentrate on getting Diane out.

He moved to the other side and saw that Valentine had Diane in front of him, using her as a human shield.

"I'm coming out!" Valentine shouted. "Don't try anything or she's dead!"

A bullet tore past Belgrad's face, searing his nose and ricocheting off the concrete beside him. A piece of the floor went into his right eye and sent a burning hell through the nerves in his head. Belgrad rolled back behind cover and clutched his face, writhing in agony. It must have been Tuff or the third guard. He had to take care of them before he could deal with Valentine, if he could.

Belgrad rolled to the other side of the boxes and scanned the room with his one good eye and found that the third guard was not quite ten feet away and was indeed moving closer. Belgrad pointed the Browning just as the man spotted him. Both guns went off at the same time.

The guard's bullet perforated the carton near Belgrad's head. The Browning's round pierced the guard's chest, whirling him around once and then dropping him to the burning floor.

Belgrad went back to the other side of his cover, his right eye still shut, and saw that Valentine still had Diane. They were fifteen feet away from freedom.

"Stand up and throw down your weapon!" Valentine shouted. "Do as I say or she's dead!"

Belgrad slowly stood and held up his hands, the Browning's trigger guard still around his index finger.

"Drop it, I said," Valentine commanded.

Diane's eyes met Belgrad's good eye. She suddenly reached for Valentine's gun arm and used it as a lever. She expertly flipped Valentine over her shoulder and he crashed into a pile of boxes. She then turned to kick the man in the face but Belgrad yelled, "Leave him! Come on!"

She wouldn't do it. Instead she leaped at the man, feet first, flawlessly using the skill that she had taught Lincoln High School girls for years. Valentine's body jerked as the kick broke his ribcage. The King of Porn collapsed over the spilled boxes, his massive body unevenly supported like a whale on scales.

Diane spent a few more seconds examining the man to make sure he was incapacitated and then, satisfied, she ran toward Belgrad. The fire raged behind her and had by now engulfed more than half the interior.

Belgrad caught her and they embraced. He kissed her once on the mouth and then shouted, "Come on!"

He took her hand and led her under the loading dock door and out into the fresh air.

"Your eye is hurt," she said.

"Only if I open it," he replied. They heard a siren in the distance and reacted quickly. Not wanting to be seen by the authorities, they jumped off the dock, ran down the street toward the Lexus, and got in the car just as a fire truck turned the corner and roared past them. Belgrad waited until the firemen got busy at their jobs before starting the car and slowly pulling away from the disaster.

CHAPTER FORTY-THREE

It was nearly dawn when they walked into Belgrad's hotel room in Hollywood. Belgrad was exhausted but Diane was curiously euphoric.

"This was just an amazing night!" she said for the fourth time. "It's over! It's finally *over!* I don't have to worry about them anymore."

He turned on the lights and was grateful that the room had been made up and cleaned. "Make yourself comfortable," Belgrad said. "I'm going to do something about my eye." He went into the bathroom and ran water in the sink until it was warm.

"Can I help you?" she asked.

"Actually, you probably can. You might be able to see what's in it better than I can."

She joined him, washed her hands, and turned his face toward the light. "Try to open your eye," she said. Belgrad attempted it but his eyelids kept closing reflexively. Diane used her fingers to hold them open and saw that the eye was bloodshot and teary.

"I see it," she said. "There's a little piece of debris . . . hold on." She took a washcloth, wet it in the warm water, and then carefully pulled his bottom eyelid down as far as it would go. Using a corner of the washcloth, she dabbed his eye until the tiny piece of concrete came out.

"There!"

"Oh, thank you," he said, immediately feeling the relief. He turned to the mirror and looked at his eye, blinked a few times, and smiled. "Good as new. Sort of."

They came out of the bathroom and he asked her if she wanted something to drink.

"What do you have?"

"Well, let's see." He went to the wet bar and unlocked it with the tiny key that came with the room. "Looks like the usual stuff. Beer, wine, some of those little airplane bottles of hard stuff. Sodas, water."

"Wine, please. Red or white, it doesn't matter." She sat in the easy chair by the desk and said once again, "I can't believe it's over."

Belgrad opened a small bottle of red wine for her and poured himself a glass of vodka on ice. He handed her the wine and said, "It isn't over, Diane. You still have to deal with the authorities in Illinois, remember?"

"That seems so trivial compared to what we did tonight. Nick, Aaron Valentine is *dead!* He can't haunt me anymore. I can't tell you how great I feel. It's like a huge weight has been lifted."

Nick sat on the bed and held up his glass. "Cheers."

"Cheers," she repeated and took a sip. The taste of wine was welcome and for once she wasn't using it to combat anxiety.

"Diane."

"What?"

"*Are* you Dana Barnett?"

She blinked. "No. I thought you believed that by now."

"Who are you, then?"

"I'm Diane Boston. Before I was married I was Diane Barnett."

"No you weren't. Your name was Diane *Wilson* when you got married."

She put her glass on the desk. "That's just a name I was using. I didn't want Valentine or his people to track me down."

"Why would they track you down? You're not Dana, right?"

"No, but I look like her. She was my twin."

Belgrad contemplated the woman sitting across from him. She was a bundle of contradictions and paradoxes. At times he believed everything she had to say but too often he was never sure she told the truth. Just in the half-day he'd been around her, Belgrad was certain she was consciously careful not to reveal her true self. She wore a mask and protected it with fervor.

In normal circumstances he could have used a dozen tricks to penetrate the façade but the problem was that he was intensely attracted to her. He had always liked Gentile women although in his heart of hearts he knew he'd never marry one. If he married at all.

"You're Jewish, aren't you?" Diane asked as if she had read his thoughts.

"Yes."

"Do you practice it religiously, if you'll pardon the pun?"

"No," he answered. "I grew up in an orthodox home, kosher and all that. And I was orthodox well into adulthood and while I was working in Israel. I kept kosher and observed the Sabbath, obeyed all the laws. But I suppose you can say I became jaded. The things I saw in the Middle East turned me against religion in so many ways. That's not to say I don't believe in God, because I do. I'm still religious and I still take pride in my heritage, but I'm no longer orthodox. Am I making sense?"

"Sure," she said. "I was raised a Baptist but I'm not anything now."

"I did a lot of undercover work in Israel, infiltrating terrorist cells, that sort of thing. When you're undercover you can't always stop what you're doing to say your prayers or stop using electricity at sundown on Friday night. I slowly lost the need to do those things, and frankly I lost the will to pursue my spirituality. There's just . . . too much evil, too much death. Too much hatred."

They were silent for a few minutes, basking in the stillness of the room. Diane finished her glass and poured the rest of the wine into it. "What are you going to do now?" she asked.

He shrugged. "Go back to New York."

"When?"

"I don't know. When I'm ready."

She nodded. Her earlier joy had dissipated into something more melancholic. "Poor Eric," she said. "What happened to him was horrible."

Belgrad frowned. "Yeah. But you know, Diane, he was involved in a world that had a lot of dark corners. He knew the risks."

"He had a good soul," she said. "So did his sister."

He narrowed his eyes at her. "You knew her?"

Diane looked away and took a sip. "Uh, no. Dana knew her. I heard about her from Dana."

"And you don't know what happened to her?"

"Are you interrogating me?"

"I just want to know."

"No. She died in that incinerator, along with my sister."

Belgrad felt that it was a lie but he also sensed that *she* believed what she was saying. Whatever had happened to her back then had permanently affected her perception of what actually occurred. He supposed he'd never know.

She changed the subject and attempted to lighten up. "So, you really think you can fence my diamonds?" She smiled and wiggled her eyebrows like Groucho Marx.

He laughed. "I'll make some calls tomorrow—er, today. After I get some sleep. I'm pretty sure I can get you something nice for them. I, uhm, know a lot of Moses and Hiram's customers."

"I won't take less than a million," she said, half-kidding.

"You won't have to. And now I'm going to take a shower," he said, standing. "You can, uhm, you can sleep in the other bed if you'd like, or if you'd like to shower after me, you can . . ." He felt awkward and tongue-tied.

"Go ahead, do what you need to do," she said. "I'll just sit here."

He went into the bathroom and shut the door. Diane could hear him unbuckle his trousers, slip them off, and turn on the water. She heard the shower door close when he stepped inside.

Diane stood and slowly walked to the bathroom door. She quietly opened it and looked inside. Already the room was steaming up but she could see the blurry image of the hairy man through the glass door. She felt a stirring within that she hadn't experienced in a long time. She had not had a lover since her ex-husband and suddenly she wanted one.

The heat and steam brought back a memory of two blond women standing beneath a spigot and making love while a camera rolled. For them it wasn't acting. Diane didn't know where the recollection came from and thought that perhaps she had seen it in one of Dana's films.

Why did she remember that?

Diane slowly removed her clothes and opened the shower door. Belgrad looked at her but didn't seem surprised to see her. Wordlessly, she stepped into the small stall and closed the door. He put his arms around her and drew her to him. Their wet bodies pressed together, warm and slippery, and their mouths joined, and then their tongues, and then their hands began to roam and touch and caress. . . .

CHAPTER FORTY-FOUR

Darren Marshall had breakfast at a Denny's in Midland and then drove back to Garden City to hunt for the Barnett ranch one more time. This time he stopped at the gas station where the toothless old man worked to ask him if he knew where the property was. The old man recognized him and inquired, "Are you enjoying our fair city?"

Marshall answered, "It's truly the garden spot of Texas."

The sarcasm flew over the old man's head and he grinned wider. "We think so. How can I help you?"

Marshall explained what he was looking for and the man replied, "Sure, I know the place. I remember ol' Roy. He was a character. Kept to himself up there on his ranch, didn't come into town much. He's dead now."

"Can you help me find the ranch?"

The old man gave him the same directions as the librarian did. Marshall said, "I tried that last night but couldn't find it. Maybe I'll have better luck now that it's daylight?"

"I should think so. Reckon there's enough daylight today!" The old man laughed. The West Texas sun was painfully bright and the temperature was close to one hundred degrees Fahrenheit.

Marshall thanked him and drove on. He followed the directions to a tee and sure enough, this time he found a break in the barbed wire fence exactly seven and a half miles north on Route 33. A cattle guard separated the highway from a dirt road lined with mesquite and sagebrush. Marshall turned left and followed the rough drive for nearly two miles until he finally spotted a building on the horizon. As he got closer he saw that the property consisted of a large two-story house, a barn with a weather vane on top, a tool shack, a small cabin, and what appeared to be a wood building used for processing cattle. There were no animals in sight, though, except for some chickens clucking in a pen on one side of the big house. A woman's white sundress was flapping in the breeze, hanging on a clothesline on the opposite end.

Marshall pulled in front of the house, got out of the car, and went to the front door. There was no sound aside from the wood creaking in the wind. He knocked on the door and waited, but nothing happened. He knocked again and called, "Hello? Anyone home?" There was still no sign of life.

He walked around to the back and saw a woman some fifty yards away in what appeared to be a vegetable garden, only there weren't any vegetables. To Marshall it looked like a patch of mud.

"Hello?" he called.

The woman looked up. She was Hispanic and not a young woman. It was difficult to say how old she was from this distance. She gave him a little wave and began to walk toward him. When she got within ten feet he could see that she was probably sixty or thereabouts.

"Good morning," he said. "Uh, do you speak English? *Habla Anglais?*"

The woman smiled and said with a strong accent, "Yes, I speak English." She had a pleasant face.

"I'm looking for Manuel Delgado. Does he live here?"

The woman's smile remained on her weathered face as she answered, "He died three years ago. I'm his wife, can I help you?"

Marshall felt embarrassed. "I'm sorry, I hope I'm not disturbing you."

She shook her head. "I never have visitors. Unless you're selling something, I'm happy to have you here."

"I'm not selling anything, ma'am. I'm, uh, well, I'm a journalist. A reporter, from California. My name is Darren Marshall. I'm doing some research on . . . well, is this the Barnett ranch?"

"It used to be. It belongs to me now."

"Actually I'm trying to find out some information about the Barnetts' nieces who lived here, I think in the sixties. Would you have known them? Diane, or maybe Dana?"

"Yes, sir, I knew them. My husband and I worked on the ranch back then. Manuel was Mister Barnett's foreman for years and I helped out in the house. Would you like to come in for some iced tea?"

"I'd be delighted." Marshall was elated. Had he finally hit the jackpot?

He followed the woman to the back porch, where she removed her muddy boots and revealed bare feet. She opened the screen door for him and they went inside.

The place looked and smelled old. There was no central air conditioning—all the windows were open. This helped some, but the house was stuffy and warm. Marshall loosened his collar as the woman led him through another door and into the living room. "Make yourself at home, *Señor* Marshall," she said, disappearing through an archway. "I'll be right back." Marshall figured the kitchen was in that direction.

The living room was tidy and furnished with what were now antiques from the early twentieth century. The easy chair looked well used, as did the sofa and rocking chair. There was an old-fashioned stone fireplace on one side of the room, the mantle of which was covered with fading black and white photographs in frames. No television.

Marshall examined the photographs while he waited. Most of them were of a Hispanic family and he recognized the woman in a few of the pictures. The man he presumed to be Manuel was a large, burly fellow with short black hair and a mustache. Apparently the Delgados had a child, a girl, as there were several shots of her at various stages of growth.

Marshall picked up a frame that was particularly interesting. It was a shot of Manuel with a tall Caucasian man in a cowboy hat. He had a stern, rugged face and looked as if he wasn't pleased that his picture was being taken.

"That's Mister Roy and my husband, Manuel," the woman said as she came in the room, carrying two glasses of tea. She placed one on the coffee table and then sat in the rocker.

"Mrs. Delgado, I didn't catch your first name?" Marshall said, replacing the frame on the mantle.

"Marisol," the woman said.

Marshall sat on the sofa and took a long drink.

"You know, I was wondering if someone would ever come around asking about those girls," Mrs. Delgado said.

"So they really were twins?" he asked.

"Yes. They were beautiful children. So . . . white, with golden blond hair!"

Marshall got out his notepad and said, "Suppose we start at the beginning—you know, how you came to be here and all that."

"Manuel and I came here in nineteen fifty-eight. Mister Roy hired Manuel 'cause he was good with cattle and had experience down in Mexico. And he was cheap. Mister Roy wasn't a big spender, but at the time we couldn't find anything else. I didn't get a wage. We lived in the cabin next to the barn. That's before I had my daughter."

"What were the Barnetts like?"

"Miz Edna was real nice to us. She was a good person, a Christian. Mister Roy, well, that's a different story. He was probably the meanest man I ever met in my life."

"Is that so?"

"I don't think I *ever* saw him smile or laugh. I know he treated Miz Edna pretty bad. He hit her. He even hit me a couple of times. Manuel couldn't confront him, though. He needed the work. Couldn't afford to get fired. So he kept his mouth shut. I don't blame him. There was nowhere else for us to go. Manuel was a good man."

Marshall had the feeling that the old woman really wanted to talk. It was as if she had a story to tell and she'd been waiting decades to relate it.

"And the Barnetts raised cattle, I take it?"

"Uh huh. Did pretty well, too."

"Now, what about the twins?"

"Diane and Dana came to live here in nineteen sixty-six. They were very young, not yet in grade school. I remember that day distinctly because Mister Roy made such a big fuss about it. He got drunk before they arrived and broke one of Miz Edna's china dishes. He didn't want them here. They came down from Illinois, where they lived until their mother died. Their father died of a heart attack, very young, not long after the girls were born. Their mother died from—I think—cancer. Roy was their father's older brother and he was the only kin so he had to take them. He didn't want to. He hated having those girls in the house."

"How come?"

"He hated children," the woman said. "He didn't want me having kids either. I didn't have my little girl until after Mister Roy died."

"When did he die?"

"Nineteen seventy-six. I thought I was too old by then to have children, but I did all right. Manuela was born a year later. We named her after her father. Miz Edna was good to her and to us after Mister Roy passed on. In fact, she willed us the ranch. That's why I still live here. Miz Edna's in a nursing home now. She lost her memory."

"Where's your little girl now?"

"In Dallas and she's not so little anymore! She works as a nurse. I don't see her often enough." The woman smiled warmly.

"How long were the twins here?"

A cloud passed over the old woman's face. "That was a bad time," she said. "A lot of unhappiness in this house. A lot of secrets." She shook her head. "I fear the devil was in this house during those years."

"Why is that?"

"Bad things happened."

When she wouldn't elaborate further, Marshall moved on. "Tell me about the girls."

"Like I said, they were so pretty. Always together. You couldn't separate them if you tried. They shoulda been joined at the hip, they were that close. They did everything together. Slept in the same bed, too, and Mister Roy didn't much like that. He was very strict. He wouldn't let them go to school, so Miz Edna had to teach 'em here on the ranch. He made 'em work, too. They had to milk the cows, feed the chickens, work the hay. He made 'em read the Bible every day. He called himself a Baptist but if you ask me he didn't have a Christian bone in his body." All of a sudden the woman smiled broadly. "I just remembered something. The girls always called each other 'Sweetie.' It was a game they played. It was always, 'Hey, Sweetie, you wanna do this?' 'No, Sweetie, I'm doing that.' 'Come on, Sweetie, or I'll go without you.' 'You better wait 'till I'm finished, Sweetie, then I'll come, too.' That sort of thing. It drove Mister Roy crazy."

Marshall took a sip of tea and then asked, "So what kind of bad things happened?"

It was clear that this was something that Marisol Delgado was uncomfortable discussing but she said, "*Señor* Marshall, I've wanted to tell someone about this for so many years but I didn't dare. I thought it would be doing wrong to Miz Edna."

"But if she's got dementia, how would she know?" He realized it was a tacky thing to say but Marisol responded favorably.

"That's what I'm beginning to think, too. I've held this secret long enough and I'd like to get it off my chest."

He looked at her expectantly.

"Around the time the twins went into puberty, I guess they were nine or ten, Mister Roy started to change his attitude toward them. You know what I mean?"

Marshall thought he did but didn't want to say. "Uh, not really."

"First he separated them at night. Made them sleep in separate bedrooms. This happened after one awful night when he caught them, uhm, well he caught them without their pajamas on. In bed."

Marshall wrinkled his brow and the psychoanalyst in him took over. "Well, girls—and boys—of that age often experiment with sex. Especially siblings. It's part of adolescence."

She raised her eyebrows and said, "I suppose so."

"And Mister Barnett took umbrage to that," he ventured.

"Took what?" she asked.

"He didn't like it."

"No," the woman answered. "He did not. He had to face the fact that these two pretty girls were growing up and had sexual feelings. So, after separating 'em into two different rooms, he became extra nice to 'em. He let 'em off easy on their chores and brought home ice cream— something he never used to do—and other little presents. The thing is . . . he was going into their bedrooms at night after Miz Edna had gone to bed."

Marshall felt his stomach turn. He was afraid it was something like that.

"He . . . abused them?" he asked.

The woman nodded. "Diane wouldn't let him. She fought him and fought him. I'd say that he probably had his way with her, by force, and then he lost interest in her because Dana . . . well, Dana was a more willing victim. I fear that poor girl suffered terribly but she relished the attention he gave her. Naturally, the relationship between the two girls changed. All of a sudden they became rivals. Mister Roy started focusing all his good will toward Dana and ignored Diane. Soon it was just Dana who got presents and favors. Diane got jealous. The girls fought."

Marshall realized that it was a classic case of abuse. Many times young girls who are sexually abused by their fathers or other family members go along with it either out of shame, fear of being caught, or because they are finally receiving affection from the patriarch of the home.

"Did Mrs. Barnett know what was going on?" he asked.

Marisol nodded. "She did. But she would never say anything. Mister Roy would just smack her if she did. It was a bad, bad situation."

"How long did this go on?" he asked.

"Until the girls were around twelve maybe, I can't remember."

Marshall shook his head and made a note. "That's terrible."

"Not as terrible as what happened that summer in nineteen seventy-three," the woman said, her eyes welling with moisture.

He looked at her and urged the woman to go on.

"Why do you want to write about these girls?" she asked suddenly.

"One of them has become famous. Do you read the papers?" he asked. "Watch television?"

She shook her head.

"Diane is wanted for the murder of her husband," he said.

The woman blinked. "Diane?"

"Yes."

Marisol looked as if she might cry. "Then Dana never got well," she whispered.

Marshall wasn't sure he heard her right. "What did you say, Mrs. Delgado?"

"Come with me, *Señor* Marshall, I want to show you something." The woman stood and walked toward the back door. Marshall followed her outside past the barn on a dirt path through the brush. They eventually got to a small clearing where a single tombstone stood, surrounded by freshly cut flowers. The name on the tombstone was "Manuel Jesus Delgado," along with the dates of birth and death.

"Here's where my Manuel lies," she said. She gave the sign of the cross and then walked on, for the path continued. After walking forty more feet they came to yet another clearing, but this one was unkempt and overrun with weeds and wild vegetation.

Two eroded tombstones stood in the ground. One read: "Roy Wayne Barnett, b. 1908, d. 1976."

Written on the second gravestone were the words: "Diane Louise Barnett, b. 1961, d. 1973."

DAVID'S JOURNAL

We're finally on our way home! At this moment we're driving out of Los Angeles, headed back to Illinois. Mom's driving a new Malibu she bought on the way here (it's really a used car). We should be home in a couple of days, maybe three.

A lot has happened since I last wrote in my real journal. The one note I wrote in the hospital was the only time I put pen to paper while I was there. I don't know why but I just didn't feel like writing. I used some tape to stick that note in my journal so it's in the right order.

I was in the hospital for three days! I was still having some arrhythmia with my heart (the nurse told me how to spell that word) and they wanted to keep me under watch. Mom came to see me every day and stayed until they kicked her out. Mister Belgrad came all three days, too, but he didn't stay as long. He hung around for an hour or two and then left my Mom with me. I think she was staying with him while I was in the hospital. I can tell they like each other.

I feel pretty good now and I'm more or less back to normal.

When I checked out of the hospital this morning, Mom had her things in the car, ready to go. Mister Belgrad wasn't there. She said that he left earlier to go back to New York and that he said to tell me "good-bye" and "good luck." I asked Mom if we'll see him again and she wasn't sure. I guess that means maybe.

It looks like I'll have that operation on my heart pretty soon. They'll have to repair the valve that leaks and do some other minor things. The doctor in L.A. said he thought I was old enough now. Mom said she would look into it as soon as we're "settled." I didn't know what she meant by that so I asked her. Mom said that things might be different when we get back to Lincoln Grove. She said there's a possibility we'll have to leave our home there and go live somewhere else. She wasn't sure. She has to work out all her legal problems.

She did have some good news, though. She talked to her lawyer in Illinois—his name is Mister Lewis—and told him that she was on her way home. Mister Lewis told her that they've dropped the murder charge! What happened was somebody smart looked into the case and determined that my Dad was killed much earlier than when my Mom was seen running from his house. Like a day or two earlier! They also determined that his murder was similar to one that happened in Chicago and another that happened in New York. Mom told me that Mister Belgrad helped by telling the police in New York and Chicago about the details of my Dad's murder. The Lincoln Grove chief of police was all set to hang Mom for Dad's murder, but some "Feds" came in and took over the case. In no time they discounted the police chief's suspicions and figured out right off the bat that Mom didn't kill my Dad. They now know who the prime suspect is.

It turns out that Emo killed him.

I hate that guy now. He was pretty nice to me on the way to California, even if he did kidnap me. But now I know for sure that he really is a killer. Or he was. Mom said I don't have to worry about him ever again. He most likely died in a huge fire with his boss, Aaron Valentine, the "King of Porn." That's what the newspapers are calling Mister Valentine. His death was big news, in all the papers and on TV. He and Emo were at some kind of warehouse and it burned down. Police said there was some gunplay involved, too. The fire was probably arson *but they don't know who did it. Maybe one of Valentine's men. Who knows and who cares? I'm just glad they're gone.*

To tell you the truth, I think Mom and Mister Belgrad had something to do with it, but she's not talking.

When we get back, Mom has to give a statement to the DA about my Dad's murder and tell him what she knows. She told Mister Lewis that she would be ready to cooperate when she gets back to Lincoln Grove. The other thing is that Mom has to face her school board regarding her job. I don't know how that's going to turn out.

Anyway, I'm just glad to be out of that stupid hospital. I feel like I've aged a few years since I was kidnapped.

Thank God I'm not any taller, though!

CHAPTER FORTY-FIVE

The worst part about Diane's appearance at the District Attorney's office in Rolling Meadows, Illinois, was getting past the reporters in front of the building. It seemed that every newspaper and television station in the world was represented and they all wanted a piece of her. She was the Porn Star Mom who was cleared of murder charges and then returned home after a mysterious trip to California. They all wanted interviews. *60 Minutes* wanted to do a story about her, Jerry Springer was dying to have her on his show, a well-known Hollywood film producer was interested in the rights to her life story, and *Playboy* offered a lot of money for her to pose in the nude.

Through Scotty, she refused to talk to anyone except a reporter named Darren Marshall, from Los Angeles. He had been particularly insistent and when he mentioned that he was a friend of Eric Gilliam's, she made an exception. She agreed to see Marshall at Scotty's office after the hearing with the DA.

It was actually Nick Belgrad who had advised her to be extremely selective with regard to the media. It was best that she not come under more scrutiny than was necessary. After all, she was now in the possession of three million dollars in cash.

Belgrad had worked out the deal in Los Angeles during the three days that David was still in the hospital. While Diane stayed by her son's side, Belgrad did the legwork and procured two buyers for the diamonds. The men were customers of Hiram Rabinowitz—two tough old Jews who had been trading the gems to a pro-Israel organization in the Middle East that, in turn, used them as bargaining chips in a number of clandestine transactions. The diamonds served as international currency for buying food, arms, medicine, and intelligence to support Israel's never-ending war against terrorism and anti-Semitism. The money was to come in two payments. Half was delivered to Diane in a large brown suitcase. The second payment would be rendered to Belgrad himself, in New York, and he would hold it for her until Diane could find the time and a way to get there to pick it up.

But being wealthy beyond her dreams didn't make her life worry-free. Since witnessing the fire in the warehouse, Diane's nightmares had increased and the nervous anxiety she had fought for years returned with a vengeance. Every hour of each day she craved a glass of wine—anything to calm her nerves—but she knew that if she started drinking again then she wouldn't have it together to face the DA and the district school board. The night before the hearing was particularly rough. She had gone into one of her trance states again and if David hadn't shaken her out of it at three in the morning she might never have gotten any sleep.

So it was with an unsteady constitution that Diane Boston entered the law office of James R. Tilton, the district attorney for her county. It was to be an informal interview, not a "hearing." Scotty Lewis was obliged to approve the presence of several other interested parties other than the DA—the Lincoln Grove chief of police, and school board president Judy Wilcox. The DA assured Lewis that Diane was not in any kind of legal jeopardy and that the session would be "painless."

Diane felt faint when she walked into the conference room. She couldn't understand why she was so nervous, for her life appeared to be on the upswing. She was rich, she had been cleared of murder, and although it had taken her a day or two away from Belgrad to convince herself that it was true, she was in love. She hadn't felt such an emotion in years and she wasn't sure how to handle it. Diane figured it was one of the many things exacerbating her anxiety.

"Can I get you anything, Mrs. Boston?" DA Tilton asked her after he had greeted them.

"Some water, please," she said. Feeling weak, she took a seat before looking around the room. She recognized the chief of police and Judy Wilcox.

When he brought her the water, Tilton said, "You know Chief Grabowski and Mrs. Wilcox." Diane nodded at them and smiled faintly. Mrs. Wilcox forced a smile back at her and Grabowski merely grunted.

Tilton took a seat and began by asking Diane about the day when she found Greg Boston dead in his house. She related how she had met with Lewis at his office and then came home to learn that her son had been kidnapped. Her sister Dana's producer of adult films, Aaron Valentine, had some kind of a grudge against her. When the porn king found out about Diane's existence, he, too, mistakenly identified her as Dana. He had David abducted and brought to L.A. in an effort to lure her there. She quickly made plans to leave town and stopped at her ex-husband's house to tell him of those plans. That's when she found his body.

The revelation of David's kidnapping was news to Tilton. He sat forward and asked, "Why didn't you call the police? The FBI?"

"Because my son's life was at stake," she said. "I couldn't."

"And what happened when you got to L.A.?" Tilton asked.

"Nothing," Diane answered. "David got away from his captors during one of Valentine's wild parties. He was able to call me on my cell phone and I found him. We were very, very lucky."

Tilton consulted his notes and then asked, "I understand that this Aaron Valentine was killed a few days ago in a fire. Do you know anything about it?"

She shook her head. "No. I was in the city when it happened, though. It was the same night that David escaped from Valentine's home in Woodland Hills. There was some kind of big party going on. David called me, like I said, and I picked him up in West Hollywood. I brought David to Cedars-Sinai Hospital's emergency room because of his heart condition. That's where I was when the fire at Valentine's warehouse occurred. David was in the hospital for three days. You're welcome to check."

Tilton asked, "The police now suspect this man, Emo Tuff, to be the killer of your former husband. Do you know him?"

"No."

"Do you have any idea why he would kill your husband?"

Diane shrugged. "He worked for Aaron Valentine. Valentine wanted me. Mister Tuff must have come looking for me and he found Greg instead." It was the best she could do.

Tilton continued. "I'm sure that Mister Lewis told you that an informant supplied the information that linked your husband's case with two similar murders, one in Chicago and one in New York. Are you aware of this?"

"I heard that, yes," she said.

"Did you know the victims in these cases?" Tilton looked at his notes. "A Mister Moses Rabinowitz and a Mister Hiram Rabinowitz?"

"No."

"Why do you think Tuff killed them and then your husband within the space of a week?"

"How should I know?" she asked. "I just said I didn't know them. Aaron Valentine and his people were criminals. Perhaps what Mister Tuff did in New York and Chicago was his business, completely separate from his interest in me."

Tilton nodded and wrote something down. "Well," he said, "that's not our concern. The Chicago and New York police are handling those investigations. Do you have any idea where Emo Tuff is now?"

She didn't want to say that he had perished in the fire with his boss. How would she know that?

"No," she answered.

Tilton seemed satisfied with that. "Mrs. Boston, now I'd like to ask you some other things that have no bearing on your former husband's murder. However, I'm asking these questions to satisfy my own curiosity about your case and I also think your answers will have relevancy to the school board case, which is why Mrs. Wilcox is here."

Lewis spoke up. "Is this necessary? It was our understanding that Diane only had to answer questions relating to Mister Boston."

Tilton said, "Again I stress that Mrs. Boston is under no obligation to answer these questions. I'd like to ask them anyway."

Lewis looked at Diane and she said to Tilton, "Go ahead."

Tilton nodded and read his first question. "Mrs. Boston, is your name really Diane Boston?"

"Yes, it is."

"And your name was Diane Barnett before you were married?"

"Yes, but I was using a different name. Diane Wilson."

"Why were you using an assumed name?"

"Because I was ashamed of the name Barnett. It meant too many painful things to me. I spent many years trying to forget that name. I thought I had until—" She glared at Judy Wilcox and continued, "—all that porn star business came out."

Tilton cleared his throat. "And it is still your contention that it was your twin sister, Dana, who starred in Aaron Valentine's adult films?"

"That's right."

"And your sister is missing, presumed dead?"

"Yes."

"I thought it went well," Lewis told her on the way to his office. "Although I wish you would come clean about your sister."

Diane had a headache. She rubbed her brow, closed her eyes, and said, "I just want to get all this over with. Will this interview be long?"

"As long as you want it to be, Diane."

Darren Marshall was already at Lewis' office when they entered. Pleasantries were exchanged and the three of them went into Scotty's small conference room for the interview.

After providing everyone with glasses of water, Lewis began by saying, "Mister Marshall, I understand that you're writing a story about Mrs. Boston for your paper, is that correct?"

Marshall answered, "That's right."

"How do you know Eric?" Diane asked.

"We met a few years ago and have been in contact every now and then," Marshall replied. "I saw him again last week, twice. He was a great guy, it's a shame he's gone."

Diane nodded. "So. Let's get started."

Marshall went through some preliminary background questions that appeared to be completely above board and standard. Then, out of the blue, he hit Diane with a stinger.

"Mrs. Boston, isn't it true that your name is really Dana and that your sister Diane died when you were both adolescents?"

Diane felt a sledgehammer hit her chest. "What?" she managed to ask.

"Isn't it true that you and your twin sister lived for a time with Roy and Edna Barnett in Garden City, Texas, after your natural parents died?"

Lewis shifted in his seat. "Uh, I think we can stop right here. Diane, you don't—"

"Yes, it's true," Diane interrupted. She reached for the glass of water but her hand shook so badly that she spilled a little.

Lewis put a hand on her arm and said softly, "Diane, you don't have to continue if you don't want to."

"It's all right, Scotty," she whispered. She seemed to have lost her voice.

Marshall went on. "And isn't it true, Mrs. Boston, that the circumstances surrounding your sister Diane's death were never fully, how shall I say—explained? That you were accused of being instrumental in her death?"

Diane shut her eyes and softly said, "Sweetie . . ."

"I beg your pardon?" Marshall asked.

"It's not true," she answered. "I didn't do it. . . ."

"But didn't your guardians, Roy and Edna Barnett, send you away to the Fulbright Center in Dallas, Texas, shortly after Diane died? An institution for the mentally ill?"

Diane bowed her head and started to cry. "Yes."

"And you were there for four years?" Marshall asked gently.

Tears dropped onto the table at which she sat. "Yes," she said, barely audible.

Now Lewis was silent, staring at Diane. He couldn't believe what he was hearing.

"And isn't it true, Mrs. Boston," Marshall asked with as much compassion as he could muster, "that it was *you* who went to Los Angeles when you got out of the Fulbright Center? Not your twin sister but rather *you* who went and starred in adult films, using your given name of Dana?"

Diane sobbed and finally nodded her head. Marshall sat back in his chair, the interrogation complete.

The two men didn't move as they waited patiently for the broken woman in front of them to pull herself together. Lewis finally broke the spell by offering her a tissue. She took it, blew her nose, and wiped her face.

"It . . . it was an accident," she said, her voice cracking. "Sweetie and I were in the barn that day and she was angry with me. I remember . . . we were up in the hayloft. Uncle Roy had given me a present, a necklace. It was probably some cheap thing from the dime store in town but I thought it was nice. She was mad that we weren't close anymore and we got into an argument. She tried to grab the necklace and I grabbed it back. She reached for it again and it became a tug-of-war . . . and I let it go. She went tumbling backwards off the hayloft and . . . landed on her head down below."

She paused to take a sip of water. "Uncle Roy thought I did it on purpose. He sent me to Dallas and after I was there for a year, even *I* started to believe I had done it on purpose. I . . . I don't remember too much about that period or the time after that in LA. I just remember that I started using drugs and . . . I . . . lost myself . . ."

"Perhaps I can shed some light on what happened," Marshall said. "I was in Garden City, Mrs. Boston, and I spoke to Marisol Delgado. Do you remember her?"

Diane nodded.

"She told me how your Uncle Roy abused you and your sister."

Diane didn't deny it.

"Afterwards I went to Dallas and I spoke to Doctor Springfield at the Fulbright Center. Do you remember him?"

She nodded again.

Marshall continued. "He's retired now, but he was willing to talk about you. Mrs. Boston, he knew that you were innocent with regard to your sister's death. But your uncle had you believing that you were responsible, and, well, you became delusional. You were very close to your sister, as most twins are. The guilt over her death combined with the tremendous abuse both of you suffered at the hands of your uncle caused your mind to shut out the truth. However, Doctor Springfield said that you showed improvement during the four years you were there and you were released. But you didn't go back to Texas, did you?"

Diane shook her head no.

"Instead you went to Los Angeles. Doctor Springfield theorized, and I believe him, that you went to work in pornographic films and took drugs as a means of punishing yourself. You see, you'd never really gotten over the guilt you felt for 'killing' your sister."

Diane stared at him blankly.

"And then you met Angela Gilliam."

"Sweetie," Diane whispered.

"Yes, the *other* Sweetie. The woman who replaced the Sweetie you loved and lived with until she died. Angela resembled you. You were both blond, beautiful, sexy . . . for all intents and purposes, she was your twin, all over again. And you became lovers. For a while, everything was as it was before the tragedy happened. Your sister was alive again, in your mind. Am I right?"

The tears began to flow again. "Yes," she whispered.

"And then," Marshall continued, "later, after you disappeared from the adult business in nineteen eighty, you somehow convinced yourself that you could keep Diane alive by becoming her. You began to use her name from then on."

Diane was numb. She merely nodded in agreement.

"The only thing I don't know," Marshall said, "is what happened that night at Valentine's warehouse, when you and Angela Gilliam disappeared. You obviously got away, but what happened to Angela?"

CHAPTER FORTY-SIX

Angela came back to the apartment at nine o'clock in the morning. She'd been out all night.

"Where have you been?" Diane/Dana asked. She had been drinking for hours, ever since she'd realized that Angela was with Eduardo. Wearing a tattered terrycloth robe, she sat watching an old rerun of *I Dream of Jeannie* on television.

Angela ignored the question and sat on the sofa beside her roommate. "You look like hell, Sweetie," she said.

Dana glared at her and said, "Fuck you, too, Sweetie. I asked you a question."

"I was with Eduardo," she said. "I got us some stuff." She opened her purse and removed a baggie full of white powder. This improved Dana's mood a bit because she enjoyed a snort in the mornings. It picked her up and shook off the effects of the wine. But the way Angela used it worried her. It hadn't been that long since she had OD'd on heroin and was at Cedars-Sinai for a week.

"Don't you think you do too much of that stuff?" Dana asked.

Angela was already busy preparing two lines on the

coffee table. "What are you talking about?" She took a straw and inhaled the cocaine through her nose. Angela closed her eyes and sniffed hard, forcing the drug into her sinus cavities. "It's better than what I *was* doing, don't you agree? You want some?" she asked.

Dana couldn't resist. "Sure. I just don't want to get another call in the middle of the night telling me that you're in the hospital again."

After they were both pleasantly high, Angela said, "You're not mad, are you?"

Dana felt like pouting despite the euphoric effects of the coke. "What can I say? You're fucking Eduardo."

"It's no big deal. It's you I love, Sweetie," Angela said. "I do it for the stuff, you know that. He has influence over Aaron and can get me some better roles."

"You believe that?"

"Well, yeah."

"And have you gotten any better roles?"

"Not yet, but Eduardo says it'll happen soon."

"Eduardo's a slime, Sweetie. He's in charge of all the dirty business that Aaron's involved in."

Angela frowned. "What do you mean?"

"Come on, Sweetie, you know what I'm talking about," Dana answered. "The drugs, the money laundering, the guns. Who knows what else he deals? Look who he hangs out with."

"Who? You mean Vincent?"

"Yeah, him and all his slick-haired friends. They're all mobsters, Sweetie. Mafia. Cosa Nostra. Whatever you want to call them."

Angela grew quiet as Barbara Eden rambled on about pleasing her master on the television.

Dana eventually said, "I thought you said we were gonna try to quit together."

"You mean the coke?"

"No, I mean the *business*. Get out of this hellhole. Do something else. Get away from Los Angeles."

Angela said quietly, "You know what would happen if we tried, don't you?"

Dana sat up and took a sip of her wine. "What, you think we'll end up like Julie?"

Angela abruptly turned to Dana and said, "Sweetie, listen. I found out something last night and it might be something we've been waiting for."

Dana was intrigued by Angela's sudden enthusiasm. "What?"

"I overheard Eduardo talking on the phone. He's gonna make a big haul tonight. He's gonna sell a lot of coke for a bunch of diamonds. These guys from Africa are meeting with him at the warehouse around midnight. Sweetie, he said those diamonds could be worth a couple of million dollars. Maybe more."

Dana snickered and said, "So? How's that gonna help us?"

Angela shrugged. "Maybe we can get some of them. Somehow."

"Oh, right," Dana said. "Eduardo's just gonna stand back and let you grab a handful? Fat chance."

Angela shook her head. "Sorry, it was just an idea." She started to clear the coffee table of the now empty wine bottle and glasses. Dana put a hand on her arm to stop her.

"Sweetie . . ." she said, softly.

Their eyes met. It was amazing, Dana thought, how much it seemed like she was looking into a mirror whenever she gazed upon Angela's lovely face.

Dana placed her palm on Angela's cheek. "Let's go to bed," she suggested. Angela smiled and nodded.

Dana had a preliminary meeting with a film director that afternoon. She had gone to the Erotica Selecta office in Hollywood, not looking her best and with very little sleep, and discussed an upcoming feature tentatively titled *Invasion of the Body Snatches*. She didn't make a good impression. The director told her flat out that she was losing her looks and he was considering signing a newer, up-and-coming starlet. Dana told him where he could stick the role and left.

When she got home that evening, Angela was out.

Probably with Eduardo, Dana figured. Unbelievable. And after that warm and fuzzy morning together. Still, Dana couldn't be too angry at her Sweetie. After all, they were like sisters, weren't they?

She went to bed and was fast asleep when the phone call came at twelve minutes after midnight.

Dana groggily picked up the phone. "Hello?"

". . . Help me . . ."

Angela sounded drunk. No, she sounded ill. In pain. Out of it. Hearing her this way snapped Dana out of her dream state. "Sweetie? What's wrong? You sound—"

"Please . . ."

"Where are you?"

". . . Warehouse . . ."

"My God, what's happened? Sweetie?"

". . . Shot . . ."

"What? I can't hear you! Did you say—?"

The phone went dead. Angela had either dropped the receiver or hung up. Dana called her name several times but there was nothing at the other end of the line: She hung up and sat on the edge of the bed. What should she do?

Dana decided there was nothing else to do but go to her. She dressed and got into her 1973 Chevy Nova, a car that was on its last legs, and drove toward Santa Monica. She had been to the Erotica Selecta warehouse before. One of her films had been shot there but she couldn't remember which one—she had been stoned out of her mind. She did recall having to perform a variety of uncomfortable sex acts on top of boxes and crates.

The warehouse was quiet and dark although some illumination was on in the rear, where the loading dock was located. She recognized Eduardo's limousine parked back there, along with three other cars and a motorcycle. The roll-up metal door on the loading dock was shut. The light came through the window on a standard door at the top of a few steps, next to the dock ramp. Dana got out of her car, ran to the door, and tried it. It was locked, of course.

She peered through the window and saw that a couple of work lights were on inside the warehouse but she couldn't discern much besides stacks of cartons. Should she dare knock?

Dana rapped on the door. "Hello? Anyone there?" she called.

When no one responded, a sick feeling hit her stomach. Something had happened. She came down the steps and searched for another way in. She went around to the side of the building and noticed that there was a line of horizontally hinged windows approximately eight feet off the ground. A pile of empty crates had been stacked beneath one. Perhaps she could climb the crates and get inside the window . . . ?

It wasn't difficult getting on top of the crates. The window, however, took every ounce of her strength to open. It probably hadn't been budged since the building was built, and who knew how long ago that was.

She snaked through the slender window and dropped to the floor inside. Wherever she was, it was pitch dark. She lay there a moment to allow her eyes to get used to the lighting and eventually she could make out the interior of a storage room. She had barely missed falling on top of a mop bucket. Dana stood and went to the door. She cracked it open and looked out into the warehouse.

She saw nothing but boxes. She left the storage room and crept quietly through the stacks of product until she got to the center, open area of the building.

Her heart skipped a beat.

There were bodies. Dead, bloody bodies.

Dana scanned the room to make sure there wasn't anyone still alive. Then she darted out to take a closer look.

Eduardo was on his back, his Colt .45 lying nearby. His chest was ripped full of holes. Three of his henchmen were dead as well, draped over tables and chairs like rag dolls. Close to Eduardo was the body of a black man whom she didn't recognize. He, too, had been shot repeatedly. Further away, three more corpses were strewn—black men, very bloody, very grotesque.

A large open briefcase sat on top of a card table that had been set up near where Eduardo lay. The case was full of the biggest, most beautiful sparkling diamonds Dana had ever seen.

Angela was nowhere in sight.

"Sweetie?" she called.

Then she noticed the trail of blood leading off between the stacks of boxes. Dana carefully followed it to the warehouse office, and there she found Angela lying in a pool of blood. She had somehow sustained a gunshot wound in the head, crawled to the office, and phoned Dana from there before collapsing.

Dana examined her and listened to the girl's chest. The heart was beating! Sweetie was breathing!

They had to get out of there. Valentine and his people would surely come soon. Maybe the police, too. Dana dragged Angela's body out of the office toward the loading dock. Before taking her outside, though, Dana removed Angela's blouse, tore it, and laid it over the lip of the open incinerator. Then she removed her own blue jeans and dropped them on the floor next to the furnace. She also dropped her wallet next to the pants after retrieving her driver's license and what money she had. Perhaps it would appear that both Angela and Dana Barnett had been thrown into the incinerator. Dana had heard the rumors floating around Erotica Selecta that this is what had happened to some of the other actors who had gone missing.

Dana struggled with Angela's limp body, pulling it toward the roll-up steel door. She wasn't sure how to operate it but she examined the controls, punched a button, and watched as the door rose slowly with a horrible grinding noise. Dana glanced at the top of the tall opening and saw that the mechanism wobbled and appeared to be on the verge of collapsing. No wonder it was so noisy. . . .

Once the door was all the way up, she pulled Angela out onto the dock ramp and stood there for a moment to catch her breath. "I'm gonna save you, Sweetie," she said to the blond, bloody girl lying in front of her.

Eventually she got a second wind and picked up Angela's body, carried her to the car, and laid her in the back seat of the Nova. Dana went back inside the warehouse to make sure she hadn't left any other signs of her presence besides the torn clothes in front of the incinerator. She then stood over the case of diamonds and carefully picked one up to examine it. It glittered and shone like nothing she had seen before.

These belong to Sweetie, she thought. Without a second thought, she closed the briefcase, picked it up, and took Eduardo's Colt .45 from the floor.

And as fate would have it, the loading door mechanism came loose from the ceiling and fell directly on her head just as she was walking outside.

She wasn't sure how long she was out. When she opened her eyes, she lay on the loading dock ramp, the night sky above her. All was quiet.

Her head hurt like hell.

She sat up and the earth tilted. She immediately felt nauseated, crawled to the side of the ramp and vomited. After a few minutes, she was able to stand.

Where was she?

Oh, right. The warehouse. Sweetie was in the car. Dana had been a bad girl and was hurt. It was up to her, Diane, to see that her sister was taken care of.

Diamonds. Sweetie's diamonds.

The briefcase was there on the ramp, where she had fallen. So was Eduardo's gun.

What had happened? Something had hit her on the head.

She touched the back of her hair and felt something wet and sticky. She wiped her bloody hand on her bare leg.

Where were her pants?

She had done something with them but couldn't remember.

Best to get the hell out of there.

Diane took the gun and the briefcase full of gems, and then went down the ramp to her car.

The girl with the gunshot wound was in the backseat.

"Dana?" Diane said. "Sweetie?"

She made sure her twin sister was still breathing by holding her finger under the unconscious woman's nose.

Have to get her to a hospital. But not in L.A.

Diane got behind the wheel and drove away from the scene that would haunt her in her nightmares for years to come.

She was going to save her sister this time. Dana wasn't going to die. Not this time. She wouldn't be blamed for her sister's death this time. No sir.

The drive to Nevada was a blur. Somehow she got across the state line, driving into the desert, the sun appearing magically in the sky and brightening the rugged landscape. All the while, brief flashes of memory shot in and out of her brain as she drove.

"I want to see the necklace, Sweetie . . ."

"You can't; it's mine!"

"Let me have it!"

"No!"

She found the small church by accident. The white building with a cross on top of the roof was on the opposite side of the highway. As she drove past, Diane noticed three nuns getting out of a car and walking inside. Diane took the next exit, turned around, and got on the service road back to the building. Nuns were nurses, weren't they? They always were in the movies.

She carried Dana's body into the church and begged for the sisters to help them. One of the women insisted on taking Dana to the hospital but Diane said that she and her sister had to remain anonymous. No police. No authorities. Men were after them. Men with guns wanted to kill them. Surprisingly, the nuns took pity on her.

One of the sisters had an idea. She had a colleague who ran a medical center in a small town not far away. She would see that the two bloodied, blond women would get medical care—no questions asked.

Diane stayed with the nuns for a month while Dana lay in intensive care. Eventually she was told that nothing could be done for her sister. Dana was in a coma. Alive, but dead to the world. Diane made arrangements for the nuns to keep Dana there until she made up her mind what to do. She left Nevada and drove east, eventually winding up in Chicago, near where she and Dana had been born.

Diane missed her parents. The only memory she had of her father was that he was a tall, lanky man with thick glasses and a bad heart. He had died when she and her sister were three. Or four. She couldn't remember.

Her mother had died not long afterward.

Could she start anew in Illinois?

Diane made arrangements to transfer Dana to another quiet, clandestine convalescent center run by nuns, situated in central Illinois. It was isolated, off the beaten path, far away from where the bad men might find her.

Diane would never let Dana die. It was her promise to her sister. She had let her die once but it wasn't going to happen a second time. The diamonds would pay for her continued care. That's the way it was going to work from then on. Diane would start a new life, change her last name, go to school, and get a job. Maybe even get married and have children. She would leave the past behind her.

   And never pull the plug on Sweetie, for someday she'd get well. . . .

CHAPTER FORTY-SEVEN

Someone once said, "The truth shall set you free." This was certainly applicable to Diane. Facing the facts about herself and her past was just the beginning of a long road to recovery from a mental illness she didn't realize she had. As the story of that fateful night in the warehouse came out between hysterics and tears, Diane experienced a catharsis that left her trembling and exhausted. Scotty Lewis helped her out of his office and offered to take her to the hospital but she refused to go. She just wanted to go home and sleep for a day.

And that's what she did.

When she awoke, birds were chirping outside her window and the sun was shining brightly. She looked at the clock and saw that it was 7:45. In the morning?

She got out of bed, went to the bathroom, and then checked on David. She looked in his room and saw that he was in bed, asleep. Something would have to be done about his schoolwork but Diane didn't have the strength to deal with that now. She had herself to think about first. There was a lot to be done.

Diane went into the kitchen to make coffee. There were messages on the answering machine so she listened to them one by one. The first was from Scotty, who expressed concern for her wellbeing and asked that she call him when she could. The second message was from Darren Marshall, the reporter who had successfully forced her to look into the mirror of her soul. He, too, expressed concern for her and hoped that his revelations had not upset her too greatly. He then added that he wanted to be the first to offer a sum of money for the rights to her story so that he could write a book.

She had to laugh at that. She *hated* Darren Marshall for what he had done. At the same time, however, she was grateful to him. It was as if he had turned on the lights in her dark heart so that she could clearly see the depths of her madness. For that was what it was, she admitted to herself. A shrink would eventually help her understand everything better but she knew enough about psychology to realize that she was ill. She could see that her delusions about her sister were at the core of her problems with Greg and the marriage, her self-destructive life in LA as an adult film actress, and her inability to properly deal with Angela Gilliam. After nearly twenty-five years, Angela had shown no signs of recovery from a coma and Diane had stubbornly kept her alive because of a promise made to a phantom. She thought that perhaps it was time to finally let go of that part of her past.

There were other messages from reporters and newscasters and another one from *60 Minutes*, but she deleted them all without bothering to write down numbers.

The last message on the machine was from Nick Belgrad. He stated he was back in New York and for her to let him know when she was going to come and collect the other half of her "belongings." He wished her well and said he missed her.

She smiled at the memory of his scruffy beard, the long Jesus-like hair, and his solid body that smelled of musk. The man had given her more physical pleasure in three days than she had received from anyone in her life, except possibly Angela. Perhaps there really was something there with Nick. It was worth exploring.

Diane took the fresh coffee into the living room and turned on the television. She sat on the sofa and found a local morning news show. She watched as the anchors discussed a deadly fire that had occurred in one of the suburbs and a bank robbery that was reported in Chicago. Then the handsome newscaster was handed a piece of paper and he stated, "This just in. Lincoln High School in Lincoln Grove has yet another public relations problem following on the heels of the Porn Star Mom scandal that hit it last week. A teacher has been accused of having sexual relations with a student. Peter Davis, a social studies instructor, has been suspended indefinitely for having an improper relationship with a female senior. The girl's parents filed charges against Davis after their daughter informed them that she was pregnant."

Diane's mouth dropped open and she sat forward in the seat. The TV showed a video clip of Davis, accompanied by a lawyer, ascending the steps of the courthouse. He looked haggard and attempted to shield his face from the camera.

She had to laugh. She set down her coffee cup and laughed so hard that her side hurt. Diane knew who the senior had to be—the lovely Heather. This was rich, she thought. This made her day.

After a while, David got up and wandered into the living room.

"Hi, honey," she said. "Sleep good?"

"Yeah," he said. "You were really out of it yesterday. Are you okay?"

She held out her arms. He went to her and let her hug him. "I'm fine, honey," she said. "And I'm gonna get better and better. You'll see."

"What are we going to do now, mom?"

"How would you like to go live in New York?" she asked.

His eyebrows went up. He had never considered anything that exotic. "Sure. I guess so. I sure want to leave this place."

She nodded. "Me too. You hungry?"

"Starving."

After they had eaten an elaborate breakfast of pancakes and eggs, she picked up the phone and called Scotty Lewis.

"Scotty," she said, "I'm sorry you had to witness my nervous breakdown yesterday. At least that's what it felt like."

"Don't think anything of it, Diane, er, Dana," he said. "What the heck am I supposed to call you now?"

"I'm going to keep the name Diane," she said. "In honor of my sister. She was the good one. I guess I had the right idea back then after that piece of metal fell on my head. Diane was reborn in my mind and I became her. I can't go back now, it'll be easier this way."

Lewis didn't comment. "How are you feeling?" he asked instead.

"Much better, thanks."

"I hope you're going to take my advice and get some professional help?"

"I am. Listen, I need you to do something for me."

"What's that?"

She took a breath and said, "Call Judy Wilcox. Tell the school board to forget it. I'm not coming back."

"Really? Are you sure? We can still fight them."

"Are you kidding? I'm sure she wouldn't want me anywhere *near* her students. And after what happened this morning with Peter Davis . . ."

"Yeah, I saw that," he said, chuckling. "Sweet justice, eh?"

"David and I are going to leave Illinois, Scotty. So just tell the school board what they can do with their job. Not in those same words, of course."

He laughed. "Sure. When do you think you'll be leaving?"

"As soon as possible."

She drove south with David, leaving the sprawling Chicago suburbs behind and into the wide-open plains of central Illinois. The two-and-a-half hour drive passed quickly with her son in the car, for they sang along with the radio and made fun of highway signs.

As usual, there were no other cars in the visitors' spaces in front of Saint Mary's Convalescent Home. The place was just as quiet and inconspicuous as it had been the day she brought Angela there in 1980.

The nun at the reception desk escorted them to Sister Jarrett's office, where the head nun was busy on her computer.

"Oh, hello," she said. "Come in. And who's this young man with you?"

"This is my son, David," Diane said. "I've brought him to see, uhm, my sister." Diane had decided that she wouldn't confuse the nuns with the details of Angela's real identity. Every legal document that pertained to the patient bore the name Dana Barnett. The only people who knew that she was really Angela Gilliam were Diane, Scotty, and Darren Marshall. Scotty had prepared the life support termination papers and Diane had decided to make the deal with Marshall in exchange for a sum of money and an agreement that he would never reveal the woman's true identity as well as her own.

After presenting the appropriate paperwork to Sister Jarrett, Diane asked, "When will this be done?"

The sister replied, "Doctor Patterson will of course need to see this and be on hand. I imagine it will be done in the next day or two. I can let you know—"

"I don't want to be here," Diane said. The sister looked surprised. "I mean, I just, want you to take care of it and let me know when the funeral home should come and pick her up. I've made all the arrangements, as you can see there in the folder I just gave you."

Sister Jarrett nodded and said, "Yes, everything appears to be in order." She looked hard at Diane and asked, "Are you sure this is what you want to do?"

Diane sighed. "Yes, sister. It's been a long time. Dana needs to rest in peace, don't you think?"

"I'm sure that Christ will welcome her into Heaven. Mercy is a subjective term and can be interpreted in a number of ways, on a case by case basis. It is not my place to pass judgement on what family members should do in a case such as this one, but if it will make you feel better I can say this with a clear conscience—and that is I think you're doing the right thing."

"Thank you, sister," Diane said. "May we see her now?"

"Of course."

The nun led them into the private room where Angela lay like the Sleeping Beauty. When they were alone, Diane said to her son, "This is your aunt, David. I'm sorry you never got to know her. But it's time for me to say good-bye to her, so I suppose you must, too."

David looked at the comatose woman and didn't know what to say. He just nodded and held his mother's hand.

Diane leaned close to Angela, kissed her on the forehead and then lightly on the lips.

"Good-bye, Sweetie," she said. "Take care of yourself."

Diane brushed back a tear, touched Angela's hand one last time, and then left the building with her son.

CHAPTER FORTY-EIGHT

It was dark by the time Diane and David returned to the little apartment in Lincoln Grove. The drive back from central Illinois had been remarkably different from the journey down. David noticed that Diane was quiet and introspective, despite his attempts to start up some car games. She had put a stop to it by simply saying, "I'm not in the mood, honey." The entire experience at Saint Mary's was bizarre for David—he never knew he *had* an aunt, much less one that was in a coma for twenty-five years. It was difficult for him to feel any kind of emotion for the woman.

"What do you want for dinner?" his mother asked him as they pulled into the one-car garage.

"At this point, anything," David replied. "I'm hungry, are you?"

She shrugged. "I guess." They got out of the car, unlocked the door to the kitchen, and then punched the button to close the automatic garage door.

David turned on the lights in the kitchen and proceeded to walk through the living room toward his bedroom. Diane put her purse on the kitchen counter and then opened the refrigerator to see what she could improvise for supper.

"Hey, Mom," David called from the hallway.

"What?"

"Come here."

"I'm trying to figure out what to do for dinner, honey. What is it?"

"You better come here."

He sounded strange. Diane closed the fridge and went to the front hall where David was standing.

"Look," he said, pointing to the front door. It was slightly ajar.

"Didn't I lock the front door?" Diane asked, horrified. She went closer and then saw that the lock was smashed. Someone had broken into the apartment. "David," she said softly. "Go back into the kitchen."

"Mom?" David's eyes went wide.

"Just do as I say."

As he turned to go, Diane peered into the dark hallway leading to the two bedrooms. She flicked on the light and saw nothing amiss. Taking one step at a time she first looked in David's room. She turned on his light and everything appeared to be all right. Her own bedroom door was closed but she always kept it that way. She stepped softly to the door and listened for the slightest sound on the other side. There was silence.

She abruptly flung the door open, reached inside, and turned on the light.

The room was empty. Her bed was made and the same clothes she had left draped over a chair were still there. Nothing seemed disturbed.

Diane put a foot over the threshold, looked in all the corners, and breathed a sigh of relief. The break-in was puzzling but apparently whoever had done it had gotten cold feet and left without taking anything.

"It's okay, David," she called. "No one's here."

Her heart was pounding and she needed a drink of

water. She walked into her bathroom and turned on the light, then reached for the plastic cup on the counter.

The black figure appeared in the corner of her eye and she screamed. The tall, hulking man swung an arm at her and she felt the sharp sting of a blade on her upper arm.

Diane's training in martial arts came into play and once again saved her life. It was pure instinct for her to raise her left arm and block a second attack. She simultaneously twisted her body to deliver a kick to the assailant's groin but she missed, hitting the man's thigh instead. Although the two maneuvers successfully surprised the attacker long enough for her to leap backward out of the bathroom, she lost her balance and failed to land on her feet. Diane tumbled onto her rear and back, slamming her head on the side of her bed.

"Mom?" David came running when he heard her scream. Standing just outside the bedroom, he saw the intruder as the man stepped out of the bathroom.

It was some kind of monster. He was dressed in black but the leather was torn in places. The face was also dark, with repulsive red splotches covering most of his features. The thing had long, dirty hair but there were patches missing from a blackened scalp.

David suddenly realized he was looking at a burn victim. The skin on the man's face, scalp, and hands was hideously ulcerated, the open sores having been scabbed over with black and brown crust.

It was Emo Tuff.

The eye patch was gone and there was a bottomless pit where his eyeball should have been.

David screamed.

Tuff turned to the boy, his one good eye ablaze with hate and fury. Something like a snarl escaped from the man's deformed mouth.

"Run, David!" Diane yelled. She attempted to scramble up the side of the bed to get out of Tuff's way but he had focused his attention back to her. He grabbed her leg and pulled her toward him, ready to strike her in the thigh with the stiletto but she kicked him in the stomach with the free leg. The blow did little damage but it caused his aim to go off as he thrust the blade deep into the mattress. He had to let go of her leg in order to pull out the knife, giving her the chance she needed to get away.

David was frozen, unable to move.

"David! Run! Call 911!" Diane yelled as she flipped her body over the bed to the other side. The boy snapped out of it and quickly ran down the hall toward the living room and kitchen.

Tuff moved to the edge of the bed, blocking Diane's way out of the bedroom. He held the stiletto in front of him, underhanded, ready to stab or slice his prey as soon as she got close enough.

David made it to the kitchen, picked up the phone, and punched 9-1-1. Nothing happened. He tried again and then realized there was no dial tone. The phone was completely dead. Tuff had most likely cut the wires.

He cursed to himself and wondered what he should do. He could run outside and try to get help or he could stay and attempt to defend his mother. David looked around the kitchen for some kind of weapon, then opened the utensil drawer. He grabbed the biggest and sharpest knife he could see, the one his mother always used to carve turkeys on Thanksgiving. Without thinking of the peril, he ran back to the hallway in time to see Tuff, the man's back to him, facing his mother with the bed between them.

David rushed at the attacker, jumped, and plunged the carving knife into Tuff's back. The blade caught on something hard—probably a rib, David thought—and glanced off without penetrating too deeply. It was enough to hurt the man, though. Tuff roared like a beast and twisted his torso fast and hard, knocking David off of him. David crashed into his mother's dresser and fell to the floor.

"David!" his mother cried. A primal, protective instinct motivated Diane to jump on top of the bed and leap at Tuff, throwing all her weight at him. He grappled with her but her momentum was too great—Tuff fell back through the open bedroom door and into the hall with Diane on top of him. She pummeled him repeatedly with both fists but his strength was far greater. He rolled her onto her back, gaining the dominant position. He raised the stiletto and prepared to bury it in her chest when David picked up the ceramic lamp from his mother's nightstand and shattered it on the back of Tuff's head.

The big man stiffened and collapsed on top of Diane. She shrieked and wiggled out from under him.

"Oh my God, David!" she sobbed as the boy ran to her. They hugged each other and then moved back, realizing how close they were to the killer.

"Is he dead?" David asked.

"I hope so," she said. "Are you all right?"

"I hit my head but I'm okay. What about you?"

"I think I'm okay." She got to her feet and took a quick look at herself. There was a nasty bleeding cut on one arm but otherwise she was just a little bruised.

"Did you call the police?" she asked.

"The line's dead."

"Then let's get out of here." She took his hand and they went to the living room. "There's something I need to get first," she said. Diane stopped long enough to open the bottom of her china cabinet, where she usually stored linens and tablecloths. Lately, though, it had been the hiding place for the suitcase full of the cash she had received for the diamonds.

David stood and watched her pull out the heavy case. "What's that?" he asked.

"Our future," she said.

She stood with the suitcase in hand, ready to carry it

to the kitchen and out into the garage—but Emo Tuff appeared from the hallway and grabbed David from behind.

David yelled and struggled but Tuff's arm was like a vise. The killer put the stiletto to the boy's neck and looked at Diane with the mad, bloodshot eye. Tuff grunted something unintelligible.

"Don't hurt him, please!" Diane pleaded. "What do you want?"

Tuff gestured for her to drop the suitcase and she did so without hesitation. The killer then motioned for her to back away. She retreated a few feet and the man came forward, the boy still in his grip. Tuff stood by the suitcase, now faced with the dilemma of choosing which hand he should use to pick up the case—the one holding David or the one clutching the stiletto.

Diane continued to back up until she was against the kitchen counter. She felt her purse, turned slightly to pick it up, and clutched it in front of her body as if it might protect her. "Let him go. Please? Take me instead."

Tuff snarled and said something but the sound that came out of his mouth was more like a grotesque gurgle.

Diane snapped opened the purse with one hand as she spoke. "He's just a boy. It's me you really want. Let him go."

Tuff held his captive tightly but Diane could see the doubt in the man's bloodshot eye. He stared at her for a tense half-minute, grunted, and finally released David.

As her son bolted toward the kitchen, Diane drew the Colt .45 from her purse, pointed it at Tuff, and squeezed the trigger. The earsplitting report echoed in the small living room as the bullet propelled Tuff backward. He fell into the television, twisted, and plummeted to the floor, face down. Diane and David didn't move. They were too traumatized to act, fearful that the killer would just get up and chase them again if they ran.

When the pool of blood began to spread on the carpet beneath the man's torso, Diane lowered the gun.

"Is it over?" David asked.

Diane fell to her knees and dropped the gun as David went to her. They hugged again and she answered, "Yes, David. This time it's over."

David's Journal

I'm writing this in the car. We just crossed the state line from Illinois into Indiana.

Mom made the news again. They still call her the "Porn Star Mom" even though it's been established that her sister Dana was the porn star. I guess she'll have to live with that name the rest of her life. Anyway, after that night at the apartment all the newspapers called her a hero. "Porn Star Mom Saves Son" and "Porn Star Mom a Hero" were just a couple of the headlines. She was on TV and everything.

That sure was an incredible night. After we were positive that Emo was dead, Mom had to call the police but our phone was dead. When she tried to use the cell phone in her purse, she found it was dead, too. We went to a nearby convenience store to use a pay phone. She called the police and she told a convincing story of how she struggled with Emo to get his gun and then shot him with it. That way she won't get in trouble for having a gun without a license. The police believed her.

We both had to go to the police station after Mom's arm was doctored and make statements about what happened. They questioned us separately but our stories were exactly alike. Everything turned out okay and the next day the case on Dad's murder was closed.

Mom decided that we'd move to New York. That guy Nick is going to help us find a place to live. He's already got a doctor for Mom (she says he's a "shrink") that's going to help her with all the junk she's been through lately. I'll probably go see him, too. I've been having nightmares ever since I was kidnapped and Mom says the doctor will be able to help me with that.

Nick also told us that he's lined up a heart specialist for me to see in New York. As soon as we're settled, they'll arrange things so I can get my operation. I used to be scared about having it, but after all that's happened to me in the past couple of weeks, that'll be nothing!

The last thing we did before leaving town was go to a funeral service for my Aunt Dana. It was at this little funeral home not far from our apartment. The only people there were Mom, Mr. Lewis, and me. Mom decided to have Aunt Dana cremated, so they gave her this metal thing called an urn that was full of her ashes. Pretty yucky. I looked inside but it didn't look like the kind of ashes you see in an ashtray. They were whiter and finer. Mom said she'd take the urn with us to New York and then find someplace cool to dump the ashes. Central Park or something like that.

The drive to New York is going to be fun. We'll play car games and sing along to the radio, like old times. I've already noticed a big change in Mom. She's not as moody as she used to be and she seems happier. I'm really glad about that. Leaving Lincoln Grove is the best thing we could have done. And living in New York City will be so damn cool, I can't wait!

Mom just turned on the radio and there was a song on that she liked. It was an oldie (for me) by Paul Simon called "Mother and Child Reunion." Mom started singing along with it. I knew the chorus so I joined in—"I would not give you false hope on this strange and mournful day. But the mother and child reunion is only a moment away."

It fit the mood.

PRETTY GIRL GONE

DAVID HOUSEWRIGHT

Mac McKenzie has had a lot of girlfriends. But only one went on to marry the governor of Minnesota. So how can Mac refuse when First Lady Lindsay Barrett tells him that someone has sent her an anonymous e-mail claiming to have evidence that Governor Jack Barrett killed his high school sweetheart.

As soon as Mac starts poking into Jack Barrett's past, he riles up a wide array of goons—including some political insiders who have big plans for Barrett and aren't above using kidnapping and murder to get their way. Mac has no choice but to keep digging for the facts…and hope he isn't digging his own grave.

SHELL GAME

JEFF BUICK

When NewPro Stock collapses, Taylor and her husband Alan lose millions, forcing them to sell their home and business. But they're not going down without a fight. They're determined to track down the elusive Edward Brand, the mastermind behind the enormous fraud….

Taylor and Alan are about to learn two hard facts: A man who doesn't want to be found can be extremely dangerous…and in the world of high-level scams absolutely nothing is what it seems. If they're going to pin Brand down and recover their money, they're going to need an ingenious—and very risky—plan of their own.

ACCIDENTS WAITING TO HAPPEN
SIMON WOOD

Josh Michaels is worth more dead than alive. He just doesn't know it yet. When an SUV forces his car off the road and into the river, it could be an accident. But when Josh looks up at the road, expecting to see the SUV's driver rushing to help him, all he sees is the driver watching him calmly…then giving him a "thumbs-down" sign. That is the first of many attempts on Josh's life, all of them designed to look like accidents, and all of them very nearly fatal. With his time—and maybe his luck—running out and no one willing to believe him, Josh had better figure out who wants him dead and why…before it's too late.

GATES OF HADES
GREGG LOOMIS

Jason Peters works for Narcom, a company that handles jobs too dangerous or politically risky for U.S. intelligence agencies. But when his house is attacked and he barely escapes the smok-ing wreckage, he knows this new case is out of the ordinary, even for him.

Jason will travel the globe—from Washington, D.C., to the Dominican Republic, to the volca-noes of Sicily—in a desperate race to uncover the ancient secret that lies at the heart of an unimaginable—and very deadly—plot.

ISBN 10: 0-8439-5894-4
ISBN 13: 978-0-8439-5894-2 $7.99 US/$9.99 CAN

SMOKE

LISA MISCIONE

A late-night visit from an NYPD detective rarely brings good news. But true-crime writer Lydia Strong is especially surprised to hear that one of her former writing students has been missing for more than two weeks. Before she disappeared, Lily had tried to get in touch with Lydia, seeking her help. Could it have something to do with the death of Lily's brother, the one Lily refused to accept as a suicide? If she wants to find the truth, Lydia will have to follow the trail Lily left behind, a trail that—like Lily herself—seems to disappear like smoke.

- -

SHAME

ALAN RUSSELL

Gray Parker's execution is front-page news and his case inspires a bestselling book. Everyone wants to hear about the man who strangled all those women. Everyone except his young son. As soon as he is old enough, Caleb starts a new life and denies any connection to his infamous father.

But now new bodies have started to turn up, marked just as his father's victims, and all the evidence points to Caleb. His only ally is the sole survivor of one of Parker's attacks, the woman who turned his crimes into a bestseller. Together, these two must desperately try to prove Caleb's innocence—before the law or the killer catches them.

- -

GOLDILOCKS
ANDREW COBURN

Lawrence, Massachusetts, is a quiet little town. But it's only quiet because the deals have already been made, the police are working hand in hand with the mob, and everyone knows where they stand. That quiet is about to be shattered. Louise Baker has married her way to the top and her mob connections have brought her the power she always wanted. She doesn't worry much about jilting her latest lover, handsome Henry Witlo, known as Goldilocks. But Henry's got a vicious streak and maybe he's a little crazy. Crazy enough to set in motion a chain of events that could blow the town sky high.

Dorchester Publishing Co., Inc.
P.O. Box 6640
Wayne, PA 19087-8640

_____5707-7
$6.99 US/$8.99 CAN

Please add $2.50 for shipping and handling for the first book and $.75 for each additional book. NY and PA residents, add appropriate sales tax. No cash, stamps, or CODs. Canadian orders require an extra $2.00 for shipping and handling and must be paid in U.S. dollars. Prices and availability subject to change. **Payment must accompany all orders.**

Name: _____

Address: _____

City: _____ State: _____ Zip: _____

E-mail: _____

I have enclosed $_____ in payment for the checked book(s).
CHECK OUT OUR WEBSITE! www.dorchesterpub.com
_____ Please send me a free catalog.